THE TAKING SHORE

Book One of The Vidarbjǫrn Saga

© Troy Harwood-Jones

20250907

ISBN 978-1-0696985-8-2

Contents:

CHAPTER 1: THE WIND TURNS

1000 A.D. — SUMARMÁL

It was the last day before the wind turned.

The sun lay flat across the fjord, casting the slope-meadows in amber. Goats shifted in the light, smoke drifted from turf-roofs, and Bjarni Herjólfrsson's knarr rocked gently against the mooring-stones below Brattahlíð.

The ship bore a red sail, keel-split and tar-dark, built for seas deeper than Greenland's narrow inlets could bear. It rode low in the water, broad-beamed and thick-ribbed, its hull curved like a whale's belly — made for burden, not speed. Black pine and larch, steamed and hammered into shape, held the weight of distant weather still in their grain. The planks overlapped tight, caulked with wool soaked in sheep tallow and pine pitch, tamped deep with iron tools and sealed over with hot resin to harden in place. Sea-scars streaked the hull, barnacles clung below the waterline. Its prow rose blunt and steep — no dragon's head, no carved eye. Just a trader's boat that had seen too many storms to pretend at beauty.

It was no warship. It lived by the wind. The single mast stood thick as a man's thigh, wrapped in climbing lines braided from walrus hide. The ropes sagged with wear. The sailcloth bore patches where it had split and been stitched again by coarse hands. The rudder — steered by a side-mounted tiller lashed with leather cord — was worn at the grip, polished by years of hard hands and harder seas. It was built for freight: for timber and fur, for wine and men. It wasn't fast. It wasn't elegant. But it had crossed the open sea, and returned—scarred, creaking, whole. More than most ships. More than most men.

Vidarbjǫrn Ketilsson stood above the inlet where the land curled like a hook.

Son of Ingólfr Ketilsson of Breiðafjörður, who worked salt pits and raised barley at Hólmlátr. Grandson of Bjǫrn Ketilsson, who claimed land with a bloodied axe and lost it to a winter that left no cairn. Great-grandson of Ketill Hroaldsson, who followed the whale-road west when Norway turned sour. On his mother's side, he bore the line of Thorolf Hrafnsson—sheep-farmers near Hof, who planted rye in frost and outlasted better-named kin. No chieftains. No saints. Just salt-hard blood and names whispered into law at the Thing, long after the bodies were gone.

He stood downwind, thirty paces from the mooring-stones, where frost-slick grass grew through the blackweed. From there, he could see the tilt of the sail and the line of Leif's back. His cloak hung open, earth-toned and sea-stained. Bitabrjótur, the short axe he used for wood-splitting, hide-cutting, and marrow-cracking, rested at his hip—worn smooth at the grip, edge dulled by labour. Across his back, half-concealed beneath the cloak's fold, lay Dökk Tönn— long-hafted, black-bladed, a pattern-welded blade of dark iron, its edge layered like river stone. That one stayed sharp. That one was never used lightly.

His hair was thick and wind-tossed. His beard, close-cropped but full. His face held the shape of weather: cheekbones carved by years, brow built for squinting into snow. His eyes were steady and deep-set—dark, layered, the kind that waited before they answered.

Ten paces off stood Leif, framed against the red-sailed hull—gold-haired, upright, every word like a hammer strike at the centre of camp.

They had met at fifteen, before either had been shaped by names. Sailed to Norway together. Bled in the same brawl. Knelt beside the same king's fire. Leif had risen, baptized with salt still in his beard. Vidarbjǫrn had watched and stayed unbowed. Since then, they had never stood far apart: flame and ash, crest and undertow. One led with voice. The other with silence that men followed, though no word had called them.

Now they gathered on the headland above the landing stones. The wind came up sharp from the sea, pressing the wool of their cloaks flat against lean frames. But none turned from it. Not while Leif was speaking.

Leif Erikson—son of Erik the Red, grandson of Thorvald Asvaldsson, whose exile traced back through Norway's hard kings and Iceland's harder winters. Blood that had burned its bridges westward for three generations. He carried that history like a keel bears storm-scars—beneath the surface, shaping every line. He stood taller than most—broad across the chest, shoulders hardened by sail and oar. The men of Brattahlíð watched him not as a chieftain, but like a shipwright studies a keel for fault lines. His skin was wind-burnished, the colour of sunlit barley. His hair, long in the Greenland style, shone like hammered bronze where it caught the westering light. A trimmed beard framed his jaw—not thick, but shaped to show the strength beneath. His eyes, pale and ice-flecked, never drifted. When he looked at you, it was as though he took a full measure—weight, intent, blood—and tucked it away without comment.

He stood with chin high and feet firm, as if praise and warning were the same weight — and neither enough to shift him. But in his quiet moments, there was something else — a stillness from Thjóðhildr, his mother. A listening quality, as if he waited to hear what others could not name. When he spoke of Norway, of court and Christ, of the black-robed monks who sang at morning, he did not preach. He recited, as if from memory. But his voice carried the weight of someone who had knelt and meant it.

He had returned that summer with gifts: glass beads strung in braids of red and green, a gospel book bound in calfskin and edged in gilt, and iron tools fine enough to draw quiet stares even from the shipwrights at Brattahlíð. He laid them out without ceremony, as if they were nothing.

But more than the treasure, Leif had come back with a hunger — to do what his father had done. To sail west and find a place no man had named. A land glimpsed once, by chance, by Bjarni Herjólfrsson.

Leif returned determined to buy Bjarni's ship — the hull that had seen that coast, and, he said, could find it again. He wasn't just buying wood and sail. He was buying the right to finish what had been left undone — shouldering it without boast, because someone had to.

"You saw it," Leif said, watching Bjarni. "But you didn't land."

Bjarni was leaner than Leif, and older. His hair had thinned since last they met, his boots cracked from too many hard winters. He wore no ring on his hand, but he looked like a man who wanted one. He looked inland when he answered, toward the slope where a woman stirred a cooking-pot beside a turf house.

"I saw it," he said. "Three times. Forested ridges. Low hills. A broad shore. But I'd lost my course, and had no men willing to land where there was no chart, no claim."

"No courage, you mean," said Ranhildr.

She was sitting on a rock just above the tideline, knees drawn up, back straight, sharpening her belt-knife with short, deliberate strokes. The edge hissed. She didn't look up.

Her body was long-limbed and upright, the kind of strength carved not in muscle but in endurance — the wiry resilience of someone who had hauled fish nets and chopped ice through four winters without help. Her tunic, rough-woven and stained with salt, clung at the elbows and darkened at the seams. The sleeves were pushed up to the forearms, showing skin pale and freckled with sun-scars, a line of fine cuts just below the wrist where the fish-hooks bit.

Her face was narrow, wind-reddened at the cheeks, and under the taut line of her jaw, a muscle ticked faintly every time the stone met the blade. Her hair was braided tight and high, black and oiled, the braids looped through carved bone pins with spiral marks — not decorative, but something older, something carried. Around her neck hung a strip of rawhide bearing three objects: a fishhook, a knucklebone, and a smooth, flat stone polished black. Each one meant something — hook for hunger, bone for chance, stone for the weight of what waited beneath. They weren't ornaments. They were warnings.

She moved like a curse unfinished — quiet, taut, meant to finish what someone else feared to start. Everything in her — blade, breath, bone — felt meant for proving.

Bjarni ignored her. Or tried to.

"I was captain," he said, calm. "The sea wasn't calm with me. That makes a difference."

Ranhildr snorted. "So does a spine."

Vidarbjǫrn felt it before the shift—a silence in the air, like when a gull changes course without flapping. Then Leif's head tilted. That same pull. He always felt Leif's gaze as a current, but now it pointed toward Ranhildr, and something tightened behind his ribs.

Ranhildr had that effect. She was his sister, yes. Four years younger, the only sibling Vidarbjǫrn had left. Trouble, always. Born sharp, raised harder. Their mother died the year she bled her first seal. After that, she walked with bone in her pocket and warning in her eyes. He'd once broken a man's jaw for speaking of her wrong—but never tried to stop her. But more than that—she'd grown up gutting fish with hands men called too fine—until one bled on her hook and never made the same mistake. She fought like a hook in the dark — small, sudden, buried before you saw it coming. He loved her like a brother who believed the gods had made a mistake—not in giving her that fire, but in giving it to a daughter. He never dared tell her that.

Leif smiled, slow.

"I remember you," he said.

"I remember being ignored," she answered.

There was a pause—but not a cold one.

Then Bjarni stood. "The ship is sound," he said. "But I've no need of her. There's a roof here. A woman with land. She'll have me if I stay. I've chased ghosts on the water long enough."

Leif nodded. Not unkindly.

"You'll take coin?"

"And four goats," Bjarni said. "The white ones. Yours are good-blooded."

Leif didn't haggle. That told Vidarbjǫrn more than any words. He wanted the ship, and he meant to use it.

That night, the longhouse breathed low. Smoke slipped through the rafters, touched with seal-fat and pine soot. You could taste it before you swallowed—sour in the back teeth. Beds lined the walls—raised planks softened with moss and sheep wool. They passed the mead hand to hand—thin, bitter, sharp at the back. Barley-boiled, with just enough bog honey to call it sweet. Despite the warmth, the room didn't hum with laughter—it shifted, quiet, like men waiting for weather.

Leif sat at the edge of the long hearth, elbows braced on the board, his cloak shrugged back. He wasn't holding court. He was just there, and that was enough.

"So," he said, mostly to his cup. "I bought his ship. Bjarni wasn't using it. Said the gods gave him a glimpse and a warning. I said—fine. I'll take the glimpse."

Vidarbjǫrn raised his cup without smiling. "And if it was a warning?"

"Then I'll try not to be what he was warned about."

Dry laughter stirred among them.

Finnvið Snake-Tongue, born of no one famous in Husavík and proud of it, leaned over the bench with a glint of teeth, fingers drumming against the bench edge.

"You paid too much," he said, voice pitched light, half-laughing, half-accusing.

He was thin as a fishing rod, restless as a wind-chime. His belt hung low with charms, knives, and pouches—half trader, half trickster. His fingers twitched near the knife at his belt—not from threat, but habit. His hair, half-tamed into small braids threaded with bone and copper, framed a face too quick for stillness. He spoke six tongues, or claimed he did. Swore in twice as many. Said he was the son of a skald's daughter and a whaler with no name. Claimed his grandmother could speak to the dead if given enough mead. No one entirely believed him. No one entirely disbelieved, either. Every word he spoke danced with mockery or charm—no one was ever quite sure which.

"It's a strong hull," Leif said. "Deep-bellied. Good timber, sound lines. I'll need thirty hands, give or take. Ten who can sail. Ten who don't panic. And ten who'll shut up and do what they're told."

"Right," Finnvið said, grinning. "Because men like that just hang around outside hoping for a cold death."

"I have names already. Eirik Hrólfrsson—he'll want the front. Geirr of Hvalsey, if the wind doesn't break him. Tyrkir the Saxlander, if he's sober. He can feed thirty men from a bone and a prayer—though he spoils seal broth with fig-skin and clove and calls it a blessing. And I'll take anyone who knows which end of a rope goes skyward."

Thorvald, the eldest of Leif's brothers, grunted near the fire — low and thick, like a man who chewed stone. "Let me know when there's something to kill."

Leif didn't look over. "It's not that kind of voyage."

Thorvald raised an eyebrow. His face was square, half-shadowed by the flames. "No voyage ends clean. If it starts with a map, it ends with a wound."

"Not if I can help it."

Beside the fire, Thorstein — slighter, paler, always quieter — turned his prayer beads between finger and thumb. His voice barely carried. "Will you take thralls?"

"No," Leif said.

"Then you'll be trimming your own sail."

Leif shrugged. "I'd rather row with free hands than be cursed with shackled ones."

Across the hearth, Ranhildr paused in her work. She was grinding a bone hook, edge long and wicked, the rasp of stone against bone like the sound of a tooth being sharpened. She didn't look up.

"What about women?" she asked.

Leif's eyes found her. "Depends on the woman."

"Good," she said. "Then you'll take me."

A beat.

Vidarbjǫrn asked, quieter: "And who's captain?"

Leif looked into the flame. "Father."

Freydis whistled. "Has he agreed to that?"

Freydis had no interest in joining. Said she had goats to mind, debts to settle, and better things to do than chase wind over water. But she listened to our talk as if it might unfurl a tale worth stealing. She was Leif's sister, after all — sharper than him in some ways, and more dangerous when crossed.

"Not yet. But he will."

The room shifted again. Not in noise — just in weight. Even the logs seemed to burn more slowly.

Thjóðhildr moved behind Erik's high seat, tending the fire. She had been his wife for thirty winters — long enough to know when not to speak. As for Erik, the old man hadn't said a word since dusk. He didn't look at anyone. But he hadn't left, either.

The silence pressed.

Thorvald, broad-shouldered and loose-limbed, sat with one boot hooked under the bench-leg, watching the sparks rise. He had never taken the cross. Neither had their father. "Does your Christ know what lies west?" he asked, too casual to be sincere.

Leif turned to him fully. "He knows the sea. The priest's reading last winter was: 'The harvest is ready, the labourers are few.'"

Thorvald gave a tight smile. "I've never known a harvest that didn't draw blood."

Ranhildr's voice cut in — calm, but shaped like a blade. "And the old gods? Or are you just hoping the new one reaches Vinland first, before the others wake?"

Leif answered, soft but not ashamed. "I made sacrifice in Norway. Before I left."

"To who?"

"To the one who listens."

He didn't say the name. He didn't have to. You only said that name if you wanted him to answer. And if he answered, it cost.

This time, they didn't let it hang.

Vidarbjǫrn's head dipped once, slow. Ranhildr's eyes narrowed, not in doubt — but in recognition. Even Thorvald gave a grunt that wasn't mockery.

Only Thorstein looked away, lips pressed white around the prayer beads in his palm.

Finnvið poured another drink. "All right then. When's the boat ready?"

"By the end of thaw," Leif said. "She needs new pitch and a prayer."

"And when we you leave?"

"When the sea lets us."

"And when do we come back?" Vidarbjǫrn asked.

Leif didn't look up right away. "Long enough to find the coast, map it, take what can be taken—and turn back before the sea seals us out."

He turned the cup in his hand once, then added, "But I've had them pack for longer. Enough to last through winter, if we must. Or if the land proves rich enough to warrant staying. If gold lines the streams, or the trees bleed resin worth its weight."

Ranhildr picked at a meat scrap—seal tendon, boiled hard then smoked near-black—working it loose with a fishbone pick. "And if it doesn't?"

Leif looked at the flame. "Then we drink. And sell the wood."

That night, Finnvið carved a knot into the mast with a nail from his dead brother's sled. Tyrkir burned dried angelica near the keel, scattered dried sweetgrass at the bow, and muttered saints' names in Saxon. Ranhildr tucked a red-threaded stone beneath the deck seam, just behind the mast, and spat west over her left shoulder before sleep. Vidarbjǫrn whispered over the tiller in Old Norse too old to name. No one spoke of it. But everyone did what they could to make the ship less visible to what watched.

The sea didn't test men. It fed on them.

By the time the snow began to melt at the edges, the hard

ones had come.

Not the loud ones. Not the braggarts who spoke of conquering seas and drinking down storms. Those men faded with the dark months — their promises left behind like thawed rope and rotting seal-fat. What remained were the ones who worked. The ones who knew how to brace a keel in ice-mud, who kept their tools sharp and their hands busier than their tongues. Some were sea-tested, used to hunger and storm. Some were young, still eager to prove themselves before men who had no need to boast. A few came for land. A few for God. One pair came as kin and would not be parted. Most just came forward when others stepped back.

They brought little. A blade. A bundle. A charm. Not enough for comfort — but enough to show they meant it.

Kristján the Ledger-Keeper, blond and composed, with shoulder-length hair tied back in a leather thong and a short beard combed flat, marked each man's name on a wax tablet as they swore in. His codex was sealed at his hip, hands clean despite the salt wind. Oddi stood just behind him — quiet, sharp-eyed, the boy he'd claimed but whose birth had split his household. None spoke ill to his face, but more than one man had asked why Leif took him — book-widowed, unloved, with only a bastard son for witness.

Ketill Flat-Nose came first. Shorter than most, broad through the shoulders, with salt stiff in his long, coarse beard and boots cracked from frost and age. His cloak hung heavy, the salt crusted into seams. He moved like a man made of old oak — weathered, slow, but unsplintered. Near fifty winters, and still eager for the sea. He had more years on saltwater than most of them had breath. His mother, he claimed, died under sail — some said near Iceland, others said farther, but he'd never named the place. He touched the prow once. Just a hand to wood. Then nodded. The younger men took it as a blessing. None said it wasn't.

Skagi Arnkelsson came next. Seventeen, maybe. Flax-haired, lean, with limbs still growing into themselves and boots tied too high on one side. His tunic was belted tight to hide how it hung loose. His face was unlined, freckled at the nose, the kind that caught morning light and held it. His eyes — wide, pale — watched everything too long, like the world was full of signs he hadn't yet learned how to read. There was a grace to him, not trained but given. He moved like someone afraid of being in the way — but more afraid of being left behind. There was nothing threatening in him, and that unsettled some men more than steel. He'd run errands for Leif all winter — fetching oil, counting nails, relaying messages he was too careful not to misquote. Never quite part of the planning, but always nearby. Always waiting to be included.

Rúni the Twice-Bitten showed up with a silent step, squat and knot-muscled, his eyes narrow, his axe slung across his back. A scar split his mouth like a hacked-in grin. His arms were marked with old burns and newer cuts — ritual, not accident. He said nothing. But the air near him felt watched. Said to be the son of a woman who whispered charms to the dirt and a man no one remembered. Bitten once by a man, once by a bear — though which had left the deeper wound was unclear. He rarely spoke. But he could split bone through fur with a single blow, and that mattered more.

And among them, though not yet assembled, would be Leif's priest, Father Arnlaugr. The one he'd brought from Norway. The one who still prayed aloud before meat, and who had written the voyage's blessing in ink stiff from the cold. Leif trusted him more than most. Not for comfort — but for certainty. There would be days, Leif knew, when certainty would weigh more than courage.

When thirty-five stood ready, Leif said no more names would be taken. He'd meant to take thirty. That had been the plan. Enough to sail, to build, to hold ground if needed — but no more. The extra five were a choice he didn't explain. More hands meant more strength. More defence, if it came to that. But it also meant less room. Less food. More boots between tempers and sleep.

Vidarbjǫrn thought it wasn't the wisest decision. But it was Leif's to make. And no one questioned him to his face.

And still, Erik had not touched the ship.

His name stayed in the hall like smoke. Leif used it when he spoke of command, but never when Erik sat near. The old man hadn't looked up at the mast, hadn't stood long without leaning, hadn't said yes. But he hadn't said no.

Some things wait for the tide.

The night before they sailed, the hall was quiet.

The ropes were coiled. Salt meat sealed. Cloaks rolled tight. Thirty-five had sworn — not with oaths, but with hands on timber and shoulders bent to work.

No singing. No boasting. Just bowls scraping wood and the wind pushing at the seams like it wanted in. A stew pot hung from the iron fork, seal bones split for marrow steeping in grey broth. No herbs, just salt and old onion peel. The smell clung low — sour and thin, but warm.

Thorvald kicked the bench-leg—loud, deliberate. "You've no shield wall. You'll need one. The ones out there—if they exist—won't bow to your God. They'll slit your throat and piss on the cross."

No one answered. Leif held a cup but didn't drink. His jaw tightened, just once.

"You should take me," Thorvald pressed. "You'll need someone who doesn't flinch when it's time for blood."

Leif didn't raise his voice. Didn't look at him, either. "You're not coming."

Thorvald snorted. "Right. Because I won't kneel."

Leif looked up now—calm, cold. Everyone knew why. Thorvald would never take orders. He had their father's temper and none of his cunning. The voyage couldn't afford that.

From the hearth, Thorstein looked up. His prayer beads clicked softly in his fingers. "This is a mission for God—as he promised the king of Norway. Christ needs to be brought to new lands."

A few men stirred at that. Not scoffing—but tight around the mouth. Greenland had heard that promise too. Leif had preached it five winters running—at the Thing, in the longhall, even by graveside. But the old gods had deeper roots. Most men nodded, then lit fires the old way.

Leif didn't answer at once. He only turned the cup in his hand.

Thorvald laughed, dry and sharp. "You think this a holy

errand? It's not. It's a grave. You'll die naming a place that doesn't care if you live."

He shoved the bench back and stood. For a moment, it looked like he might lunge. But he only held Leif's gaze—long enough to make the silence stretch—then turned and walked out.

"Some fields are stonier than others," Leif said at last. "But the seed's the same."

No one called him back.

Erik hadn't moved since dusk—hadn't spoken, hadn't met a single gaze. Just sat beneath the old wolf-hide, fingers loose against the carved armrest. The fire threw his face in and out of shadow, but the stillness didn't shift.

Leif took one step forward. Then stopped.

He turned instead toward the hearth.

Thjóðhildr was stirring the stew. Not with urgency—just the same slow circle, over and over, though nothing was burning. The pot steamed. She did not look up.

"Has he eaten?" Leif asked, quiet.

Her ladle kept its rhythm. "Not tonight. Not yesterday."

"And the pain?"

Her mouth tightened. "His knees swell by sundown. He shivers under two pelts. He hasn't touched the tiller since the thaw."

Leif glanced back toward the high seat. "I should speak to him."

"You should," she said. "But not as a captain."

That held him a moment. He shifted his weight.

"Speak to him as a son," she added. "You'll only get one chance to ask."

A voice broke in—firm, quick, and a little too loud.

"He won't say yes," said Freydis, standing beside their mother. Barely twenty, with the same red in her hair, but a sharper mouth. "He'd rather rot here than challenge the sea again."

"Freydis—" Thjóðhildr began.

Freydis didn't look away from the fire. "If he sails and dies, he'll blame no one. But he'll die angry." There was defiance there—but no cruelty. Just the sharpness of someone who hadn't yet been told no enough times to doubt her footing.

Leif met her gaze for a beat.

"I'd rather him angry than absent," he said. He turned back toward the high seat.

Erik sat as ever, unmoving in the high seat. The axe that cleared Greenland hung above him, untouched. Leif stopped at the hearthstone.

"Father," he said.

Erik gave no response.

"We sail with the tide. If you're to captain, you have to say it now."

Erik's eyes opened. He gazed at his son, and his look was neither weary nor warm. Still sharp.

"You think I haven't seen what's out there?" Erik's voice was low, rough-edged—not anger, but warning.

"No," Leif said. "I think you've seen more than I ever will. And your hand on the tiller could steer us to something greater than any of us alone."

Erik stood. Slowly. His spine cracked with the motion. He gripped the chair-post like it might sway beneath him.

"Fine," he said. "I'll come."

A breath passed.

"I'll be at the mooring by dawn—unless the gods take me first."

Then he turned, each step slower than the last.

"Now leave me," he said.

He had been outlaw once.

Not just from court, but from the land itself. Blood on his hands, some buried, some not. A law-thing at Thorsnes named him wolf's-head, unfit for kin or hall. Cast from Haukadalr like spoiled grain.

He sailed west with nothing—no blessing, no crew but ghosts. Just exile and the kind of fury that survives on salt.

And he found land. Cold, jagged, cruel. Enough to survive him.

"Greenland," he'd called it—laughing, because names were weapons. "Men'll come for a name like that," he said, "even if it bites." They had. It did.

Vidarbjørn had seen the map Erik made: soot on calfskin, coastlines etched from memory, fjords shaped like broken teeth. Not claimed. Named. Like planting a flag in a wound.

Now the old man sat still in the hall he'd raised with his own hands. The axe that cleared his stead hung cold on the wall.

Not broken. Just still.

Leif turned from the hearth and walked the hall's length, boots striking stone like they meant to count the distance. Vidarbjørn followed.

At the door, Leif paused.

The wind had changed.

Vidarbjørn didn't feel it in his face—not at first. He felt it in his knees. Less stone, more salt. That shift that tells you the ice will lift soon, the whales will return.

They walked in silence, cloaks tight, soil hard beneath their boots.

Down by the water, the tide had slipped far enough to show the slick ribs of the landing stones. The ship sat low, the red sail furled, the hull a black seam at the fjord's edge. The water barely stirred, but the mooring ropes creaked faintly — like the ship was waiting.

Leif stood with his hands on his hips, staring at the prow.

Vidarbjørn let the silence stretch. "He doesn't want to go," he said finally.

Leif didn't move. "He said he would."

"Anger's not agreement. It just looks similar when you're standing too close."

Still no motion from Leif.

"Your mother's right," Vidarbjørn said. "His joints are swelling. He's cold even under furs. If he boards that ship, he won't see Greenland again."

"I know."

Leif said it without blinking. No emphasis. Just dropped it like a stone into the cold.

"I know," he repeated. "But I can't be the one to stop him. Not without making it worse."

The wind caught a loose strand from Leif's braid and whipped it across his cheek. He pushed it back absently.

"I'll never be what he is," he said. "Even if I map the whole coast of the world. He bore exile like armor. I carry only hunger."

Vidarbjørn snorted. "You don't have to carry it. Just let it fall where it's meant to."

Leif almost smiled. Almost.

"Easy to say."

"Yes," Vidarbjǫrn said. "But true."

They stood there a while longer. Not waiting—just sharing the silence. Listening to the creak of the hull, the breath of the sea.

Then Leif turned. Walked back toward the hall.

Above them, the sky held a hard grey—flat, pale, empty of omens. The kind of sky that watches, but doesn't speak.

They began loading the knarr two days after the thaw lifted the ice from the shallows.

The hold lay beneath the central deck boards—open but covered—between the keel and the men's sitting space. Cargo was packed early, before the planks were fixed, though loose hatches allowed for access mid-voyage. Seal-hide pouches of dried fish, barley meal, and sea-biscuits went in first, lashed low near the keel where the ship's sway was least felt. Barrels followed—water, mead, and whey—wedged in place with turf blocks to stop them rolling in storm-surge. Charcoal. Blubber pots. Whetstones. Buckets clanked against coils of hemp rope and tar-sealed caulking wedges.

Kristján scratched weight marks into a wax tablet and frowned at the growing crowd.

"This was meant for thirty," he said. "We've no room for thirty-five and three goats."

The goats were tethered near the stern, hooves wrapped in cloth to muffle them, a measure against both noise and omen.

Leif just pointed to the mast. "Then stack it tighter."

No one argued. But no one liked it.

The frost still clung to the gangplank. Silver along the ropes. A rime on the sail's edge. The ship sat quiet, low in the fjord, its seams tar-dark and scarred. The slope above still lay in shadow, but the sky had begun to pale.

Skagi stood at the stern, counting barrels of dried fish, goatskin flasks, and a crate of iron hooks lashed with seal sinew. Again. For the third time. The load hadn't changed.

Rúni sat cross-legged, axe across his knees, sharpening it without urgency. His breath came slow and steady, like he could carve patience into the blade.

Tyrkir from Saxland — tallest among them, broad as a barrel stave, thick-necked and slow-stepping, with forearms freckled from sun and scarred from brine. His voice was low, his temper steady, and his tunic carried the smells of broth, pitch, and old cloves. Wherever he went, the smell of salt and sweetness followed, like a hearth built in a larder. He spoke little, but his hands moved with certainty — whether gutting a hare, binding a wound, or stirring broth that always seemed to know what it was for. His cookfire back in Brattahlíð had kept half the crew from abandoning the voyage outright — his stews sweet with roots, his hands always stirring or blessing something.

Tyrkir moved through the crowd without fuss or command, a small cask balanced on one shoulder like it weighed nothing. He paused beside the hold, sniffed once, and muttered something in a tongue none but Leif half-recognized — old Saxon or older prayer, half-chant and half habit. Then he set the cask down, knocked its rim with his knuckle, and nodded.

"Whey's still good," he said. "Fish too. But not together." His voice was calm, rasped slightly at the edges by years of smoke and salt.

Finnvið knelt nearby, tying a loop into a strip of hide, humming some nonsense verse to himself. When he tucked something inside the knot — something small, glinting — he said to no one in particular, "Best not to leave the spirits empty-handed. They get… enthusiastic."

Then they heard it — hooves. Not rushed. Just sure. Stone cracking under iron. A figure above the field.

Erik.

He came alone, riding a grey horse with foam on its flanks. The reins were just rope. The stirrups didn't match. His cloak hung uneven, lined in wolf-pelt rubbed thin. His beard was loose. His eyes were fixed on the ship.

He didn't look at the men. Just the water.

The horse stepped onto the slope. Slipped.

Not a fall. A buckle. The horse's foreleg folded, the hind stepped too late. Erik hit the turf like a sodden beam, no curse, no cry — just a grunt and silence.

Thorstein moved half a step forward, then stopped.

Erik pushed himself up to his knees. One hand to the ground, one to his hip. His face pale, mouth pressed tight.

He didn't swear. Didn't blame the horse. Didn't even glance at it.

He looked at the sea.

Then, at Leif.

There was pride in his gaze, and fury—and something quieter still. A kind of surrender only old men know—one that comes not with peace, but with limits.

He didn't raise his voice.

"It is not meant for me to find any other land than this which we now inhabit. This will be the end of our travelling together."

He turned. Limped up the hill.

The horse followed.

No one spoke.

Vidarbjǫrn felt it—not grief, not relief. Just the weight of something closing. Like a door shutting on a storm behind you.

Then Leif stepped onto the gangplank. The plank groaned beneath Leif's boots. Not loud. Just enough to remind the men watching that it bore more than his weight.

He didn't look back.

He knew if he did — if he turned toward that hill, toward the shape of a man limping into the past — it would change something inside him. Bend it. He wasn't sure it would bend back. So, he kept walking.

The frost cracked beneath his step. Rime crushed under heel, leaving dark footprints on the grain. He didn't pause at the midpoint — where the plank arched above the stones, and the whole fjord opened like a wound. Just walked, straight-backed, eyes forward.

At the stern, the seat waited.

Just a board — flat, nailed across a brace, without carving or runes, but every man knew what it meant when someone touched it.

Leif stood over it. He looked down for a breath, maybe two.

Then he sat.

The air shifted. Not the kind of shift that comes with a gust or gale. It was the absence of noise — like the world holding its breath through another's lungs. Beneath the hull, something vast moved slowly in the deep. No splash or ripple, just a shadow in the sea's memory.

No one spoke of it, but no one moved until it had passed.

Then Skagi let out a breath, sharp and short, like he hadn't realized he was holding it.

"Right," Finnvið said. "Well. That's one omen survived. Should we push off before the next one shows up hungry?"

Rúni stood. Said nothing. Just hoisted his axe and walked to the rope.

Ketill nodded once, as if that was permission for the others to start moving.

Ranhildr joined them at the plank. Her braid was tight. Her knife was visible.

Tyrkir muttered something under his breath and stepped aboard, pouch clinking with whatever figs and faith he carried.

Skagi lingered a second longer on the stones. Then looked up at Vidarbjǫrn.

"I didn't say goodbye to anyone," he said, voice too light, as if naming it might make it not true.

Vidarbjǫrn shrugged. "Then there's no one to haunt you if you don't come back."

Finnvið followed, still talking. "Glory, blood, and a belly full of bad luck—that's my guess. But I'm ever the hopeful one."

Vidarbjǫrn stepped up beside Leif. "You don't need to be him," he said. "You only need to see farther than he did."

Leif didn't answer. But he didn't deny it, either.

"Cast off," he called. "Before the ice remembers."

The ropes were loosed. They pushed off and drifted a moment. Then the sail—patched, dark, marked with stitches and salt—was raised just high enough to catch what wind the gods had seen fit to give.

The knarr moved. Not fast or not dramatic — but it moved.

Past the mooring stones and the slope. Past the place where Erik had once stood watching the sea like it owed him everything.

The men stood or sat, their eyes set west.

No one cheered or sang.

Ranhildr sat near the prow, her belt-knife laid across her lap. She didn't speak. But her fingers traced the bone hook on her rawhide necklace — slow, deliberate.

Finnvið leaned toward Skagi, voice too light for the hour. "First man to weep goes overboard."

Skagi blinked. "What if I spew instead?"

"Then over twice. That's even measure."

Leif looked ahead. The water opened wide in front of them — cold, empty, and unclaimed.

Vidarbjǫrn said nothing.

But he felt it. The wind had shifted. He glanced skyward — not at the sun, but at the cloud fringe, reading the high wind by its curl. A gull wheeled eastward, silent. That, more than anything, told him the sea was opening.

It wasn't omen or promise. Just the crack of frost under boot, and the sea pulling west.

And something — out beyond the line where sea met sky — waiting.

1000 A.D. — HARPA

The wind had teeth.

Not cold alone—dry, angled, rising sharp from the inland ice. It came quartering off the inland ice—east by north, clean-edged and rising. No storm behind it. No break ahead. Each morning it bit deeper. Each night it pressed them farther than they meant to go. It did not howl. It drove. It learned the shape of their sail and waited for the knots to slip.

The knarr bore it poorly—a cargo vessel deep in the belly, broad-ribbed, with a square sail best suited for following seas, not a quartering gale. When the gusts struck wrong, the hull shuddered like a cow struck behind the shoulder— heavy, startled, wrong-footed. She fought the wind with weight, not grace. Leif had meant to travel slow. Keep land to the starboard, anchor in lee-water, let the men dry their cloaks and sleep off the damp.

But the wind had other plans.

It drove them past Brattahlíð, past the fjords where snow clung in cuts of stone too narrow for sun. The cliffs sharpened. The sea turned glassy between gusts. The cold threaded joints and collars and cracks in old seams. It snapped the sail like wet hide stretched too thin. Every rope rasped skin. The knots bled through callus.

They sailed in shifts. Half on deck, half curled in the stern under a hide slick with brine and sagged from rain. Shields were tied flat below the benches, boss to rim, wrapped to keep from clatter. Chainmail was stowed in sailbags near the mast, too heavy to wear at sea. No man wore helm or mail underway—not from fear, but from sense. Iron drags you down when the hull splits. Men lay hip to hip. Boots on. Eyes red. Cloaks stank of fish and wool rot. Men relieved themselves over the side if the wind allowed. Otherwise crouched forward. The rest—a bucket. Once it spilled. No one spoke for hours.

Food came when it could. Cold porridge, clumped with husk. Dried fish tough as bark, the salt rasping the tongue. Tar-sealed skins of water stank faintly of pitch. The mead was gone by the fifth night. Bread by the sixth—mould-spotted and bitter at the crust. After that: hardtack, brittle as bone. Softened with spit. Swallowed without breath. Salt crusted every seam. Skin sloughed beneath wool. Brine yellowed the whites of the eyes.

Hafgrímr—barely fourteen, wrists thin as gull legs—moved like a boy pretending at a man's labour. His tunic hung loose. His hood slipped down one eye when wind caught it. He tied knots too slow. Pulled too fast. Tried to make up for his size with speed. Laughed too easily, too long. No one joined him. He slept with his arms crossed tight around his chest. Like he hadn't yet learned to take space.

Tyrkir kept the pot going, as long as it held. Boiled saltweed with fish oil. Seal-bone broth, bones cracked with stone to bleed the last marrow—grease pooling thick at the rim. Boiled in a soapstone pot slung low over the embers, thickened with bread-crumbs or moss scrap. It tasted of smoke and salt rot, but it filled the belly and stayed down. He worked with what they had, muttering to saints no one else named, sometimes crossing himself, sometimes not. The smell of Tyrkir's stew changed with the weather—

sometimes sweet with dried root, sometimes sour with fish-turn, always clinging to the breath.

On the fifth day, Hafgrímr's cloak snagged on a hauling line. Skagi was nearest. He stepped in without pause, untangled it with quick fingers, and offered a quiet joke—flat, not cruel. Hafgrímr flushed and turned away. Skagi didn't press it. Didn't smile again. But when the wind shifted that night, Skagi shifted too—making space at the bench edge, turning his side to block the gust. Hafgrímr sat closer than usual. Just near enough to catch warmth, not touch.

The boy kept a charm: whale tooth, carved to a gull-wing's curve, strung on gut cord. He gripped it when the hull lurched. "Keeps the sea from calling," he said once. Too loud. No one asked what he meant.

The wind turned harder near the broad coast. No fjords. No safe water. Just bare stone sloped into black surf. The gusts struck like grinding wheels. Once, the sail caught wrong—square and full—and cracked the rigging. The tiller jumped. The hull moaned. They made no headway. Just endured.

By then, no one sang. The wind peeled sound from the throat. Hands blistered. Eyes streamed. Cloaks stiffened into posture. The hull groaned—not with motion, but with memory. Like weight it had carried too many times before. What dry remained stayed wrapped in oiled hide—kindling, wool, a change of tunic sealed near the tiller. All else ran to salt.

But no one named it.

They passed a high bluff where the cliffs turned white with frost and guano. No trees. No hollows. Just a ridge of black rock streaked pale. Ranhildr stood at the rail, squinting up through the spray.

"The bone-curve," she said.

No one corrected her.

That night, with no word, she opened her palm on the prow. One cut, sharp and clean, then she pressed the blood to the pitch. It beaded, then sank into the grain—slow, dark. Not to a god or to a name. Just to what waited west. The thing that always took before it gave. She wiped her blade on her tunic and sat back down.

Leif saw from the tiller—her palm opened, the cut pressed clean. He said nothing. Not then. But his grip on the tiller shifted. Not in recoil—though he has accepted Christianity and brought it to Greenland—in something heavier. The act disturbed him, not because it was heathen. Because it mattered. The sea had heard her. He had seen it.

He looked away too late.

She hadn't done it for him to see. Or perhaps she had. Leif wore faith like salt-wet cloth—heavy, obedient, cold. Yet when she bled to the sea, he had flinched. Just slightly. That was enough. Let him hold to his gospel. Power recognized power, even if it spoke another tongue.

That night, the sea changed. Not louder. Not rougher. Just watching. As if something had accepted the mark—and begun to weigh its reply.

By the seventh day, Hafgrímr had folded into himself. He sat near the mast, knees tight to his chest, arms wrapped close, as if trying to hold himself steady while the ship pitched and moaned beneath him. His hands trembled at times—barely, but enough. The salt wind had blistered his lips, chafed his knuckles raw. His face, still too young for a beard, was marked now with the raw red of cold and brine. He blinked often, but not against spray; it was the look of someone trying to unsee what he'd seen. The older men watched him, but kept their silence. He didn't look like someone enduring. He looked like someone lost inside the storm. Even Finnvið, who mocked everything, left him to his shadows after dusk.

Rúni whispered to his axe—slow, rhythmic, as if feeding it the names of things he feared.

Finnvið knotted his beard at the jawline. When asked why, he only smiled.

Hafgrímr vomited over the rail each morning. Always tried to laugh after. No one joined him.

They saw no sails. No fires. No men. Just the coast, curling like a blade too long to sheath. Then even that vanished. Just the scrape of water. Just the stone.

On the twelfth day, the cliffs ended.

Past the last headland, the land fell away into wind-scoured nothing. No shelter. No wood. Just water—still, flat, cold as hammered pewter.

No one pointed. No one spoke.

Their boots were soaked, their hands torn, and their eyes hollowed to sockets.

Still the wind came off the ice.

West, beyond chart or blessing, waited the thing they did not name.

Leif said only, "We keep west."

Then turned the tiller, and they followed.

<hr>

Fog came on the second day west. It fell like wool across the sea's face. Low, full, and unmoving. The sail vanished above. The sea vanished below. The mast dissolved into cloud. The world shrank to the length of the hull.

No sun. No stars. No sky. Only drift, and silence thick enough to press against the teeth.

No lamp was lit. Oil soaked the wick, but no one dared break the dark — lest it name what waited.

No one spoke. Even breath came shallow.

They had slipped into another realm — not Niflheim, but near it. A seam in the world, where even gods must walk carefully. The kind that made gods listen sideways. Where names stayed close to the chest, and silence kept shape from being stolen.

The water made no sound. Even the waves forgot how to rise. Only the ache of oar-callused hands remained — gripping what the sea might take. The fog dulled sound, sight, and shape. It stripped the world of edge. Even the cold changed — less biting, more waiting.

Rúni tied bone to the rigging — knucklebone, tooth, antler shard. Wrapped in sinew. Set high where the last wind had passed. He whispered as he worked. Not to men. Not in prayer, but names. Old ones. Ones the Christ-priest would not know.

"Fog listens," he said, low. "If you speak before it names you, it can't take your shape."

He did not sleep. Sat by the mast, blade across his knees, head half-shaved and low, whispering in a crouch like a wolf waiting for dark.

Finnvið offered a carved seal-tooth to the sea. Held it over the rail. Said something soft. Not Norse. Or not fully. His braid swung loose behind one ear, wind-snared with charms. He grinned sidelong, like a boy making a dare.

Leif said nothing. Hands on the tiller. Jaw set. He steered by feel alone—weight, pitch, what the hull whispered through the boards. No sunstone showed path. No bird marked land. Just the swell, the keel, and what his hands remembered. He watched the fog like it had a tongue.

Father Arnlaugr had stood like stone at departure. Pale-lashed, strong-voiced, robe lashed at the waist, hand gripping the cross not as a relic, but a weapon made bare. Rope-muscled arms, hands veined and raw from frost, his skin blued at the knuckles where prayer met cold. Not a court priest—not soft, not cloister-born. He had followed Leif from Norway, ten years past, when the sea still bent the boy's voice and pride hadn't yet hardened. Back then, in a stone-walled school at Nidaross, Leif had learned his letters from monks and his faith from Arnlaugr—a man who spoke of Christ not as a lamb, but as a spear-broken king, nailed upright like a warrior left for wolves. A god who bled, fought, and rose again not meek but marked by fire.

Leif had listened. And when the king offered him a charge—to carry Christ west, to Greenland—it was Arnlaugr who had stepped forward, saying, "Where the cross goes, I go."

They had returned together. Preached together. Five winters of baptisms, refusals, frostbitten rites in halls that still hung Odin's hammer over the door. Arnlaugr did not falter. He did not curse the old ways, only outlasted them.

He knew Leif's faith better than Leif himself did. Knew where the cracks ran, how much came from conviction, how much from duty, and how much from the desire to be more than Erik had ever been.

Now, Father Arnlaugr stood steady. He did not yield. Not for fear of the fog, but for what he believed waited beyond it. When the holy book froze shut, he recited from memory—words hammered into him like runes, meant to hold fast when parchment failed. Though his voice cracked and his fingers split, he still spoke, steady as the keel. When Hafgrímr cried out, Arnlaugr knelt beside him—not gently, but with purpose. Behind them, Skagi shifted—half-rose, then knelt again when he saw the priest's hand at the boy's brow. He stayed close, just beyond the reach of panic, his presence quiet but fixed. When Arnlaugr spoke, Skagi mouthed *amen*—not with certainty, but like someone afraid the silence might take shape if he didn't answer it.

Ranhildr did not kneel. She stood near the mast, feet wide, knife bare—obsidian-dark, scar-etched. Her stance was coiled, shoulders square, eyes tracking something no one else named. She sang once—slow, low, with no warmth in it. Older than Christ. When one of the younger men spat and cursed the gods, she said only, "They're watching."

Then added, "If we're lucky."

Vidarbjǫrn watched the fog like it might split. He thought of Erik—his exile, his silence, his arrival in a land no god had blessed. Greenland had not been a promise. It had been a punishment. Still, Erik had raised halls from stone. Not chosen—just endured.

Vidarbjǫrn did not pray. But he watched the sea like Erik might have. Waiting for the crack in the world.

The gulls had gone.

The sea, too, had fallen silent.

Once, something drifted past. Pale. Long. Hairless. It floated near the hull, then vanished into grey. No one reached for it. No one asked.

That night, the fog glowed faint—like breath held too long.

Ketill, who had not spoken in three days, stood at the rail. Shoulders stiff. Face wet with wind.

He didn't speak loudly. "It's something else," he said. "Something older. And watching."

No one answered.

The fog stayed.

By the twelfth morning, the light changed. Not broke—just lifted at the edges. Grey gave way to pearl. Then to steel. The air sharpened—clean, but hollow. Like the breath had been pulled from it.

And then—land.

Not green. Not soft.

A jagged ridge of stone, rising straight from the sea. No slope. No harbour. Black cliff scoured white in streaks—frost and guano and old wounds. No trees. No curve. Just bare rock leaning into the wind like it had been waiting to be named.

Leif said nothing for a long time.

Then, flat: "Helluland."

It was named—but not claimed, not welcomed.

The rock seemed to sink heavier into the water, as if it recognized the word and meant to stay.

No one moved to lower the sail.

Skagi sat with his arms around his knees and rasped, "We made it."

Rúni stared at the cliffs. Then spat. "Even gods rot," he said. "Fog's where they forget they're dead."

The ship drifted close enough to feel it—the hush beneath the wind, the stillness where sea meets stone with no beach, no shoal, only the sheer face of the land. The way the air thickens when something remembers it was once alive.

"We land?" someone asked.

Leif shook his head.

"No wood," he said. "No shelter. No point."

But his gaze stayed fixed. Like he was memorizing something he'd never speak of.

Ranhildr stood beside him, blade still drawn.

"No welcome," she said.

"No curse either," Vidarbjǫrn answered.

But just then the cliff cracked — low, distant, like bone giving under old strain.

Leif stepped to the gunwale. From the bundle lashed to the mast he pulled a piece of driftwood — pale, warped, curled by sun and salt. He carved it quick with his seax — short-bladed, bone-handled. It was not a rune or a plea, only a mark — a witness.

He threw it into the water.

It floated. Turned once. Sank.

None watched it vanish into the depths. As if seeing it go would give it meaning.

They let the current take them on.

That night, the wind returned.

Not as breath. Not as weather.

As wrath.

No warning. No rise. Just impact. It struck the sail like a fist — ripping canvas, bending spar. The mast groaned — not like wood, but like joint and sinew pulled beyond limit. The tiller snapped sideways.

The sound was clean.

Like something breaking in flesh.

Rúni reached it first. Shoulders down. Boots skidding. He threw his weight across the brace.

Leif followed — jaw clenched, rope wrapped in bloodied hands. He pulled as if he could turn the sea in reverse, bracing with boots against the hull's rise, rope cutting across callused palms.

The sail tried to split. Lines screamed. One snapped past Skagi's ear. He didn't move. Didn't blink.

They tried to reef it — hauling the stiff, salt-hardened hemp and sinew lines by hand. Each loop cut and burned. The ropes had gone iron with salt. Stiff with cold. Finnvið fell. Slammed the mast. No sound. Crawled aft with one hand bleeding, the other dragging.

The sea rose wrong. Not wave by wave. All at once. From beneath. From within.

The hull lifted sideways, loose planks groaning beneath. Rain fell like gravel — sharp, wind-driven, stripping warmth from skin and sail alike.

The deck vanished. Returned. Vanished again. Every roll shook the loose planks above the hold. Some buckled, slamming back with a crack. Men braced their boots to keep the hatches from giving.

The sky had gone. The sea had taken its place.

Then the wave struck. Broadside. Heavy. Not a blow — but
a verdict.

The ship rolled — not fully. Just enough.

One of Rúni's bone charms snapped loose from the rigging. It skittered across the deck, vanished into the sea. He didn't move to recover it.

A small form went over. Too fast for anyone to stop. Too small to stay.

No shout. Just the scrape of boots.

Hafgrímr, last seen gripping the rail, the charm swinging loose from his neck.

The sea shut like a mouth.

No name was called.

There wasn't time.

The storm didn't end. It passed. Like a hand pulled back after a blow.

What remained was wreckage that hadn't yet given way. The creak of timber strained but unbroken. Water slapped the hull in slow, exhausted rhythm. Men breathed — slow, shallow, half-believing they still could. The sail hung in strips. The tiller cracked and bound with rawhide. One rope was ruined. Two others went stiff as bone. The mast leaned but held. Below deck, a board had given near the mid-hold. Water lapped in knee-deep, sloshing through sacks and bedding. One goat was dead — drowned in its pen, half-submerged when they dared look. Another still stood, slick and shivering, its tether frayed to a thread and caught fast in the slats.

Leif stood at the rail, both hands torn. Rope burns open, scabbed with salt. He looked into the dark as if it still owed him an answer. Then forward.

Rúni didn't touch the tiller again.

Skagi had retreated to the mast. Arms locked around his knees. His eyes never left the water. Once, he mouthed a prayer — but made no sound. His lips froze halfway through the name.

No one lit a torch or reached for a rope.

The sea had already decided.

The sea had taken what it wanted. That was its way. It never told you why. But it always took enough.

Tyrkir gathered what hadn't spoiled. Boiled hardtack with salt grease. Stirred until it thickened. Passed bowls in silence. He didn't speak either — not in Saxon, not in Norse. Just sang once, low, a hymn with no name they recognized.

Arnlaugr stood at the mast. One hand braced to the wood, the other still lifting the cross. His lips moved — maybe scripture, maybe just breath made into form. The wind tore the words. But not the weight behind them.

The birds came before dawn.

Three of them — gulls, pale against the grey, screaming thin and high as they cut north and west. Not storm-followers. Land-birds.

Vidarbjǫrn saw them first. Then Leif.

Neither spoke. But Leif moved to the tiller.

He turned them after the birds.

The sail hung loose, patched with knots and blood. The mast leaned, collar-splintered where the bracing ring had cracked under torsion. Men clung to benches and posts with hands swollen, broken, split.

One lost. One gone silent. The priest still whispering.

But they followed.

Near midmorning, the fog began to retreat. Not vanish. Withdraw. Like wool pulled from a wound. Each gust took a little more of it. The sky lightened — not blue, not yet, but steel. The sea flattened.

And ahead: a line.

Low. Dark. Unmoving.

At first, it looked like fog again. A wall of it. But it held shape. Held still. Grew sharper with each breath of sail.

They weren't cliffs or bare stone, but trees — dense, upright, dark with root-memory. Spruce, maybe. Or pine. Too many to count. Too close to dismiss. They held shape through the mist, as if the land had grown a wall with no gate.

No one spoke. The ship creaked like something holding back a break.

The gulls wheeled once more overhead. Then vanished

inland.

Ranhildr squinted. "Could be an island."

Vidarbjǫrn shook his head. "Too broad."

Skagi leaned forward, jaw set. "It fits," he said—quiet, but sure. "What Bjarni saw. Forested. Sloped. Dark inland." His voice cracked on the last word, but he didn't flinch. Just looked to Leif, like he needed the name to land aloud, not rot inside.

No one moved. They let the sail pull what it could.

The ship gave a long, low groan—wood swelling, old joins straining—not from injury, but from some deeper memory stirred by shore.

Leif stood at the prow, his hands braced against the salt-slick beam. He had held silence since the boy vanished beneath the ice. Now, at last, his voice came—low, weathered, almost unwilling.

"Markland."

Not a claim. Not a shout. A naming drawn from recognition, not triumph. Bjarni had seen this coast once and turned away. Left it unnamed. That burden—and right—had passed to Leif.

"If this is land," he said, "we take it like men who meant to find it, not ghosts crawling from the sea."

Though no one answered, they moved. Straightened. Shifted weight. Checked line. Not because they believed. Because they remembered who had led them this far.

They came in slow. They did not beach—not yet. Just near enough to see tree-root and rockfall and the line where tide met loam. The forest stood still. Spruce, maybe pine—too dense to see through. Old trunks. Old root. The kind that remembered.

The ship scraped once—rock grazing hull—and made landfall. No wind stirred the trees, and no bird gave warning. Even the sea had fallen silent behind them. They stepped ashore one by one, not in haste, not together—boots sinking slightly into the tide-packed loam, hands still braced for motion.

Geirr staggered slightly as he crossed the gunwale, catching himself with a grunt. Skagi reached to steady him—not forcefully, just an open hand, braced and waiting. Geirr shook his head, half-smiling. "Salt in the chest," he said. "Shakes out soon enough." Skagi didn't answer, but he stayed there, just long enough to be reached for if the next step failed.

Leif knelt on the shore. Many followed.

Father Arnlaugr knelt beside him. Back straight, hands unshaken, eyes skyward. He crossed himself with salt-cracked fingers, then spoke—not as plea, but as claim. A blessing first. Then a prayer of thanks for safe passage.

He drew a small cross in the sand with his thumb, firm and slow.

"By the Father who made the sea, by the Son who walked upon it, by the Spirit who moves across its face—this ground is set apart."

His voice caught in the windless air.

"No spirit may cling to us. No dead may answer our step. Christ ward our going in and our coming out. He who brought us safe through the deep — be praised."

Leif corrected him — quiet, but firm. "Not safe. Only through."

Then the priest prayed for Hafgrímr — not loud, but clear. "Lord of the deep and the firmament, receive your servant Hafgrímr. Not whole, not crowned, but marked by salt and fear. The sea has taken — but not to keep. We commend him to your mercy. Not lost. Not wasted. But returned, as all flesh must be, in time, to the hands of God."

Some men looked toward the stern, half-expecting to see him still there. The boy with the gull charm. But there was only rope and spray and the space he had once filled.

Ranhildr turned from the priest. She knelt — but not as he did. Low, still, one hand pressed to the soil as if listening for what lay beneath.

Then Leif rose. His hand still bleeding. He stepped forward, not toward the trees, but toward the sky above them — as if the shape of clouds might speak what the land would not.

Vidarbjǫrn waited longer. Watched the treeline. Still. Close. He stood apart — broad, unmoving, the haft of his axe pressed into the loam like a second spine. He did not believe the priest. But he hoped. Hoped that was the only payment required.

CHAPTER 3: THE FOREST THAT WATCHES

1000 A.D. — SKERPLA

They called it *Vatnslaugr*—Water Hollow. Leif spoke the name first, kneeling by the bank, carving it into driftwood with his knife. Each rune notched with care. Not for memory. Not for poetry. For severance—a line cut to tell the land: we are here now.

Ottar Sigmundsson had asked him, later, why that name. A broad-shouldered man with seal-scars on both wrists, eldest of the fishers, and first to read tide by taste alone. Leif hadn't answered. But Kristján had nodded like it made sense. And Father Arnlaugr, watching the current, had said, "A clean stream is a blessing."

No one had corrected him. But no one repeated it either.

The stream ran cold and narrow, descending from the ridge above like a vein laid bare. It pressed through shale and root, shouldered alder aside where it could, wore down the clay in long, slate-grey lines. Birch leaned overhead—thin, upright, shedding their bark in curling strips like flesh in fever. Their trunks were speckled, their limbs high and brittle, as if they'd grown tall only because nothing nearby had lived long enough to shade them.

The water itself moved quietly. Too quietly. It didn't churn like seawater, didn't foam, didn't carry salt. There was no voice in it. No taste of rot. Just glass-smooth current, shallow enough to show the flicker of fish in gravel—trout, likely. But they didn't break the surface. Didn't rise to bait. They held still, shadows stitched to stone.

Skagi had said once, almost to himself, "It moves like it never meant to be seen."

He crouched near the bank as he said it, one hand trailing just above the water, not touching. His voice was soft, like he feared waking it.

Finnvið had replied, "So do things with teeth."

It was a clean stream, yes. And maybe that was the danger.

They had worked the bend hard — drove willow stakes deep into the banks, lashed them with gut cord, angled the frame to narrow the run. Basket traps were set upstream: gut-twine weaves weighted with river stones, the reed-bellies dark with silt. Bone hooks baited with eel scrap hung from alder branches. Some men rose before light to tend them, walking into mist with hands cracked and faces raw from wind. Others laid eel-weirs downstream, patient and hopeful.

But more than half returned with nothing.

Some lines snapped, as if pulled from below. Some traps vanished entirely. One was found days later downstream, caught in a root-snarl, the weave crushed flat, half-unpicked from within. What fish they had were strung from green ash by the shallows — thin salmon, bleeding slow, flies already at their mouths. One smoked in the trench-pit, hung over alder kindling. The skin had blistered to copper, but the meat inside was still grey.

Less than needed — again.

They chewed what they caught, but no one smiled. The fish left an aftertaste like bloodweed — dull, metallic, faintly sour. Better than hunger. But not by much. They ate in threes—silent, crouched, shoulders hunched against the cold. A single pot served seven. The broth stung of fish-turn and bitter root.

Oddi took his share with both hands, careful not to spill. As he passed the pot, his elbow brushed Kristján's. The boy lingered—just a second too long—like he meant to speak, or meant   to   stay.
Kristján shifted his weight. Not sharply. Just enough to make   space.
The moment passed. The pot moved on. Kristján waited until the end. No one offered a second ladle.

Ranhildr drank standing, bone hook still in her grip. The clink of the spoon on stone was louder than breath.

No one blessed it. But no one dared waste it.

Vidarbjǫrn knelt at the waterline, forearms streaked with pitch, the cold bracing his frame like a held breath. One knuckle was split to the joint, opened earlier lifting a beam—the skin torn where the grain twisted wrong. Blood beaded along the cut, slow and dark. He dipped both hands into the water. The cold hit sharp, bone-deep. He held it. Watched the blood fade from his skin as if the creek itself refused it.

He let the ache root in. Let it still him. Then withdrew his hands, wiped them dry on the damp reed-grass, and turned uphill.

The hall-frame waited above. Half-built. Unroofed.

Six main posts, sunk deep, reached skyward like ribs from something long dead. Cross-joists notched between them—

crooked, green-cut pine still weeping sap. The tar pitch they'd spread to seal the grain had thinned overnight. Bark had peeled. Two rafters had split lengthwise, twisted clean out of socket. They'd tried birch poles from the low grove, but fog warped them. Half now lay smoking in the trench fires. The rest were gone to rot.

Still, they slept under it. Hallbjørn had lined the sleeping ground with spruce tips, bark down. Not for comfort—just to keep the wet from soaking up. He moved without fuss, balm-stained hands never idle.

The south wall had not yet risen beyond a man's waist. Birch bark, stripped too early, curled inward and leaked sap dark as blood. The wind crossed the space without hesitation. Inside, the floor was raw. Earth unturned. No drainage laid. Rain had pooled beneath the firepit tarp and had to be bailed each morning.

A shallow trench near the centre held fire. Tarps pegged low above it made the smoke cling, thick and heavy. A blackened soapstone pot hung from a forked stick at the edge, its rim streaked with broth and pine soot. A dozen lay beneath hides along the east wall: Leif among them, eyes shut but not sleeping; Hallbjørn Bent-Nose, the herbalist, snoring soft through broken cartilage; Oddi Kristjánsson, Kristján's son and apprentice, lettered, sleeves too long, shivered beside a pile of wet timber. Knives lay sheathed beside every bedroll—not from caution, but from ritual. A blade kept close was habit among sea-farers—not just for threat, but for warding sleep.

Geirr of Hvalsey clearing his throat once—rough, but quiet. He didn't sleep much. Not deeply. One hand always rested near the knife at his belt, eyes half-shut, tracking shadow like it might grow teeth. In Iceland, he'd served three winters on the eastward posts — night watch in pine groves so cold they cracked. His jarl feared draugr more than blades. Geirr learned early that not everything in the dark comes with steel or voice.

Vidarbjǫrn passed through the open wall, his hand trailing along a beam where the pitch had dried to scab. The pine bled slow, like something still trying to live. It wouldn't hold come frost.

He stepped beyond the half-raised wall, into the perimeter — brush thinned, undergrowth half-burned. A ring of clearing carved into forest, but only barely. Spruce and alder pressed in tight. Larch trunks wrapped in dry thorn. Roots like claws. Branches bent low and bristling. Every movement of wind caught like a question.

He paused. Not for sound. For lack of it. Then — a soft crack behind him.

He turned.

Leif stepped out from shadow, boots sodden and heavy, cloak dragging low. His broad shoulders hunched against the weight of wet wool and unspoken threat. Pale eyes swept the treeline — not frantic, not searching — just fixed, like a man counting dangers he'd already begun to regret.

"They still watch," he said.

Vidarbjǫrn waited. The silence held.

Leif gestured toward the ridge. "Take a group. Find what saw us. Before nightfall."

His tone wasn't tight. But it wasn't open either. It had the cadence of a man who gave orders only when he had already begun to regret them.

Inside the frame, someone turned in sleep. A blade knocked against stone. Another breath caught in a cough and never finished. The fire hissed low, half-choked.

Vidarbjǫrn crouched near the coals, drew one line in the ash with a forefinger, and let the wind erase it.

He stood.

Smoke curled against his shoulders as he crossed back through the half-frame. Men stirred in the corners of the hall, but none rose. Knives remained within reach. The quiet held — no longer just silence, but something thicker, grown from what hadn't been spoken.

Outside, near the timber stack, Kristján stood with one hand flat to the broken beam, jaw tight, tracking the resin like it might confess where they'd failed. He said nothing.

At the waterline, Ottar was gutting what little they'd caught. Fish opened in his hands like scribed bark — always too clean. No rot. No muck. Just flesh, and the sound of knives.

Ottar crouched low, brine-rough hands steady, eyes pale as shallows, gutting fish like the work might anchor the world. He was called *Fish-Lord*, half in mockery, half in truth — had netted seal and salmon enough to earn the name, though no lordship clung to his voice or back. His beard was coarse and sun-bleached, braided once for function, now left to fray. Salt crusted the hem of his wool tunic. He carried no charms, only a gutting blade and a pouch that smelled of brine and old oil. His eyes were the colour of shallows: pale, unreadable.

"You saw it."

Ottar's knife hesitated. He wiped it clean on the rocks.

"Maybe. Not well."

Vidarbjǫrn waited.

"It wasn't right," Ottar said finally. "Too tall. Too smooth. Not beast. Not elk. It slid, didn't step. Not man."

He said nothing more.

By the old cooking trench, Rúni sat crouched, oiling the leather grip of his axe.

Vidarbjǫrn stopped before him.

Rúni looked up from the blade he oiled, eyes unreadable, the tilt of his head closer to a wolf than a man. "You want me to walk into the trees with you."

It wasn't a question.

Rúni stood, slung the axe across his back with a single motion, and smirked—only the left side of his mouth moving, as if the right had forgotten how. "If we find anything, I'll try not to kill it before it speaks."

Skagi crouched by a sapling, fingers sunk lightly into the soil, posture as still as if he might coax the ground to speak. His hair, sun-caught, fell loose across his brow, unmoving. He didn't startle when Vidarbjǫrn approached—just tilted his head slightly and said, "There's no frost-line here."

Vidarbjǫrn said, "So?"

"So anything that dies here rots without waiting."

"Let's just find it. Worry about death later," Vidarbjǫrn answered, looking to the forest.

Skagi straightened. His eyes were pale. "You'll want someone quiet."

Finnvið chewed a fish-strip into thread, grin waiting behind it, one brow lifted like he'd already heard the punchline. He liked to chew when nervous — said it kept the gods from chewing him. When he saw Vidarbjǫrn, he spat the strip into his palm and grinned.

"Finally going to chase the watchers?"

Vidarbjǫrn said, "You've named them already?"

"Just voices," Finnvið said, slipping the strip into his belt pouch. "One whistles. One clicks. One sounds like wet leaves."

"You'll come."

Finnvið clapped once. "I was born to follow things I can't see."

Ketill honed the blade in slow, measured strokes, shoulders stooped, hands moving like they'd once carved bone instead of meat.

He didn't look up. "I heard you pick the boys."

"They aren't boys."

Ketill wiped the blade clean on his cloak. "Then I'll come, before they prove you wrong."

Vidarbjǫrn said, "Ranhildr, too."

This time, Ketill looked up.

He said nothing. But his gaze was not empty.

Ranhildr crouched by the trenchfire, sleeves rolled, her hands working the birch with precise, silent pulls—jaw tight, red hair damp and catching light. The knife she used had no hilt—just a bone shard wrapped in tarred thread.

When Vidarbjǫrn told her, she didn't stop cutting.

"Someone needs to see what you won't name," she said.

Behind them, Finnvið murmured, "You always bring her when it feels wrong."

Skagi asked her, voice quiet but steady, "Do you know their name?"

His gaze didn't press—it offered. She looked at him, just for a beat, before answering.

"Not yet. But I will," she answered, sheathing her blade.

Rúni glanced at Ranhildr's hands. "Just don't ask me to follow her into anything older than the trees."

From the frame's edge, Leif watched—one hand clenched hard at his belt-knife, thumb pressing the hilt in rhythm with his jaw. He seemed about to speak. Then turned back into the smoke.

They packed light. Salt, flint, torches wrapped in pitchcloth. Blades oiled and bound. Rúni carried two coils of rope. Skagi tucked a sealed pouch of birch fungus into his cloak lining. Ranhildr filled a small clay pot with ash from the trenchfire and stoppered it with cloth. Finnvið whispered to each of his tools before wrapping them. Ketill wrapped a godsmark in linen, tied it to the inside of his belt. Not as a ward. As memory.

No one asked where they were going. Only how long.

They left without farewell. No horn. No gaze backward. Just the press of feet against moss, the weight of silence carried forward.

By the fifth step, the clearing was no longer behind them — only trees.

This forest was not of Eiríksfjǫrðr — the fjord in southwestern Greenland where Brattahlíð lay.

Here, the trees bent low not from wind but from weight. Larch with thorn-wrapped trunks, spruce in knots, roots curled like claws. Moss coated everything. No animal track, no snapped branch. Just damp and earth and the thick green light of water slowed into wood.

It smelled not of pine, but of wet stone and forgotten smoke.

Skagi paused beneath a leaning birch, touched one side of the trunk. His fingers came back ochre-stained.

Finnið traced a spiral in the moss with a boot heel.

They passed into the first gully. Roots rose high from the soil, interlaced like rib cages. Water trickled beneath them without sound.

Ranhildr crouched, feeling the ground with an open palm.

"What is it?" Skagi asked.

She walked on, blade hand loose at her side. "I don't give shape to what already listens."

In the second hollow, the brush thickened. No birds. No fur-sign. Just twisted bramble, old scat dried white, a single antler wedged upright in the soil like it had grown there.

They circled it.

Skagi snapped a rowan twig and stabbed it deep into the mud—blade-end down, not as warning, but like memory pinned

"Not for them. For us."

Vidarbjǫrn said nothing, but did not stop him.

In the third gully, the ground changed.

Ranhildr paused. Crouched again. Dug her hand into the soil.

"Feel this."

Vidarbjǫrn crouched beside her. Ran his palm along the surface. The loam pulled strangely—clung to the fingers. Too damp. Too warm.

Skagi knelt opposite her. He didn't speak at first—just ran one palm flat along the soil like smoothing cloth, then drew his knife and cut. The blade met resistance halfway down. He didn't force it. "Root mat. Dense," he said.

Finnvið watched him. "It's not growing. It's holding."

Ketill stepped wide around the cut, as if circling something not visible.

Vidarbjǫrn marked the place with a bone peg. Another beside it. One at the treeline.

Then he stood. "We turn back."

No one objected.

They didn't say it aloud. But they had all felt it.

Something beneath the soil.

The ridge rose, knife-sharp, a stone tongue between the trees. No moss grew there. Birch stood sparse, their bark peeled like old scars. Each step landed soft, but not loose — as if the ground remembered other feet. And didn't want them back.

They climbed without torches. No one said it aloud, but the fire would have shown too much.

Skagi led. He moved ahead without sound, like something the forest had forgotten to fear. Where his boots touched, no leaves stirred. Some men watched him and felt steadier just for knowing he walked before them.

No wind. No birdsong. Not even the stretch-creak of old

trees. Just that thick, rib-humming quiet that came before either worship or killing.

Finnvið crouched beside him, whispering close. "They don't hunt with breath."

Skagi didn't blink. "They don't hunt at all."

Rúni drew his axe—slow, spine curved, shoulders flexing like an animal slipping loose of restraint. His eyes kept to the angles between trees. Not scanning for bodies—watching for shape repetition. A pattern. A trap.

Vidarbjǫrn came forward next, shoulders loose, knees absorbing the slope. His axe stayed sheathed, but his left hand hovered over it, fingers curled but not closed. A readiness without threat.

Behind him, Ranhildr knelt in the brush, one palm pressed to the soil.

"It thickens here," she said.

"Roots?" Vidarbjǫrn asked.

"No. Something deeper. As if the ground's been holding still too long."

Skagi raised his hand again. Flat. Absolute.

They froze.

Then came the sound.

Dry. Clean. Not voice. Not wind. A crack like heat-split timber. Bark breaking from inside.

Another sound followed—a clicking series, high and wet. Almost avian. Almost human. Then silence again, too complete to be trusted.

Ketill turned in place, widening his stance. His hands hung open, loose at his sides. His mouth didn't move. But his breath came shallow.

And then—they saw them.

No approach. No rustle. No sound of footfall. Just presence.

Two figures between the birch trunks. Then more. A dozen, maybe. Maybe fewer. But it felt like more. They stood still. Not posed. Not human. Just present— like trunks that had once been men, then forgot. Long-limbed. Wrapped in hide or plank or bone. Materials lashed to their bodies with sinew cord, but not as armour—as burial. Nothing shone. No iron glint. No horn curl. Just surface and mass and shape.

Their torsos bent at the wrong tension. Not broken— restrained. Their heads were covered in paint—smears of ochre, charcoal, chalk—crossed in lines that contradicted the body beneath. Runes not of language, but refusal. The marks didn't follow bone. They defied it.

The eyes—if they were eyes—were deep in shadow. Not glinting. Just empty, like something had burned the looking out of them.

Rúni stepped forward, just half a pace, like his ribs forgot how to hold back. His axe dipped. His face twitched, as though struck from inside.

Vidarbjǫrn raised one hand. Not in warning. Not in peace. In recognition.

The figures did not move.

Ranhildr stepped laterally, keeping low. She took ash from the pouch at her hip and smeared two streaks beneath her eyes, thumb to cheekbone. Not a ward. Not a rite. A signal. You are seen. You are known.

Then one of the watchers shifted. No footfall. No step. Just a movement like a trunk under slow wind.

A bow lifted.

Not drawn high. Not aimed.

Just raised.

Another figure echoed it. Then another. The motion wasn't coordinated — but it answered.

Not in speech. In rhythm.

Finnvið stepped forward.

Not bravely. Not recklessly. Just unwilling to let silence hold shape too long.

He wasn't the strongest among them. Wasn't the most devout. But he understood the power of words — and how stillness, if left too long, could harden into judgment.

He moved slow, each step placed with care. Not in ritual. In recognition. His hands stayed where they could be seen — not raised, not pleading. Just open.

"We mean no harm," he said. In Norse first — clear, even, without edge.

Nothing.

He tried again, shifting tones. The Greenland trade tongue—thicker vowels, shorter ends. "We bring no claim. No theft. No cross."

Still nothing.

Then his voice changed—something older. The words came slow and water-weighted—part chant, part shoreline echo. A dialect dredged from coastal tongues and tide-mutter. He didn't perform it. He let it happen. His breath matched its rhythm.

He bowed his head slightly—not in worship. In respect, given without knowing the rank.

Still nothing.

He drew breath again, ready to try once more.

A bark broke the air—sharp, guttural, wrong in the mouth. Almost canine. Almost command.

A second followed—shorter, tighter. Like bone struck against stone.

Then the arrow.

It came clean from the dark—fast, without tremor. It struck the earth three paces from Finnvið's feet and stood humming, unmoved. As if the air itself had agreed to hold it there.

Finnvið didn't flinch.

He looked at the arrow.

Then at the figures. And gave a single nod.

"That's a no, then," he said — low, dry. The grin that flickered was real, but didn't linger.

Vidarbjǫrn stepped forward, hand to Finnvið's elbow. Drew him back. One pace. Two.

Finnvið let him. But his eyes stayed fixed — not on the weapons. Not on the masks. On the pattern behind them. The rhythm. The refusal.

The watchers did not follow.

They did not retreat.

They ceased.

One by one, or all at once — it was impossible to say — they dissolved. Not into fog. Not into night. Into bark. Into the lean of branches. Into the crooked posture of trees. As if they had never been separate. As if to see them had been the transgression.

The ridge stood empty again.

Only the arrow remained — still upright. Still humming. A boundary, or a breath.

After a moment, Ranhildr pulled it from the ground, and they retreated.

They did not speak on the descent—not by choice, but because nothing in them could rise to shape a word. Speech would name it. Naming would fix it. And none of them—none of them—wanted that burden on their tongue. The ridge fell away behind them, and still they felt watched. Not followed. Watched—as if the trees had turned their roots upward and were listening with the dirt.

The trail back was not the trail they'd taken. The forest had shifted. Or perhaps they had. Moss coated the rise in a thicker film than before. Thorn caught at Rúni's cloak. He didn't cut it free. He just let it cling until it tore loose.

Skagi stopped without signal. He crouched low, pulled flint and dry shavings from his pouch, and struck once. Twice. On the third, the torch took—flame blooming soft and golden in the wet dark. He shielded it with his body until it steadied. He held it low. Watched the flame as it guttered, then steadied.

Ranhildr turned the arrow in her hand, studied the shaft. Feather fletching. Rough sinew binding. No metal. The head was sharpened bone, not stone—split, barbed, still wet at the tip. It hadn't struck blood. But it could have.

She snapped it over her knee and tossed the pieces in opposite directions.

Skagi turned. Watched her. "Why not keep it?"

She met his eyes. "I break the line so that it cannot hold us."

Ketill stepped to the edge of the cut sod they'd marked earlier. He lowered himself to one knee—slowly, like the act cost more now than it had an hour ago. He pressed his hand to the earth beside the bone peg.

It was warm.

Not from sun. Not from touch.

"Still fresh," he murmured.

Finnvið crouched on a flat stone, one hand at his throat like he was trying to swallow a laugh that had curdled. His mouth moved, but nothing came — only the twitch of a man who knew sound itself might be a mistake.

Vidarbjǫrn stood a little apart. He hadn't touched his axe. Not during the approach. Not during the retreat. He didn't need to. He had already recognized them, whatever they were, and they had answered without gesture.

Rúni leaned against a low-limbed larch, both hands loose now, axe hanging by the leather tie. He let his head rest against the bark. Then: "They chose to leave us."

Finnvið looked up. "No words. Just seen, rejected, and gone."

"They spoke," said Ranhildr. "Just not kindly."

Skagi stood now. "Not men."

Ketill replied without emphasis. "Not living ones."

No one spoke after that.

They returned to camp near dusk. No one noticed them at first. The smoke from the half-hall clung low to the ground. Someone had stoked the trenchpit too hot — resin smoke curled from the damp pine, stinging the eyes.

Kristján stood by the beam line, sleeves rolled, one arm flecked with sap. Arnlaugr was tending a bundle of soaked parchment by the fire. He looked up, then down again.

Leif came from behind the frame.

He saw the line of them — Vidarbjǫrn at the front, Ranhildr beside him, Skagi behind, Ketill steady, Finnvið sly-eyed, Rúni unreadable — and his jaw worked once before he spoke.

"Anything?"

For a moment no one answered.

Ranhildr walked to the fire, stirred the ash with her knife, and spat into the flames. The fire popped and went silent.

Only then did Finnvið speak. "Whatever's out there... it isn't lost."

Leif looked at him. "Then what?"

Finn006 stared into the fire. "It's already named. Just not in the language of men."

They gathered at first light.

No one called it a council.

There was no horn, no ring of stones, no place of honour. Just men and woman moving toward the firepit like smoke had pulled them there, shoulders hunched, cloaks soaked through. The mist hung thick and low—knee-high, pale as marrow, clinging to boots and beard alike.

No one stood at the centre. They formed without intention—ring-shaped, uneven, uneasy. Not for ritual. For shelter.

The fire spat low heat. Pine sap cracked. Birch bark hissed.

Vidarbjǫrn stood just behind the flame, unmoving. Ranhildr stood near him, arms crossed, ash still faint on her cheeks. Skagi crouched to one side, hands bare despite the cold, one eye on the trees. Finnvið lingered further back, eyes red from smoke or thought. Ketill kept his place at the edge, where the clearing frayed into brush. Rúni leaned against a post, arms folded tight, jaw working like he was chewing through something too tough to swallow.

Kristján stepped forward first—not as command, but as measure. He looked at the fire, then at the faces. "Not all threats come with steel," he said. His voice was quiet, as if he feared echo. "We have water. Timber. Meat, if not enough. The land hasn't failed us. Not yet. We can build higher. Post watchers. Wait."

He looked at Leif, then away. "That's how we hold."

A few heads nodded. Not many.

Father Arnlaugr followed. He held no cross this time. It hung from his belt, half-wrapped. His hands were empty.

"Fear," he said, "has turned better men than us from better land than this." His voice was firm, but not raised. "Fear forgets what faith builds. Christ walked into storms. Not around them."

He paused. Let that settle. Turned slowly.

"Christ called fishermen, not kings," he said. "We are no less." His voice rose — not loud, but laden. "God does not abandon the faithful."

Rúni pushed off the post. "You're both wrong." He looked at the fire, not the men. "That thing — those things — let us walk away. They don't care about your god, or your watchers. They didn't strike. Because they didn't need to. They've already drawn their line."

Finnvið's voice came low. "And we're standing on the wrong side of it."

Murmurs. Not full speech. Words passed under breath. Some scoffed. Others nodded.

Skagi didn't rise. He tossed a pine shaving into the flame. "They didn't want us gone," he said.

"Then what?"

"They wanted us seen — and made uncertain."

"Like bait," Rúni said.

"No," Ranhildr said. Her voice wasn't loud. But it carried. She looked around the ring. "If they'd wanted blood, we'd be smoke and ash. They didn't strike. They marked."

"Marked what?" someone muttered.

"The edge of their world," she said. "Or the start of ours."

Silence.

Then Ketill spoke, slow. "Warnings don't come twice."

Leif stood at the edge of the ring. His arms were crossed. His cloak was soaked. His eyes looked toward Vidarbjǫrn, not the fire.

Vidarbjǫrn stepped forward. He didn't raise his voice. He bent. Took a strip of birch from the woodpile. Held it over the coals until steam bled from it, curling like breath. Then dropped it in.

He turned to Leif.

"You want this place?" Vidarbjǫrn said. "Then take it."

No one moved.

Vidarbjǫrn stepped closer. "Your father named coastlines with fire and salt. He spilled blood at every boundary stone. You wait for the trees to bless you." He pointed toward the woods. "But they wont. They already have a god. And he doesn't speak our tongue."

Leif's jaw tensed. His hands stayed at his sides.

Rúni spat into the dirt. "It's not land. It's a trap."

Kristján stepped forward again, voice lower now. "A trap only snares the careless. We can make it answer."

Then Leif raised his head.

He didn't speak to the group. Only to Vidarbjǫrn.

"We leave."

There was no vote.

No hand clasp.

Just that.

And the sound of rain beginning again — soft, steady, uninterested.

They left at dusk. Not in fear. Not in haste. Just certain. Because they'd seen enough to know that staying would require forcing the land to answer, and that answer was not yet known.

None of them — not even Leif — was ready to make it.

No horn sounded. No gospel spoken. No ash circle drawn to bind the leaving. They simply packed.

They took only what could be carried without cost — iron, gut-sealed pouches of salt, the last slabs of dried meat, the herb bundles Tyrkir had wrapped in waxed wool.

Kristján bore the fire-seed, slung in a horn packed with dried moss and birch fungus to cradle embers, tight against his ribs. Arnlaugr reached for the ember horn — but Kristján stepped in first, took it without word. Packed the moss himself, wedged the old coals with care. Slid the horn beneath his cloak, tight against the ribs.

Father Arnlaugr wrapped the soaked pages of the Gospel in hide and tucked the cross beneath his belt.

Skagi walked wide, one pace outside the line, blade sheathed but uncovered.

Finnvið teased the bones in his belt pouch as he walked.

Rúni walked rear, eyes to the trees.

They did not burn what they had built.

But they did not mark it either.

The half-frame of the hall stood unroofed above the ridge, smoke long since thinned, tarps slack. The storehouse had been sealed with pitch that morning. Fish still hung from the crossbeams, drying in the cool air. The trenchfires had been smothered with brine and ash.

They left them standing.

Whether as a gift or a warning, no one said.

Behind them, the clearing settled. Slowly. As though unsure whether to release them or call them back.

No one sang.

No one asked if they would return.

As the line passed the edge of the clearing, Vidarbjǫrn paused.

Only once.

He looked back—not at the trees, but at the firepit, where they had knelt, spoken, bled.

In the ash, something had been drawn.

A loop, a slash, a jagged cut through both — not a rune, not a letter, not anything he knew.

But it remained.

He did not call to the others. Did not move. Did not even breathe, until the wind passed around it. He watched the wind move around it, but not over it. As if even the air held back from touching what had been traced.

Then he turned and walked on.

By morning, the rain had washed their tracks. By nightfall, the stream ran clear — cold and forgetful. As if no one had ever settled. Only the ash-mark lingered. Then that, too, was gone.

And the trees resumed their silence.

CHAPTER 4: NO LAW BUT THE LAND

1000 A.D. — SÓLMÁNUÐR

The wind came from the northeast — steady, cruel, and old. It didn't strike in bursts, but pressed, as if the land itself had exhaled a long refusal. Sleet carved across the deck, threading its way into every layer of wool and hide, sliding beneath fur and skin with the certainty of something that had done it before. The mast bowed under the strain. The sail creaked, stiffened by patches gone salt-brittle, its seams drawn tight and pale as frostbit knuckles.

Above, the sky refused structure. No lid. No opening. Just a flat expanse of bone-grey cloud, marbled with something yellow and unclean at its edges — like light spoiled in its keeping. It sagged, not with threat, but with judgement. Watching. Pressing.

The knarr did not move well. She was broad in beam and deep in hull, built more for burden than grace. Against crosswind, she dragged like a sodden ox — stubborn, slow to heel. The crosswind pulled the keel sideways. Ropes thrashed, stiff with ice. The mast moaned in long, unbroken tones. Water spilled along the deck's seams and gathered at the tiller's base — dark, slow, thick as blood where it pools beneath a wound left open too long.

Leif stood with both hands gripped to the rudder, shoulders broad and soaked, the wool of his cloak clinging like sodden bark. His jaw was set hard beneath wind-reddened stubble, eyes narrowed — not scanning, but holding the line like a man keeping himself from breaking. His gloves had long since soaked through; the skin beneath was raw. When

Kristján passed him a command — sharp, shaped for wind —
Leif didn't turn. Didn't nod. Only held the line, as though
the act of steering was all that remained between his breath
and whatever waited just past the edge of seeing.

Kristján moved along the deck, issuing orders twice — once
to the men, once to the wind that stole them. His voice came
short now, clipped from the cold and from trying too long
to be heard. His cloak flared, soaked to the hem, and each
footfall echoed as if it too had grown tired of falling.

Beneath the low drop of the sail, Arnlaugr crouched, one
shoulder pressed to the beam, his knees drawn in beneath
him. He held the Christ-book tight against his ribs, wrapped
in oilcloth slick with salt. His mouth moved, silently
forming words only the parchment might know. Each time
the wind lashed the rigging overhead, he flinched — not
from fear, but from something deeper: the tremble of faith
when the signs come cold and unwelcoming.

High in the rigging, Skagi clung with both hands, his
knuckles blue, the straps biting through to bone. His hair,
wind-lashed, had come loose across his brow. He watched
the land. Not the sea, not the horizon — but the treeline
sliding past, dark with pine and snow-streaked stone.
Something in his stillness made even the wind hesitate. A
few men glanced up. No one called him down.

Finnvið huddled midships, knees drawn up, cloak sagging
across his lap. He muttered nonsense, but not idly. Bits of
Latin, half-prayers, old curse-ends and cradle-sounds. His
fingers danced lightly in the puddled water beside him,
tracing patterns that might have been charms, or might have
been fear made ritual. Twice he tried to stand. Twice he
slipped. Ketill caught him both times, without looking, as
though lifting Finnvið was no more burdensome than

raising a hand against the rain.

Ketill stood near the prow, rooted. His boots locked to the deck by habit more than need. Salt hung in his beard, thickened it. He stared ahead as if the wind were only memory, and he was watching for something older—something he had seen once, long before, in a place the sea would never let him name aloud.

Rúni broke silence only once. He named the wind in the old tongue. Then the rain. Then the dark. The syllables caught in the air, as if the wind paused to hear them. After that, he moved to the mast, tied a charm just below the head—a twist of fishbone, gut, and hide. It swung crooked in the sleet. Arnlaugr saw it and frowned but did not speak. Leif saw nothing. Or did not want to.

Tyrkir stood apart. Chewing something from his pouch—dark, dried, clove-scented—and watching the coastline as though it were moving wrong. Not watching the trees. Watching what moved between them.

No one spoke unless a rope snarled or a line gave. The ship moved southward, each plank groaning under the strain. Men pulled as they were told, but no one laboured loudly. They worked as if each action must pass unnoticed.

By the time the sleet gave way to rain, it no longer mattered. The cold had gone into them. Rain ran the spine, soaked tunics, gathered in boots. The coast pinched in again, then opened into a shallow bay, pines leaning so close a man could strike them with a stone—though none did.

They ran the knarr aground in black gravel and weed-slick rock. Not fast, not recklessly, but with the resignation of those who knew they had no choice. The sail came down in a practiced haul. When the keel ground, not one man leapt to the water. Each paused. Each glanced to the trees.

Mist pressed in as they heaved the boats above the tide, hulls grinding through pebble and weed, bows coming to rest half-swallowed in rock-slop. The beach was steep and narrow, its pebbles dark with old wet. Just beyond, the forest crouched—pine-tall and close-grown, bark stripped raw by wind, trunks slick with lichen. Smoke from the cookfires coiled low, unwilling to rise, drifting like breath from a dying mouth.

Leif sat beside the firepit where damp wood spat and hissed. Tinder kept dry in seal bladders—moss, birchbark, slivered root. Struck with flint until lichen caught, then breathed into smoke. The fire rose slow, grudging. One boot hung half-laced, the leather stiff with salt. His gaze held on nothing. The lines of his shoulders stayed drawn, pulled tight as if still bracing against wind that had not touched him in hours. Light caught in the water on his brow, but did not reach the skin beneath.

Vidarbjǫrn sat near—not close enough to speak, but within reach of the cold leaching from Leif's body. His frame, broad and quiet as always, cast no shadow in the fire's weak glow. He sat like stone left half-buried—seen, but not easily moved. The fire's heat didn't reach them. What came off Leif's body was not warmth, but a kind of tremor—like steam rising off a stone too long frozen, cracked from within.

They had sailed more than one hundred thirty miles since last laying eyes on Greenland—not marked in chart or star, but in ache, in wear, in the brittle way hands began to tremble when the sail snapped too loud or the sky pressed too low. And still, it had not felt like gain. Only that the land had tolerated their crossing.

If the gods had ever cast their gaze this far, they had long since turned away. Or else the land answered to something older—something that swallowed not only men, but the names they carried.

Leif's eyes flicked to the tree-line. The pines did not move.

"Three months," he said. "And still the land bears no true name. Not one that stays."

His fingers curled slightly. "We speak blessings. Oaths. The wind carries them off. We mark the soil, and the rain clears it. Runes don't take. Even the Cross—"

He stopped there. Jaw clenched.

"It's like the land belongs to something else. And whatever watches... it doesn't speak our tongue."

Vidarbjǫrn stood a few paces off, near the firepit where steam curled low from the ash. He didn't lift his head. Only answered.

"Then we go farther," he said. "Until it speaks. Or until we carve a place it can't refuse."

Leif's mouth tightened. "And if there is no answer? If this place is outside them all—Old and New?"

Ranhildr's voice cut in sharp.

"Then force one."

She stepped into view—tall, braid heavy down her back,

hands bark-darkened and jaw held tight. Her eyes caught what little light the fire offered—green-flecked and unflinching, like frost under flame.

"If the gods go quiet, speak louder. If the land gives no name, take it from its throat. You wait like something sacred must grant us leave. But we didn't come to be welcomed."

Leif turned to her. Not fully. Just enough to show the strain beneath his stillness.

"And if the land was never meant for us?" he said.

Ranhildr's gaze didn't shift. "Then let it learn our names in blood and smoke."

Evening descended. The silence between their trunks was thick enough to drink. And cold as anything drawn from the belly of the sea. The shapes seen two nights past—glimpses between the trees, too fast for certainty—were still spoken of, but not as threat. Most claimed they were men. But no one crossed into the woods unarmed. Not even to piss.

Father Arnlaugr rose slowly, oilskin bundle clutched close. The book—warped, salt-bent—gleamed dully in the light. His voice did not rise above the wind.

"For those who would," he said, "let us give thanks for the day."

No one moved. One man cleared his throat. Another adjusted his cloak. The rest sat silent. Wet from brow and beard dripped onto the stones, feeding the hiss of fire. Leif did not look up. But Vidarbjǫrn felt the tautness in him—a held string, stretched past tone. Not refusal. Not belief. Only tension. The kind that comes before sound breaks.

Leif rose. His words were clipped, but carried no venom.

"Hold shape. We don't kneel to dark. We speak. We watch."

Then they kneeled.

Arnlaugr stepped forward without flourish, robes heavy with salt. The oilskin wrap crinkled as he unfolded it, slow and exact, hands callused from work as much as worship. The Gospel sat within—warped, sea-warped, salt-bent at the spine—but intact. He did not look to the fire or to the men. Only the book.

He knelt in the ash—*not before the storm, not before the land*, but to mark that the shape of belief still held. Even here.

When he opened the Gospel, the pages clung. Damp. Reluctant. As if the sea still wanted them.

His voice came low, shaped by breath not command. He did not preach. He *anchored*.

"Our feet are on cursed ground. So we speak blessings."

He paused. Let the hiss of fire pass through him. "Even Christ walked into storms. Not around them."

His voice cracked on the word *Christ,* not from fear—but from cold. And something deeper.

He raised the book. Just a hand's height. "What is not named cannot own us."

Then he read.

The words struck the fire's spit and came apart in the steam—Latin shaped in frost and mist. But the rhythm held. The cadence still carved space.

A few others joined him—bare murmurs, soft as insects on old mead. Not harmony. But structure.

And for a moment, the dark held off. Not gone. Not weakened. But met.

Then Tyrkir moved.

He said nothing. Just shifted his weight, slow and deliberate, and knelt by the packs. His knees cracked as he bent—not with age, but with long use. He unwrapped a twist of hide, movements calm, like the cold had no hold on his hands. From within, he drew a pouch. Sealskin, dark with oil. It gave a soft sound, not unlike breath, when opened.

Inside: fruits. Shrivelled, brown, split at their seams. Apples dried in mead, salted plums from a jar long empty. Most had split in the cold, the sugars hardened to skin. They were not pleasant to look at. But they had lasted. And that was the point.

He passed them without speech. Hand to hand. Never more than one at a time. His fingers moved with the patience of someone who'd done this before—in a holdfast during famine, in a blizzard with the dead still warm beside him, in a cave where the fire had gone to smoke.

"Sweet holds rot back," he said.

His voice was soft, but the words sat deep. Not proverb. Not ritual. Just truth, spoken by someone who had lived it.

They ate them slowly. The taste was bitter-edged—preserved too long, mead-sour and iron-tinged. It caught between the teeth and clung to the tongue. But it gave something back. Not warmth. Not strength. But memory—of harvests sealed in salt, of fire that had once been easy, of hunger endured and not worshipped. When the pouch emptied, he wrapped it again, tied the leather with ash-stiff fingers, and set it back beneath the tarp. Tyrkir did not speak again. But his presence remained—a weight, not a flare. Not faith like Father Arnlaugr's, but something older. Something built in the gut. In the jaw. In the act of chewing through what had to be endured. And when the wind shifted, and the fire flared, and the dark pressed inward once more, it met not silence, but breath that had been steadied. Bellies that had remembered sweetness. That was enough.

Later, when the wind softened and the fire caught clean, shoulders eased. Cloaks opened. One man even laughed—low, brief, like a muscle unclenching.

Then a branch snapped in the dark. Sudden. Wrong.

Voices came fast.

"Spirits followed," Rúni said. His voice cut clean. "They rode the sleet."

Ranhildr answered at once. "Stop naming what's not there."

Rúni turned. Not slow. Not cautious.

"You think naming makes it real?"

His shoulders braced. "It's behind the wind. In the rootline. I smelled it before your charm failed."

Ranhildr stepped forward, blade still in hand, ash still on her face.

"You chase ghosts to feel needed. Fear doesn't make you wise. Just loud."

Rúni's hand flexed near his belt. Not threat. Readiness.

"And you think the land listens just because you've painted your face. It doesn't. It watches."

They stood eye to eye, the fire between them. Her fingers curled around the hilt. His breath fogged fast.

Neither blinked. No one stepped in. The fire cracked.

Tyrkir stood.

His voice came soft, but it settled the air.

"We should drink."

Kristján nodded once.

"For strength," he said. "Not carelessness."

His smile had no curve in it. Just the shape of endurance.

The mead was thin, sour with smoke, but it burned its way down. They passed the horn once, then again. Fire was fed. The green kindling smoked thick, catching slow.

Two guards were set — one at the tide, one at the trees.

Neither liked their post.

The woods gave no sound, but did not sleep.

No one turned their back on the dark.

The morning did not break. It seeped—grey and low, drawing itself out of the trees and shoreline like steam from spoiled meat.

Mist peeled back from the rocks with slow reluctance, as if the land itself shed a skin it hadn't meant to wear. The pines stood still—not in welcome, nor in warning. Only watching. Smoke from the last fire rose in a single line, thin as sinew. The wind had stilled in the night, or turned. Cold remained, but it no longer clung to the throat. That absence felt like mercy, though no man named it aloud.

They moved without command. Boots found the wet sand. Ropes ran through raw hands. Breath smoked in the air, low and slow. No one grumbled. No one spat. It was the silence of those who listen for answer.

Father Arnlaugr stepped into the shallows. His robes dragged salt. He waded to the waist, turned east, and crossed himself with both hands. The Christ-book he lifted high, salt-warped and shining in its oilskin wrap.

"We give thanks," he said. His voice was low, but it held.

No man mocked it.

By midmorning the sail had caught. The sea bore them even and clean, the wind steady enough to press their cloaks to their backs. Salt air tasted right again. Stiff wool dried into shape. Some opened their cloaks wide, letting the sun beat through as if it might leach the last of the camp-smoke from their skin. A few blades were unwrapped and checked for rust. Oiled with care. One man hummed, and another joined, and a work-song took shape—old, fjord-born, no one's in particular. Its rhythm set in their boots and boards alike.

Then Tyrkir sang.

The words were thick in the throat, round and wide in the jaw. Not Norse. Not Latin. Not Faroese. Older. He sang low, grinning—not to mock, but as if the song itself mocked the need for meaning. The crew leaned close, drawn not by melody but by some shared memory they couldn't quite name.

Skagi tilted his head, blinking into the wind. "What is it?"

Tyrkir shrugged. "Drinking song." As if that were all the answer needed.

The wind pressed behind them—broad and firm now. The waves no longer chopped. They rolled, long and slow, like something returning to rhythm. The hull shifted beneath their feet, not as if carried, but as if it remembered how to float.

Skagi climbed the rigging like a hare up birch—quick, clean, careless. He reached the cross-spar and stood with arms flung wide, catching all the sky he could. Kristján looked up, squinting.

"You're no gull," he called. Dry. Without bite.

"There's a fish!" Skagi shouted down. "Big as the boat. Just under us!"

No one else saw it. But heads turned. Men leaned. Whether it had been there or not no longer mattered. It had been named. That was enough.

Leif stood near the mast. He had said nothing all morning. But now he reached to his belt, pulled loose a leather token — hair-bound, sinew-twisted — and tied it beneath the tiller, three turns and one half-knot. A seal sign had been seen. It had to be answered.

The sea was feeding again.

The gods — if they still watched — had not yet turned their faces away.

***

Evening did not come gentle. But it came clean. The sky cleared sharp and deep, blue as bone carved and polished. Light struck cold from above, and the sea beneath darkened into steel.

The wind dropped. Not soft. Just thinner. It scraped, now, rather than pushed.

The men gathered low by the firepit, backs still hunched — not from cold, but from the memory of cold. Spirits had lifted. One man gnawed at meat too dry to spoil. Another trimmed a leather patch to fit his boot-seam. A third whetted his knife, not in fear, only to feel the edge sit right in his hand.

The trees no longer pressed.

Kristján turned toward Leif — not deferent, but measured, shoulders squared beneath a cloak stiff with dried salt. His eyes tracked Leif's profile — the jaw tight, the brow drawn into that unreadable stillness Leif wore when judging men or fate.

"When we settle," he said, voice steady, "we'll need law. Not just to bind. To name us."

Leif stared into the fire. The flame danced in the cracked salt around his eyes.

Kristján didn't wait. "A Thing. Not like Greenland's. Nothing bent by old lineages or debt. Something clean."

Father Arnlaugr gave a quiet nod. His thumb ran the wrap-edge of his book, slow, reverent. "Land needs law like beams need joints. Even if the house is never raised."

Vidarbjǫrn muttered, almost without breath, "I've seen the joints in Greenland."

The men laughed—low, brief, real.

Leif's voice came at last. "My father was outlawed by those joints. His father too. Not from weakness. Only because they didn't fit."

Kristján met the words with a half-smile. "Then we build new ones. Not theirs. Ours."

The fire cracked. Sparks rose in a spiral, wind-lifted, flame-bitten.

No one answered. But the silence held weight. The kind that speaks of hammer-blows still to come.

Ranhildr sat apart, cloak pulled tight at the shoulders, hands steady as her knife split driftwood into barbs. Her mouth stayed set, unreadable. But her eyes—dark and bright with intent—never once lifted from the work. Her jaw locked with every pull. The pile grew. She did not glance up. No one asked what she made.

Ketill slept first. Not curled for warmth. Not shielded. Just still, laid long against the boards as if he'd grown tired of motion.

One guard walked the waterline. Another patrolled the trees. Neither looked back toward the fire.

The dark settled thick between the pines. But the wind did not rise. And no man turned his back to the woods.

Later, when the talk had stilled and the coals had caved in on themselves, Vidarbjǫrn rose without word and walked the edge of firelight to where Ranhildr crouched.

She didn't look up. Her hands worked still.

"Come to ask?" she said, voice flat.

"No."

She drew the blade again. The driftwood split down its grain like it had been waiting to break.

"It wasn't mine," she said. "The land. The salt pit. The nets. They were Father's. His barley. His slope. His name."

Another cut. Clean. She didn't watch it fall.

"Hrafn Eiriksson took it when Father fell ill. Claimed debts, showed forged oaths. One signed by a man long dead. No one questioned it."

Vidarbjǫrn waited.

"The Thing let it stand. Said Father should've spoken sooner. But by then his tongue was thick. Couldn't hold a word. Just blood."

Her knife paused above the next piece.

"I should've done something. Slit Hrafn's throat. Or his dog's first."

"You were thirteen," he said, low.

She didn't answer that.

"You were in Norway," she went on. "Learning to carry steel. I was digging rotgrain from the shed floor. Watching our timber go to his new hall. I knew every beam by its scar."

The wind shifted her braid across her shoulder. She didn't brush it back.

"They called him clever," she said. "Said he outfoxed an old man. But it wasn't clever. It was rot. Dressed in law. Dressed in smiles. And the Thing crowned it just."

Vidarbjǫrn gave a small nod. She saw it. Didn't return it.

"I let them call it justice," she said, quieter now. "I was thirteen. And I let them."

He stepped closer, slow, then sat—not close, not within reach, but enough to catch the cold she carried and offer some of his own in return.

The knife stayed still in her hand. Her thumb pressed into the hilt. Blood welled at the edge of a callus.

"If we build a Thing here," she said, not looking at him, "it won't be their kind. I'll see to that. No soft edges. No debt-games. No sons of chieftains slipping into power like skin into glove."

She drew the blade once more. The wood split into a jagged point.

The sky above her had gone sharp and starless — clear in the way that cracks before it breaks.

He watched her, not with pity, but with the long quiet of a man who had once believed law could bind the world rightly, and no longer did.

Ranhildr's hands didn't still. The pile beside her had grown. Not to a purpose. Just sharpened wood and effort, the kind that fills silence because nothing else will.

The last guard passed at a distance. Saw them. Said nothing. Kept walking.

The fire at their backs gave its last hiss and died to ash.

No one named the land.

The third morning held its breath.

No wind rose before dawn. Just a stillness left behind, thick and pale as bone beneath skin. The trees stood silent, their needles unmoved. Even the gulls came late, wheeling in slow arcs as if unsure they were wanted.

Frost cracked in the ash-rim near the firepit.

Rúni moved barefoot across the grass. His heel pressed into the dirt like it might yield a sign. The cold did not break him. He stepped slow, unblinking.

Finnvið hunched on a log, spine crooked like a raven's perch. He cleared his throat, spat sideways into the frost, and began a tale no one had asked for.

"Eastern god," he said. "Dog head. Fish tongue. Drowned himself for wisdom. Held his breath 'til the river forgot his name. Came back with ash-bones and frog-skin secrets."

His grin flashed like a knife too thin to cut. No one laughed.

A twig snapped under someone's heel. The fire hissed, low and sharp.

Rúni looked up. "Wisdom doesn't float."

No one asked if it was curse or proverb. No one had to.

Ketill crouched near the tiller, where salt and strain had worked a rope to threadbare ruin. He fingered the fibres gently, ran them flat across his palm, then began the binding. A fourfold weave. Tight. Fast. Each tuck exact. A sailor's splice, done clean by hand — no iron, no hook, only memory pressed into sinew. With the final twist, he murmured something — not loud, not for others. Just old. It moved through the air like water under stone.

Arnlaugr heard. His brow shifted, but he spoke no word.

Vidarbjǫrn watched. He didn't know the tongue. But he knew its shape. The rhythm of belief inside it. That rope would not break. That much he knew.

Near the fire, Skagi passed Ketill a strip of dried trout. Ketill tore it in two, chewed once, then shifted his weight a hand-width to the right.

Skagi sat beside him. Quiet. Close.

Later, when no one watched, Skagi tried to mimic the knot Ketill had tied. The rope slipped, unravelled. He stared at it. Let it fall. Did not try again.

The morning wore on like a damp shirt — clinging, chilled, but bearable.

And the sea, for once, showed no teeth.

Vidarbjǫrn sat low in the hull's curve. The boards had caught some sun, and the warmth held. His hands rested on his thighs — neither tensed nor idle. Just waiting.

He tasted the wind. Westerly. Soft. No bite in it.

No gulls screamed wrong. No tide fought the keel.

Just the long lean of the boat, its patched sail holding firm. No strain. No snap. A steadiness that felt, for a moment, undeserved.

A kind of mercy.

The thought rose in him — perhaps the test is done.

He drew breath through his nose. Held it. Let it go. Let the sea take it. Then he drew his knife and tapped the gunwale twice. Bone on pine. Quiet, but heard. A sign, not a flourish. A whisper, not a shout. The word that followed was not for men.

He touched the haft of Bitabrjótur, still sheathed. Still asleep.

A plank creaked behind him.

Rúni stood nearby, watching. His eyes narrowed in that way of his — not challenge, not question, only presence.

He said nothing.

Vidarbjǫrn did not turn.

He kept his gaze on the horizon, where light met water in a strip too narrow for peace and too wide for warning.

They saw the seals just after noon.

A flat outcrop rose from the shallows like a god's tooth left to rot — broad, kelp-slick, steaming under the sun. Thirty heads or more, grey-backed and long-eyed, lay sprawled across the stone. Some barked in dream. Most slept — bellies pale, slick with tide, ribs dark with breath. One lifted its head, sniffed the wind, and lay back down. Like it had known worse.

Leif stood at the bow.

"We land," he said.

No vote. No reason. The sign had come. It had to be answered.

He turned and named six: "Rúni. Ketill. Ranhildr. Skagi. Vidarbjǫrn. Myself."

No man questioned. Each name marked a soul long-proven—weathered, blooded, and known.

But one voice rose from the boats.

"Let me come."

Hallkell the Red.

The two brothers had come together like stones cut from the same fault-line—same grain, same fracture, but worn to different shapes by use. Hallkell the Red first. Windburned, broad across the chest, hands calloused from rope but not yet from blood. His beard still thin in places, more rust than fire. Eyes too bright—always seeking, always measuring. Older than Skagi, though still young. Hungry in the mouth, like he'd been raised one meal short of contentment. He stood with weight forward, as if waiting for the world to flinch. His boots still held the salt of the western fjords.

After him had come his brother: Haraldr. Darker in beard, slower in movement, older by five winters and carrying them like stone in the joints. His face was flatter, less eager. The nose had been broken once. He bore the weight of a man who'd learned what didn't need saying. His belt held a sailor's knife, his gaze held a warning.

They were brothers. Not by likeness, but by rhythm. One tested. One endured. And both had come to stake claim in Leif's uncertain fire.

Now Leif studied Hallkell the Red. Let the silence stretch until it touched the edge of insult. Then gave a single nod.

"Bring your spear."

Hallkell's mouth twitched—something not yet a smile. He turned to fetch it, boots biting into gravel.

Vidarbjǫrn said nothing. But his eyes moved—from Skagi to Hallkell, then to the space between them. One limped from pride. The other hadn't noticed the limp.

Back on shore, the camp held steady. Driftwood was gathered. Spoiled fish were gutted. No complaint from Kristján—only a sharp call for salt and a double watch. The salt was kept in leather twists, dried hard as horn and tucked in the shade of the tarp. Pulled from seawash pans at Greenland's edge, boiled down to flake and grind.

Arnlaugr sat near the tide with the Christ-book shut in his lap, his thumb stroking its spine like he remembered the heft of something heavier.

The hunters moved low.

Bows unstrung. Blades bound. They crept the ridge above seal-crag, boots wool-wrapped, weight spread wide across fernroot and alder mulch. The wind came steady from the west. Their scent held behind. That was the only grace.

Rúni whispered to his axe. Ranhildr bit blood from the inside of her cheek. Skagi's mouth had closed. His gait no longer quick—head bent, careful. Hallkell mouthed charm-words—three lines, bone-hung and leaf-stuck, passed hand to hand from men who no longer stirred at the taste of blood.

They bellied to the edge. Shields stayed behind—too loud for seal-stalking, too wide for fern-thickets. They crept light, each man trusting blade and boot to serve in silence.

Below: the crag. Broad and flat, kelp-hung and stone-warmed. Seals lay thick across it—grey-backs breath-pulsing, bellies pale as gut parchment. Some twitched. Some blinked. None stirred.

Rúni nocked first. Then Skagi. Hallkell already held draw—full pull, no tremor. Leif raised his hand. The moment held. Wind still west.

Then—a silence. Sudden. Wrong.

Not gull. Not seal.

Vidarbjǫrn felt it first, in the gut, like a held breath that turned.

A twig snapped uphill.

He turned toward the alder rise.

Too late.

She came down through the scrub without warning—a sow, massive, her white coat slicked grey with brine and old blood. No gleam left in her fur, just the clotted drag of kelp and muck. Two cubs flickered behind her—ghosts in the underbrush—then were gone. But she didn't bluff. She didn't rear. She came on, low and fast, all weight and silence.

Not like a beast. Like the slope itself had broken loose.

The crag below erupted—seals scattering, slapping foam, screaming into surf.

"Back—!" Leif's voice cut high, but wind or fear took the

rest.

Skagi turned toward the sound—and never finished the motion.

Her paw slammed him across the ribs, full sweep. His cloak split. Blood followed, dark and sudden. He spun, fell, rolled once, and lay still.

Ketill shouted his name.

But the bear was already past.

Rúni moved first. Low, fast, axe drawn clean.

He struck behind her rear hock—deep, fast, angled to lame.

It barely slowed her.

She twisted. One paw caught him mid-swing. Raked through wool, hide, then bone.

He folded hard. Blood sprayed from his mouth before he hit the ground.

Then Hallkell.

Wordless. From the flank. Spear low, two hands.

He drove it deep above the foreleg—clean to the haft.

The rib turned it.

The shaft shuddered in his grip. He had time to grimace. Nothing more.

The sow reared.

Steam rose off her mouth. Her jaw opened wide — black and hot and wrong.

Then she came down.

One paw. One stroke. Jaw to ear.

Hallkell's skull cracked sideways. His body hit the stone like it had been flung by the gods.

He did not rise.

Ranhildr threw from crouch. Fifteen paces. No chance to close.

The spear flew true — caught her in the throat. It stuck. She drew her knife before it landed.

Ketill was already moving. No voice. No shout.

He slipped in low, past the front leg, and drove his seax deep behind the shoulder.

Blood welled thick, fast, choking on the heat.

Then Leif.

He came from behind, silent.

One step. One cut.

His axe caught behind her skull — through hide, through bone, into the eye.

The haft jolted in his grip. He held on.

She spasmed.

The legs gave.

She collapsed with a grunt like thunder rolling into bog.

Silence returned—fast, complete.

Steam rose off her flank. Blood soaked the ferns.

Vidarbjǫrn stood frozen, three paces off. He had drawn too slow. Moved too late.

He had felt it—back at the stream, in the twitch of Hallkell's eyes—but said nothing.

He let out his breath, slow and cold, and stepped forward.

Behind him, Ranhildr pressed hard into Rúni's side. Her hands were red to the wrist.

Ketill knelt beside Skagi, already binding. Skagi groaned once, low and wet.

There was no shouting now.

Only the rhythm of aftermath: bind, seal, bury, burn.

Hallkell lay twisted by the treeline, one arm flung into shadow. His eyes stared up. His mouth stayed open, as if still trying to name what had come.

No one spoke.

But the land had.

Leif stood over the fallen bear. Axe low. Knuckles crusted in blood. His eyes stayed locked on the sow's body, like he was waiting for it to rise.

"We burn it," Leif said.

Vidarbjǫrn gave one nod. Then stepped forward and drew Bitabrjótur —not for killing, but to begin the work that follows when the killing is done.

The thicket stilled around him—no birds, no branch-ache, only breath, blood-heat, and the stink of ruptured muscle.

The silence pressed into his ribs like a cairn laid wrong.

He had felt the shift back at the stream. The unease. The twitch in Hallkell's jaw. The glance sideways. The pause.

And he had said nothing.

He had waited for words the land was never going to speak.

That would not happen again.

This ground didn't deal in omen or sign. It spoke in blood and root-stir, in the stillness before bone breaks.

Next time, he would answer.

Hallkell's body would be washed and sung over.

The bear would burn. Its spirit loosed and driven east, past the salt-lands, beyond the reach of sleep. Not for revenge. For balance.

The wind turned. Shifted west to east.

They hauled the carcass before dusk.

No meat was kept. None salted. Meat struck by fate drew rot. The flesh was laid out in strips and hunks, arranged like butchered penance on stones warmed by the sun's last heat. The bones were stacked high in a pyre — not with reverence, but with finality. A hill of failure. A weight owed. When the fire caught, the fat hissed, bubbling through muscle like blood beneath blistered skin. The smell turned at once — sweet, then spoiled, then thick as boiled horn. It stuck in the throat. It salted the eyes. It would not leave.

No one spoke.

Even Finnvið stood still. His mouth moved, but the syllables came bent, half-forgotten, like a drunk man whispering a spell he didn't believe in. Arnlaugr read from the Christ-book, voice low and slow, as though repeating words meant for someone else. His robes clung to his shins, soaked through from knee to hem. The words came like warnings half-remembered.

Haraldr, Hallkell's kin, knelt near the corpse. He drew a ring around the stacked bones — salt mixed with charcoal, crushed fine and poured in careful arcs. The powder soaked into the dirt. No one crossed it.

Kristján stood at the clearing's edge. The smoke wrapped his shoulders and curled into his beard like a crown of ash.

"This wasn't punishment," he said. "It was proof."

Kristján did not look at the body. His gaze held instead on the crouched form of his son—mud at the knees, smoke at the shoulders, eyes too wide for his age.

He did not say what it proved. But he knew.

They had tried to stake a claim—and the land had judged.

He knew that rhythm. He had lived it once already, in a longhouse where his name was no longer spoken. When his wife sent him out and would not take the boy. When no one called it exile, but all upheld the verdict.

He had thought once that failure came quiet, without cost. Now he knew: a threshold broken does not mend. Judgement comes, whether named or not. His hands stayed at his belt, but his fingers curled hard enough to blanch the skin.

Hallbjǫrn Ketilsson was already waiting at the treeline—lean, long-fingered, built like a root pulled from frost-ground. His hair lay flat, dark with sweat, and his tunic hung loose except where it was cinched by a belt heavy with pouches, twine, and carved tools. No blade. Just a cedar staff for walking—and sometimes bracing others.

He didn't shout. He didn't gesture. Just spoke, clear and unsentimental.

"Get them down. Not in the mud. And not where the wind cuts."

He'd once served as herb-ward to a chieftain's house in Iceland, though he never said which. His voice had a rasp to it, like bark dragged on stone, and he was quicker to correct than praise. But he had hands steady as drift-ice and strength where it mattered — in the grip, in the spine, in how long he could hold someone together before the blood told its final truth.

The wounded were lain on wool and bark. Skagi, bound thigh to ankle, sweat beading hard at his brow. Rúni, chest rising sharp and thin, eyes half-shut but not fading. Neither groaned. Neither wept. The pain was too close for that. It held them like weather.

Hallbjǫrn crouched beside them, his belt already unbuckled, tools laid out in order on a square of hide. He opened a clay jar sealed with waxed cloth, then broke apart a hardened lump of pitch-dark paste with his nails. The scent hit: sharp spruce, old whale-oil, crushed juniper. Not sweet — never sweet. A medicine made to offend the mouth but save the flesh.

He handed the first smear to Skagi, nodding once. "Press deep. Don't chase the pain."

Skagi took the balm without word. His hands trembled. He smeared it over the wound, clumsy-fingered but deliberate. He didn't look up. Ketill reached to steady him without comment — just touch, brief but bracing.

Next, Hallbjǫrn turned to Rúni. He eased the cloth from his ribs. The tear ran deep — skin split, blood weeping slow and dark where the bear's claw had dragged across the bone. No moan. Just breath catching in the throat.

From his kit, Hallbjǫrn drew a pouch wrapped in waxed wool, inside it a flat leaf folded over dried slivers — kelp-black and sharp-smelling. He crushed them between stones, added ash, spat once, stirred. The mix steamed.

"This will sting," he said, not as warning. As fact.

He pressed the paste into the wound with bare fingers, slow and exact. Not fast. Not gentle. But right. The smell thickened — pith and pitch and crushed berry, sour oil and sweat. Then came the heat. Rúni flinched. Bit the inside of his cheek.

"You'll keep the lung," Hallbjǫrn said. "If you breathe clean."

Hallbjǫrn bound the ribs with layered wool. Tight, not cruel. He tied it with twine and ash.

Hallbjǫrn finished the last binding and stepped back. Only then did Tyrkir rise, slow and broad-shouldered, wiping his palms on his tunic. He pulled a pouch from the coals — dried apples soaked two nights in honeyed mead. He set them to warm at the edge of the coals. The scent spread slow: sweet, rich, wrong for the moment. He set a strip of birch beneath the pan.

He didn't explain. Just stirred the pot and said, "Men eat first. Spirits can wait."

Hallbjǫrn grunted. Not agreement — just tolerance.

No one spoke. But the air shifted. Men leaned closer. Someone breathed easier.

Ranhildr stood nearest the flame. Her jaw was locked. Her arms still streaked with Rúni's blood. Her gaze fixed on the centre of the pyre where the skull had cracked open and poured.

Then — she sang. Her voice rose from low in the chest,

roughened by cold, smoke, and old blood. The song came low, from somewhere marrow-deep, where breath met bone. It rose without words at first—just tone, raw and earth-heavy. A sound like pine roots split under frost. A sound that did not ask to be heard, only *held*. A carrying-song. A binding-song. It curled into the smoke, twisted with the burning—blood, ash, pine. The sound scraped the throat. It wasn't meant for men. But the men held it. It bound what had happened. Named it, without naming. And when Ranhildr began to sing, the steam from Tyrkir's pan curled with it—smoke and honey and grief.

No one joined. No one moved.

Even the fire quieted.

The seal meat was left behind.

No one said why. No vote was called. No prayer said. Hunger knew its place.

That night the flames burned long, fed slow. No boasting followed. No mead-praise. No tale.

One man was gone. One burned into ash. Two bound in cloth and silence.

The land had taken its due. But gave no name in return.

CHAPTER 5: THE TEETH OF THE COAST

1000 A.D. — SEIÐHULA

The land no longer opened to them. It curled inward, meaner with each headland — black stone shelves bouldered and slick, crowding the sea with tide-smeared weed. Surf broke shallow, struck late, and left no clear passage. Bladderwrack tangled in the strakes. The last headland had scraped her low — deep enough to rasp pitch from the grain. The knarr heeled — not in fight, but confusion. Dragged like a beast by a tether it couldn't see.

The wind had dropped — but not kindly. The sail sagged on the spar, the luff slack and twitching. What motion remained came from the sea itself — an uneven pull, crosswise and inland, like the coast was drawing breath through a broken jaw.

Ranhildr crouched forward at the prow, one hand on the gunwale, the other tightening the knot on her wrist. Her hair lifted in the slack wind, red-streaked and damp, looped back through bone pins. She squinted into the mist, then turned — not toward Leif, but toward the hull's underside, where the sea spoke first.

"No depth under us," she called. "Too sharp. It folds in here."

Skagi stood behind her, braced but eager, his eyes bright against the grey, tracking light like it might name the safest path. A strand of hair caught at the edge of his mouth, and he didn't brush it back.

Leif said nothing. One hand rested loose on the tiller, his frame braced as it had been since first light. Salt traced the corners of his mouth. When the tiller kicked, he corrected without thought—habit, not choice.

"Where?" Vidarbjørn asked, stepping to the forward beam. His voice was even, but the question turned the ship toward him.

Ranhildr pointed off starboard—southwest—where a narrow break in the cliffs opened between two sloped basalt shoulders, still wet from the last push of tide.

"It's not good," she said. "But it's open."

Skagi nodded sharply. "Better than what's coming. That cut ahead—" he motioned toward the broader gap further down the coast, already narrowing as the cliffs converged— "it's teeth. Can't even see the back wall."

Vidarbjørn stepped beside them, squinting into the sea-mist. The air didn't smell right. The wind had shifted—not enough to fill the sail, but enough to twist the lines of pressure across the hull. Something here had slipped its pattern. Not chance, not weather—but something else unspoken.

"We won't clear the cut," he said. Then, after a breath: "Take her in. Through the basalt."

He didn't raise his voice. He didn't look at Leif. But Leif nodded.

The knarr coasted without command. She was built to bear weight, not outrun it—her square sail more burden than wing when the wind fell wrong. Lines were drawn in. The sail trimmed—tight enough to slow her, loose enough to steer. Haukr moved forward to the bowline, knife already loose in hand—not drawn, just unbound. If the line caught wrong, he'd have to cut fast. Ketill braced himself with one foot on the outer hull planking, just above the waterline, using it as a footing and leaned into the lean of the ship, eyes narrowed as if scenting shoals ahead.

Then the sound—wood on stone. Not a break, but a drag—slow and deliberate, like a hand searching along the hull.

"Brace!" Kristján shouted, but the hull had already shuddered—low on the nose. Not fully caught—only wrong enough to chill the spine. No one cursed. That silence meant more than fear. They only looked—some to the water, some to each other.

"Take the wind out," Rúni said, voice low, hand raised in supplication. "You don't fight a current when it's speaking."

"Ranhildr, back," Leif ordered. "Skagi too."

They shifted without argument. Only Skagi muttered as he passed Vidarbjǫrn. "I said it was teeth."

Vidarbjǫrn did not reply. He moved to the side rail and watched the water run thick with churned kelp. Beneath the foam, dark streaks ran counter. The coast wasn't just resisting. The water beneath threshed in reverse, as if something deep-mouthed and unseen tugged at the knarr's bones.

They drifted until the current loosened its hold—like something testing their weight, then choosing to release. Beneath the foam, stone flashed black through the churn, too close beneath.

Leif angled the knarr toward the shallows. She rode deep — four feet of draft beneath her, too much for the surf — but the current had slowed, and they had no clearer way in.

As the hull slid into calf-deep water, the keel brushed bottom — just once. No jolt — only warning, enough to mark the frame with tension.

Then Ketill dropped over the side. The surf reached mid-shin. His boots — seal-oiled and leather-soled — sank into the grit, but he did not stumble. He had crossed like this before. Twice in Greenland, once in storm, once in ice-thaw — always with silence ahead and the weight of someone else's orders behind. He never liked coasts that met you with stone. The ground here felt wrong in the arch of his foot. He turned and braced both arms against the hull, holding her steady. Haukr followed, rope in hand. Then the others — Tyrkir, Rúni, Hallbjǫrn. They moved in silence, no word between them.

The rest waded through. Boots struck slick rock. Some fell. None cried out.

"Keep her from biting again," ordered Asleikr the Keel-Setter.

He didn't shout. He never did. Broad-jawed, with a nose bent long ago and never reset, Asleikr spoke rarely, and only when the wood or wind demanded answer. Born at Borðarfjǫrðr, raised in sheds that stank of pine and whale-tar, he had shaped ships for men long buried, or lost beyond the reach of wind. Leif had brought him not for faith, but for fear — because Asleikr knew which knots held, which grains split, and when a charm was worth more than a brace.

After they had drawn the knarr ashore, he knelt beside the keel and touched his thumb to the seam—not for heat, but for drag. If it stuck to the pitch and held, it meant the resin had thickened just enough to set. That thumb was ruined—blunted and blackened from years of pitch burns—but he used it more than most men used their eyes.

They built the fire close to the hull, where the stone dipped just enough to shield it from the wind. Haukr lashed one corner of the sail over the stern post, pulling it tight between two drift staves—half shelter, half windbreak—then struck the flint. Rúni fed it bark blackened from a previous burn. It caught slow—too much damp in the moss, too little sun—but it held. No one spoke while it caught. They didn't build the fire for warmth—but for binding.

Kristján was already hauling moss down from the cleft above, each handful still cold with soil.

Asleikr crouched near the fire. He worked the resin bowl with a driftwood spoon, his ruined thumb tight along the rim. The nail was black. The joint swollen. But he stirred with steady rhythm.

"Do not boil it," he said. "It pulls thin."

Vidarbjǫrn stepped past him, made for the prow. The wind had changed again—now coming from inland. Cold, but sour. Not sea-salt. Leaf rot. He touched Bitabrjótur where it hung. Drew it slow. Set it flat to the keel, haft aligned with grain, edge turned inward.

"Is that a rite?" Skagi asked. His voice was tight. Too young.

"No," Vidarbjǫrn said. "Recognition."

Behind him, Leif crouched. He said nothing. He dug a line in the wet stone with the butt of his knife—two arcs, overlapping. Not for direction. To mark where the keel first took harm. When he stood, he wiped his hand clean on his cloak and turned inland.

"We climb," he said.

Ranhildr glanced up from the hull. Her hand lingered on her charm, now loose at the wrist. "No rite for landfall?"

Leif's gaze didn't shift. "Later."

The keel was still open. No rite was clean while a wound bled.

She looked away.

Skagi looked at her, then at Leif, then down.

Still, it was Skagi who moved first.

Most stayed behind to work the hull. The seal wouldn't hold long, and the pitch hadn't yet set.

Kristján was already packing moss.

Haukr sorted tools by the bowline—adze, caulking iron, bone-handled awl—laying each by use, not name. He always worked this way. Quiet, focused, hands just quick enough to keep others from noticing they shook. His father had shaped barrel hoops in Sandnes and beat him for poor knots. Haukr still tied every bundle twice—once for the job, once to keep himself steady.

Rúni knelt by the fire, warming the blade for the binding.

None looked up when Leif stood. He didn't call for volunteers. He only named: "Vidarbjǫrn. Skagi. Ketill."

The named moved without question.

Ranhildr stood as well. No one had asked her, but Lief made space for her.

They climbed above the tide-line. Roots twisted under shale. Dwarf pine clawed at their sleeves. The wind leaned—no edge, only weight.

Ketill kept pace. He did not speak.

Skagi pressed forward, long limbs quick over root and shale, eyes bright with that restless, seeking sharpness the older men no longer wore.

Vidarbjǫrn walked slow but steady, reading slope and grain.

Ranhildr followed, her stride sure, shoulders square, but her gaze stayed fixed on Leif's back—not the trees, not the trail—watching not where he led, but what it cost him to lead.

At the ridge, they stopped.

The view northeast, the way they had come, showed only that broken stretch of coast—low cliffs stripped bare, kelp wrack lining every inlet like entrails. The water below still churned shallow, foam-slicked and streaked with rock.

But south —

"There," Skagi said. He pointed toward a dark island cutting across the strait. It rose jagged at the back, sloped seaward like a jaw out of socket. A land without smoke or trees. Only rock — wet, ridged, and watching.

"And there," Ranhildr said. Her fingers pressed against her charm. Her eyes had narrowed. "Beyond it. Do you see?"

Through the island's broken shoulder, a dark line ran low along the horizon — ridge-backed and treeless, as if land had forgotten to rise. Not close. Not clear. But there.

Leif stepped forward. Dropped to one knee. Set his palm to the stone.

"A new land," he said.

Ranhildr watched the wind touch his back. It didn't press. It circled — like a thing considering whether to pass or stay.

To the right, the water moved wrong. No river mouth. Just a narrow strait — shallow at the shoulders, fast through the gut. Ice threaded it thick, riding low, veined and jagged like bone thrown to dogs.

Ketill stepped to the ridge's edge, eyes narrowed, breath steady. "This channel will split us," he said. He didn't raise his voice. He didn't need to.

Leif looked to him. "It opens east."

"Into deeper teeth."

For a breath, neither moved.

Then Leif turned to Vidarbjǫrn.

Vidarbjǫrn felt it—not in the wind, but low in the chest, where old instincts settle before they name themselves. He knelt beside Leif. Not close enough to crowd him, but near enough that their weight pressed into the same stone. He set one hand down beside Leif's—steady, flat. The rock was cold. Damp with sea-air. But it held.

It wasn't trust. It was contact.

He let his eyes trace the distant rise—land or shadow—and drew a breath deep into the ribs. Then let it go.

Leif stood. Turned his face from the sea. "We cross."

Vidarbjǫrn didn't nod. But he rose. And turned first.

Behind him, Ketill and Skagi fell in without a word.

Only the two of them remained.

Leif stood at the ridge's edge, posture set but not at rest. Below, the channel ran black, splintered with ice. Beyond it: land they had not yet named.

Ranhildr stepped beside him—close enough that the air between them tightened, but not enough for touch. Her cloak dragged wet stone. Her breath misted slow. The charm at her wrist shifted as she moved, the leather twist brushing her skin with each breath. She didn't hide it.

Leif's gaze flicked to it, then away.

"You touch it every time the wind shifts," he said.

"And you mutter gospel, though no one listens."

His jaw tightened. Just enough to show. "That's different."

The breeze pulled at her braid. She adjusted the charm without thought—bone and sinew, worn smooth from use. It didn't shine. It didn't speak. But the land didn't bite when she wore it.

Leif watched her hands. The way they moved—deliberate, sure, shaped by old rites. He hated that he'd memorized them.

"You know it's not power," he said. "It's habit. That's all."

Ranhildr turned to him. Her gaze was clean of scorn—and of mercy.

"It holds the old names," she said. "The ones your Christ never touched."

Leif's breath caught—half-inhaled, never finished. He wanted to say she was wrong. That the old ways were shadows, carved for firelight and fear. But he couldn't.

Because he'd seen the land quiet when she spoke. Because he'd followed her eyes more than once, and they'd been right. Because she stood here now—between cliff and tide, charm wrapped tight—and he could not push her away.

He looked to the sea.

Ranhildr said nothing. She let the silence weigh. Then she turned and walked back down the ridge.

By the time they reached the fire again, the light had changed—more yellow at the edge, not sunset but something else, as if the fog had thinned in places only to let through a different kind of brightness. It touched no faces. It coloured no stone. But it lingered in the air like smoke without fire.

Asleikr was still crouched by the pitch. He had not moved from the bowl, only stirred. Slow, circular, with one thumb dragging along the lip between motions. The resin had thickened to its working state—no longer smoke-slick, but molasses-dark, bubbling at the centre with the sound of wet knots splitting in flame.

Rúni was setting knives—not for food, and not to threaten. He laid them one by one on a flat stone, each handle aligned. He wiped the blades clean—not with water, but with a square of bark blackened by fire.

"Too cold to hold the seal oil," he said. "It'll skin wrong."

"We'll press it through," Kristján said. "Moss first."

"No gaps," Asleikr muttered.

Kristján packed the moss—deep, tight, each strike like he was sealing a wound that wouldn't clot. The brine-soaked tufts swelled to fill the seam, giving the seal oil something to bite before Asleikr spread the pitch. Rúni followed with the oil, ladled from a flask wrapped in wool. It steamed slightly in the bowl but not on contact. Just thickened. Then Asleikr smeared the pitch, dragging it like a seal across torn hide. No one asked if it would hold. Everyone knew it had to.

Geirr sat nearby, pounding bark slow, as if each strike took more out of him than it should. He cleared his throat once, low, and shifted position like the air had turned sharp. When Asleikr passed the flask, he nodded once and drank — measured, but without complaint.

Tyrkir glanced east, where the moon's thin edge had begun to rise. "Tide turns at moonrise," he said. "Two hours to clear the rock."

Leif stood just beyond, hands behind his back. His fingers moved occasionally — wrapping and unwrapping the ends of a cord that trailed from his belt. It wasn't prayer. Just movement. His gaze was fixed south, but not into the water. Into the air. Where the mist shifted like wool pulled apart.

Vidarbjǫrn paced the length of the boat twice — not to oversee, but to listen. Near the mid-keel, he bent low and pressed his ear to the hull. The wood spoke — not loudly, but with a tension in the grain, like a rib not yet set.

"This isn't holding," he said.

Kristján looked up from the moss sack. "It is."

Vidarbjǫrn shook his head once. "You sealed a wound. But the bones are still loose."

Kristján stood. Not fast — but sharp enough to challenge. "You have a better fix?"

Vidarbjǫrn turned toward him — not with anger, but with certainty. "It can't be fixed. But something's wrong."

The pause stretched. Unwelcome.

Kristján looked away first — jaw clenched, one hand curling at his side as if to still something that didn't belong to the body.

Skagi said nothing, but his eyes darted between them — bright, worried, too young to hide the fear. When the wind died, he turned toward the prow and did not speak again.

Rúni spoke first, voice low. "The fog is wrong."

It had crept in while they worked — not off the sea, but down from the cleft above, sliding between root and shale. It didn't billow, only clung — thin but unmoving, like breath held too long.

Leif's gaze moved from the fog sliding down the ridge, to the hull, then to the sea beyond.

"We can't hold here," he said.

No one argued.

"The coast curls too tight. The tide will lift wrong." He pointed across the channel, past the ice-veined current and toward the distant shape beyond the gap. "We cross."

Ranhildr rose before he finished. She didn't look at him. She only adjusted the loop on her wrist where the charm still clung.

Skagi didn't speak. He looked to the fog, then to the sea, then followed.

Asleikr raised his voice. "Time to move her."

Each man took position. Haukr braced the forward line.

Ketill and Tyrkir at the mid-beams. Kristján and Hallbjǫrn flanked the stern. Vidarbjǫrn stood to the side, feet bare now, boots left on the rock to feel the slant of the hull through his soles.

"Steady on her weight," he said.

The knarr shifted—not violently. Just enough to change its mind. The pitch held. The moss darkened where brine tested the seal.

"Push," Leif said.

And they did.

The vessel slid slow into deeper water, the surf tugging gently, then stronger. Then a small lurch, and the hull rocked forward. They scrambled up along the sides as the stern lifted.

"Off the rock," Kristján called.

But before they cleared the land a new sound came. A knock—soft, deliberate—beneath the keel. Then another. Not violent. Rhythmic. Like testing. Then silence.

Ranhildr froze. One hand on the rim, the other to her charm again. She said nothing.

Leif looked at Vidarbjǫrn.

Vidarbjǫrn didn't answer, but he moved—quicker now, back onto the deck. He watched the water.

The fog didn't roll in. It clung—still, deliberate. The shore vanished first, then the surf, then the dark lines of the cliffs.

Not swallowed, but withheld, as if the land itself had chosen not to be seen.

"No wind," Rúni muttered. "But we move."

The sail flapped once, then fell still. Then rose again—not from above, but beneath. The hull rocked with a swell that hadn't come from sea.

"Steer us south," Leif said.

"Steer?" Skagi asked. "There's no line."

Leif didn't respond. He turned the rudder slightly, enough to angle for the gap beyond the shoulder of the black island.

The knarr moved slow. Against no tide and without wind.

Then the first ice passed.

Flat, black at the surface. But it turned as it passed—a depth to it, just under the swell, slick and broad as a whale's back.

Another. Then a third—white-veined, but gouged, as if something had clawed the side. No noise. Just slide and vanish.

Ranhildr stood at the prow, silent. Her body tensed—one hand gripping the rim hard enough to strain the cords in her wrist.

Then came one beneath them.

It struck with no cry, no flash—just a pull. A weight. Like being seized by something that did not want to rise, only drag.

The hull shifted—bow low.

"Buckets!" Kristján shouted.

Haukr grabbed for the pail, missed, slipped hard against the wet deck.

Ranhildr moved—not rushed, not panicked. Her hands stayed steady as she unfastened the charm, even as the pitch rolled beneath her.

The water at the prow had soured—white at the edges like spoiled milk.

"Don't—" Vidarbjǫrn said.

Ranhildr stepped from the gunwale. One foot onto the nearest slab—flat, wide, slick with melt. It dipped slightly under her weight but held. She shifted her balance and stepped again, onto a second piece, where the ice had buckled and left a narrow channel of dark water between.

She crouched. She crouched—not slowly, but with a fighter's control, knees wide for balance. Her left hand reached to her wrist, unwrapped the charm. With her right, she gripped the oar—and carried it like a spear. At the channel's edge, she planted the charm deep into the gap— the old way to mark passage or plea, when the sea watched and judgment had not yet come. The water surged once around her hand, then stilled. Then she drove the oar in after it, haft-first, as if setting a post in a grave. Her face stayed hard—wind-rough, mouth set in discipline that didn't seek witness.

Then the ice moved. Not outward. Down.

It took the charm.

Took the oar.

Then her hand, knees, and body.

There was no splash. No cry. Just a fold—sharp and soundless—as if the water had made space for her and then closed it behind.

"RANHILDR!"

Three voices. Skagi's loudest. Leif's first.

She was gone.

Vidarbjǫrn leapt from the hull. The water swallowed him to the chest—freezing, fast, no footing beneath. He kicked hard, cloak dragging, axe still slung and forgotten at his back. One hand caught the knarr's side, just enough to hold him afloat. With the other, he reached—toward the ice, toward the gap where she had vanished. Nothing. Only churn.

Cold climbed his spine like knives pressed flat against bone.

Leif seized a rope from the rail. Twice it slipped—soaked wool, blood-slicked. He caught it the third time and hurled it toward the ice. Not to reach her. To anchor someone who might.

Vidarbjǫrn twisted the rope around his chest—three loops, fast, wet—and let go of the hull. The current took him at once. He kicked forward, the rope taut behind him, gasping from cold.

He plunged both arms into the water. His fingers scraped ice. Then fabric. Then a jolt — something kicked. Then stilled.

"There —" Skagi's voice cracked. "There! Beneath!"

They saw her between the slabs — half-submerged, tangled in her own cloak. Her face turned upward. Mouth open. No sound.

Vidarbjørn lunged, water churning past his chest. His fingers caught not her skin but sodden wool — and held with a blunt, bone-deep grip that did not ask permission.

The charm still clung — bone thread coiled tight beneath the ice, refusing release.

Leif threw more rope. Vidarbjørn dove again, reaching for her hand. The water closed over him.

"Pull!" Skagi shouted. His voice broke.

No one answered — but hands seized the line and pulled. Hard.

The rope ran taut.

The ice groaned — loud now. It didn't crack — it shifted, like ribs under strain.

Then she came free — sudden, hard — spat from the water like something refused. A heave from beneath, or the ice itself cracking wide. Her body rose limp, half-turned, hair plastered across her face.

They slammed into the hull. Vidarbjørn caught the rail with one hand, the other still locked around her. His grip slipped — her tunic slick, water running in sheets.

She hit the side of the knarr hard. Her thigh struck just below the gunwale, where a broken brace jutted sharp — a split of wood. The impact tore a gash just above her knee: deep, and far from clean.

The water darkened around her leg.

"Blood," Kristján said, sharp, voice flat with shock.

She slipped again — almost lost back to the foam.

Kristján caught her shoulder. Leif grabbed her belt. Vidarbjǫrn shoved his arm beneath her and hauled, not carefully but with force. They heaved her bodily into the boat.

Her skin was grey. Her lips moved, but no breath came.

The others pulled Vidarbjǫrn up next. He fell beside her, half-sprawled, one knee banging the mast as he caught his weight.

She lay still, legs twisted awkward, water running in rivulets from her boots. The wound on her thigh streamed red. One flap of the fabric was torn wide, soaked dark already.

Her eyes were open. Unseeing. The lashes rimmed with ice. The freckled skin greyed from cold. Her hand twitched — then curled, by reflex, around the broken charm still tied at her wrist. Then stilled. She did not breathe.

No one moved.

Then Skagi—all grace and no fear, like a thing the sea forgot to mark—pulled his cloak from his shoulders and laid it over her. It was too thin, still damp with sea-spray. But it was his. He spread it gently across her ribs, then stayed crouched beside her, hands trembling. He didn't speak. Just watched her mouth, waiting for another breath.

Vidarbjǫrn knelt at her side, one hand on her shin—as if anchoring her body to the hull.

Father Arnlaugr crossed himself once, then again. Slower.

Rúni turned to the mast and muttered. Not a prayer. The words didn't ask. They bargained. He'd bargained once before—in the woods above Haukadalr, when the fever took his sister and he walked barefoot for three days to bleed his own skin at a hollow stone. She lived. Or something that wore her voice did. He'd been running since. He crouched nearby in silence, close but not touching, his eyes fixed on her chest.

One breath. Then another. Shallow. Wet.

But there.

She was alive.

The water held. No swell stirred. No tide spoke. Only weight—as if something vast had chosen not to move.

Then a knock.

Low. Deliberate.

Then silence.

Overhead, a gull passed. It did not call.

Vidarbjǫrn reached to his belt and untied the token he kept there—a seal-knot, coiled and charred at one edge, worn soft by years of sweat and salt. He held it a moment. Then pressed it to the hull above the bilgewater. The wood darkened, and the knot slipped through—taken without ripple or sound.

The wood accepted it.

"That vow's spent," he said. Quiet. A voice pitched for gods, not men.

Skagi looked up. "What vow?"

Vidarbjǫrn didn't answer. His eyes were dark, unreadable, still fixed on the place where she had vanished.

The sea didn't calm. But it settled. As if whatever had been watching turned its gaze aside.

The fog thinned slightly. Then thickened again.

The hull rocked once to starboard. Then centred.

Ranhildr stirred.

She coughed—sharp, ragged, wet. Her hand tightened around the broken charm.

"Ranhildr," Leif said.

She did not respond. Her eyes moved, but not toward him. She studied the charm as if seeing it for the first time, then let it fall. It struck the planks with no weight, rolled once, and slid into the bilge.

She did not reach for it.

Kristján moved to retrieve it.

"Leave it," she said.

The voice was hoarse. But hers.

Ranhildr lay beside the mast unresponsive. Breathing. Barely. Her skin grey-blue at the lips. Her fingers still curled, but without tension.

Leif crouched beside her, one hand near—but not touching—her shoulder.

He stayed too long, crouched by her side, the tautness in his jaw giving him away. Then he stood—slow, heavy, like something pulled from weight.

"We're not clear yet," he said. He didn't speak to the men—but to the waiting air.

He crossed the deck. Looked aft.

"Skagi—off the prow. I'll take it."

Skagi blinked. "Captain?"

"I'll watch." Leif's voice was flat. "Ketill—tiller. Hold us off the worst of it. Don't trust the wind. Just the flow."

Skagi stepped back without protest. Ketill moved to the

stern.

Leif didn't turn.

"We carry on," he said to those at rudder and line. "Keep her moving. If we stall, we lose the passage."

"The current's too strong for that twist in her spine," Kristján warned, keeping one hand braced to the keelline. "We're rigged for drift, not drive."

"Then ride her clean," Leif snapped. "No stalls. No turns. Straight ahead."

Vidarbjǫrn's voice followed, quiet but iron: "She's wounded. If you force her, she'll open again."

Leif took the prow without another word. Braced one boot to the rail. Gripped the stay with both hands. His eyes watched forward, but kept flashing to back to Ranhildr.

The knarr drifted slow, half-guided. Ice floated loose now — broken sheets, some flat as skin, others ridged and half-tilted. The fog was lifting in strands, but the air stayed heavy. No wind, no guidance — only current and mass.

Kristján kept to the mid-keel. Haukr checked the patched seam every few breaths.

Tyrkir and Hallbjǫrn stayed near the steering lines and pole gear, ready to shift ballast or angle her if the wind returned — or if the current dragged her wrong.

The knarr moved faster now — more slide than steerage, her wounded frame pushed through current by urgency, not readiness.

"We need to slow her," Kristján snapped. "She's taking too much—"

Then the hit came.

Not ice—shore. Hard. Unyielding. The stone rose fast: flat black, sea-slicked. No sand, no ledge—just a shelf, narrow and rising.

The keel struck.

Not a stop—a twist.

A mid-beam cracked at the joint. Beneath them, the frame gave. The knarr jolted upward, then slued sideways. The bow lifted, then dropped. Water surged across the deck.

"Brace!" Kristján shouted.

The crew staggered but held. No one was thrown. But they were stuck.

The fog parted behind them—just enough to show the coast ahead: a narrow run of bare stone sloping gently inland, broken by marsh and scrub. A place they could reach.

Leif pointed. "There. We pull her in."

They moved without order. Haukr and Ketill took the bowline. Kristján and Hallbjǫrn over the sides. Rúni left the tiller and joined them. Ice shifted around their boots, but none cut.

They heaved by rope and shoulder, guiding the knarr off the stone shelf and toward the inlet— guiding the knarr off the stone shelf and into a narrow cut in the rock, low and slick with weed, barely broad enough to take her keel.

The water thinned beneath them. Then cleared.

The keel rasped once — low, deliberate — then held.

She drifted no longer. Fixed now, held in the stone's quiet grip.

For a moment, no one spoke.

Ranhildr still lay near the mast, chest rising faintly.

Vidarbjǫrn crouched beside her, one hand at her shin. Watching the shore.

Skagi dropped to one knee in the surf. Palmed water over his face.

Kristján looked to the horizon behind them. Just fog. Just ice.

No cheers — only breath, and the weight of stone beneath their feet.

Then Leif stepped forward.

He slid one arm beneath Ranhildr's shoulders, the other beneath her knees, and lifted her in a single motion. She gave no sound. No stir. Her head lolled slightly against his collar.

The crew stilled. No one spoke.

Tyrkir's hand froze on the line. Rúni turned away. Kristján looked as if he meant to object — then didn't.

At the bow, Skagi dropped the gangplank without being told. The timber landed with a hollow slap across the rock.

Leif stepped onto it.

He bore her across the plank with measured steps, boots loud against wet wood. The tide lapped mid-calf. Inland, the ground sloped in patches of slick lichen and wind-bent grass.

"Get a fire built," he said.

They obeyed.

CHAPTER 6: THE GROUND THAT WAITED

1000 A.D. — HEYANNIR

No fire that night. Only the thick dark, pooled low across the cove like a tide that had risen and refused to fall. The wind had dropped inland, but the cold did not ease — it pressed from the earth itself, rising through stone and marrow. Mist clung tight to the roots of bent pine and alder, worming between the grasses. The sea didn't break. Just a dull, shifting thump — like a wounded thing breathing against stone.

Ranhildr lay wrapped in every spare hide they had not soaked through in the storm. The outer layer — a fox-pelt cloak stiff with brine and pitch — reeked of seal-oil, old blood, and moulded salt. Beneath it, she was smaller than she should have been. Her skin had gone a waxy pallor, and though the wound at her thigh no longer bled, the flesh around it had turned tight and blotched. The linen dressing had already soaked through once. Her breath came high and shallow, lips parted without sound. She did not shiver anymore.

Tyrkir crouched on his heels nearby, massive shoulders hunched like a hearth-beast gone still. His bulk pressed against the mist like something the land had shaped and kept. He didn't touch her, but his hand hovered just above the furs. "When they stop shaking, it's not a blessing. It means the cold got inside."

Leif sat beside her, one arm behind her head, the other draped over his own knees. His sleeves were pushed past the elbow, forearms glistening with salt-damp and sap from the last alder he'd stripped for kindling they hadn't dared to light. He hadn't spoken since they'd made landfall. Not a word—not to the men, not to Vidarbjǫrn, not even to Kristján.

"She went under too long."

Vidarbjǫrn stood nearby, arms crossed. "But she came back."

Leif didn't speak for a moment. His hands were still, open across his knees.

"She had the charm in her fist. Wouldn't let go, even under the water."

Tyrkir crouched beside them, eyes on the fire. "And afterward?"

"She dropped it," Leif said. "Told Kristján to leave it."

Tyrkir gave a small nod. "Spent, then."

"It did what it was meant to do," Vidarbjǫrn said. "That's all."

They looked toward Ranhildr. She lay wrapped in furs, her breath thin but steady. One hand half-curled. Empty. Her jaw moved slightly. No sound. But her throat worked once—like a swallow that had forgotten its path.

The fire cracked once. Then held.

Behind them, the knarr sat slumped on her side, bow half-buried in kelp-strewn gravel. Her sail was down, rigging loosened, lines slack and tangled where Kristján had tied them off for the night. Ice-scarring ran in long white streaks down her hull. A piece of seaweed flapped slowly against the rudder like a tongue gone limp.

Vidarbjørn exhaled.

"You should sleep," he told Leif.

"She's cold."

"She's not yours."

"I never claimed—"

"The others are watching. They see how you sit. How you hold her."

"I don't care what they wonder."

A silence stretched out between them. Leif didn't move. But his hand settled more firmly atop hers.

"I didn't see it coming," he said, too quiet for the others to hear.

"You saw the ice," said Vidarbjørn. "You hauled her out. That's what matters."

Behind them, Hallbjørn stood. "I'll steep bark in the morning. For heat. For pain. If it's not already past mending."

Leif flinched—but barely. Hallbjørn didn't soften the words. Only adjusted the strap of his pouch and vanished into the trees.

After a moment, Father Arnlaugr stepped out from the dark. His steps made no sound on the wet grass. He carried no lamp—only a leather-bound psalter wrapped against the damp, and the crucifix slung from his belt. The fog caught faintly in the pale hairs of his lashes.

"She's still breathing?" he asked.

"Still," said Leif.

"Then she can be named before God." The priest opened the book but did not read from it. Instead, he reached for her forehead and pressed a cross there with two fingers—gentle, but firm.

"She's not yours to name," said Vidarbjǫrn. His voice was soft, but not deferent.

Arnlaugr did not look up. "Christ knew fishermen. Knew wild women too. I'll name her for protection, not conversion."

"She didn't ask for it."

"Many don't. At first."

He spoke—not loud, but clear. Latin first, then Norse. A short prayer. No flourish. Just a naming. A giving over. Leif watched without interruption, his breath slow but uneven.

When it was done, Arnlaugr stood. He offered no benediction. Just turned and walked back toward the knarr.

Vidarbjǫrn stayed.

"You intend to claim her," he said—not as accusation, but

with the same plain tone he might use naming a type of tree or knot of wind.

Leif's shoulders were hunched, face unreadable in the dark.

"You should know before you act this way," Vidarbjǫrn responded. Then quieter, "You held her. You stayed. If she wakes—she'll know, and your path may be set."

Still no answer.

Then, finally, Leif said only, "She will wake."

The land held no sound. No cry of gull. No drip of branch. Just breath—his, hers, and Vidarbjǫrn's. Held close in a silence that seemed not empty, but expectant.

"Then you better be ready," Vidarbjǫrn said. "Because she's as wild as this land. If she is reborn here, it won't be gentle."

The light came slow. Not with glory, but with certainty. It soaked the eastern mist until it turned the colour of ash and bone. Then it reached the water, where frost still clung to the strandweed, and found the curve of gravel above the tide. It passed over the knarr where it was run aground— her oak hull wedged into stone and sea-wrack, ribs groaning with every change in tide. It climbed the alder rise beyond, catching there on damp leaves and crooked roots— until, all at once, the trees seemed rimmed with fire.

And beyond the grove: birds.

Terns wheeled above the inlet, silent in their numbers. Loons rode the pooled marsh farther inland, heads twitching with the weight of fish in their gullets. Ducks passed low across the shallows, wings catching the copper light. A heron stood stilt-legged in the grass, unmoving.

The air wasn't still, but hushed. Not lifeless — just the land holding breath while it was seen.

Kristján was the first to rise — shoulders squared, cloak high, every motion clipped and deliberate. He rose first, as always — not from rest, but from refusal. Order first, before the day could take shape without him. He walked the perimeter slowly, spear in one hand, the other brushing tall grass as he moved. The quiet was bearable, so long as it obeyed him. When he reached the ridge above, he crouched — not to rest, but to test the ground. He pressed his palm to the moss. Brought it to his face. Smelled it. Damp. Clean. No rot.

He turned and looked downslope.

"Wake the others," he said. His voice did not carry far. It didn't need to.

Leif was already rising, joints stiff, back bent from the night spent cross-legged on cold ground. He brushed a layer of dew from

Ranhildr's furs with his palm, careful not to disturb her hand. Her breath still came shallow. But still it came.

Vidarbjørn stood behind him. He said nothing. He had watched the same light crawl across the stones. Seen the same birds gather without cry.

"She's through the worst," said Leif, eyes rimmed with red.

"No," said Vidarbjørn. "She's between. Not claimed. Not released."

A gull called once from above — sharp, unbroken. The sound cut the silence, and with it, the men began to stir.

One by one, the crew emerged from their cloaks and sailcloth bundles, voices low, limbs slow. No songs. No oaths. Only small words passed from hand to hand as boots were checked, gear tightened, cloaks shaken out. Hunger surfaced but did not yet speak.

Kristján moved among them, pointing — here for the gear, there for the firepit. He said no orders aloud, but the men fell to work.

Asleikr the Keel-Setter emerged last from behind the hull, sleeves rolled to elbows scarred by pitch and old burns. He carried a scrap of tarred cloth and a sliver of pine he'd stripped to test the grain. His thumb ran across it as he walked.

"She'll need lifting," he said to no one in particular. "Spar's no good. Crack runs past the mount. Ribs are torqued."

"Workable?" asked Kristján.

"On better ground. Not here."

"Then we move her."

Asleikr grunted. Nodded once. But his gaze stayed on the split seam — like it might speak again if he waited long enough.

Kristján moved through the camp with quiet efficiency,

marking the slope with his heel, directing gear toward the leeward side. He tapped shoulders, pointed to bundles, redirected tools — all without raising his voice. There was an intensity driven not by pride, but by the cost of failure.

"Skins here. Keep the pitch near the fire. Ropes off the sail — dry, not stretched. The foodstuffs come last."

He often drove the hardest edge toward Oddi — never shouting, but quicker to correct, slower to nod. The boy moved without question, gaze fixed forward, jaw tight. There was no praise waiting at the end — only another task.

Haukr the Half-Built — so named for his broad shoulders and low frame, short as a woodstump but built for hauling stone — fell in beside him. The smith's apprentice didn't speak much, but he watched Kristján with the wary steadiness of someone who knew which strikes could warp iron. He took on half the weight when Oddi's load shifted. He said nothing, just adjusted the lashings and kept pace.

Tyrkir had already tied his pouch and vanished toward the tree line with a small blade and a coil of bark rope.

At the stern, Skagi was cinching the last of the gear sacks. His long frame folded easily, one knee to the gravel, the other braced. His hair, still damp, clung at the brow. His fingers — raw at the knuckles where rope had scraped — moved with quiet precision. A few men glanced toward him but said nothing. When he moved, they gave him space.

Leif stepped up behind him.

The boy turned. "Yes, captain?"

Leif glanced toward the alder line where the mist still clung low.

"You and Finnvið. South and inland. Three half-days out, one to return. No deeper."

Skagi straightened. A flicker of pride crossed his face—small, but visible.

Across the line, Finnvið looked up from his perch, long limbs folded like a hawk's, knife dancing through green wood with the bored grace of someone too used to danger.

"For what?" he asked, grinning. "Friendly neighbours? Wood sprites? I promise to speak respectfully to anyone who isn't already nocking arrows."

Leif didn't smile.

"You see smoke—mark it. You see people—leave them be. You see anything that sees you first—don't linger."

Finnvið lifted one brow. "And if we see a goddess?"

Kristján, overhearing, called. "Don't talk to it."

Finnvið lowered the stick. "Not even if she's beautiful?"

Leif's eyes stayed on Finnvið—pale, unsmiling, unreadable. Not cold, just full of weight he didn't share. "Words won't help if they don't want hearing."

Finnvið shrugged, but the grin stayed. "Then I'll let the boy do the talking."

Skagi made a sound—not quite a laugh, not quite a protest.

Leif clapped Skagi's shoulder. "You walk straight. Let Finnvið wander."

Finnvið twitched his cloak into place. To Skagi he said, "Well boy, make sure you dress not to be seen." He pulled the pitch-stained hem down to his thighs. "If we meet a bear, or worse, I intend to be mistaken for a shrub."

Leif muttered. "Just don't forget your way back."

The two moved off together—Finnvið loose-hipped and casual, Skagi upright, already scanning the trees.

By midmorning the sun had cleared the mist, but not the cold. The light now struck sideways across the slope, throwing long shadows from every alder and man. The beach gravel steamed faintly where it caught warmth, but the ship herself stayed dark—pitch-slick, salt-rimed, her hull slumped like an old animal too long ashore.

Asleikr circled the knarr in a slow, deliberate spiral. He stopped every few paces to crouch, press a hand to the timber, then rise and mutter something under his breath. His ruined thumb—blackened and swollen from an old boil that had never drained—hovered constantly at the hull, brushing each seam as if reading with it.

"She's off her line," he said at last. "Starboard lean, three handspans by the stern. The weight's wrong. If we haul her like that, the midrib might crack."

Kristján stood nearby, arms folded. "We lift evenly."

"Wont work," Asleikr muttered, looking over the slope.

"Too many arms. Not enough backs."

"Then how?" Kristján replied.

"There," he said. "Clean incline. South-facing. We dig brace-holds wide, six hands deep. Set roller-poles beneath the hull. Birch or fir. Not pine—it'll twist under weight."

The others scattered into motion—thirty men, no wasted breath among them. Some cut, some stripped bark, some cleared stone with hands raw from salt. Rúni and Haukr moved in tandem with felling axes, bark peeling in long curls. Tyrkir returned from inland with a bundle of green saplings and lashing-fibre. When asked what they were, he only said, "For binding. Bark's too fresh, but it'll hold."

Below, Víg-Bjǫrn the Joiner moved along the hull's starboard side, a curved drawknife at his belt and a wooden wedge behind one ear, hands reading the grain with the same touch others gave prayer. His hands were callused but fine-jointed, knuckles scarred from chisel slip and burn, not blade or frostbite. He wasn't chosen for strength or speed— he'd been brought for the places where wood must marry wood without fail. Raised near Lagarfljót, trained by shipwrights but shaped by longhouse work, he could join timber to hinge without iron, and doorframes so flush they kept snow out without pitch. Now he knelt by a deadfall spruce, cut wedges smooth and narrow, and laid them out in a clean arc—spaced by instinct, not measure. Each one he slid beneath the forward keel, one after another, adjusting pressure to match the lean. The hull shifted—not breaking, but easing, like a rib settling back into place. His gaze didn't leave the grain.

Kristján approached then, wiping sap from his palms. "That ground will freeze again tonight. If she's not lifted by dusk, she won't move without tearing."

Asleikr grunted. "Then we lift."

He passed word to the others—short phrases, spoken only once.

"Rollers under the keel. Lash lines to the sternposts. Pull even. No shouting."

Haukr and Rúni set the rollers—three beneath, one leading. Vidarbjǫrn aligned the frame stones, palms flattened to cold granite—hands scarred and quiet, working like someone who'd shaped graves and walls in equal measure.

Asleikr adjusted the aft line himself, his ruined thumb pressed hard to the knot as he tied.

"Cross-braced," he said. "Pull without stagger and she'll follow."

Kristján took position at the stern line. Haukr, Rúni, and Tyrkir manned the mid-tension, joined by others—boots braced, shoulders low, eyes fixed on the ground. Asleikr took the bow.

Leif, silent until now, moved behind him.

"Let me take forward," he said.

Asleikr looked at him, just once. Then stepped back.

Leif gripped the line without flourish. He did not look at the men. His eyes stayed on the hull.

"On my count," he said. "Three. Two. One—pull."

They pulled.

The hull groaned—not high-pitched, not fracturing. Deep and guttural, like a thing roused from unwilling rest. The rollers shifted, caught, then turned. Gravel scattered beneath. One brace cracked.

"Don't stop," Asleikr called, low but sharp.

They hauled again. Ropes cut red lines across palms. Someone stumbled. Tyrkir hissed through his teeth. Kristján braced with both legs wide, arms rigid. Vidarbjǫrn drove a wedge into place just before the keel passed over it.

"She's lifting," Haukr said, voice surprised. "She's—"

"She's not done," Asleikr snapped. "Next pull."

This time they moved in rhythm. Gravel gave way, and the keel rode up onto the frame stones with a loud thunk. The hull settled onto the timber bed, sloped slightly toward the firepit. She sat quiet.

No one spoke for a moment.

Asleikr stepped forward and laid his hand flat on her side, just above the seamline. He did not smile. But he nodded— once—and let out a slow breath.

"Tomorrow," he said, "we cut her open."

Kristján rolled his shoulder. "And pray she hasn't sprung all the way through."

"She hasn't," Asleikr replied. "I'd have smelled it."

Kristján didn't argue.

The men scattered slowly, rubbing wrists, checking palms. Blood had broken through in more than one place. Haukr had a splinter beneath the nail. Rúni's knuckles were split.

Tyrkir crouched at the marsh-edge. His fingers moved through grass wet with dawn. He lifted an egg—small, white, unbroken. Turned it once in his palm. Then wrapped it in a cloth and tied the knot tight. He didn't always name the reason. The land had its own grammar. An egg before sun-up. A branch bent the wrong way. These were signs his mother had marked and muttered over, back when he still spoke her tongue in sleep. He wasn't a priest. But the men listened all the same.

Kristján watched. "That for food?"

"For broth," Tyrkir said. "Or blessing. Or bait. Depends what she needs."

Kristján didn't scoff. Just nodded once—sharp, like tallying risk—then said, "She?"

Tyrkir's gaze drifted—not evasive, just elsewhere. The answer was older than the question. He looked toward Ranhildr's shape beside the firepit, still beneath the fox-pelt.

"She," he said.

They left just after the mist began to lift.

Skagi moved with care—eyes up, boots placed without break or scuff. He walked the way Kristján had taught him: no pace too sure, no path too easy. The trees bent low where frost had softened the soil beneath, and mist still hung along the creekbeds in thin strands.

Finnvið moved differently. Cloak snagging. Hands never quiet. His voice low, more to the air than to his companion.

"Don't," Skagi said, voice tight.

"Why not?"

"You'll scare game. Or worse."

Finnvið paused, sniffed the air, and grinned.

"If this land has ears, best it hears me first. I'd rather speak than be spoken to."

Skagi didn't answer. He touched the bark of an alder as they passed—a habit he didn't name. Not reverence. Not fear. Just a wish to be counted by the land.

"Spring runs thick here," he murmured.

Finnvið squatted beside him. "That's not just spring. That's root-water. Deep-fed. This ground's been drinking for years."

They rose again, moving south by shadow. Three gulls circled overhead without sound. The land sloped upward, then flattened into a hummock, where bramble and red osier tangled with thorn-vine.

Finnið drew his knife and sliced a length of bark from a low stem. He turned it in his hand, sniffed it.

"Dogwood," he said. "Good for fire-start or fever. The bark stinks when it's wrong. This one doesn't."

"You're not a seer," Skagi muttered.

"No," Finnvið said, "but I know what bites. I know what rots. I know when something's waiting."

He turned then—suddenly—and pointed. "There. See that?"

Skagi squinted. "Where?"

"There. Between those boulders. Track sign. Two sets. Deer. One lame."

Skagi crouched, moved forward on instinct, brushing aside a vine. The soil was soft. Two hoof-prints, one deeper than the other, angled eastward. He nodded.

"Good eyes."

"Always," Finnvið said. "Just rarely pointed at people."

They crested a rise. On the other side, a shallow hollow opened—a clearing no more than ten paces wide. At its centre, a cluster of pale stalks rose together, slick and wax-white, no leaves, no bloom. Silent as breath.

Finn07ið drew short.

"Ghost pipe."

"What does it mean?"

Finnvið crouched low. "It grows where things have died. Not once. Long and often. The ground remembers." He reached out, then stopped. Didn't touch. "You don't cut this. Not without offering."

Skagi looked around the clearing — no tracks, no branches broken, no sign of wind. Just the pale stalks in their still ring. His breath caught. "We should go," he said.

Finnvið stood, brushing dirt from his palm. "That's the first right call you've made."

He'd drawn a knife — not for cutting. He slit the edge of his thumb. A thin line of blood welled, dark against the cold. He let it drip — one drop only — into the soil just beyond the stalks.

Skagi hissed. "What are you doing?"

"Same thing you do when you cross a grave and nod to nothing. I'm paying what's owed."

They pushed west, skirting the clearing. As they moved, the birds returned — quiet at first, then wheeling again, thin shadows against the sky.

Skagi stopped once to drink from the stream they'd crossed earlier. When he knelt, something caught his eye in the bank — a small cluster of dark reddish-purple berries, half-sunken in moss beneath the rot-leaf. Their skin was taut like fish-scale. The stems were wrong — too thin. The leaves too broad.

"Finnið," he called.

The older man doubled back and crouched beside him. He didn't speak. Just stared.

"Those shouldn't be here," he said.

"I thought so."

Finnvið reached into his pouch and drew out a scrap of broadleaf bark. He used it like a tongue, curling it under the berries, careful not to split the skins. One dropped, and he caught it in his other hand before it hit the mud.

"We take them back. Let Tyrkir speak to them."

"They look like grapes."

"Not grapes," Finnvið said. He chewed one. "Close. But there's rot in the sweetness. Something like bark. Or blood."

They didn't speak again until dusk. When they reached the alder line where the camp smoke curled thin above the rise, Finnvið muttered, "We found green things growing in bones."

Skagi adjusted the wrapping on his foot—strips of linden bast layered with reindeer moss, binding pressed soft by water and stone, wrapped tight to wick the wet and keep the chill from his bones.

"New things," he said.

Finnvið's mouth twisted. "Or old things that don't remember dying."

They crossed back into camp with the shadows long behind them.

The fire was low when they returned. Just embers tucked into a ring of damp stone. Smoke drifted sideways, chased by a thin salt wind off the marsh.

Ranhildr lay on her side, one arm bent beneath her head. The fox-pelt had slipped, revealing a strip of linen wound tight across her thigh. The linen bandage—coarsely spun, once clean—had been changed twice now. Bruising spread up the muscle in blotches black and purple, edged with the sick yellow of blood gone stagnant beneath the skin. Her skin shone with a thin sheen of sweat. But her chest rose steady.

Vidarbjǫrn sat beside her, legs crossed. His axe lay untouched. His fingers worked mosswater into a folded cloth, changed rhythmically, not tenderly, but with the practised stillness of a man too used to bleeding things.

Hallbjǫrn knelt opposite, laying out bark, leaf, and bone across hide with a dry mutter of measurements. His fingers worked quick, unadorned—crushing bitter root between stone and thumb, adding salt, scraping it to a paste without pause.

Hallbjǫrn had lived among wound and wasting since his boyhood on a farm in Herjólfsfjörðr, where winters thinned children's lungs and herbs were hoarded like coin. He'd never been taught—only watched. Animals knew what eased them: how to roll in mud when fevered, to chew bark when in pain. That was his schooling. Healing, to him, was not mercy. It was labour.

He brushed her brow, once. Then pressed behind her knee with two fingers.

"Fever's rooted," he said.

Vidarbjǫrn stood over her. "From the wound?"

"It is. But not just."

"What do you need?" Vidarbjǫrn asked.

"Time," Hallbjǫrn muttered. "And quiet. And a thing that wants to live."

A movement behind him — a shadow — then Leif stepped forward, carrying a waterskin. He knelt without looking at Vidarbjǫrn and tilted the water against Ranhildr's lips.

Ranhildr stirred once — sweat slicking the hollow of her back, hair stuck to her brow, mouth parted with breath that fought to stay. She drank, then opened her eyes — clouded, burned — but seeing.

"Leif," she rasped.

He almost dropped the skin. Instead, he lowered it, touched her hair, and said, "You're back."

She blinked slowly. Her fingers moved across the cloth at her thigh, searching. She winced but didn't cry out.

Vidarbjǫrn looked at his sister again. She had drifted back into sleep. Her breath was steadier now — but not strong.

"She said your name first, when she woke."

Leif didn't look up. "I was closest."

"That's not what I meant."

Leif stayed quiet.

"She carries old signs. Her blood still smells of the ice. You shouldn't try to bind her with prayers she hasn't spoken."

Leif looked at him. "I haven't."

Another pause.

"The sea gave her back," Vidarbjǫrn said. "But it still might want something in return."

Leif's voice came low. "Then it can come for me."

They both looked inland then. The alder bent wrong. The birch bark curled like old skin. And yet—beyond it all—green shoots pushed up through the frost line.

Kristján approached them slowly.

"The deer came again," he said.

Vidarbjǫrn raised a brow.

"Low in the marsh. Haukr brought it down with a thrown spear."

"Clean kill?" Leif asked.

"Almost too clean," Kristján said. "It bled easy. As if it had been waiting."

They didn't speak for a while.

By dusk, the meat was hung. The deer hide was pegged between saplings using split bone pins and rawhide lashings—tight-stretched for scraping, already stinking of first cure. The camp smelled of smoke, blood, and rendered fat—smoke pitched low to dry tools, fat warmed slow to treat wounds and soften pitch.

Ranhildr drank broth that night. Tyrkir ladled the broth—seal-bone and moss-root, thick and sour. Not a cure, but warmth. Hallbjǫrn said nothing, only watched the sweat break clean across her brow. Her fingers curled stronger each time Leif lifted the horn to her lips. Her eyes stayed open a little longer each time—though not fully clear, not fully here.

"She looks at him like she's remembering something he hasn't said," Rúni muttered to Ketill, just beyond the fire's edge. Rúni had always spoken sideways, as if afraid a direct sentence might summon something that already watched too closely.

"She almost drowned," Ketill replied. "There's memory in that."

Rúni's mouth twisted. "And if she brought something back with her?"

Ketill said nothing. He did not rise for omens or kneel for gods. He'd spent two years under a jarl who thought prophecy hid in frost patterns, and another with a crew that didn't make it past Bjarneyjar. What Ketill trusted was the cut of ice, the heft of a hull, and whether men shut their eyes when they slept.

Across the fire, Vidarbjǫrn sat sharpening Bitabrjótur with short, careful strokes. He wasn't watching them—but his pace changed slightly when Ketill spoke.

The wind had not returned. The mist did not lift. The trees beyond the camp leaned slightly west, as if pulled.

Hallbjǫrn crouched low, sniffed once, then spoke: "Brine and fever. But the sweat's clean now. The worst has passed."

"She's not sweating it out," Leif said. "It left her."

Hallbjǫrn had said nothing since before first light — just checked the dressing, sniffed the wound, and nodded once. Not past danger. But not lost.

The scouts returned just after dark — limping, scraped, streaked with burrs and bracken. Skagi had bound his ankle in linden fibre, his gait uneven. In his hand: a crushed stalk, pale-seeded, bent.

"Wheatgrass," he said, though it sounded like a question. "By a stream. Still green beneath."

Finnvið's hands cupped a bundle of broad leaves, pressed tight. He opened them slowly, not smiling now. The others drew close.

Inside: berries. Small. Dark. Dull-skinned, unbroken. Not quite grapes, but near enough to spark memory.

Tyrkir leaned in, his voice low. "These do not belong. Not in this soil."

Leif stepped forward, silent. He plucked one between thumb and forefinger and turned it in the light of the fire. Then bit. Juice flooded his mouth — sweet, dense, strange.

He closed his eyes.

When he spoke, it was not loudly.

"Vinland."

A shift passed through the group. No protest. No echo. Just that word, and the way it hung.

A loon called once across the inlet. Then silence. Then the fog stirred—not blown, but drawn back, like breath pulled slow between teeth.

Leif's gaze climbed the slope—where the sailcloth sagged between crooked saplings, where the knarr lay hoisted on wet braces like a carcass drying for winter.

"This camp," he said. "Leifsbuðir."

Kristján exhaled through his nose. "We'll need to drain the slope. And dig the firepit deeper."

Asleikr added, "And raise a windbreak. Something that holds."

Finnvið muttered, "And a woman who doesn't fall through rivers."

No one laughed. But no one left.

Vidarbjǫrn stepped past them. He crouched and pressed his palm flat to the moss. Cold seeped up through it, slow and steady. Beneath: firmness. Not rock. Earth.

He kept his hand there a while, listening through his skin.

Then he nodded once, to no one.

CHAPTER 7: WHERE THE GROUND GIVES

1000 A.D. — TVÍMÁNUÐR

The keel had cracked deep along her hog seam — that critical cross join where tar-soaked oak met tide-worn grain. They'd raised her high on skids, lashed between alder trunks and staked through the frame. But the shape sagged wrong. Not like a resting ship. Like something broken in silence, mid-breath.

Asleikr knelt in the shadow of the cradle, thumb pressed to the ribline. His nail was long gone — lost weeks back under a sled-runner. The skin had sealed rough over the pulp. He dragged the thumb slow along the split. Pitch clung to the grain. Not dry. Not soaked. Just slack.

"She's flexed beyond hold," he said. "The grain runs wrong. Still breathing at the seam."

Kristján crouched beside him, tablet braced to his knee. He'd marked two columns already: surface patch and full replacement. Now he dragged a third — diagonal, sharp — meant for what could only be reforged.

"Keel's sprung," Asleikr continued. "Twist along the midline. Two ribs shifted. And the scarph joint's open where the patch ran."

He spat into the dust and bent again to the seam. His eyes did not lift. "If she's to float again," he muttered, "it won't be this year."

Kristján paused, tapped the wax with the stylus.

Asleikr scraped at the pitch with a sliver of pine. It came away soft. Not foul. Just spent.

"A bit of rot starting at the forward edge," he muttered. "But not enough to blame. She split on the strike. The sea just finished the work."

Behind them, Leif stood braced, one boot hooked on a sled rail, the belt drawn hard across his side. His weight settled like someone holding more than just posture. He'd not spoken since they began.

"Say it plain," he said.

Kristján didn't look up. "We're stranded."

A gull shrieked once from the bluff. Wind moved only at the edges—up the slope, through the last scrub pine. The tents below did not stir. Far off, wind caught in the birch tops. The trees made no sound, only leaned. The sea rose and fell without rhythm, as if waiting for something to break. The men gathered behind the cradle held their silence. They'd come to hear it. Now they had.

Kristján stood, one hand braced on the hull, the other tight at his belt. He turned to Leif, but spoke for all. His voice was clear, but the rhythm came forced—measured, like tallying weight by habit.

"Forming a new keel will be six months. That's felling, shaping, bending, slow-curing every length. And only if the winter's kind." He exhaled through his nose, steady. "We'll need shelter. A timber longhouse, earth-sunk and ridge-braced, raised before frost sets the clay. Not just a lean-to—posts driven deep, proper drainage. Rafters pitched for snowload. Roof sealed tight. Wood must be felled and shaped."

"Not from the slope," Asleikr said, thumb rubbing the knot of his belt. "Too bare. We'll cut inland—spruce and alder up the stream rise, where the wind hasn't twisted the trunks thin. What driftwood we find, we use. But not the ship." He nodded toward the knarr, still hoisted in her cradle, pitch-dark and still listing. "She'll sail again, come spring. Not if we gut her like a cod."

Kristján continued, setting the pace without pause. "We'll need trenches cut before the rains come. Firewood—at least four stacks—sheltered from wet. Bedding must be off the ground. And a smoke vent, or the hearth will choke us out."

Oddi was among them—watching him. Kristján didn't meet his son's eyes. Not now. Not with failure drawn so sharp across the wax.

Oddi shifted. "That's—"

Kristján cut him off. "It's possible—if we start now. We'll also need a smoke-rack. Salt, if any's to be had. A forge. Water sealed in barrels before the topsoil freezes. A midden. A latrine. And a system for tool tracking—if we lose even one axe—"

Leif raised a hand. Not sharp—just final.

"Enough."

Kristján's mouth shut, jaw still working.

Leif looked at him, not unkindly. "Can it be done?"

Kristján hesitated, but only for a breath. "If we work to the hour. If no one's foolish."

Leif nodded once. "Then it will be done."

He turned away from the group and started uphill, toward the alder edge.

"Kristján," he said without looking back. "You'll see to it. Assign the crews. I want progress by dusk."

And then he walked on—not toward the frame-marks cleared for the longhouse, but toward the slope where Ranhildr's tent had been staked, slightly apart from the others—a space neither joined nor cast out. She had not moved it closer. She waited, perhaps, for a sign.

Vidarbjǫrn watched Leif's back as he climbed the slope, his steps measured, not slow—as if the world behind him had already faded. He did not look back. He did not speak. Vidarbjǫrn noted, instead, that the men had not moved— how two of them glanced sideways, tracking Leif's path. How none followed. How silence held—not as stillness, but as cost.

At meals, Ranhildr took a place beside Leif.

She sat at his left. He made room without speaking. Her staff rested behind him. Their bowls often shared the same trencher. Once, he reached to hand her salt before she asked. She passed him fish with her fingers.

Not yet lovers. Not quite kin.

The space was claimed, not spoken for—but held in silence.

Leif grew quieter.

He walked slower, listened more, but spoke less. His eyes tracked her when she crossed the slope. He flinched once when she laughed. He stayed long after meals, elbows on knees, while the others cleared the trenchers.

Kristján began to speak in his place.

He gave the orders. He set the watches. He stood when Arnlaugr preached and nodded at the right times. He stepped into silence without claim, organized drills, night watches, and spoke to the settlers of weight, wood, and winter-readiness.

And Leif did not contradict him.

They gathered on the dry rise above the stream-mouth where alder stood thin and the ground drained clear. Kristján, who the men had started calling the Ledger-Keeper, called the meeting. More came than asked—formed, as all necessary things did, under the weight of silence, and with tools still on belts. The keel lay gnarled between the stakes, split by frost and tide, warped like a jaw broken from its skull and left to stiffen in silence.

Kristján stood at the centre, tablet tucked firm to his side, the stylus pressed behind his ear like a blade waiting draw. He kept his cloak folded back, exposing the belt-loop where his tally weights clinked faintly as he shifted. The tablet weighed heavy at his side, and he rubbed at the pressure-line where the stylus pressed behind his ear. His eyes swept the circle, not for threat, but for sequence.

"Right," he said. "Then this is where it begins. We have four days of clear weather — if the sky holds. And if Rúnar has read it right."

A few heads turned. Rúnar Thorsteinsson stood at the rear of the group, wrapped in his sea-cloak, eyes half-lidded beneath his heavy brow. Born near Dýrafjǫrðr, he had once read the swell-line off Iceland's northern coast and guided a crippled ship back by starlight alone. He said little, often nothing, but when he spoke of sky or sea, the wise listened.

Kristján continued. "Nine good axes. Two blades near worn-through. Pitch low. Rope frayed at half the coils. But the ground's dry, the land holds beast, grain, and fruit, and we are here."

Ranhildr limped through the alder last, Leif trailing half a step behind — not guarding, but following. She leaned on a birch stave — cut clean and bark-stripped — and favoured her right leg, still wrapped tight from thigh to shin. The wrapping had bled once that morning — just enough to darken the edge — but it stayed dry now. She stepped unevenly, breath held sharp in her chest, each planting of the stave precise, as if daring the leg to fail. The wound was healing, slowly. But strength had not returned. Not yet.

Eyes turned as she entered the gathering. Some with concern, some with quiet respect. She said nothing, only took her place just outside the main ring, planting the stave with controlled force. Leif stepped toward her — reflex, not command — but she moved first, steadying herself with a stiff breath and no backward glance.

Kristján glanced toward them, then continued.

"We're not calling this a council," he said, "but some things need order, and the time for waiting has passed. We settle here. Which means before snow, we need four things: a longhall, a hearth, a food store, and a plan for thaw."

He tapped the stylus to the tablet. It slipped once against the wax, and he steadied it with a thumb-calloused grip.

"I'll speak plain. We'll need two dozen trees downed by week's end. Ten pace width, twelve length, raised on stone and floored with plank. That's forty-eight foundation cuts. Rafters cut and cured. Ridgebeams sunk at frost depth. Turf from the dry bank to slab the walls. The forge ring cleared and firesafe. Charcoal started before rot sinks in."

Hrafn Sigurdsson had raised frame walls in Eyjafjǫrðr with his father, and laid ridgebeams tight enough to hold under whale-bone weight. He shifted his stance, but did not raise his eyes. His hands hung low, thick-knuckled, scored with splinters and lime-etch.

"Green fir won't carry a ridge," he said. "Set it wet, and she'll sag before the snowline's first fall."

Beside him, Stígandr Hroaldsson grunted. Bald and thick-necked, arms freckled with old slag scars, his voice came slow.

"We'll need pitch for joinery and iron to anchor it. Not much spare. And a forge needs clearing before it needs stoking."

Kristján didn't flinch. "Then we start both." His stylus paused a beat too long over the wax. He made a new column.

From the far side of the ring, Father Arnlaugr stepped forward. His voice stayed low, but it carried.

"Prayer must come first. Before the cutting. Before the fire."

Father Arnlaugr raised the cross at his chest—not high, but steady. "This land is not yet claimed. Not by axe. Not by shelter. Only by God. We must consecrate it. Then the cross is raised. Then work begins."

The men bowed their heads—not all deeply, but with respect. Several crossed themselves. Others simply stood still, the way they would before a grave or a storm.

Then Ranhildr's voice came quiet, but clear: "And if the land does not yield to your God?" She pressed her fingers briefly to the earth, then to the edge of her stave, where a carved line curled like a serpent's spine. A god sign, but not that of Christ.

Kristján looked to Leif. So did many.

Leif's posture was composed, but his jaw worked. After a moment's breath, he answered, "We'll do it in order. Arnlaugr will bless the ground. We raise the cross. Then build the longhall. The forge. The storehouse. The church, if spring finds us."

Kristján turned one of the wax leaves. Struck through a line. Began again.

"Asleikr oversees carpentry and timber shaping. Eindriði will lead trenching—stone and run-off. Ketilbjǫrn, turf-cutting."

He tapped the stylus once.

"Tyrkir directs on food and its storage. That includes you, Hallbjǫrn, for herbs before the frost comes, as well as Ottar, for the fishing crew, and Ranhildr for hunting."

He turned the tablet.

"Vidarbjǫrn, Ketill — you're with me on foundations. Stígandr runs the forge. Haukr with him — go where he says. And don't burn your hands."

Finnvið muttered something to Haukr that made him flush, but the boy said nothing.

"The rest, rotate labour. Someone asks you to lift, you lift."

Kristján looked up. "Three men each morning on cutting. One for sharpening. Two on peg-shaping. One to watch the sun's climb — mark when the trench shadow shortens. Four-hour cuts."

Hrafn added, "And we stagger our meals. If everyone leaves the trench line to eat, we lose half a day."

Finnvið, who had been quiet too long for comfort, leaned in slightly toward Skagi and said low — meant to be heard:

"Dry trout, wooden walls, and one-legged hunters. Vinland, our promised land."

Grani Bjornsson, axe slung at his back, spat once and said flatly, "Promised land or not, we came to voyage. Not to plant roofs."

A silence followed — short, but taut. Then came the voice of Ketill, low and dry as rope rubbed smooth: "We came to live."

Grani held his tongue after that.

There were no cheers. But the silence after felt taut—not empty. Like a hide stretched taut before scraping. Or rope pulled tight around a frame not yet raised. The men began to shift—toward tools, toward slope, and hard work. Behind them, a cold breeze moved through the alder and blew westward, back toward the sea.

They raised the cross at Arnlaugr's direction.

He chose the morning: mist low, grass wet to the knee, birch leaves yellow but still clinging. The wind carried sea-rot and old ash. Since landfall, the ground had held its breath.

The cross stood seven feet tall, cut from fir heartwood, squared by wedge and adze. Its base was scorched black—fire-hardened for planting. Squared by Víg-Bjǫrn Arnesson's hand. The carpenter was short and squat, with fingers flattened from decades of hafting and joining, and his eye could square timber by the sun alone. Among the men he was called the Joiner—not as jest, but with a craftsman's respect.

It was not shaped for beauty, only for endurance. A rough stave, weighty at the base, blackened at the foot where it had been scorched for hardening. There was no gilded Christ, no painted edge. Just wood and iron nails.

They tried to drive it deep. The earth pushed back. When set too shallow, it tilted. When too soft, it sank. Father Arnlaugr walked the slope alone until he found it—a break in the stone, just above the northern rise, where the land had cracked long ago. The fissure cut through the slope like a fault. He called the men to bring the cross.

With Leif, Kristján, Haukr, and two more, they lowered the foot into the split. Arnlaugr guided it down himself, pressing cloth-wrapped hands against the grain while the others steadied it. They hammered stones in beside it until the fit was tight, then wedged an iron spike through the base. The cross held. Firm in the split. Tilted slightly, but visible from both sea and land.

When the wind turned, it caught the upper beam. No creak. No groan. It stood.

The blessing was short.

Arnlaugr wore no vestment—only his work cloak, salt-stiff at the hem, dark to the knee. His wooden cross hung plain at his throat.

"Vinland belongs to God," he said. "Not by conquest. But by truth."

His voice came even—not loud, but no one missed it. Fog swirled at their boots. It did not lift.

"The ground yields to Him, because it was made for Him. And now it is marked."

He took a small iron nail from his pouch and pressed it into the base of the standing cross. It vanished into the grain, dulled with rust.

"In the name of the Father," Arnlaugr said. "And the Son. And the Spirit."

The priest stepped back. The mist stayed low. No bird called. But the silence no longer felt empty. It held shape now: a stake driven deep, a mark the land could not ignore.

Leif knelt first—quiet, steady. His eyes were low. He crossed himself once, hand to shoulder.

Kristján came next, lips moving slowly through the Latin. He made the sign precisely, and remained on one knee a moment longer.

Then Skagi stepped forward. His boots left no mark on the mist-wet grass. He knelt without hesitation, hands flat to the thigh, hair falling forward like flame dampened.

One by one, the crew came forward.

Even Tyrkir stepped forward. He did not cross himself. Only bowed, hands folded, eyes half-closed.

Three stood apart.

Vidarbjǫrn stood near the edge, arms crossed, but did not kneel. Bitabrjótur hung at his side. His arms were folded across his chest, and his gaze was fixed on the split in the stone—not the cross. At his feet stood Ranhildr, leaning on her carved staff, wrapped in a thick cloak with her charm-bundle visible at her wrist. She did not bow. But her eyes, just once, flicked to Leif—as if to see if he would speak in her place, or stand beside her if she did.

Behind them stood Sveinn Brandsson, hands loose, face still, eyes on the fog-wrapped trees. Long-limbed and narrow-shouldered, he carried the look of a boy still growing into his reach—but no one doubted his worth. He could find fish where others found nothing, coax eels from stone beds with two fingers and a length of gut-line, read tidepull from the twitch of weed. His father had taught him to whisper to the sea when the wind held its breath. Sveinn did not whisper now. He stood quiet, belt knotted twice around his narrow waist, gaze sharpened not by fear but by some inner sense honed in deep waters. He had never taken the faith, but did not mock it. Now, as the others bowed or crossed themselves, he simply stepped aside. Fishing, salt, and the wordless trust of his father held firmer than Christ ever had.

When the others turned away, Vidarbjǫrn remained. He approached Father Arnlaugr in silence.

The priest did not look up, but did not dismiss him.

At last, Vidarbjǫrn said, "You've marked the ground."

"I have," Arnlaugr answered. "And it holds."

"There's stillness in it. But not peace. Like a breath drawn and kept."

Arnlaugr studied him—not with distrust, but with care. "Stillness is not always danger. It can be readiness."

"Yes," Vidarbjǫrn said. "But this is closer to a whisper in the dark. I can feel the shape of it. I just cannot make out the word."

Arnlaugr folded his hands behind his back. The skin was cracked at the knuckles, salt-worn and ash-creased.

"Your instincts have served Leif well," he said. "They serve us still. You hear what others miss. I respect that. But I've heard no voice here but our own. And what we've found—shelter, fish, fruit—is favour, not warning."

Vidarbjǫrn nodded once. Slow.

"I believe you," he said. "But something in the land has not yet breathed out. It watches. It waits."

Arnlaugr's eyes shifted — briefly — to the tree line, then back.

"I feel nothing dark," he said. "But yes — something old. Not cruel. Not welcoming either. Just — vast. I've prayed on it. I believe God watches over us. Even here. Especially here."

He paused.

"Or is it that you've carried your axe at the ready so long, you no longer know how to set it down?"

Vidarbjǫrn's brow lifted slightly. "Does your God take back what he gives?"

Father Arnlaugr was quiet for a breath. Then another.

"Not when we stand where He intends," he said. "But knowing where that is — that's the harder part."

Vidarbjǫrn let the words settle between them.

"On that," he said, "we agree. It's the knowing that bites."

His eyes drifted to the cross — tall, well-joined, but tilted slightly in the cleft stone.

"I would like your words to be true," he said.

"I know," Arnlaugr replied, voice low. "That's why you stayed."

He stepped forward and placed one hand on Vidarbjǫrn's shoulder. Brief. Not light.

"God keeps His own," he said. "And He sends warnings—when He must—by the mouths of those who'll speak. If you see more, speak."

"I will," Vidarbjǫrn said.

But as he turned away, the weight in his chest did not ease.

Behind them, the cross held fast in the split stone. The wind did not stir.

By mid-sun, the wind turned landward. The mist thinned. Fish guts had already drawn gulls to the slope, and the hides laid out on the gravel began to curl at the edges.

Ranhildr stepped from her ring of turf with a basket slung at her hip and a skinning knife half-tucked in the belt of her tunic. Her wrapped leg moved stiffly, but she did not lean on the stave. She walked with purpose—toward the slope where the trout had been strung and split, drying over ash sticks. Leif was already there, sleeves rolled, hands blackened to the wrist. He looked up when she came. She handed him the basket without speech, as if the act needed no asking.

Beneath the cook shelter, something boiled—too thin to name, but warm enough to hold men close. Finnvið watched from behind it, an unlit reed-pipe bobbing between his teeth.

"She walks like she owns the place," he murmured, to no one in particular.

Kristján looked up briefly from where he was scraping

scales into a clay bowl. "She nearly died for it."

"And now she's queen." Finnvið smiled — not mocking, just amused. "Tell me that's not a story the gods would approve."

No one answered.

Kristján set down the bowl.

On the slope, Leif rose. His eyes flicked to the bandage. Ranhildr said something — inaudible at this distance. He shook his head. She handed him the basket.

Then, unhurriedly, Leif removed the cross from around his neck.

He paused. Glanced once toward the longhouse, where Father Arnlaugr's white cloth still hung in the doorframe. Then forward again. Not to discard it. To give it. He stepped toward her, looped the cord gently over her head. His hands touched her hair. His gaze did not.

Ranhildr let him. Her mouth did not change, but her chin rose a fraction. The wooden cross sat light against her collarbone — foreign, but unrefused. She touched it once with her fingers — slowly, almost as if accepting more than wood — then touched the stave at her hip.

From the shelter, Finnvið spoke low to himself. "Oh, she'll wear it. But not for his God."

He lit the pipe. The flame flared briefly, then caught. A curl of smoke rose across his face.

Skagi had just returned with water. He stopped mid-step,

both pails swaying slightly on the yoke across his shoulders. His face was still freckled, still open, but something in it pulled tight—like fabric caught on a nail. He said nothing. But he stared too long.

Finnvið turned his head slowly. Saw the boy's clenched grip on the beam. "Careful," he said, still not looking directly at him. "If you stare too hard at a flame, it might look back."

Skagi shifted. One pail tipped, water sloshing over his boot. He didn't flinch. Didn't blink.

Up on the slope, Ranhildr had turned away. She was speaking to Tyrkir, who had come to inspect the drying racks. Leif remained behind, half-turned, still watching her back.

Vidarbjǫrn passed through the scene without stopping.

He looked once at Leif. Then at the cross, stark against Ranhildr's collarbone. "Careful who you crown—and why."

Up the slope, Ranhildr's back remained turned. But her hand touched the cross again. Not softly.

They raised the forge at the edge of the clearing, where the wind met the slope but did not scatter the ash. Stígandr had shaped the fire-bed himself: stone-lined, dry-packed with crushed shell and black earth. Bellows, stitched from goat hide and pegged to alder ribs, hung over the pit. The anvil sat low on a cedar root. All built with care. All by old form. But when they lit it, the fire ran wrong. Not dull. Not weak. Just—crooked. The wind did not feed it. The air around it refused to breathe. Smoke curled low and slow, then dropped, sinking into the soil instead of rising. They fed the crucible three times. Each bloom came out brittle—flaked, unruly. The fire curled wrong. The coals hissed low, like spit on cold stone.

"It's not the ore," Haukr said. "Same stuff we used in Helluland. Same cut."

Stígandr did not answer. He sat beside the firepit, jaw clenched, both hands flat on his knees. His sleeves were rolled, arms scored with ash. He stared at the slag cooling in the trough as if it had betrayed him.

Kristján crouched near the bellows. He touched the frame where one seam had come loose from strain.

"It's the seal," he said. "Or the feed. Too much draw." He looked to Stígandr. "We'll reseat it. With pitch or wax."

He said it like a cure. As if fixing what cracked was as simple as sealing a seam—if caught soon enough. If not left too long.

Still, no answer.

From the path behind them came the sound of approaching boots. Arnlaugr. His cloak open, cross bare, a scrap of psalm stitched into the cuff of his left sleeve. He stopped just outside the ring of soot.

"This fire has not been blessed," he said.

Kristján stood, brushing soot from his knees. "We blessed the land."

Arnlaugr's voice sharpened. "But not the forge. Not the tools that shape. You think the earth yields iron by chance? It yields what God allows. Not what you demand."

Stígandr rose slowly.

Not abruptly. Not in challenge. But with a deliberate, almost ritual stillness. His fingers brushed the edge of the crucible. His thumb pressed to the rim — where the heat still lingered — and held.

He did not look at Arnlaugr right away.

At last, Stígandr spoke.

"The forge is not a place for prayer," he said. His voice came low, cracked at the edges from years of smoke. "Nor for blessing. It is for shaping. And shaping has its own rites."

Now he looked to the priest — not in defiance, but with the flat steadiness of someone who had been burned before and still stepped close to the flame.

"I taught a boy once. Fast hands. Slow feet."

He brushed ash from the rim of the crucible.

"He slipped near the bloom. Slag caught him. Arm lit in seconds. He lived. Didn't shape again."

He looked past Arnlaugr, not through him. "Since then, I bless the coals with care. But not with words. You raise your cross at the threshold. That's right. But past the coals, Father — " he nodded toward the anvil, " — this place answers to older rites. Let it stay that way."

Arnlaugr's mouth thinned. His voice came harder, clipped.

"No work of the hand thrives in rebellion."

Kristján held still, jaw clenched. "It wasn't rebellion. The fire just failed. That's not the same." Too late he realized he wasn't defending just the forge, but himself. He knew the feeling: heat flaring too fast, control lost in a breath. Not rebellion. Just a hand slipped too far, too late.

"No," Arnlaugr said. "But it leads to the same place."

Stígandr knelt again beside the slag. His face gave nothing. But his hands moved slower than before, as if remembering the heat too long. Haukr, standing nearby, shifted his weight and glanced between them. His fingers twitched at his belt-strap, then stilled.

He didn't speak.

The others busied themselves — adjusting tongs, hauling coals, restacking wood. No one looked up.

Only Vidarbjǫrn lingered near the treeline. He looked not at the forge, but at the smoke itself — still dragging low, sinking along the dirt. As if the land meant to swallow it.

The ground had been cleared in a day — birch scrub cut low, roots burned out with fat and coal ash where they ran shallow. Timber came from inland — hauled rough by sled from the stream rise, where the trunks grew straight. The longhouse frame ran southeast to northwest, its rear braced against the slope for windbreak. But the doorway faced north, toward the bay and the knarr — watching the water they'd crossed. Corner posts were stone-padded and wedge-driven, sunk deep to carry turf weight. The hearth would sit central, shielded from sea-draft by the sloped bank behind.

Vidarbjǫrn marked them out with ash lines.

Ketill drove the stone braces with his heel and weight.

Asleikr brought rope and tensioned each joint clean.

But the soil wouldn't hold its shape. The freeze line ran shallow. The ridge was dry, but the belly held old melt and muck — hidden, soft beneath the hardpack.

Eindriði Kolsson, ditch-cutter and foundation-placer, short and broad, all shoulders and quiet economy, wanted a full digout and drainage trench.

Kristján disagreed.

"We don't have time," he said. "Walls up first. If the ground gives, we brace it then."

By dusk the frame stood — angled, thatched in part, smoke-hole ringed but not sealed. The beams were lashed but not pegged. They planned to brace it with stones in the morning. For the night, it would hold.

Then the wind shifted.

Not strong. Not even sharp. Just enough to lift one of the sailcloth covers and carry it sideways — caught in the join between ridgebeam and post. The weight pulled wrong.

There was a pop.

A groan of wood. The lashings slipped. One joint—barely set—gave way.

It happened fast.

The roof twisted, then folded inward—heavy and slow, like a limb hollowed by rot.

Sveinn lunged for the falling rope—too slow. The support post slammed down beside him, jarring the half-framed wall. The crossbeam, unmoored, swung wide and dropped. It caught him full across the right arm, just above the elbow, and drove it hard against the footing stone behind him. There was a crack—sharp and wet, more than bone. The beam pinned his forearm across the stone's edge, and the joint snapped sideways under the weight. The wood bounced once, then settled with a groan, and Sveinn's arm twisted beneath it—flattened and held.

Haukr screamed. Rúni dropped the pitch bucket, hot tar splattering his boots. Geirr, farther back, turned and vomited into the gravel before the dust had even settled. Blood darkened the packed dirt fast.

Sveinn screamed—a raw, tearing sound—then bit it off. His breath caught in the middle, and turned to silence. He rolled half onto his side, the shattered arm twisted underneath him, jaws clenched so hard the muscle jumped in his neck. He only breathed—short, wet bursts through his teeth. He choked once. But never cried out again.

The arm was not broken. It was crushed. Not clean. The skin held, but nothing inside did.

They rushed him.

Vidarbjǫrn reached the beam first. He tried lifting at the far end—nothing. Haukr knelt beside Sveinn, hands fluttering uselessly at the pinned arm, too afraid to touch. Kristján came in fast and shouted, "Roll it! From the brace end!" They heaved as one, the wood groaning as it tipped and rolled from the stone.

Sveinn screamed again—short and sharp—as his arm slumped free.

It was wrong. Bent where it should not bend. Swollen already. Skin unbroken but darkening, the flesh beneath mottled and loose. When Haukr tried to lift it, the forearm flexed the wrong way and Sveinn hissed through bloodied teeth.

"Don't move it," Ketill snapped, appearing at his side. He slid a hand beneath the wrist, testing weight, then pulled back. "The bone's gone to pulp."

"We can splint," Kristján said, though his voice was dry. "Set it straight, bind it high, pack it in pitch."

Ketill stayed on the arm. Once, in Greenland, he'd seen a bull break its leg in ice. The sound had been the same. He said nothing then, either. Just did what had to be done.

Still, they tried.

Ketill split willow rods—bent for give, bark left on to hold damp—then packed them tight with wool and pitch. Hallbjǫrn brought the mead—steeped in honey and bitter herb. Tyrkir stood nearby, warming cloth over the fire. Haukr fetched linen. Arnlaugr stood off to the side, lips moving in low prayer. No one asked him to stop.

They sluiced the limb with hot mead—sticky with honey, sharp with herbs—and turned the blade with breath held. Sveinn didn't move. His eyes were wide, but unfocused—breath shallow, jaw working, no words. When they lifted the arm to bind it, blood came fresh again, thin and fast.

"Still bleeding," Ketill muttered. "That's something. Not much, but something."

They bound it tight and prayed the heat would hold.

The swelling came fast.

By the second day, Sveinn shook with fever. The arm turned grey, then black at the joint. It stank—sweet and wrong. Skin blistered and thinned.

By the third, they cut it off.

Not in the longhouse. Not near the hearth. Vidarbjǫrn forbade it.

"The wound must face the open," he said, "and the smoke must not carry it into the hall."

So they laid the boy on the flat stone by the cookpit, where fish were gutted and blood washed into moss. The stone had been warmed by fire, then scraped clean.

Tyrkir burned juniper. Not for cleansing—but for memory. The smoke coiled sweet and bitter, like the old hearths back home. Father Arnlaugr drew the sign of the cross on Sveinn's brow with ash. Rúni twisted the tourniquet—birchfibre and deer-hide. Haukr held Sveinn's good shoulder, his knuckles white. Ketill knelt again at the feet, but this time, he spoke no words.

Vidarbjǫrn did the cutting.

He did not look at the boy. He looked at the blade.

Bitabrjótur gleamed once in the firelight, then fell.

One stroke. Not loud. But it stayed — like an echo caught in bone.

Sveinn screamed once — the sound tore from him like gutline snapped mid-haul. Then nothing. His eyes rolled, and he went limp, breath shallow as banked coals.

Hallbjǫrn said little — checked the stump once before the blade fell. His face was stone, his hands precise. After, he packed it in ash-moss and birch pitch, tight as seal-hide.

The priest stood behind them and whispered three Latin words into the smoke.

Sveinn lived.

Not well. But lived.

Haukr buried the arm beyond the clearing — a flat stone laid over top. The moss held the blood. The wind did not rise. And still the land watched.

CHAPTER 8: WHERE THE ICE DOES NOT BREAK

1000 A.D. – HAUSTMÁNUÐR

The air had thinned—not cold yet, but sharp as a blade drawn slow across skin. The mornings left frost at the base of the sedge grass. The gulls had fallen silent.

Since the wind broke the first frame-line of the longhouse, the settlement had reshaped itself. The second line held. Now half its ribs stood—lashed with alder, sunk deep into clay-packed trenchwork. The roofline had not yet risen. But from a distance, the bones of it showed. Birchbark and turf would come last—laid thick atop the ribs to seal in warmth and keep out the thaw. For now, the frame stood bare against the sky.

The nearest straight trunks lay a league inland, and each beam hauled down cost half a day and four backs. Not the felling, but the dragging—always the dragging—slowed the frame. With no oxen to yoke, the sleds ran on shoulders alone. Every idle hand not bound to forge, hunt, or fish was turned to the timber line. That meant a crew of ten to twelve walking, cutting, and hauling back through bog and brush. The work was long and grueling, with more curses spent on wood snagged in root-clutch than on the axe-stroke itself. And the build went slower than Kristján liked. He often looked at the sky as if trying to read its mood, weighing how eager it was to turn toward snow.

Near the slope, the knarr still lay in her cradle of alder trunks and pitch-smudged stakes. The keel had split at the lowest seam, and brine still wept through the grain. Her mast and sail had been pulled weeks ago—lashed now into the longhouse frame—but the hull remained whole. Asleikr the Keel-Setter had marked her beyond use for the season. They no longer spoke of sailing before thaw. But they had not stripped her bare. If she was to float again, it would be in the spring.

Smoke curled from the forge every second morning. Stígandr Hroaldsson claimed the draft still failed—too much ash in the throat—but he hammered iron blanks all the same. The chimney rose too low, and the throat narrowed too sharp. Smoke choked the fire when the wind swung wrong.

Near him, Víg-Bjǫrn the Joiner and Haukr Asleiksson had thrown up a lean-to for tools and dry stock, marked with charred stave-lines to ward off loss.

Geirr of Hvalsey had staked a low bench beside it, where he carved arrowshafts and fletched by touch. He worked seated now—less for comfort than breath. When the wind shifted wrong and smoke curled his way, he paused, let it pass, then resumed.

Six drying racks ringed the windbreak. Gull feathers clung to the lower slats. Tyrkir hissed them off with the back of a ladle.

It still felt like a place caught between. Less brine-rot, more ash and bark—but no corners yet. No true hearth. No true roof. A place still asking whether it would hold.

Kristján knelt beside the meat trench, where fishbone curled white at the bottom. His wax tablet had gone soft in the sun. The beeswax took heat poorly—its surface dulled, edges blurred, and the stylus carved more mess than mark. He scraped figures carefully: smoked fish, dwindled to half-stores; dried roots, curled and bitter at the edges; meat, not enough. He remembered his father's voice, calm even over ledger-fire: "The weight doesn't lie. Only the man reading it." But the wax blurred in the sun, and the fish count turned to smear.

"We need six full carcasses," he said without looking up. "Not lean. Not scattered. A kill we can gut and hang whole."

Tyrkir nodded once and spat. "Seal, maybe. Moose, if the gods are drunk. But seals don't walk to us. They bed low. They wait on stone."

Kristján's stylus paused. "Then go to stone."

They gathered before sunbreak — five in total.

The hunters stood near the saltline where fish hung dry and gulls kept distance. Ranhildr stood at the centre, wrapped in her bone-white cloak, bow in hand. Her braid lay tight along her spine, red-copper catching light at the crown. The limp she'd carried after the sea had faded. She moved evenly now, if not yet lightly. Her breath held steady. The weight she bore — bow, spear, belt-knife — she carried without strain.

The cross Leif had given her — carved wood, scraped bone — hung plain at her throat, sharp against wind-roughened skin. She wore it plainly. Not hidden. But when she touched it, it was never in prayer.

She moved between the men with purpose. Not speaking much. Not smiling.

"Vali," she said. "Your bow's true, and you don't talk in the bush. You're with me."

Vali Skeggjasson, born of the Eastern Settlement, nodded once. Tall, reedy, with a wide-eyed look like he'd never quite adjusted to surviving. He had hunted fox across blown ridges and seal from tide-cracks before signing on. He hummed when he worked—once loud enough that Rúni threatened to break his fingers. That morning, he carried three arrows fletched in osprey feather—for luck.

"Eirik," she said. "Flank me. Watch for movement. Hold formation."

Eirik Hrolfsson was younger—barely marked with beard—but already quiet in the way older men learned to be. He had proven himself spearing rabbit near Brattahlíð. His uncle had taught him to trap hare with no bait, just stillness and scent-masking. He'd gone days without a word once—just listening to the frost speak through the brush. She'd seen how still he stood when birds rose. He said nothing. Just gripped the haft tighter.

She turned toward the butcher.

"Orm. If we drop more than one, I'll need you cutting fast."

Orm Hallfredsson grinned through dried cod. A gutting knife the length of a forearm hung from his belt. He wore a salt-stiffened apron split down the middle. The expedition's animal tender, his wrists were thick, his steps slow, but he gutted animals with a calmness that unsettled even Tyrkir.

"Seal's no good if it's spoiled by midday," he said.

Then she motioned toward the forge.

"Eindriði. You're no hunter. But I've seen your feet hold true across stone. You carry your weight clean. Prove yourself, and you'll keep pace."

Eindriði didn't blink. Just checked the strap on his hook and stepped into place.

She turned toward the inlet path, ready to move.

Then Leif stepped forward, dressed for the hunt. His Greenland cloak hung salt-warped and darkened by age. His boots were seal-hide, laced high. A spear rested across his back.

"I'll lead the hunt," he said.

Ranhildr looked up. "This hunt is mine."

She didn't look at him. But her voice dared him to name what neither had spoken.

Silence followed—not frozen, but suspended. A bowstring drawn, not yet loosed.

Leif's gaze didn't falter. "We're low on meat. If anything goes wrong, I'll answer for it. Not you."

"You'll answer for it either way," she said.

Her hand rested lightly on the bowstring. Not drawn. Not threatening. Just there.

He exhaled once, slow. "Then I'll walk behind you."

It wasn't a win. Wasn't a loss either.

The others said nothing. But when they turned toward the inlet path, it was Ranhildr who moved first.

Leif walked third.

That, too, was seen.

The route curved north over shale, the sea to their left, the sky flat and pale. The stones clicked underfoot like bones knocked loose. The tide had gone out, leaving slick brown kelp draped over the stones like dead hair. Flies lifted and settled again in silent swarms. Seagulls circled high, but not close—they'd learned the difference between drying racks and drawn bows.

They moved without speech.

Ranhildr kept to the front, crouching when the stone narrowed, then rising again to scout ahead.

Eindriði moved nearest her—his tread as quiet as his build allowed.

Vali followed light, checking wind with a dampened feather tuft. The air moved from the sea inward. Good. They would stay downwind if they kept to the ridge. Ranhildr ran spruce tips across her palms—a sharp bite to mute the skin. They would stink of sweat, but not meat.

Behind him, Leif's steps were heavy but measured.

Eirik brought up the rear, eyes always scanning—stone, brush, sky.

They were two hills north of camp when they dropped into a scrub-lined hollow where the alder grew short and bent. A shallow stream braided through the stone, and beyond it, the coast fell into a low basin of tide-scoured shelf. Flat, dark, and wet-looking — like a tongue of basalt stretched to drink from the sea.

Ranhildr dropped to one knee and signalled. The others halted.

Vali crept beside her, leaned in, whispered, "It's the shelf?"

She nodded.

This was the place. Skagi and Finnvið had first scouted it five days back. Low tide revealed bedding stones flecked with lichen and seal oil. Wind curled back toward the forest. The slope from here to the shore was open — no trees, only knee-high grass and scattered boulders pushed in by past ice.

They waited in the brush, breath low.

The sun had climbed by then — not high, but warm enough that the blackflies had woken. Orm slapped one lazily and was hushed sharp by Vali.

Then: motion.

Six shapes hauled from the sea — heavy, pale, slick with brine. One large, four middling, and a smaller one trailing wet.

Harbour seals.

Fat from fish, bellies glistening in the sun. They moved with half-grace, undulating until they found the stone, then settled — snorting, shifting, eyes blinking wide in the brightness.

None had spotted them.

Ranhildr watched their spread. The large male anchored the group at the centre. One of the younger ones nosed toward the sea again, unsure.

She whispered, "That one. At the edge."

Vali nodded.

Peripheral kill. Cleaner.

They would move low, keep stone between them and the basking group, then rise in sync.

Vali with the arrow.

Eirik backing with spear.

Ranhildr ready to close if wounded.

Leif shifted behind her.

 "They'll bolt if the wind turns," he said.

"I know," she answered. "We won't give it the chance."

Eindriði rubbed pine-pitch onto his palms.

Orm unwrapped his knife.

No one spoke of Hallkell. But every man had thought of

him—the way he'd screamed once, then stopped, and the blood that stayed on the snow. That had been a bear. This wasn't. But no one trusted the quiet anymore.

Ranhildr signalled.

They began the crawl.

Ranhildr moved low—elbows brushing grit, bow hugged close to her chest. She angled behind a spine of stone tall enough to mask their rise. The seal at the edge flicked its tail once but did not stir.

Vali followed, feather-light. Eirik mirrored her crawl, spear laid flat against his forearm to keep it from knocking.

Eindriði moved slower. But he kept his weight forward, boot-edges lifted, no drag.

Leif brought up the rear. Not clumsy—but heavier. His breath rasped louder than hers. His shoulder brushed against hers once.

She stilled.

"I'll circle wide," he whispered, voice low near her ear.

She didn't look back. Her jaw clenched.

"No. One rise. One shot."

He hesitated. Didn't nod. Didn't speak. But stayed behind her.

The seals lay stilled by the sun, bellies up. The chosen target—the young one at the edge— raised its head once, snorted, then flattened again. Flies drifted in slow circles above the rocks.

Closer now. Thirty paces.

Ranhildr raised two fingers.

Vali notched his arrow. Eirik braced to rise. Orm crouched low, hand resting near the belt-knife.

Then behind them—stone shifted.

Leif had moved. Just half a step. His boot grazed gravel.

It scraped.

A small sound. Barely a breath. But the seal heard it.

The animal jerked—head up, nostrils flaring. Its whole body tensed. The others stirred.

"Now," Ranhildr hissed.

Vali rose and loosed.

The arrow struck—but high. The shaft drove into the meat above the shoulder. Not through the lung. He'd missed once before—on a fox in the settlement hills. His father broke the bow. This time, he cursed soft, and reached again.

The seal screamed. A shrill, braying cry that echoed off stone, louder than it should have. The rest scattered for the sea.

Ranhildr surged up, already running. Seax drawn. The blade was wide-bellied, single-edged—made for splitting hide and muscle in a single stroke.

Eirik followed, slower.

Vali cursed, knocked another arrow.

Leif surged past, shoulder striking hers with more weight than grace. She stumbled, caught herself. He reached the seal first. Drove the spear down. Missed the heart.

The animal shrieked again. Blood sprayed in a red rope.

Ranhildr hit next. She drove Leif aside—controlled, blade swinging as he slipped. He staggered, boots slipping. She dropped to one knee and plunged the blade deep—angled in, then down, clean through the neck. The seal gave one last heave. Then stilled.

No one spoke.

The tide lapped below. The shelf was empty but for blood and steam.

Leif stood panting, his face drawn tight. Her hand remained in the wound a breath longer before she stood.

She didn't wipe the blade. Didn't meet his eye.

"I told you not to move."

Leif opened his mouth.

She was already past him.

"Vali—bleed it proper. Orm, keep the gut high. Eirik—watch the bluff. Eindriði, stones under the flank. Move."

The others obeyed.

Vali didn't look at Leif. Neither did Orm.

Only Eindriði glanced once — between the sea and the trees.

"Did you hear that?" he said.

Ranhildr turned. "What?"

"Nothing," he said. "But... it echoed wrong."

There were no cliffs nearby. No face to throw back sound. And yet the seal's scream had bounced — not outward, but inward. Toward the trees.

She looked up. The birch along the bluff leaned, though no wind moved them. The sun behind them was strong. But the shadows bent too long.

She rubbed two fingers together — blood slick in the grooves — and looked out toward the water, where no birds had returned.

"Get it cut," she said. "Fast. We don't linger here."

They worked quick.

Ranhildr knelt first, drawing a deep line from throat to flank. Her thigh ached beneath the old scar, not sharp — but deep, threaded like bark-split under frost. She knelt anyway. The others didn't see her breath catch. The fat was thick, layered. Orm joined her, steady as always, lifting blubber from meat, peeling back the skin.

The blood soaked into the stone. It steamed faintly in the

warmth.

Eirik knelt by the bluff with his spear ready. He did not speak. Did not shift.

Orm set stones beneath the carcass, angling the belly upward to keep the gut from bursting. His hands moved with the calm of someone used to unseen weight.

The air stayed still.

But no gulls came back.

The flies circled slow. Not many.

Vali stiffened first. He crouched near the blood-slick hide, head angled toward the trees.

A flicker of motion—dark shapes near the treeline.

He nudged Eirik.

"Wolves," Eirik said, not rising. Just watching.

Eyes blinked in the half-shadow. One. Then three. A fourth, farther back.

They didn't approach. But they were close enough to see. Close enough to smell blood.

Ranhildr saw them too.

"We take what we can carry," she said. "Leave the rest."

No one argued.

They worked fast now—cutting thick haunches, coiling blubber into gutline wraps. The hide was peeled and folded over the meat to keep it warm. Every gesture stayed quiet.

The wolves did not move closer.

With the meat packed and the hide knotted tight, they moved inland—backs hunched under weight, eyes dragging to the trees. The wolves did not follow. But the forest watched.

Ranhildr stood only when the last wrap was bound.

"Back," she said.

They moved inland. The weight of the seal hung low against their backs.

Blood had dried dark on their sleeves.

The gulls had not returned.

Nor had the silence.

The wolves didn't follow close.

But every man felt them in the trees.

Orm muttered—low and steady, not words but habit.

Even Eindriði looked back, mouth tight.

Leif walked behind Ranhildr, steps matched to hers. Not beside. Not behind. Just off. A shadow that watched the trees. Then he shifted half a step. Enough to place himself between her and danger.

She noticed.

She said nothing at first.

Then: "Don't."

Leif looked sideways. "What?"

"You stepped in front of me."

He frowned. "I'm watching the trees."

"You stepped between me and the threat."

He exhaled. "It's instinct. That's not—"

She stopped walking.

He did too.

The others moved ahead—slow, watching—but didn't interfere.

Ranhildr faced him.

"You moved without my word. Broke the shot. Forced the close. And now step between me and the threat."

"I'm not—"

"You are. You think it's protection. But it's claim."

His jaw worked, but he didn't speak.

"You treat me like something to guard. A thing owned. You gave me a cross, not a name. No vow. No word. Just this — shielding. As if that were enough."

She didn't raise her voice. Didn't need to.

"You want to walk beside me? Then walk."

She turned. Walked on.

He followed. But slower now.

Offset again. But not shielding.

She saw him fall back. Did not slow. Did not smile.

Behind them, the path bent low beneath the alder.

The light was wrong. Dusk-coloured, though the sun hadn't dropped.

Even the wolves did not return.

The meat came back heavy.

Two shoulders. Half the haunch. Coiled blubber still warm. The hide wrapped tight and knotted with gutline.

The blood had soaked through by the time they reached camp.

But no one complained.

Tyrkir had cleared a space near the slope, where the smoke

pulled best. He laid birch bark flat and set stones to drain the fat. He would smoke the meat at dawn, stringing it high in the windbreak. The blubber would be rendered slow, the hide cured if the cold held.

Finnvið helped untie the bundles.

"God's breath," he muttered. "That's fat. Grease enough to light the priest's beard."

Vidarbjǫrn crouched beside Tyrkir, saying nothing. He placed the gut-basket to one side, took up a bone blade, and scored the hide.

His hands were slow. Exact.

"Do I say it?" Finnvið muttered. "Or do we all just pretend we didn't watch the swan-lovers rip each other raw?"

Tyrkir grunted. "Say it quiet. Meat listens."

Finnvið snorted. He chewed dried trout, then nodded toward the ridge.

Ranhildr and Leif stood apart. Not near the hearth. Not near the others. They spoke in low tones, but not gently. Their shapes moved—tight arms, a gesture, a half-turn, a step back. Her hand lifted briefly to the cross, then dropped away.

Too far to hear. But not too far to see.

"She's flaying him finer than this seal," Finnvið muttered. "And still he thinks he holds the blade."

Vidarbjǫrn didn't answer.

He watched a moment longer — his sister and his friend.

Then lowered his eyes to the blubber.

He sliced long, even strips. Steam lifted from the fat.

The flies hadn't come yet.

"Won't end well," Finnvið said, softer now.

"No," Vidarbjǫrn said. "But it has to run its course."

He paused.

"She won't be claimed," Vidarbjǫrn said. "And he won't follow."

Tyrkir said nothing. Just worked.

Above them, the light thinned — flat and white, though the sun still held. The wind shifted again. Too fast. Wrong for the hour.

Ranhildr turned then, walking toward the treeline, away from Leif, from the hearth.

She passed through light like mist.

Not claimed. Not followed.

Just gone.

CHAPTER 9: THE LAND KEEPS WATCH

1000 A.D. — VETRNÆTR

The men had felled the trees, and Asleikr had shaped a new mid-beam from pine — fresh-cut, set clean into its socket. A replacement plank had been laid into the keel where it had split, fitted tight and sealed with pitch and moss. It still cured under turf, untouched by tide. Each morning, Asleikr walked the hull, pressing his thumb to the joins, muttering when the grain dried too fast. He traced the ribs like a bonesetter feeling for hairline wounds. She sagged where she lay in the cradle. She held. But she was not ready for sea.

The longhouse had risen slower. Alder ribs stood from clay-packed trenches, braced with spruce and pegged tight with split stakes. Half the roof was laid — turf-weighted, wet with the season's breath. They laid it root-side down, cut long from the slope's south face, each strip overlapped for drainage. A sod knife borrowed from Hrafn's kit scored the seams. Inside, the ground steamed at dawn. Men slept close, pressed shoulder to shoulder, breathing each other's warmth. Lice had already come. So had silence.

The forge, built under a turf lean-to near the slope, still failed to draw. Smoke hung low, refused the flue, and curled back into the hammer-space like breath turned wrong. Stígandr had stopped speaking when he worked. The boy, Haukr, blackened his arms daily but learned nothing of heat, only how to endure smoke that made his nose bleed. Still — the longhouse stood.

Kristján's tally-board hung by the door. The rows were notched clean: trees felled, ribs fitted, seal meat lost. One mark held the day Sveinn's arm was taken. Another, the night the gulls went quiet. A new mark was carved yesterday — for the forge's failure to spark true.

The meat stores had begun to hold. Seal hunts came regular now, and the caribou had run twice through the lower valley — enough to hang flesh, dry strips, and boil down bone. Fish still came from the traps each morning, small but steady, and the racks near the slope smoked well when the wind held. But the greens were nearly gone. The first grapes had dried to husks, and the roots grew thin in the colder soil.

Only herbs remained in any number — bundled tight above the firepit, already losing strength. The last barley was kept in a wrapped skin and used only to thicken broth. No one spoke of the butter. It was down to two pots, hidden in Kristján's ledger count. They had meat, and some oil. But no grain. No sweetness. No sure supply. If the traps froze or the wind turned, they would feel it fast.

They already felt it. Jaws clenched at night. Coughs deepened. Skagi had begun licking the rim of empty bowls, when he thought no one watched. Tyrkir watched.

Tyrkir set the search. Not for meat this time, but what the meat could not give — leaf, root, bitter stem. There were six, including him. Hallbjǫrn Bent-Nose, who could tell plant from poison. Skagi and Rúni, chosen for their eyes and quiet feet. Finnvið Snake-Tongue, who could follow a trail even through silence. And Vidarbjǫrn — not to lead, but to read the land.

They left at first light, just ahead of the gulls. No prayers. No boasts. Just the weight of baskets and the breath of cedar in the air.

The first patch came fast—crowberries along a mossed ridge. Skagi spotted them first. He crouched low with the grace of someone taught to move without break or noise. "Black enough to hold through frost," he said, lifting a clump with his fingertips—not squeezing, just raising.

"Take the whole stem," Hallbjǫrn muttered, already cutting with a bone-handled blade. "Don't twist. They'll rot faster."

Tyrkir knelt beside him. "These ones will be sharp with less sun—harder to bruise, better for drying."

Finnvið leaned against a birch and spat a seed. "Still better than salt-bloat and marrow broth."

The words landed uneven. Skagi's fingers stilled. His jaw moved, but no words came. He didn't look at Finnvið—just slightly away—like the line had turned bitter on the tongue.

Hallbjǫrn's blade scraped louder on the stem.

Tyrkir's eyes narrowed. "Say what you mean," he said flatly.

Finnvið held up both hands. "Only saying they'll taste more like leaf than leech."

"Words that play both sides tend to cut," Tyrkir said.

Finnvið only smiled, but said no more. Behind his boot, a small cluster of low-stalked green caught the light. He toed it sideways, bent low, and scraped a sprig into the seam of his glove. No one saw. Or no one said.

Rúni gathered rough and fast—fingers blackened, nails chipped, movements like a man pulling meat from bone.

"Slower," Hallbjǫrn said without looking up. His voice carried the rasp of age and ground bone—he had outlived two winters more than most men managed, and knew the difference between haste and ruin. His fingers worked with calm precision, separating stem from fruit as if sorting fever from cure.

"I'm not cooking it," Rúni muttered—short and sharp, as he was with nearly everyone.

Hallbjǫrn looked up, slow. "Then don't spoil it for the one who will."

Rúni didn't answer, but his mouth pulled tight. The silence wasn't peace. Just pressure, held too long.

Skagi shifted away from him without thought.

They moved inland, away from the wind, where low roots and fog held to the earth. Finnvið moved wide around a sunken patch, then called back. "Sedge bulbs here. Deep ones."

Vidarbjǫrn remained uphill, crouched beside a patch of alder. He pinched a sprig between his fingers, sniffed once, then crushed it in his palm. His eyes lifted—not toward the bulbs, but toward the slope above, where no light moved.

Skagi dropped beside Finnvið with a digging stick. "How many?"

Finnvið shrugged. "Enough for one good meal. Or two hungry ones."

Tyrkir's voice cut through from above. "We're not here to feed ourselves."

"Foragers need to eat to keep their strength," said Finnvið, winking at Skagi. "Besides, there's not enough for thirty — so really, it would be greedy not to eat them now. We lighten the load. Economical. Noble."

Tyrkir stepped closer, voice low now. "Try noble again with dirt in your teeth."

Finnvið didn't smile this time. He placed the bulbs in the basket. His hands lingered a moment too long before he pulled away.

By midday, their baskets were half-full — berries, sedge, two bundles of sweet gale. Hallbjǫrn snapped a sprig and sniffed it. "Still wet with oil. It'll draw flies if we dry it wrong."

Vidarbjǫrn hadn't spoken. He trailed behind them all, touching bark, breathing through his mouth. Once, he stopped and laid his palm to a rock slick with lichen. The others moved ahead.

Skagi noticed and paused. "Something wrong?"

"The trees lean wrong," Vidarbjǫrn said quietly. "Wind hasn't touched them, but still they bow."

They kept moving. The trail bent away from the waterline and into a thicker patch of woods, where the alder leaned low and the moss grew high around the trunks. The air cooled — no wind, only something stiller than shade.

Skagi broke the silence. "We're off the deer paths now."

Hallbjǫrn looked around, slow. "No droppings. No scrape.

Even the flies are gone."

Finnvið brushed a branch aside with the back of his hand. "Or maybe we're just the first to walk here."

"No," said Vidarbjǫrn. "We're not."

They reached a place where the ground dipped, soft underfoot, lined with fallen cedar and stone teeth. A narrow opening in the underbrush led farther down—a channel of dark, root-bound earth. Rúni had already stepped into it.

Tyrkir held back. "We've enough. This isn't for us."

Rúni didn't turn. He moved like water through underbrush—light-footed, unbothered, too sure of where he stepped. "You can go back, cook. I'm still hunting."

Vidarbjǫrn watched him a moment, then followed. "Stay close," he said.

"To what?" Rúni replied.

No one laughed.

The hollow was nearly hidden—a low seam in the land where the slope folded inward. Hallbjǫrn called it *Elgrbrott*, Elk-Fold, though he said no elk had ever come near it. A narrow creek ran through it, barely moving, its surface slick and green. Everything grew thick here: moss over stone. Rotwood underfoot. Leaves wide and curled like tongues. The air hung damp and thick with sweetness—not rot, but something cloying, boiled down to syrup and breath. It pressed behind the eyes.

Finnvið sniffed the air and frowned. "That's not elder.

That's something else."

Rúni stopped near a fallen birch, half-dead and ringed with pale fungus. One of the clusters glowed faintly with moisture, edges curled like dried meat, its surface dappled gold and brown. He crouched, sliced a lobe free with his knife, and held it to his nose. It smelled faintly of cedar and warm broth—rich, earthy, almost inviting. "Smells clean," he said.

Hallbjǫrn's voice snapped across the space. "Don't eat that."

"It's dry," Rúni said.

"Dry doesn't mean safe," Hallbjǫrn muttered.

"Safe's not a thing here," Rúni muttered. He glanced sideways at Hallbjǫrn—then bit, slow and deliberate. If the old man wanted to snap orders, let him choke on this.

Hallbjǫrn's jaw shifted. Then he spat into the moss and turned. Twigs cracked underfoot as he moved off, curses low in his beard. His hands stayed fists. He walked alone.

Rúni stayed crouched, chewing slow—wet, mouth-open, like sinew torn too long between the teeth. His teeth showed through the chew.

Skagi stared. His throat moved like he'd swallowed wrong. He stepped back a half-pace, shifted his basket, and let his bow hand hover at his belt without lifting it.

Tyrkir stepped forward and knelt. He sniffed at the severed edge. His brow creased.

"Could be bark-blood," he said. "The kind that runs when

something breaks—not wood, but the blood in a man. That's when fylgjur come near. Not to guard. To see. Sometimes to take."

Rúni snorted. "It's food. Dead bark and clean broth. The old man's just sore he can't swing like he used to."

Tyrkir shaved two slivers with the tip of his knife, folded them into birchbark, and tapped the wrap once against his palm.

"For the ledger," he said, quiet. "Or the grave."

Then, without ceremony, he scratched a mark into the nearest alder with the tip of his knife—a deep cross cut once, twice. His hand did not shake.

Vidarbjǫrn stood fixed where the slope folded deepest, one hand heavy on the darkened trunk, like he meant to steady the land itself. The trees bent too close here. The light had not changed. But the shape of the world had narrowed.

The moss began to climb—over root, under stone—thick and wet as raw fleece. Their boots no longer rang on earth but sank into it. Sound fell away. No cry of jay or flicker of squirrel. No wings. Only the drag of steps and the slow hush of bodies pushing between spruce trunks. Mist gathered low, unannounced. Not fog, but breath—like the forest had held something too long and now exhaled through its skin.

Vidarbjǫrn slowed, crouched near a slab of stone half-sunken under nettle and lichen. His hand reached out, slow and deliberate, and laid flat on its surface.

The chill wasn't cold — it held. Like something pressed back.

He jerked his hand away.

"The land watches," he said.

None of them answered.

Rúni did not stop. He ranged forward, light on his feet, both axes drawn. Head cocked to one side like he heard something none of them did.

Tyrkir called after. "We should pause here. Let the mist shift. Drink."

"We *move*," Rúni snapped. His eyes were too wide, the whites glistening. "You stop, you sink."

"Nothing's chasing us," Hallbjǫrn muttered, not kindly. "Just a hollow with too many trees."

"Then why are you all whispering?"

No one was.

Finnvið let out a short breath through his nose, not quite a laugh. "He hears spirits behind the bark now. Careful, Twice-Bitten. Start talking to trees and they might tell you they don't like axes."

Rúni turned his head, slow. His gaze dragged across Finnvið like he was sighting an animal that hadn't yet bolted.

Vidarbjǫrn stepped between them.

"Enough," he said, not loud. "If the land is listening, mockery is not the tongue to use."

Finnvið shrugged, but did not speak again.

A silence settled — worse than before.

Tyrkir crouched and touched the moss with the back of his hand, then sniffed at it.

Skagi stood apart, bow slack at his side, eyes sharp but uncertain. "I thought I saw something before," he said. "Something low. Four-limbed. It moved like it belonged here."

"Everything here does," Hallbjǫrn said. "Except us."

The mist thickened.

Rúni was gone from the path.

Not far—just uphill, just beyond the twisted root that curved like a knuckled hand. But the way his body moved had changed. He crouched as he walked, shoulders drawn like a dog tracking blood, but unsure whose.

Skagi called to him, but Rúni didn't answer.

Then: the snap of a branch.

Rúni straightened. Froze.

"Did you see it?" he said, but not to them. "It looked straight through."

It stood uphill — half-shadowed, half-still — between two

leaning spruce where the mist pooled deepest. A lynx. Or close to it.

But something in the posture was wrong. It didn't crouch. Didn't twitch. It only *watched*, its thick paws square, head too still for a cat. The ruff around its face caught no wind, though mist curled round its limbs.

Rúni's breath hissed through his teeth. He crouched low, shoulder to the slope, axes in hand.

"Not its own," he whispered. "That face — it wears it."

"Rúni," Tyrkir said, even. "It's only a cat."

But Rúni didn't blink.

"Hamsgandr," he breathed. "Skin-serpent. It wears the shape, but not the soul."

His nostrils flared.

"The bones are too long. The mouth too soft. That's not a hunter's jaw."

Finnvið moved as if to circle, but Vidarbjǫrn lifted a hand.

The lynx did not move. Its ears flicked once.

Then Rúni lunged. No cry — just breath and motion, like he wasn't hunting, but reclaiming a shape that once belonged to him. He crashed through fern and scrub, bounding low as if he meant to tackle it whole. The axes flashed wide — one caught the cat's flank, and a spatter of hair flew up with a streak of red.

The creature screamed—high, not feline, not human, something too thin in the throat. Then it struck back—one paw lashing wide, claws like thorns raking across Rúni's shoulder. Not deep. But wrong. Not a cut that bled. A cut that stayed. Like something left behind. Then it vanished into the mist with a violent rustle of root and branch.

Then—stillness.

No sound.

No blood trail.

Not even the scent of it.

Rúni stood at the edge of where it had been, axes lowered, chest heaving.

"It knew me," he said, barely more than breath. "It saw what I am."

Behind him, no one moved.

Rúni stood at the slope's edge, chest heaving. Mist curled around him but wouldn't pass. His mouth hung open. Teeth bared.

Then he turned.

His eyes swept them like a wolf scans a line of prey. Not recognition—inventory.

No one spoke.

Then Finnvið muttered, "Of gods. He's lost."

Rúni twitched.

Hallbjǫrn stepped back, then again. The moss pulled at his boots. "No fight in this," he said low. "Not for me."

Then he turned and fled, boots striking soft, fast, uneven.

Skagi reached a hand toward him—half an instinct. But when Rúni turned, something in Skagi froze. His knees bent as if bracing for a blow. His hand dropped. The bowstring quivered under his grip, but he never lifted it. His mouth opened once. Closed. He didn't call again.

"Rúni," Tyrkir said, carefully. He had not moved. His hands were down, visible. "It's done. The thing's gone."

"It left me," Rúni said. "Took the shape and left me standing here like meat. You saw it."

"I saw a wounded animal. That's all."

Rúni tilted his head. "Is it?" His voice had lowered—almost calm now. "Then why does my skin feel inside-out?"

He took one step downslope.

Tyrkir didn't flinch, but his stance shifted—more squared now, more braced. "Don't do this, Rúni."

"I'm not doing anything," Rúni said, eyes now scanning the space between them. "You are. You're all breathing wrong."

He moved.

Not toward Tyrkir—but laterally, fast, closing toward Finnvið, who had begun to draw a long knife from the wrap at his hip.

Vidarbjǫrn moved first.

He stepped into Rúni's path, axe already raised but not swung. He planted his feet. The line of his shoulders was neither loose nor tensed—just *set*, like the ground under frost.

Rúni halted.

"You want something to hit," Vidarbjǫrn said. "I'll give it back."

For a beat, nothing.

Then Rúni roared—wordless—and charged, both axes high. The sound cracked the stillness. Not a battle-cry. A *tearing*.

Vidarbjǫrn ducked the first arc, shoulders rolling low with practised weight, and stepped inside the second. His axe caught the haft of Rúni's right-hand swing and twisted hard. The weapon skidded out, thudding to the moss.

Rúni didn't slow. He used the free hand to hook around Vidarbjǫrn's shoulder and pull them chest-to-chest, driving with knees, snarling low.

They hit the ground in a tangle—one axe between them, still clutched in Rúni's left hand.

The edge scraped Vidarbjǫrn's ribs, tore cloth, drew a shallow line. He didn't cry out. Just braced a forearm against Rúni's throat, pushed, twisted his hips to reverse. The axe came up again, nearly struck—but Vidarbjǫrn grabbed the haft and wrenched it across Rúni's own neck.

They rolled again. Mud smeared both faces. Their breath came in ragged bursts. It was not clean combat—it was raw, desperate, unpractised.

Rúni bucked, spat, drove a thumb toward Vidarbjǫrn's eye.

Vidarbjǫrn bit his own cheek to stay present.

He let the axe go.

Shifted. Slipped under Rúni's arm, caught him round the back and turned them—grappled from behind now, one arm across the throat, the other cinched round the ribs.

He leaned in—not just with force, but *weight*, heavy as sodden timber. Rúni strained against it, but Vidarbjǫrn bore down like a beam settling into a socket, steady, exact. He knew what he had: reach, leverage, the greater mass. And Rúni, for all his rage, could not breathe through it.

The younger man thrashed. Snarled. Then wheezed. One elbow jabbed back. A knee found moss. But the breath went out of him.

Slowly.

And then—he dropped.

Not limp, but low. Spent. His whole weight hung in Vidarbjǫrn's grip, head down, jaw slack.

The forest did not move.

Mist gathered around them again, slow as sleep.

Vidarbjǫrn eased him down, but did not let go. Not yet.

Tyrkir passed the rope—steady, sure, no blessing in the gesture, just the quiet gravity of one who knew what must be tied, and when.

Hallbjǫrn had not returned.

Finnvið spat into the moss. "This is why we listen to Hallbjǫrn—except when it comes to *bravery*."

He didn't look at Vidarbjǫrn when he said it. But he stood nearer him than before. Then he moved to Skagi. Not fast. Just enough to enter the boy's frame.

"Hey." His voice dropped low, casual. "That was the worst of it. You didn't miss a chance—you *kept breathing*. That's worth more than swinging dumb."

Skagi blinked, once. His hand tightened slightly around the bowstring.

Finnvið didn't press. Just gave a nod, light as a leaf fall. "Come on. He'll need help walking when he wakes. We need to stand near him, so he knows who's real when he opens his eyes."

Vidarbjǫrn stayed crouched, arms still looped around Rúni's slack frame. Mud soaked his knees. Blood warmed his ribs. He could feel the pulse still pounding in the man's neck—fast, shallow, wrong. When he spoke, his voice came low. "We head back. No more path. No more harvest. This place is spent."

No one argued.

Tyrkir stepped forward, rope already uncoiled from his pack. "He'll wake badly."

"He *shouldn't* wake," Finnvið said, but his hands moved anyway—quick, practised, all talk gone from his voice.

They cut branches for a rough stretcher—sapling trunks stripped and notched, cloaks stretched across. It took all but Finnvið to lift and hold Rúni's weight. Even bound, he writhed. His head lolled, eyes half-lidded, and he spoke in a low snarl of broken phrases.

"Split wrong—split wrong—the tongue's not mine. It drank me."

"Quiet now," Tyrkir muttered. "Quiet, boy."

But Rúni didn't stop. He growled. He gnashed at air. Once he thrashed so violently the stretcher tipped, and they had to pause, rebind, breathe.

Blood streaked Vidarbjǫrn's arm. Skagi didn't meet their eyes. His fingers twitched against the bowstring every few steps, though he never raised it.

No one spoke of Hallbjǫrn. The silence he left felt thicker than the mist.

Berries lay scattered across the glade like fallen teeth. No one gathered them.

They moved downslope, slow, burdened. Toward the coast.

Just before the treeline broke, Vidarbjǫrn turned back.

Something moved.

Not clearly. Not directly. Just the shape of a shape—too tall for a man, too crooked for a beast—half-seen between trunks.

He did not call it out.

His hand pressed briefly to the welt at his ribs, where Rúni's axe had caught skin. The warmth there had nothing to do with blood.

He looked once — then walked on.

They laid Rúni beneath the half-roofed storehouse, where the turf still wept and the ground held cold. Skagi and Finnvið bound him upright to a frame-post with fish-net and cord, legs folded beneath him, back braced to the timber. His head lolled and his breath came fast from his nose. His eyes stayed shut, but the cords in his throat flickered, as if something moved behind the skin.

Tyrkir set a dish of water beside him, untouched. The water came from the spring east of camp — still running, though it tasted of leaf and stone.

They gathered outside, just off the slope where the alder hollow met the first stones of camp. The light was thinning. No one sat. No one worked.

Hallbjǫrn spat sideways and broke the silence.

"I said it before. He's wrong in the head. Always was. Talks to things no man hears. Eats wild. Like nothing could harm him. Always the first to try what grows, never the one to ask what it is. Took too many chances — this one just caught up."

Finnvið tilted his head, voice light. "We all eat wild. We eat what Tyrkir puts in front of us! Half of it doesn't even grow on this side of the sea."

"Foreign doesn't mean foolish," Tyrkir said dryly. "And none of you complain when it's sweet, or keeps your guts from turning."

Hallbjǫrn wouldn't be taken off the scent. "Tyrkir isn't wild. Rúni is. That's not a man you tie your fate to."

Skagi swallowed, then said low, "Tyrkir took a piece of it—wrapped it neat like something worth knowing. Called it fylgjur, I think. Said it didn't belong here. Rúni found it first, back in that hollow. Ate it like he always does, careless as breath. Didn't ask, just chewed and waited to see."

Tyrkir gave a slow nod and reached into the pouch at his belt. From it, he drew a twist of birchbark, unwrapping it slowly to show a pale shard of root and a clipped stem dark at the tip.

"It didn't smell of this ground," he said. "Not of leaf, nor root, nor rot. Like something old we carried with us—out of the north, maybe. *Seidplanta*, they called it, back in Trondelag. A dream-fungus, meant to open the self to its double. Never used without a seid-woman near," he added. "Without a guide, it opens more than it shows."

At that, the men shifted. Hallbjǫrn muttered a curse. Skagi made the sign against bad luck. Even Finnvið went quiet, rubbing at the spot above his sternum.

Skagi glanced toward the slope. "Then it showed. Just past the hollow's edge. Looked like a lynx—but too still. Too long in the legs. And it looked back—like it chose to wear the shape."

He hesitated. "Rúni didn't flinch. He stepped toward it like it had called him. Like he knew it wasn't just a beast. Like it wasn't the first time he'd seen a spirit wear a shape."

Finnvið crossed his arms, chin tilted like he meant to push back. "You say spirit," he muttered. "But it bled."

But his feet edged backward in the dirt, and he didn't meet anyone's eyes. "I saw fur where Rúni cut it."

"No tracks after," Skagi said. "None I could follow."

Vidarbjǫrn stared toward the storehouse. "He's not wild," he said. "He's torn."

Kristján stepped forward, shoulders high from the hard pace back. "Torn by what?"

Vidarbjǫrn half-turned, as if naming it might split something further. "Berserker," he said. "Not the frenzy born of blood—this is deeper. The god-ridden state. Odr. When Odinn presses hand to bone and breath both."

"Madness," Kristján muttered.

Vidarbjǫrn shook his head. "Not only that. This was a fault-line giving way. A shape pressed in—or something pulled free. The plant didn't cause it. It revealed it. Odinn's hand is on the back of Rúni's neck. It runs through him like marrow."

No one spoke. Kristján's fingers twitched at the edge of his ledger-board, but he didn't write.

Leif stepped forward, shoulders squared beneath a cloak still crusted from the forest damp. "Rúni's spirit is a blade turned inward," he said, voice low, deliberate. "But he came for a reason. That carries weight. We may yet need him."

Hallbjǫrn shook his head. "So we let him live? Tied like a dog in the dark?"

"Yes," said Vidarbjǫrn. "Until the spirit lets him go."

"And if it doesn't?"

Vidarbjǫrn didn't answer. Nor did Leif. The silence held.

Kristján opened his ledger and scanned it grimly. "Did we at least find what we left for?"

"A little," Tyrkir said. "Berries. Roots. Some sorrel. I marked three plants I've not seen before. Two I took samples of. One I buried."

Kristján held the stylus above the wax. Hesitated. The space for the day's mark was clean—no tally yet. Not for food. Not for the fight. He pressed once, gently. Then pulled back.

"Some things don't fit the board," he muttered.

No one replied.

He nodded, once. "And next time, we don't eat what hasn't been cleared."

"Next time," Leif said, "no one eats a thing Hallbjǫrn hasn't touched first. He gives sign. Or you go hungry."

Tyrkir gave a nod, not slighted. "I cook what he blesses. Not the other way around."

Hallbjǫrn gave a sharp exhale, part pride, part bitterness. "Assuming anyone listens."

Ranhildr, who had stood apart, now moved slightly forward. Her eyes hadn't left the storehouse door. But her gaze flicked once — just once — to Leif. "He faced a spirit and came back breathing," she said. "That's not shame. That's strength."

Skagi looked at her. "You think it's something to chase?"

She didn't smile. But there was heat behind her voice now.

"No. But it's something to respect. Especially when others turn away."

Tyrkir glanced between them, then back toward the bound figure inside. "I'll watch him," he said. "He trusts my voice."

Leif gave a slow nod. "Then stay with him. If he wakes hungry, feed him. If he wakes wrong — call me first."

No one asked what he meant by *wrong*. The wind had dropped. The slope was still. Somewhere in the timberline, a jay called once, sharp and mocking. No one answered.

CHAPTER 10: THE COLD LISTENS

1000 A.D. – GORMÁNUÐR

The cold had buried the voice of the sea in the night. It packed the roofbeams with white silence, laid its weight across the sod walls like a closing hand. No sound from the birch grove. No creak from the midden-ladder. The wind did not move.

Before the ground set hard, before the cold sank into the beams, the longhouse had been sealed. Not perfectly. Not against gods. But enough to hold a breath through winter.

The beam at the western end still slanted wrong. The turf at the eaves had to be lifted and laid again. Ketilbjǫrn Hallkelsson, the thatcher, cut his palm on the gable—too fast, too cold, the stone dropped.

Its ribs of alder and spruce braced tight, its spine of pine taken from the knarr's own hold. Turf lay thick across the roof, sod-stitched and pressed under stone, though the seams still lifted where the wind came crooked. Each sod square had been cut root-down from frost-free banks, laid with overlap to shed water. Without snowweight yet, they shifted with every gust. Smoke clung low some mornings, slow to rise through the smokehole. Without a draw to funnel heat, the smoke drifted and returned on itself. The floor steamed less now, but the back corners still wept, dark with seepage where the clay sloped wrong.

And the forge still would not hold heat. The wall behind it steamed with frost in the mornings, the anvil rim hoarfrosted by noon.

But the walls had not shifted. They held.

The house had weight now. A centre. Not warmth—but refusal.

They had chinked the wall gaps with peat and hair, sealed the beam-fits with pine pitch, crushed bark into the cracks where wind liked to find its teeth. Birch bast—the fibrous inner layer of bark—was used where the pitch wouldn't cling. They wedged it deep and hammered it flat with bone. It swelled when wet, which helped hold the seal.

The turf roof was laid thick, soaked, cured, then cut again to take root atop the bones of the house. It sagged in places, even then—but it sagged slowly. That was enough.

Asleikr had tested every post with the side of his hand. Not a word spoken—just the slow weight of knowing where strain would gather. He did not bless the wood, but he muttered to the pitch. He whispered to the frost in the air. When others asked why he worked late, he said only, "The cold listens. So I answer."

It was Asleikr who tied the final beam with gut soaked in alder ash, and Asleikr who spat into the hearth trench before it was fired. Svartalfheim, those hidden underground forgers, had him in the wrists, in the shoulder joints, in the splinters under his nails. He did not ask the longhouse to stand. He told it how.

Sveigr Sǫrkvirsson worked beside him—broad-shouldered, eager, loud in summer—but by autumn, the weight had taught him. He split a joist two days before frost. The beam had been wet, swollen, and Sveigr the peg too soon. The wood cracked down the centre like bone beneath a heel.

He said nothing at first. Then offered to plane a new one. Asleikr said nothing back. Just stepped around the ruined timber, chose another, and set the brace again.

Sveigr split wood alone. No one asked him to. Since then, he worked slower. His fingers whitened at the grip when he pulled the adze. His jaw set when he lined the wedges. He began bracing without being told.

When the early snows came—wet and pressing—the turf above the east wall began to dip. Not failure. Not yet. Just a warning. Like a breath held wrong. Sveigr mended it first. Hauled the ladder himself. No one offered to help. That was the binding. Jotunheim, that realm of wildness, chaos, and elemental strength, did not break a man privately.

They say the house does not creak now because the frost is kind. But it is Asleikr's name that keeps it quiet. If he fell, the beams would know it.

The smokehole crusted with hoarfrost, though the hearth still breathed. Somewhere in the rafters, a drop of thaw clicked once against the bone-laced beams—and then was gone.

But nothing returned. Not in dream. Not in wind. Not in the brittle fire that sputtered, dimmed, and held.

Inside, most slept above the ground now—straw-matted benches, rough-framed bunks. The worst lice were gone. So was the smell of pitch. What remained was quieter: clay breath, old blood in the cracks, the sour tang of wet wool, and the scrape of boots half-cleaned. Rúni still kept to the door-threshold—barefoot, even in frost, as if the longhouse couldn't hold his weight.

Outside, frost held the rim of the midden heap. The piss-trench ran slow. No birds. The forge had drawn once — barely — and then failed again. No one asked why. Stígandr beat metal only in the daylight now, and only for what could not wait.

The knarr lay up-slope, rib-lifted in her cradle of alder and stone.

Earlier, before the frost took hold, they had felled a yellow birch inland near the bog line — tall, straight, slow-grown in shadowed soil. Asleikr had chosen it himself, marking the grain with a notch of whale-bone. They'd stripped it clean and set it upright between two alder forks above the windbreak, bark peeled and the ends sealed with tar. It would season there through the winter — heartwood drying slow beneath a thatch of spruce boughs and snow-packed turf. Come spring, it would be split and shaped into a new keel.

The plank set at the split had sealed, but not cured. Pitch clung soft to the moss wrap. Asleikr still touched her each morning with the care of a man testing the heat of a grave. He said little now. Only, "She'll not move this season," when Kristján asked.

Leif stood just outside the half-hung doorway, jaw tight against the wind. The cold pinched his freckled cheeks red, but he didn't flinch.

The ridge-line was rimmed in frost. The frost did not melt. A scab of ice had grown along the lintel where breath leaked through in the night.

Kristján read off figures — days lost, supplies spent, what

they might finish before the frost turned brittle. He didn't name the spirit of the crew. He didn't need to.

"We've two clean mornings left before the ground hardens. After that, turf won't bend. Joinery fails. If the sealant doesn't dry before the turn, we lose the roofline. And if we lose the roofline, we sleep in steam and rot." He flipped the tally-board. "We're down to four fish-coils, and the last of the barley's been cut with ash. We need to finish before snow takes the pitch."

No one answered. Even Finnviŏ's mouth stayed shut. The air inside pressed too low for jokes.

Father Arnlaugr spoke. "Something in this place resists."

He did not raise his voice. He never did. But men looked.

He faced Leif. "I rise at dawn. I kneel alone. The forge was never blessed. Charms are hung on door-beams. Birch ash and runes tucked in pockets. You know this."

Across the hall, Ranhildr's head turned—first to Arnlaugr, then to Leif.

Father Arnlaugr's voice remained level. "It is no longer small. The smith refused my prayer. The builder turned from the cross. I have seen the blood-drop rites in the trees."

He let that hang. "They act unchallenged."

"They act as they should," Ranhildr said, voice cutting.

But Arnlaugr stepped forward. "You are captain. You have taken that charge not only over men, but over this ground. If you let the old rites fester, they will root here. We must consecrate the house. As Christ commands."

Vidarbjǫrn shifted near the rear beam. He had not moved until then—just one calloused hand laid on the turf seam, fingers reading the grain like a priest touches scripture. He did not speak. But his eyes moved—from Arnlaugr, to Ranhildr, to Leif.

Leif didn't flinch beneath Arnlaugr's gaze. But he took a breath before speaking, and his words came slow, as if each carried weight beyond the room.

"I follow the cross," he said. "You know that. I knelt when we landed. I stood with you when the ground was named. I bear its mark on the land and in the law."

His eyes moved across the hall—not to win them, but to bind them.

"But I will not drive men with the lash of faith. I will not tear charms from necks, or knives from doorposts. We are held here by wind, ice, and timber. I will not add fire."

Arnlaugr stepped forward.

"That is not enough."

His voice remained level. But it had thickened.

"You claim the name of Christ, but you rule as if He were one god among many. You let the old ways speak unchecked. You look the other way when rites are laid in blood and ash. That is not leadership. That is compromise."

Leif's jaw moved once. But he did not interrupt.

Arnlaugr pressed on.

"Faith is not a fence to lean against. It is a gate. Narrow. Hard. It divides. That is its task."

He pointed—not sharp, but steady—toward the beams above.

"You want this house to hold. Then mark it wholly. Seal it against the rot you've allowed to root."

He let the words settle.

Then, quieter: "If you serve the cross, then serve it. Not beside another altar."

Ranhildr stood.

"The house will hold," she said. "Because we have bent our backs to build it. Because the stone holds heat and the wood holds weight."

She stepped into the open space between them, voice level. "Do you think the forest cares for your prayers, priest? Or that frost bends to your hymns? You want Leif to bless it? Let him pour wine and break bread. I've walked the bounds and laid charms. That's why the hall still stands."

Her voice did not rise. But her posture shifted. Not just resistance—claim. She looked not just at Arnlaugr now, but past him. At Leif.

She turned to him. "But if you want to choose, do it cleanly. Don't let us dine together while you smile at both. It dishonours more than the rites."

Leif looked at her then—but not as a lover. "Enough."

Something older tightened in his mouth. Not shame. Not anger. A tension earned by cold nights and too many eyes.

He looked around the room—not just at her, not just at Arnlaugr. At the men who'd sunk stone and slaughtered meat and buried Sveinn's arm beneath the midden rise. At those who still rubbed their wrists at night where pitch had burned the skin. At Tyrkir, who hadn't moved from the drying line, but who stood straighter now. At Kristján, whose jaw worked as he clutched the tally-board. At Vidarbjǫrn, who never spoke unless he had to—and who was watching him now.

The wind struck the turf above like a flat palm. A fine dust of frost shook from the rafters.

Ranhildr didn't flinch.

The fire hissed and dropped.

No one spoke.

The frost clicked once at the lintel. Then again.

Kristján shifted his grip on the tally-board, as if to speak—but did not. Tyrkir's hand had gone still against the gut-strung drying rack. Skagi's eyes flicked toward Ranhildr, then to Leif, then away. Finnvið looked as though he meant to smirk, but found nothing in the room worth smiling at.

Only Vidarbjǫrn moved. Not far. Just a slight bend of the wrist, brushing frost from the post. A slow, deliberate check of the join. The way a man might test a beam before snow.

Ranhildr held her place. Leif did not look at her again.

He turned toward the hearth and reached for the long-handled coal-rake. The leather hissed as his hand closed on it. He stirred the coals, not as gesture, but judgement. Sparks cracked and spat into the dark.

"Enough," he said again — softer, this time, but it held.

He did not raise his voice. He did not move to bless the hall. He left the silence untouched.

The fire caught — then settled.

The forge had to be buried deep enough that the frost couldn't find the coals from below. That was the first rule. Stígandr Hroaldsson kept it, and it was his task to remember.

Before the ground set hard, they dug out the ash-pit a second time — deeper than before, ringed it with stones that had never held heat, then backfilled with slag and sand. The floor held firm. The smokehole was widened to let wet air out faster. The pitch seal on the roof was redone. Twice.

Charcoal had to be laid in layers. Alder, mostly — burned downwind on the salt-flats through September, banked in sand, cooled slow. Haukr and Skagi helped gather driftwood from the broken cove: dry spruce, grey pine, water-paled fir still iron-hard in the grain. No greenwood. No cuts from living trees. The forge took only wood that had already died.

They built the pile beneath the lean-to, back of the forge

wall—stacked in rows, rain-tight, wind-sheltered, banded in gut. Enough for three months' hammering, if the smith's hand didn't falter. More than enough if the snow stayed light.

When it was done, Stígandr closed the forge for one day. No coals lit. No tools touched. No voice near the ash.

He walked there alone, bare to the frost. Not cloaked. Not shod. The cold had to see him—had to recognize the body that dared shape iron in its silence. The door bore no mark. He opened it with the back of his wrist so no blood touched the latch.

Inside, the forge held stillness like breath in a buried lung. The coals were grey. The air smelled of salt-ash and old iron. He did not breathe deep.

He laid the charcoal in rings—five of them, inward, each tighter than the last. Between each he pressed bark, stripped and dried from the driftwood he'd cut himself in August. No one else touched that bark. He bound each ring with whale sinew, cured three seasons ago.

At the centre, he placed the hammer head. No haft.

Then he bled his thumb, and touched the iron. His thoughts pressed upon it: *You will not sleep. You will keep the names of what must be shaped. Listen in snow silence. Do not go deaf in the cold.*

The iron did not gleam. But the air around it warmed, slightly.

He covered it in ash and left.

Near the wall where the pitch sacks were kept, Geirr of Hvalsey had taken to working seated, wrapped in two cloaks, his breath short even in warmth. He no longer helped with the fire-pull or the snow-haul. When the forge last smoked, he'd stepped outside—face drawn, coughing into the crook of his elbow. He'd said it was the pitch. But the sound stayed with him after the air had cleared.

Before the ground froze solid, they sealed the food pits.

Each lined with spruce boughs, then packed with peat, ringed in stone, and covered with sod lashed in turf-twine. The base was sloped slightly to one side, in case of thaw-seep. Smoked fish in birchbark bundles. Venison dried to slivers. Hare. Seal fat. Dried berries bound in gut-string. Anything that would keep without light.

Above, the loft shelves were hung with nets of fish and bladder-skin sacks of ground root. Three barrels for meat. Two for meal. One for dried greens, lined with ash at the bottom and cut spruce at the rim.

It held through the first frost. But not the second.

A scent found them in the dark—faint, then sharp: rot. One of the lower barrels had spoiled from the base up. Asleikr pried it open with the spine of his knife and showed the others: soft rot at the seam, chew-marks on the inner slat. Not mice. Something larger. One rat was found days later near the forge wall, bloated and split. It had eaten too well, too fast.

They rechecked every pit. Hauled sacks. Split kindling. Haukr overturned a root crate and found six more teeth-marks. Kristján ordered the food-shift doubled. Every meal was weighed, then weighed again. No panic. Just tightening.

The next day, Asleikr boiled pitch.

It had to be done outside. The smoke from spruce pitch fouls the air, clings to skin and cloth. He built the fire downwind from the forge, near the half-dug channel where snow had not yet held. The cauldron was iron, pitted from salt use, hung over a crossbeam of alder pegged into forked stakes.

He wore his sealskin gloves and the old cloak lined with birchbark and fleece. He fed the flame with patience, waited until the sap darkened, then skimmed off the crust with a char-bent ladle.

A boy stood with him—Sveigr, no beard, no braid. A Brattahlíð youth with sharp wrists and no voice for song. He'd been caught miscounting the pitch pots two weeks before. Asleikr had said nothing then. Only pointed at the empty measure. Now, without word or ceremony, the boy stood beside him, holding the pot steady as the boiled pitch hissed down the funnel.

"Don't speak," Asleikr said. Not a rebuke. A rule.

The boy nodded. He didn't speak.

That barrel held.

So did the next.

Ketill Flat-Nose tested the east windbreak two days too

early. The ground was iced glass, and he went out before full light. Kristján found him an hour later, hand to the post, eyes white from the drift. Three fingers blackened past the nail.

They bound his hand and gave him the heated stone. Arnlaugr whispered something. He nodded, once, but never said what he heard.

He never stepped past the lintel again—just carved driftwood scraps near the door, head bowed, breath clouding slow like steam from split stone. The others didn't ask what they were for. Haukr said once that Ketill's breath smelled of burnt thyme and salt. Asleikr said nothing, but when the cloaks were laid for sorting, he left his better pair at Ketill's feet.

The fight over cloth came a day later.

Skagi and Grani both claimed the same bolt—grey wool, warped but dry, tight-woven from Brattahlíð stores. The weave was double-faced, oiled with lanolin. Good against wet, better against snow. One bolt like that could wrap three cloaks.

"I hauled it in the last shipload," Skagi said—not loud, not eager, just flat.

Grani stepped in close. "I packed it first. In Markland."

Shoving now. Quick. Not clean.

Skagi didn't shove hard—but when he stumbled, something in the room shifted.

A few men moved. No one called out. But the weight in the

air turned.

Sveigr caught a knee to the chin trying to pull them apart.

Kristján stepped in — not with force, but like a tree shadow falling across both of them.

"Enough," he said. Not loud. But Grani stepped back first.

He drew his knife and cut the bolt clean. One half to Skagi. One half to Grani. Then, without pause, he cut two narrow strips from the edge. Passed them to Sveigr.

"For the blood," he said.

No one laughed. But the room eased.

He didn't tally the bolt. Some things, he'd begun to learn, weren't kept that way.

Ketill laughed. "Shame to waste it on the living."

After, Skagi stood holding his half of the cloth, still folded. He didn't move right away. Tyrkir passed behind him without word — but set a hand briefly to the boy's back before going. Just one touch. Just enough.

The deer came back heavy. Four stags, two hinds, hauled from the east ridge where the trees thinned to frost-cracked stone. Haukr and Tyrkir brought down the lead buck with two shots — one through the lung, one through the neck. Kristján said nothing when the younger boys cheered. Leif just nodded once and turned back toward camp.

They butchered by torchlight, not because they needed to, but because the light held a shape. It cut the dusk into pieces, the same way their knives opened the hide.

The stags were laid across the gutting stones — not dirt, not moss. Stones warmed earlier by fire, then scraped bare.

Vali began the chant — not loud, not liturgical, just the low blood-hum he used when skinning: three tones, one wordless, one with breath, one broken into syllables from the old tongue. The boys picked it up without knowing the words. Their knives found the rhythm.

Haukr cut fast. Asleikr cut clean. Kristján oversaw the hanging lines. Tyrkir sharpened blades between shoulders and shanks. Sveigr watched and learned.

Blood was caught in trenchers. Bones sorted by length. The antlers were laid to the side — no one touched them. That would come later.

When the liver was pulled from the first buck, Ranhildr stepped forward. Said nothing. Took it in both hands and brought it to the fire. She dropped no blood. She did not flinch. But her hands held it like a vow — one already broken. The liver burned slow and high. Sweet smoke, thick. No one said who it was for.

They watched it burn, and the wind did not change.

Then they finished the work.

The meat was strung above the longhouse, near the smokehole, where the pitch still held and the ice kept close. The skin was stripped and stretched. Hooves tossed to midden. Hearts packed in salt.

When the liver had blackened and fallen in on itself, Ranhildr stepped back. No one spoke. The smoke curled slow and sweet into the rafters.

Asleikr moved last. Not to speak or mark. Just to place his hand on the hearth-post seam—where pitch had darkened and frost once bloomed. He pressed the join, felt for shift. Listened.

The house breathed shallow, but it held. Above, the beams held their silence.

CHAPTER 11: A RITE WITHOUT FIRE

1000 A.D. – FROSTMÁNUÐR

Arnlaugr blessed the longhouse on the third night after it was sealed. He had been waiting for Lief's order, but it did not come.

No sermon. No relic. Just meltwater from a drift-pool, and a line none could name. He touched the lintel with his palm, whispered something in Latin, and stepped back into silence.

Leif said nothing, and so no one stopped him.

Ranhildr watched from the far wall, arms crossed beneath her cloak. She watched Leif, not the priest. She did not kneel. She did not speak. But her silence was not assent. It was a demand left hanging — one only Leif could answer. When he said nothing, she held her gaze a moment longer, then looked away, jaw tight.

She did not sit with him at the evening meal. When the others gathered at the hearth, she was gone — into the woods beyond the piss trench, beyond the path.

She came back at dusk. Her hands were chapped raw. Her left wrist bore a streak — dark and dried.

No one asked where the blood came from.

Leif looked up as she passed the fire.

She did not meet his eyes.

The next morning, Leif called Asleikr to him, and Kristján too, and pointed to the bluff above the inlet mouth — where the rock turned outward to the sea, and the grass thinned to salt-bleached moss.

"Build it there," he said.

So they did.

It was not a great church. Six paces long, four wide. Pine walls, pitch-smeared and knotted. A sloped roof of sod and scavenged plank. The sod was laid root-down over birch branches, packed tight with frozen moss to shed meltwater. The ridge-pole was drift pine — cracked, but still bearing sap scent. The floor sloped with the land beneath — southward, always downhill. The door hung askew on leather hinges. It groaned when the wind caught it.

But it stood.

Leif raised the frame with his own hands, stripped to the waist. The scars across his shoulders caught the thin sun — pale against freckled, weather-hardened skin. His arms moved like oars — broad, blunt-fingered, deliberate. Kristján wedged the uprights. Arnlaugr brought a stone from the creek — broad, flat, sea-scoured — and cleaned it with melted snow. He set it at the far end, low to the ground, and placed three white shells across its face. One for each part of his god.

When the roof was laid and the door hung crooked but whole, Arnlaugr entered alone. He lit a lamp, its wick soaked with last year's fat. No hymn. No chant. Just smoke. It curled slow toward the beam above him, as if breath had returned to a dead thing.

He stood until the flame guttered.

The church was finished just as the wind turned, and the snow laid its weight upon the land. It fell dense, slow, and soundless—blanketing earth and thought alike. Tracks pressed through the snow: worn paths where the men went. One broad trail to the piss trench, where yellow steamed up through the snow. One path cut down to the shore, where fish-traps had to be freed each day. And one lone set of steps to the church, always returned upon—because Father Arnlaugr would not yield. He came back stiff-limbed, lips cracked, but still he went.

<hr>

The house was sealed. But not the ones within it.

Smoke gathered low in the rafters, unable to rise. The coals hadn't taken well, and the green alder snapped with more steam than flame. It brought heat but little fire, and the men's eyes watered in the drift of it.

Kristján worked the bronze ring of the smokehole shutter, frost-lipped and sluggish. The shutter had warped in the cold, the leather gasket stiff. The draw failed whenever ice crusted the rim. He cursed low, jaw clenched, soot grinding at the crack of his knuckles.

"It's sealing shut," he muttered. "We should leave it half-open—draw the air through, let the worst out."

"Not in storm-weather," said Asleikr from the hearthside, not looking up. He was sharpening an antler tine against slate, slow and even. "Leave it open, we invite them in."

"The draugr?" Oddi the Ledger-Whelp asked, not quite

mocking.

"Not them." Asleikr's eyes flicked to the roofbeam where the joist had groaned. "Worse."

Kristján frowned. His hands were black with soot. "If the smoke stays in, the hearth won't draw. We'll choke in it by evening."

"Then the house will learn to breathe," Asleikr said. "Seal it."

The air held. No one else spoke.

Kristján stood at the base of the ladder for a moment longer. Then he nodded once, sharp, and closed the shutter with both hands, pressing ice to ice. The latch gave. The light dimmed. The smoke stayed.

"So be it," he said.

A raven clattered against the roof, then was still.

The fire-ring ash turned wet again and the flame would not catch.

Father Arnlaugr knelt to light the flame as he did each seventh day. Three strokes of flint. A prayer in Latin. A bowl of oil pressed from nut-fat, lifted to the smokehole and turned clockwise.

"By flame," he said. "By Word. By the Spirit."

Kristján stood beside him. Not speaking, but near enough

for agreement.

The others watched in silence. Most with heads bowed. Sveinn sat silent, without protest. Vidarbjǫrn stood near the doorway, as always.

Ranhildr had held her tongue until the longhouse was sealed. While the beams rose, she said nothing. Not when Arnlaugr crossed the threshold. Not when he blessed the lintel without consent. But the house brought them close — too close. Meals shared, breath shared, prayer spoken overhead where no silence could hold. She kept her distance in gesture, in look. But now there was nowhere else to stand.

She stepped forward — barefoot, the skin raw at the arch, her cloak open at the throat. Her face held nothing soft. In one hand, the knife. The other hung loose, fingers reddened and cracked. Not raised. Just carried. The bone grip wore marks from her palm.

"Your fire doesn't take," she said, voice low. "It dies before the prayer ends."

Arnlaugr did not look at her. "It takes enough."

She crouched at the edge of the ring. Reached into her sleeve. Pulled out a small stone knife — obsidian, knapped rough. The edge had been pressure-flaked along both sides, brittle but razor-keen. It wasn't Greenland stone — more likely sea-traded, or chipped from drift-rock.

"The sea gave this," she said. "It cuts truer than your faith."

"That claim is heresy," said Kristján, sharp.

She looked to the fire. "Then your god should speak

louder."

She drew her thumb across the blade — fast, clean. Blood welled. She let it fall into the fire. Not a drop spattered. The flame hissed, then rose.

Arnlaugr turned to her at last. "That blood is not blessed. This flame is not yours to call."

"No," she said. "It was here before yours."

The smoke bent sideways. Only a little. But it bent.

Leif stood behind the others. His hands were at his sides. His eyes on the floor.

"Say something," Kristján hissed, not loud — but Leif heard.

He looked up. Met Ranhildr's eyes, then Arnlaugr's.

"The fire rose," he said. "That's all I saw."

Arnlaugr's jaw tightened. He did not speak again.

Ranhildr did not look at Leif again. She had offered her blood. And he had offered nothing. She turned and walked out. Blood still on her thumb.

Vidarbjǫrn waited until the wind touched the fire again. Then he stepped forward and stirred the ash with the butt of his knife.

"She's not wrong," he said. "But she's not right, either."

The next morning, the fire-ring lay cold. No one fed it.

Father Arnlaugr called them to the church at midday. Not at dusk, as was custom, but while the sky still held colour. "The saints must be named while the light still rises," he said. "So that the shadow does not claim them."

They gathered. The sod-roof had settled in the tilt, and the doorway hung skewed on its leather hinge, but the walls still held. Kristján lit the altar lamp while Arnlaugr prepared the bowl.

Leif hadn't spoken a command. But the men saw that he was tired of her defiance, and the rite gave him a way to answer it. They came as much for faith and for him.

Asleikr stood near the back wall, arms folded, face unreadable. Kristján knelt. Skagi watched the flame too long and blinked when the light shifted. Even Tyrkir, who muttered through most rites, stood steady beside Finnvið. Vidarbjǫrn leaned against the post outside, not within. He had come halfway. That was all.

Only Ranhildr did not come.

Leif had found her before the mass, near the slope where the snow broke thin. She was walking the line between tree and stone, eyes half-lidded.

"Just one day," he had said. "One rite. For the sake of peace."

"Peace?" she'd asked, not turning. "Is that what you think your god brings?"

"The others are watching. They follow when you defy."

"Then teach them to see."

He had not said more.

Now he stood inside the leaning church with the lamp burning low and the priest's voice rising like ash.

Father Arnlaugr named the saints one by one. Some in Latin, some in the tongue of Greenland. Some names none remembered. Some names no one had ever heard before.

"Agatha," he said.

"Crispin," he said.

"Benedict, Augustine, Martin of Tours."

The fire guttered once, then rose again.

Finnvið Snake-Tongue laughed.

Not loud. Just sharp. High in the throat, like a man trying not to spit.

"Sorry," he said when the heads turned. "Didn't know it took that much God to warm a wick."

Leif moved before Arnlaugr could. He crossed the floor in three steps and struck Finnvið with an open palm—hard enough to knock him back against the wall.

"This is not for mocking," he said.

"It's not me he wants to hit," Finnvið muttered, which almost got him another.

Arnlaugr raised the bowl, hands steady despite the tension.

"The flame bears witness," he said. "The names are not for the living only. They are to mark the path."

Leif thought of the path he had begun—and the one they followed now. Stranded. Watched by a land without kindness. And Ranhildr, claimed once, now turning from him with bare hands and blood. He looked toward the open doorway. The wind had shifted—barely. Not toward the fire. Not away. Just sideways.

When Arnlaugr finished the rite, the silence held too long.

No one prayed. They did not know to.

Rúni was not meant for winter walls.

Not after the forest. Not after the blood. Something had been torn then—opened, or let loose—and whatever stepped back into camp afterward was not the same man who'd entered the hollow.

When the beams were raised and the prayers thinned, it became clear: the longhouse could not hold his weight. He moved through the hall like a second shadow—too fast when startled, too still when angered. He slept close to the door. He ate late. He walked with bare feet until frost burn split the skin.

He would not sit with his back to walls. He flinched at fire-crack. He spoke little, and always after delay, like listening first for a voice that wasn't his.

Vali no longer hummed near him.

Kristján began assigning him posts alone.

When Haukr mocked his silence, he threw the boy against the back wall, hard enough to shake the stores. When Skagi asked about the scars on his throat, Rúni grinned wide, too long, and said nothing. When the men rose for Arnlaugr's blessing, Rúni stood with his back to the fire.

The others stopped asking questions. Even Vali, who once hummed near him, had grown quiet.

Leif spoke with Kristján. No shouting. Just words traded at dusk. The next day, Rúni was told to scout the upper coast.

"Take the drift-track," Kristján had said. "Map the land north. Count the rivers. Mark the stone."

Rúni didn't argue. He packed food, a flint kit, two knives, and the shortest of the three spears. Dried venison in gutstring, three hard cakes of barley and marrow, a sealing-bladder pouch of pine pitch for binding or burn. He left that night. No farewell.

He was gone three weeks the first time. Returned thin but not tired, bearing a map scratched into birchbark with resin-char. It showed the horn of the northern cape, where the land pulled east into broken cliff and the sea pounded from below. He spoke only to Leif and pointed with two fingers: "Here. Elk sign. Five days out. One limping."

Then he left again.

The longhouse held warmth, but not peace.

With snow tight against the walls and the cold pressing from the root-cellars to the rafters, the space inside collapsed. There was no privacy. No silence. The fire's reach marked status: who lay nearest, who dared turn from it, who woke coughing when the ash settled wrong.

Bladders swelled in the night. No one wanted to walk to the piss-trench. Some did anyway. Some didn't. The air began to sour.

Kristján kept the peace. He rationed the firewood. Rotated the sleepers. Enforced rest cycles. When Finnvið and Hallgeirr Herjólfrsson, the sailmaster, fought over bed-roll placement, Kristján settled it with a measured look and the phrase: "You'll sleep better further apart." When Sveigr went too long without standing post, Kristján assigned him to the midden patrol—not as punishment, but to keep his limbs moving. He had Leif's word. He had Arnlaugr's blessing. More importantly, he had the men's eyes. They listened. For now.

The smokehole froze twice in a single day. Kristján broke the shutter hinge with a stick and cursed until it came loose. The green alder burned thick, but not hot. It hissed more than it flamed, and let off steam that coated the ceiling with black drops that froze before they fell.

The smoke gathered early that week and stayed. Green alder, wet-split, steamed instead of burned. Each morning, the rafters held a low haze. The air stung the eyes. The clothes drank the smoke. Every man reeked of pitch and fire rot. The men rubbed their eyes when they woke, and the walls wept more than they dried. Kristján began cracking the smokehole earlier.

Arnlaugr muttered louder during prayers.

Ranhildr stepped outside more often, and not always to fetch wood.

Geirr carved from the far wall now, hunched tight in his cloak. His breathing slowed when he leaned too close to smoke. Twice, he paused mid-cut, eyes lost to something he didn't name. The smoke caught him more than it once had. He carved only in short shifts now, wrapping his cloak twice, even when others had begun shedding theirs near the warmth. He said nothing of it. But Tyrkir noticed. One night, he passed Geirr an extra stone, still warm from the firebank. Geirr took it in silence and did not return it.

By the third day, the coughing started—dry at first, then wet, then worse. At night, it echoed through the sleeping bank. No blood, at first. Just a sound that didn't end. Some shifted away. Others held breath. At night, it echoed through the sleeping bank.

Skagi turned his face to the wall.

Finnvið muttered.

By the fifth, Geirr no longer rose with the others. He blinked at the rafters, eyes bright with fever. His mouth opened sideways, like bark torn damp. Each breath rasped shallow and soft.

Kristján asked Hallbjǫrn to check him.

The herbalist touched Geirr's brow, pulled back the blanket, said nothing for a long time. Then quietly: "If it's not death's hand, it's at least his gloves."

Tyrkir brought salt-water, honeyed spruce, and a worn token of St. Thorlakr. He knelt beside Geirr's bed and whispered a prayer. The coughing paused. But the breath stayed wrong — shallow, like paper crumpling in slow wind.

Father Arnlaugr came next. His Latin was clean, rhythmic, unwavering.

Domine, miserere nobis…

But the cadence didn't comfort. It carved space around the sickbed — alien, even to those who believed.

Ranhildr dreamt of wolves that night.

By morning, two others had started coughing.

Kristján made the call. Not with anger. Not with grief. Just steel.

"He goes out," he said. "We cannot keep breath that will not hold."

Skagi tried to argue.

Vidarbjǫrn stepped forward before it could rise.

"I'll go with him," he said.

No one objected.

Not even Leif.

They built a windbreak of spruce and hide, near the slope where the cookpit smoke drifted wide. The shelter was low, dry, open at the sides. Enough for one man to die, and one to keep watch.

Geirr said nothing when they moved him. His eyes didn't track the door. He coughed twice, then slept.

Ranhildr came just before dusk. She did not speak. She brought no balm.

From her pouch, she took a strip of bark scored with runes, dark with boiled ash and fat. It was birchbark — peeled mid-summer, stored flat. The ash was goat-bone, the fat seal. Marked not for healing, but for letting go. She bent over Geirr's mouth, careful not to touch skin, and passed the bark once against the sun's path. Then once more, with it. A binding and a release.

She pressed the bark to the door-post of the shelter and whispered something low. The wind did not catch the words.

Vidarbjǫrn stayed beside him through the frostfall.

No lamp. No Latin. No runes. Just a blade on his knee, and one hand near Geirr's mouth, feeling for each breath.

In the longhouse, no one spoke that night unless spoken to. And the fire, though well-fed, did not warm the feet.

The snowfall deepened in silence. Not in flurry, but in weight. A kind of settling that changed the pitch of breath. No one tracked it that night. The fire needed tending. The sealskin at the door swelled with frost. By the morning, the sickbed held no steam. Not from breath, not from skin.

They dug with antler tines and fists. No one spoke. The ground was shallow near the southern drift where the wind cut least. The snow there had packed hard, but the earth beneath gave way in layers—cracked roots, dark loam, frostbit clay. The grave was not deep, but it took the weight.

They wrapped Geirr in his own cloak. Laid his tools beside him: the dull knife, the spoon he carved, a strip of birch marked with tally, and two arrowheads tied in waxed cord. A bowyer's hands shouldn't pass unmarked.

Arnlaugr drove the driftwood cross deep—his knuckles red, the binding cord frost-stiff. He didn't look up until it held. Leif stood beside him but did not speak.

Leif named the dead. Father Arnlaugr performed the rites— Latin low, gestures slow but sure.

Ranhildr did not come.

Later that night, Vidarbjǫrn returned to the grave. He stood, head bowed, as if listening. The wind moved across the stones, low and slow, like breath through a cracked reed.

He pressed the spear into the drift, elbow deep, until it stood without sway. He watched where it caught, eyes nearly shut against the wind. Then scored a line with his thumbnail— slow, precise, unspoken. No tally. No prayer. Just pressure and memory. Then he pulled it free.

The shaft steamed slightly in the cold. He held it upright for a moment. Not for omen. Not for show. Just to know the line.

Then he turned and walked back through his own prints.

The wind shifted behind him—barely. Just enough to move the cross.

He did not look back.

Behind him, the snow kept falling. The gods did not answer.
But the rite still held.

CHAPTER 12: THE SILENCE THAT SHOULDN'T BE

1000 A.D. — ÝLIR

The wind came low under the eaves — rasping, like breath in an old throat. The sky stayed gauzed in grey. Daylight passed like smoke. Then night.

Inside the longhouse, the roof sagged from the snow's weight. Smoke clung to the beams. Breath misted at the rafters. Turf walls bowed inward. Corner posts blackened with wet — as if the wood had grown weary of standing. They'd braced the ridgepole with spruce forks, but each week the weight pressed harder. Thirty-one men and one woman lay pressed shoulder to shoulder beneath it, sleeping in turns. The silence was not peace. It was held taut, like bowstring before the shot.

Food was salted meat and root mash, thick with lard and silence. Once a week, Tyrkir made a broth with dried berries and strips of sedge bulb and bark peel — found before the freeze. Preserved in spruce gum, they kept their sharpness. Hallbjǫrn muttered it was witch-work. Tyrkir didn't answer. He only stirred with the spine of a fir branch, slow and steady, until the fat came clear.

The hearth smoked wrong. Too low a draw, too many damp logs. They tried a birchbark cone to funnel the draft, but it softened in the heat. Nothing held long in the pitch-thick air. But the fire held. Barely.

Kristján's ledger warped with damp. Runes smudged. Even he wrote less now.

Breath pooled above them, held fast in the beams.

There was no wool. No new cloth. Only what they'd carried on their backs or lashed in chests. Tunics twice-mended. Rags wrapped at the calves, stiff with old blood. Strips of wool felt, tied with sinew, served where boots failed. The hide wore thin fastest at the heels, where no stitching held. Fur collars where the skin still held. A few had hoods. Most did not.

Rúnar wore the same sealskin he had in Markland, its back patched with fish glue.

Asleikr tied thongs of birch-bark around his feet before stepping out—to keep the frost from eating through the seams.

Ranhildr wore mittens: seal-hide tight to the skin, caribou hair thick above, both waxed stiff with spruce sap. When she peeled them free, steam rose from her palms—red, scar-creased, bone-tensed. Hands that worked and wounded— that had once warmed beside Leif's, now withdrawn.

When the wind blew down from the ridges, it scoured skin raw. Fingers cracked. Toes blackened. Ears curled with frostbite, then split. Salted fat was rubbed into cheeks and brows to hold the heat—but it stung in open wounds, and turned rancid if forgotten near the hearth.

Every step outside hurt. The drifts shifted, re-formed, packed to crust. Each layer hid another. They learned to walk flat-footed, knees bent, like men crossing spring ice— though winter had barely turned. Ice overlaid itself like plate-armour—slippery on top, sharp beneath. Ankles twisted. Knees locked. Backs spasmed. The old wounds came alive again: Kristján's arrow-split hip, Leif's left shoulder, Stígandr's wrist, broken at landfall and never set right. They moved like men twice their age.

The creek vanished beneath a lid of white. Ice had to be broken, then the water lifted and boiled before drinking. Meltwater carried flecks of ash and charcoal from the snow they burned to make it. They strained it through cloth scraps stretched over bone hoops — once used for fish — now black with soot

The piss trench froze halfway down. Men slipped. Fell. Cursed. The snow smoked yellow where it struck, then crusted over fast. The midden froze too. It steamed under the rime but wouldn't yield. Haukr dug it out with an axe. The blade caught on something frozen solid. He did not ask what. He only spat and kept cutting.

Leif watched her from the shadows — not openly, but like a man circling fire with bare hands. His mouth stayed set, but his eyes followed: pale, rimmed red from cold and want.

She had wanted him once. That first day on the Greenland shore, before the knarr was even loaded — he saw it in her eyes. After the sea took her and gave her back, they'd shared a season. Brief, bitter, but real. She had leaned against him at the fire. Taken warmth from his hands. Even laughed once — sharp and low, like it startled her.

But it hadn't lasted.

He had claimed her. For him, it had been simple: she had taken his cross, so she should share his bed. But the more space he gave, the sharper she became. She mocked Christ. Challenged Arnlaugr. Spoke where others stayed silent. He broke custom after custom — let her hunt alone, let her speak without rebuke, bore her silence when it cut deep. But each allowance only hardened her stance. When he tried to correct her, she did not cry out. But she turned her face away.

Still, she sat beside him at meals — sometimes. But always with her mouth drawn tight, words honed like hooks. He couldn't always name the grievance — only that it was him. The way he believed. The way he shielded. Even the way he looked at her — too long, too certain — seemed to offend. He cracked marrow bones too hard. The splinters flew into the fire.

He praised her in front of the men. Called her sharp-sighted. Brave. But it did not satisfy.

At the fire, when he spoke gently, she met it with a cold stare that held no softness.

She spoke with edge. She clashed with him at meals, contradicted his orders when the hunts were drawn. Once, she threw a fish at his boots, saying, "If you want meat, gut it yourself." He had done nothing.

The men heard. Father Arnlaugr did not interrupt. But his jaw set hard, and his hands remained folded behind his back — as if binding a judgement he would not yet speak. Kristján winced, lowered his gaze, and One night he tried — quietly — to settle his cloak near hers in the loft. She slapped it aside, but still it seemed to him that her eyes dared him to try again.

His temper flared. "You shame me before the men," he said, his voice hard.

She laughed, cold and sharp. "Ha! What do you know of shame?"

"Every man here knows I have made a space for you. And before, when the weather was warm, you accepted."

"I accepted what I thought you offered. But it was a false gift."

"You took the cross."

"I took what was important to you. Not your faith. What have you returned?"

He pressed his fingers to the bridge of his nose, rage clamped in his chest like a stone.

"Then what am I to you?"

"A man who wants but does not name. Who sees a flame, calls it his, but brings no kindling."

"You twist words like a skald."

She turned from him and said no more.

The next day he barked across the hall—sharp, a captain's tone. "Kristján. Leave the papers. You've counted the same tally three times. The men need firewood, not ink."

Silence, half a breath. Then Ranhildr stood.

"And who decides what the men need?" Her voice was clear, loud. "You, who once led through storm and landfall. You, who now sits in shadow while others keep the fire lit. If they need firewood, it's because no one leads them to gather it."

Leif turned toward her, mouth hard. "Do not cut across me like that. Not here. Not now."

She stepped forward. "Then speak sense. Or keep silence."

The room stilled. The hearth spat a coal. Wind hissed at the smoke-hole.

When their eyes locked, there was something fierce in her — cheeks flushed, breath fast. Not love. But heat. The kind that did not retreat.

Skagi watched wide-eyed, caught between awe and discomfort. Their words struck like lines from an old tale — but no one was guiding it, and no one knew how it would end.

A crack had opened in the centre of the hall — not wide, not loud, but deep.

The fire did not dwindle. The rage fed something else — want, rooted deep. It sat behind his ribs, rising like smoke, without outlet. The fire between them hadn't gone out. It just had no chimney.

She did not refuse him outright. When she leaned past him and her hip grazed his, she didn't pull away. But her tools stayed separate. Her cloak too. She slept near the outer wall, where the warmth thinned and the wind gnawed. She smelled of pine and blood and salt, and for a moment, he thought she lingered. Once, after a long silence, he passed her the waterskin and her fingers lingered — too long to be chance. Too brief to be certain.

The men noticed. They sorted themselves by it. Some near her place by the wall, others by Leif's hearth. The space between filled with silence. Laughter stuttered. Trust thinned, like broth stretched too many days.

He sought Father Arnlaugr by the hearth, when the others had gone out for ice-drawing. The priest sat cross-legged, palms open to the coals. His hair had turned the colour of birch smoke.

Leif stood silent a moment, then spoke. "May I ask counsel?"

A nod.

"Ranhildr," he said. "There's no peace between us. I don't know the root. She was with me once — not as wife. But still. Now she will not come near."

The priest's fingers were mottled from cold. He shifted one hand closer to the fire.

"She took the cross."

"She did."

"But she does not keep it."

"She wears it."

Arnlaugr gave no assent. No dismissal. Just silence.

"She mocks the rites. Speaks when men speak. Denies correction. All of it — one root. The old ways. The old blood."

"She's fierce, yes," Leif said, voice low. "But not false."

Arnlaugr looked up. His eyes were red-rimmed from smoke. "You want peace. There is none while she straddles two paths. No marriage. No obedience. No covenant without Christ."

Leif's jaw tightened. His gloved hand clenched on his knee, leather creaking.

"If she took the sacrament truly," said Arnlaugr, "then the way would open. A woman must cleave to her man. The flesh answers to the bond."

"So I should wed her?"

"She must be made right with God first. But yes—wed her, and the storm will pass."

The log cracked sharply. Leif did not flinch.

"You are her shield," the priest said. "You offered protection. She owes return. That is the way of things."

"She does not see it that way."

"Then she must be shown."

Leif said nothing. He stood a moment longer, then turned, and left.

Outside, the frost had set hard. No track marked his step. He walked the slope above the store-pit, where the smoke curled low. The sea beyond was sealed. The horizon gone. Ice met sky without seam.

Below, the camp sagged under its rime. No fires showed. No one moved. Even the smoke held still—suspended, directionless.

Leif crouched by a crooked pine, pressed his gloved hand to the earth. Hard as bone. Cold through to the knuckle. He closed his eyes. Tried to pray. But the words clanged in his chest—wrong shape, wrong god.

She must be made right with God. She must be shown.

He let breath out through his nose. It steamed, then vanished.

A gull passed overhead—silent. Not crying. Just a shadow on grey.

He stood. Knees aching. Then turned toward the lean-to, where axe-light flickered behind slats.

Vidarbjørn crouched beneath the lean-to, shoulders square, still as timber. Dökk Tönn rested across his lap, the black blade catching slivers of firelight. His hands moved slow—scarred, burn-ringed, sure.

Leif lingered a moment, then crouched opposite. "Still sharp?"

Vidarbjørn turned the axe in his hands. "Hasn't dulled."

The oil-stone moved in circles. Wind scraped along the wall—dry leaves, maybe. The ground beneath them had hardened but not yet taken snow.

"She looked at me different, once," Leif said. His voice barely marked the air. "On the Greenland shore. Before the shipyard."

Vidarbjǫrn said nothing.

"I didn't know. Not until after. When I thought she was gone. That's when it struck."

The cloth wiped clean the edge. It came away dark.

"One thing done in water," Vidarbjǫrn said. "Another by fire."

Leif's mouth pulled, not quite a smile. "She keeps silence now. Or draws blood."

"She speaks to you more than most."

"She's your sister."

A pause. Then Vidarbjǫrn met his gaze. "She is."

Leif didn't look away. "What did I do?"

Vidarbjǫrn folded the cloth and set it aside. "You stepped in — but never crossed the threshold."

Leif exhaled, sharp as flint. "We're not in Greenland. No fathers to ask. No bride-price to weigh. But she won't take vows under Christ. And certainly not before Arnlaugr."

Vidarbjǫrn nodded. "Even so."

Wind rose — dry, thin. A sound like breath through bone.

Leif's hand dropped to his knee. "Say a man wished to speak with honour. Say he meant more than warmth or firelight. Say he came to ask—not to take."

Vidarbjǫrn watched the blade. "You and she don't fit."

Silence.

Leif stood too fast, brushed frost from his knees as if it stung. His hand went halfway to the axe at his belt, then stopped.

Vidarbjǫrn shrugged, not without weight. He saw the hurt bloom in Leif's stillness and did not chase it back.

"Doesn't stop your feet," he said, quieter now. Not refusal. Not invitation. Just a letting-be—the kind given to men who've already made their crossing.

Leif didn't answer. He looked once toward the longhouse — its roof dark, its hearth gone cold.

Rúni came when the sky blackened at the edges. Left when the wind turned off the lake or the snow went light enough to breathe. He slept beneath the rafters only when the old wound in his shoulder—earned deep in the woods— pressed from within. Still red at the seams. Numb as old bark.

When he returned, the axe came first. Drawn low, edge turned in. He whispered at the threshold—not a greeting, not a prayer, but words that bound. No one welcomed him. No one stopped him. He asked for no fire. Claimed no place. Just crouched near the centre post, one arm looped round his knee, eyes on the smokehole, like something watched from above.

He hunted alone. No bow. No traps. Just the axe, a gutting blade, and a coil of black twine wound round his wrist. He brought back meat, sometimes. Once, a hare. Legs splayed, throat gone. He said nothing.

He spoke to the axe. Named things when fog thickened — so it wouldn't name them first. Once struck the doorframe and said, "It's listening." Then kept silence five days. Another night he poured water on his boots until they froze stiff, then shattered them with the axe's back. He laughed once — sharp, broken, like a crow cracking its own spine. Then silence again. Frost rimed the scars at his throat. He took no salt. But he was no fool. He saw frost before it came. Saw sag before the walls bent. Saw dark before it moved. And when he stood, men left on errands they didn't name.

He always came back.

And when he did, the fire bent low.

One evening, Rúni returned with dried blood in his beard and a strip of hide bound round one boot. The door swung open and stayed that way. Snow followed him in.

Eirikr Hrolfsson stood at the hearth, ladling stew. His hands slowed. Then kept going. More than his share.

Their quarrel was old — summer-born, creek-fed. Bruises traded. A stone once left in Rúni's boot. Never named. Never mended.

Eirikr didn't look up. "You eat when you earn," he said.

The ladle struck the pot. Not loud. But final.

Rúni stepped forward. Not fast. Not slow. The knife came out—flat and quiet. Slid under Eirikr's tunic, into the meat of his side, and out again. One breath. No more.

Eirikr gasped. Dropped the ladle. Blood hit the hearthstone and hissed. He fell to his knees. Not dead. But ended.

Kristján stepped forward. Voice level. "Enough," he said. "You'll sleep at opposite ends." Then, to Rúni: "The door is yours."

Rúni nodded.

That night he lay beneath the threshold beam, wrapped in skins, shoulder to the wood. The wind needled through a seam near his neck. He didn't move.

After that, he came less. Gone longer. Men began to ask—quietly—if he still hunted, or just watched. None offered to follow.

Three nights passed. Then four.

The door was open one morning. His axe was gone. So was the twine. The drift at the threshold curled in like breath. The men said there were tracks—long-stride, no heel-drag—but the wind had taken the rest.

No man could live in that cold. Not now. Not so deep into winter.

Rúni did not come back.

But one night, Haukr found prints by the midden. Deep. Clean. Toe-heavy. Beside them: a deer, half-eaten. The guts still steamed. The hide had been peeled by blade, not teeth.

No one had brought down a deer in days.

No trail. No blood. No path inland.

Tyrkir walked the ring twice, muttering in a tongue no one knew.

Skagi carved a new rune by the threshold—three lines crossed. No one asked what it meant.

That night, the men slept closer to the centre-post. No one touched the place where Rúni once crouched.

The fire cracked louder in his absence. As if the wood remembered.

The sea hissed beneath its skin of ice.

It did not speak. Did not give. It pressed upward in ridges and black cracks, shifting with the tide below—alive, but sealed. When the wind changed, the fissures groaned, then closed again. Nothing surfaced.

They cut holes with bone-pegs and backblades, chipped narrow mouths through hand-thick crust. Nets were lowered. Anchored. Watched.

Waiting took hours.

The nets came up limp. Or tangled. Or torn where the ice had shifted and bit through the twine. Once, a single capelin wriggled on the line. It froze stiff before it could be claimed.

Breath froze in beards. Fingers bled through gloves. Salt

rubbed raw on cheeks burned colder with wind. The men huddled in pairs, backs to the sea, ropes looped round gloved wrists so the pull — if it came — would not be missed.

Ketill did not flinch. He crouched at the last hole, slow in his movements, hands bare to the wind. His breath steamed faintly, but he did not shiver. The cold moved around him like around a stone. He stared into the black water and did not blink.

Skagi kept close — young limbs taut with cold, eyes narrowed against drift. He checked the line, then tugged Ketill's cloak collar higher with numb fingers. His jaw trembled, though he set it tight.

"Better catch nothing," he muttered, "than pull up the wrong thing."

Ketill gave no reply. But he stopped whispering after that.

That morning, he had come without his belt-knife. The day before, he'd salted the same fish twice. Skagi had seen him step into the wind and call a name no one knew — once, twice — then fall silent when asked.

They sharpened hooks slower. Mended cord longer. Sat in silence and let the sea judge them. Still it gave nothing.

Evening pressed weight on the camp. Fire-smoke dragged sideways in the sea wind. The men stood in a staggered line near the tarp-stockpile, shadows long across snow-crust and sled-mark. Kristján called names from memory.

"Stigr."

"Aye."

"Hallsteinn."

"Here."

One by one, they answered—blunt vowels, hoarse from damp air. Skagi scraped frost from the haft of his axe with a thumbnail. Finnvið sniffed and spat in the snow.

Kristján frowned at the end of the count. "Ketill," he said louder.

Silence.

"Anyone seen Ketill?"

Murmurs. A few shrugged. Skagi shook his head. "He was mending net cord this morning. Took it toward the cove after midmeal. Not since."

Leif rose from his crouch, brushing soot from his palms. "Fan out. Forest and shore. If he's slipped through—" He didn't finish.

They moved fast. Some inland, through the spruce-shadowed slope. Others split along the shore, snow crust giving with wet sighs underfoot. Skagi and Finnvið took the inlet ice, poles brushing aside snow ahead of each step.

Snow thickened—wet, heavy, muffling. Trees faded behind them. Cloaks slumped with weight. Skagi's boots squealed on slick patches. His beard iced over hard.

"There," Finnvið said low, pointing.

Half a league downslope, where the inlet curled against rock, a figure knelt.

Ketill.

His hood hung loose. Silver hair clumped with melt. Bare scalp red with cold. He sat still, spine bent, hands open to the ice—like a man waiting to be claimed, not found. Snow swept sideways—thick as down. It gathered on his shoulders and did not melt.

They slowed.

He had scraped a wide patch bare in front of him. Hands red and cracked at the knuckles. Skin flaked raw. The hollow he'd cleared showed only grey ice. Hard. Unbroken.

No net. No hook. No cord.

Nothing but the hollow between his palms.

"Ketill," Skagi said quietly.

No answer.

Finnvið circled wide, careful of the crust. "You alright?"

Still nothing.

Skagi knelt beside him. One hand brushed snow clear again. "There's no catch," he said. "Nothing here, Ketill."

The name dropped like a rope across water.

At last, Ketill blinked. Slow. "There was a pull," he whispered. "It scraped. Like bone on bone. I stayed still.

Didn't want to spook it."

Skagi glanced at the scraped ice. No cracks. No hole. No trail.

Ketill's hands hovered, trembling, as if they'd touched something that had touched back.

Skagi reached out, gripped his elbow. "It's night now. Come on. Fire's still up."

Ketill let himself be raised. No protest. But as they turned, he looked back—once, twice—over his shoulder, as if the thing might still rise. Out of the silence. Out of the snow-choked dark.

Just a man, fishing for what was already gone.

The land did not strike. It settled—slow as rot, quiet as meltwater.

One night, Finnvið woke to find the threshold stones wet. No melt had run from the roof.

Skagi found the firewood stacked wrong—spiral-laid, with charred ends out.

Leif sat beside Ranhildr but did not look at her. She kept her hand closed through the meal. Only after did she open it: a scrap of red thread, stiff with something dark.

No great storm came.

Only a silence that crept now—low and jointed, like

something crouched between the beams. It moved in shifts. Where Rúni once sat. Where Ranhildr once laughed.

Now cold. Now still.

CHAPTER 13: THE MASS, THE RITE, THE SEA

1000 A.D. — JÓL

Arnlaugr did not wait for consent.

He counted backward from the solstice, not by moon or tide, but by gospel measure, each day notched against the ledger Kristján kept by firelight. On the eve, he tied a strip of linen to the crossbeam above the altar, blackened its ends in pine ash, and raised the cracked book with hands that only trembled when still. The linen had once edged a christening gown—now cut thin, the ash ground fine with thawed marrow and soot. A bitter-smelling ink, meant to hold.

"The Christ Mass will be held," he said. Not loud but final. "In the church."

Leif gave no answer beyond a nod. There was no council. No quarrel. Just the cold, and the silence, and the shape of command taken on by those too tired to contest it.

They came. Not all, but enough.

Wrapped in furs stiff with smoke and old sweat, they filed along the frozen path from the longhouse. One man carried a lantern, the flame hunched low behind horn plates. Eirikr limped, favouring the leg that had turned in the frost weeks ago. Hallbjǫrn had wrapped it tight that morning—said nothing, just grunted, and moved on. Rúnar muttered into his collar. None listened. Skagi came steady behind Ketill, guiding him with a hand at the elbow—gentle, but firm enough to steer. The old man walked without seeing, eyes on some distant place the rest had left behind.

The wind dragged hard across the bluff. Snow did not fall but scoured—slanted, needled, thick with grit and salt that scraped the throat. Ice laced the eaves. The cross atop the church leaned into the gale, its shadow cast sideways across the threshold.

Tyrkir came last.

He wore the same mended cloak he'd brought from Brattahlíð, its seams restitched with gut, the collar softened with salt. No cross adorned his neck. No ring or token. Just the quiet gait of a man who had survived too many winters to argue with the shape of this one.

He stopped beneath the eaves. Looked up at the frost where it hung in long teeth from the beam. Then he murmured in his own tongue—a low, rounded cadence shaped by ash, not altar. A name, perhaps. The frost didn't melt, but it listened. Then he stepped inside.

The walls groaned.

Slabs of frost crawled down the timber joints. The turf at the base of the frame whistled where they'd patched the leak above the altar. They'd stuffed it with frozen sedge and hair-cord, packed wet moss behind—anything to slow the draft. It held, barely. The cup—brass, battered, too small—had been warmed by the hearth. But by the time Arnlaugr lifted it, ice had crusted the rim. He drank anyway.

The cut was clean. The wine, thin and sour, stung at the lip as it mixed with blood. He did not flinch.

Arnlaugr opened the book with both hands and let the pages fall to the marked place. His breath curled between him and the men. He did not meet their eyes.

"And the Word was made flesh," he began, in Latin, voice hoarse, each syllable fogging in the cold. "And dwelt among us."

The Latin dragged slow. Uneven. He paused once to swallow, then repeated the same words in Norse. The words come out rough but strong.

A silence followed. No cough. No creak. Just the frost settling in the joints of the roof.

His sermon was short. "This is no symbol. No story. No dream. The Word took on bone, and blood, and breath. Not like the old spirits. Not drift or omen. He entered the world to tear death out by the root."

He looked at no one. But the tone had turned — dense, certain, full of a faith that left no room for dusk between.

He lowered the book. Let his hand fall to his side. And said nothing more.

He read from the scroll of Isaiah, voice tightening with the cold: "The people that walked in darkness have seen a great light; they that dwell in the land of the shadow of death, upon them hath the light shined." A few voices murmured "Amen." Not all. But enough.

Then a psalm — Psalm 27, his choice deliberate: "The Lord is my light and my salvation; whom shall I fear? The Lord is the strength of my life; of whom shall I be afraid?" The cadence caught. One or two men repeated the lines under their breath. Another "Amen" followed, louder now, shaped more by habit than conviction.

Arnlaugr lifted his hand — not in flourish, just slowly, with weight—as though pressing the air toward the frost-veined beam above. The book closed. He kissed its cover with chapped lips. The silence held.

Outside, the wind pressed harder. The shutters jumped in their frames. Snow hissed beneath the door. No one lingered.

They turned together, wordless, and went back down toward the longhouse—boots slipping, eyes down, arms tucked tight against the wind. No one spoke. No one looked back.

The cold pushed at their heels, needled through seams, bit at every patch of skin that dared exposure. Breath caught in beards. Fingers fumbled at latches. Skagi half-carried Ketill across the slope. His boot slid once on a patch of glazed snow, but he caught them both—grip strong despite his size. The old man wheezed, refusing to stop. Skagi didn't ask him to. He only said, softly, "Almost."

It wasn't clear if Ketill heard. But he moved better after that.

At the threshold, the smell of smoke struck like a blow— peat, grease, old wool. Someone barked a laugh too loud, just to break the silence. Others stamped their boots, shook frost from their cloaks. The door shut hard behind them.

Inside, the warmth arrived slow. Not comfort, but contrast. Fire cracked. Steam rose from cloaks and sleeves. They moved close, instinctively, toward the hearth where the wood hissed and spat. Hands stretched. Cloaks steamed. No one mentioned the mass.

Only when they were certain the cold had been left outside did anyone speak.

"Is the stew still alive, or did it freeze to death waiting for us?" someone muttered near the fire.

"It twitched when I poked it," came the reply, dry as frost.

A few men chuckled—low, short, like breath too tired for mirth. Someone added a log. Another passed a skin of something sharp.

"Well," said Tyrkir, peeling off a stiff mitten, "if Christ was born in a barn, this isn't far. We've got the animals, at least."

"We're the animals," said Rúnar. "The ox and the ass both."

That got a louder laugh. Even Leif cracked a smile from the far bench—shoulders hunched, cloak steaming, pale eyes catching the firelight but revealing nothing.

Steam curled from cloaks. Ice melted from beards. The fire hissed and cracked like it was listening.

By morning, the snow had buried the path. No prints. No sign. Only the church, hunched in frost, holding its breath against the dark.

They went into the trees at dusk.

No horn. No order. Just a glance from Ranhildr across the hearth smoke—and Vidarbjǫrn rose to follow. She passed Leif without slowing. He didn't speak. Just watched her go, shoulders tight, one hand resting on his belt as if weighing words he'd already lost. She carried a pail in one hand, a bundle in the other. The snow parted at her steps but did not fill them. Birch branches overhead held hoarfrost like fleece. The wind left them still.

They climbed past the ash-clearing, where the firepit lay buried, and crested the second ridge, where the stones lay low and wide, slick with ice. The Jol place.

Rimed moss pressed flat beneath their boots. No wing-beat. No cry. Even the trees seemed to hush themselves.

Ranhildr knelt without a word. She set down the bundle and unwrapped it—fingers red from cold.

Laid out the offal: liver, lung, frozen black at the edges. The meat had come from that morning's cull—the last of the tethered goats. Still warm when taken. Bone-split clean with the seax. Then came the blood. Not splashed, but poured. Deliberate arcs, slow and wet against the stone. No horn. No bowl. Just meat and memory.

She took her knife and opened her palm—slow, sure, red welling over fingers already raw from cold. No flinch. No glance at the wound.

She pressed it to the stone's midline, where the lichen split and no ice had formed. Her lips moved. Too soft for him to catch.

Vidarbjǫrn stood nearby. Arms crossed, weight evenly set, breath held long in the chest. It was not the blood that unsettled him. It was the stillness in her—how she moved without seeking, without fear, as if what mattered was not answer but act. She carved shape against the dark because the gods watched—and would answer, if fed.

She struck a pine shaving alight with flint and fat. The tinder hissed. Caught. Then guttered. The smoke turned sideways and disappeared. The blood steamed. Froze.

Vidarbjǫrn stepped forward. Just reached—deliberate, slow—for the smoke-dark sinew wrapped at his belt, fingers stiff from frost but unshaking. He laid it on the stone's edge. Not a gift. Not a prayer. Just a line in the frost. A tether, maybe. Or a record. Or simply this: that someone had borne witness.

Ranhildr watched. Her voice stayed level.

"Not enough," she said.

He met her eyes. "Or too late."

She stood, brushing frost from her skirts. "The gods are not fed."

"Then they'll stay hungry."

For a moment, neither moved. Their breath hung pale between them.

She didn't look at Vidarbjǫrn. But she didn't look toward the camp either. The man she waited for was not the one who came. Then she turned, without signal or word, and walked back into the trees.

He followed, one pace behind. Not her shadow. Not her keeper. Just another soul crossing the cold.

Vidarbjǫrn found Finnvið by the sea as the last light drained from the sky.

The tide had frozen mid-pulse—white ridges tilted like shattered shields, slabs groaning as they shifted in place. Beneath, the sea still moved, but trapped, muffled, angry. Finnvið stood at the breakline—boots sunk deep, hair crusted with sea-frost, lips barely moving. His eyes were sharp, but set far beyond the ice. No breath showed.

Vidarbjǫrn said nothing. The wind was soft but rising, pulling at his cloak with a rhythm like breath, or waves, or words. As he neared, he caught fragments—names. Not those of the living.

Finnvið turned, unsurprised. "You shouldn't sneak."

"I didn't," said Vidarbjǫrn.

They stood beside one another, watching the sea heave faintly under its crust. Something long moved beneath — shadowed, slow — but did not surface.

Finnvið's voice was flat. "They don't stay dead, you know. Not here. Not cleanly."

"Do you mean the gods?"

"No." He shook his head. "The ones we brought. The ones we left. The ones who fed us, or broke us. They don't stay buried."

A silence. The tide cracked further down the coast. Ice ground against ice.

Vidarbjǫrn's eyes traced the ridges until they vanished into mist.

"Do you hear it?" Finnvið asked, low.

Vidarbjǫrn said nothing. But he knew the sound at the longhouse door was not always the wind. Sometimes it paused. Waited. Scraped once. Then was gone.

Vidarbjǫrn stood a long while with his eyes on the moon. It hung full and low, a dull coin behind gauze. The world was still. But not safe. Rúni was out there, or what remained of him. Ketill's eyes wandered more each day. The land was claiming things — quietly, without show.

He walked to Geirr's burial mound. The snow held tight, but the shape still showed. He pressed a stave into the crust. Twice, it struck soft beneath the drift — once near the base, once near the crown. He marked both.

Then he sat: knees bent, arms folded, wind-scoured face unreadable.

No prayer. No name. Just stillness.

When the moon slid behind cloud, he placed two knucklebones — tiny, pale — one at each softened spot. Goat-bones, scraped and polished. Each wrapped in red thread. In the old lands, children played fate-games with them. Here, they kept watch.

He waited until the wind changed.

Then he rose, turned, and walked back to the longhouse.

Behind him, the ground was still.

But it watched him go.

CHAPTER 14: BENEATH THE ICE

1001 A.D. — ÞORRI

Winter pressed on them—broad, cold, and merciless. It gripped the land in iron talons, held back only by the thinning thread of men's labour and whatever prayers still found breath in their chests.

The weight came from above. Not storm, not wrath—just snow that had never thawed, pressing down through beam and bone. The roof sagged under snow thick as a man's chest, and the turf seams along the rafters no longer held tight. Spruce braces had been set beneath the crossbeams, but the joints groaned each night. Without dry wood, they could not fire the smokeholes high enough to melt the inner ice. Wind found its way through. Not with violence, but with patience.

Smoke gathered low and stayed there. It mixed with the damp breath of thirty-one men and one woman, layered itself in the beams, and turned their lungs soft. The fire no longer dried the boots. It moved the wet from wool to hide. Gloves hissed faintly when laid too near, steam rising off the wool like ghost-breath.

Tyrkir stirred his broth with a carved stick, scraping the bottom of the cauldron more than the sides. Even with fish bone and spruce needle, it tasted mostly of water. Once he would hum. Now he stirred in silence.

Three men coughed blood that morning. Not much. Just red in the phlegm. Hallbjǫrn sniffed the rags, spat once, and said, "Not dead yet." Then walked off. Kristján marked their names in the ledger. The ink bled a little—he had to warm the pot by the coals to keep it from freezing in the well.

Ranhildr found mould along the salted fish skin. Not thick—green fuzz edging the meat where brine had thinned. She scraped it off with a bone-blade and set the rest aside. Her eyes did not narrow. She did not speak.

The walls wept at the corners, where the turf had softened from within. Melt came from body heat alone, soaking down into the clay-packed joints. The outer ice held, but inside the longhouse the very seams of the shelter began to sag. No rot, not yet. But something close. The smell was of smoke, sweat, and low decay.

Men passed the hours by habit, not desire. Some mended gloves or rewrapped axe hafts with rawhide strips. Others whittled tokens too odd for tools—half-formed runes, beasts with no name, spirals carved into bone discs. Skagi and Thorleifr threw shoulder-bones at a target scratched into the turf post, but even that lost its meaning when the same mark cracked and fell. Vali spent hours tracing animal tracks into a flat plank with the tip of his knife—fox, hare, elk—but never finished any one. The nose would taper wrong, or the hoof would flatten, and he would scrape it down to begin again. And still the fire was tended in turns, as if flame alone might hold the roof up.

Finnvið tried again.

It was the tale of Grettir's swim to Drangey, the one he told best—sharp-voiced, wry, full of piss and guts. He had told it in Greenland, in storms, even once on the deck of the knarr. But now, halfway in, he lost his place.

"—and Grettir, not yet grown his full beard, dove in with

nothing but—"

"That's not right," came a voice near the back. It might have been Ottar. Or Haraldr.

Finnvið frowned. "It *is* right."

"Last time he had the cloak with him."

"He never had a cloak. That's the whole point."

Another voice: "You said cloak. Twice."

Finnvið stood, threw up his hands in disgust. "Then tell it your gods-damned selves." He kicked at a bit of firewood and returned to his corner. The knife he used to carve was already in hand.

No one finished the story.

Arnlaugr rose from his bed-space near the crossbeam and gave a sermon in a voice half-buried by sleep. He did not rise fully. He only sat up, rubbed his wrists, and began with words from John's gospel. No one responded. No one moved except to shift position—half-waking, half-ignoring. He spoke until the cold caught his jaw and made the syllables slur. Then he stopped. After a moment, he folded the book shut and lay back down without crossing himself.

Across the hall, Tyrkir set his broth down without drinking.

Skagi shifted, then spat once into the fire. It hissed, briefly— then nothing. He didn't look at the others. His eyes stayed on the flame as if waiting for it to answer.

No one crossed themselves.

The only sound that marked time was the breath — rising, clouding, falling again. And the groan of the main beam when the snow shifted. It had begun to creak at even intervals, like a man exhaling through his teeth. No one spoke of it.

It was Kristján who raised the idea, but Leif who gave the nod. Not a command — just a look to Vidarbjǫrn, then to the door. No speech. No plan. Only a shift of weight and the understanding that something had to be done, or men would begin clawing each other open for noise.

They went out before dawn, when the wind had stilled and the air felt heavy enough to press the ribs inward. The snow bore the smell of old ash and rotted pine, as if the forest had been sealed too long under ice. Frost feathered the alder bark in white crusts. Each step sank with a brittle crunch, the cold so thick it hissed against nostrils and bit through wool at the joints. The land felt held in breath, watchful and unyielding — no thaw, no scent of animal, only the dry sting of cold iron and leaf-rot clinging beneath the ice.

Leif and Ranhildr had stopped speaking, though they hadn't stopped hurting each other. Once, she passed him a waterskin. Their fingers brushed, and she pulled back fast — jaw clenched, lashes stiff with frost, like she'd touched a brand. Ranhildr's silence held like drawn steel, and Leif — braced and flinching both — had taken to the far end of the hall most nights. Whatever fire they'd shared had frozen in place, too brittle now to thaw. Even the crew had grown quiet around them.

Many volunteered to go, but Kristján named Vidarbjǫrn, Skagi, Vali, Eirik, and Thorleifr. These five were the surest shots, the ones who could move quiet and carry back more than just meat—they could read the land, and they still knew how to listen when things felt wrong. The rest were needed to hold the hall—tend fire, guard the stores, prepare meals, and any number of tasks scrawled in Kristján's ledger. Leif was not named, but came anyway—pulling on his boots with slow, blunt-fingered hands, face drawn tight, eyes pale and unreadable. He looked like a man daring the cold to cut him clean. No one argued. Ranhildr had spoken just three words to him that week, and none kindly.

Kristján stepped forward, ledger still under one arm. "You weren't named."

Leif met his eyes. Said nothing. Just pulled his hood tight.

No one moved to stop him.

For a moment, Kristján stood firm—spine stiff, feet set as if he might block the way. Then his gaze dropped. Just for a breath. As if he'd seen something familiar in Leif's face— something young, rash, and ruinous.

He stepped back.

"Go," he said. "Answer the cold."

They left the open scrub behind the longhouse—low willow, frost-bitten grass, and salt-dried moss—then began the slow climb inland. The forest here did not rise sudden but crept, patch by patch, gaining density with each frozen ridge. Only after an hour did the trees thicken—dwarfed spruce, black pine, and silver birch twisted by wind.

Each man wore layers: wool tunics under fur-lined cloaks, mittens stiff with frost, hoods drawn low against the lash of cold. Wrappings of felt and skin bound the calves. Sinew ties cracked with ice. Breath iced thick against beard and brow, turning faces to masks. Even so, the chill found seams. Their boots squealed against the crusted snow, and breath came in hard white clouds that vanished before the next step. Ice bloomed up the birch-trunks in frozen lashes. Nothing stirred. No tracks. No scat. Not even the bite marks of hares on twig or bark. Only the sound of their own breath and the occasional knock of hafts against sapling.

Two hours in, Vali held up a hand.

It limped across a ridge ahead of them — gaunt, slate-furred, legs too long for its frame. A caribou buck, ribs showing like caged fingers, left hind hock twisted from an old wound. No herd. No trail. It moved as if time no longer mattered to it.

They fanned slightly, slow. Vali notched an arrow. Skagi mirrored. The bowstrings creaked in the cold. Eirik held the flank with his spear. Vidarbjǫrn gave no signal — only the nod of breath, the draw of shoulder. Two arrows flew.

The beast collapsed where it stood. No run. No cry. As if it had simply decided to lie down.

They reached it in silence. Thorleifr bent to slit the throat but paused.

The eyes were still open.

Vali crouched, hand to the belly. "Too lean."

Eirik rolled it gently with his boot. The stomach was bloated. The fur matted with pitchy crust at the haunch. When Vidarbjǫrn drove his knife into the gut to open it, the smell hit first. Sour, wrong. The liver came out in two colours—one half black, the other green-veined. Parasites ringed the lungs like rope-burn. The bile stank even in the cold.

No one said to leave it. No one argued.

They covered it with branches out of instinct alone.

The silence on the way back was thicker than snow. No one spoke of hunger. They carried their packs, but not for food—just for weight, for habit, for the faint chance of berries or bark. Vali stopped once to piss and came back shaking his head. "No steam," he muttered. "The ground's colder than the air."

It was Skagi who saw the grove.

"Wait."

Just off the trail, behind a drifted bend, a ring of saplings stood—young, birch or alder, hard to tell under the ice—but dead. The bark peeled inward along each trunk, split top to base as if something had unwrapped them from within. No animal signs. No axe marks. And no tracks in or out.

They stood and looked.

Thorleifr made a sign against the sight. Vali did not speak. Skagi adjusted his grip on the bow—but his hand shook, not from cold. He looked at the spiral-stripped tree a third time. His lips moved. No sound.

Vidarbjǫrn said only, "We walk on."

One tree, near the centre, had been scraped clean to the bone—bark peeled down in spirals, like rope unwinding.

Skagi glanced at it twice, then walked faster.

When they returned, no one asked what they had found.

They saw the change before they felt it. Not in sky, but in silence. The trees no longer creaked. The wind no longer sighed. Even the snow seemed to hold still.

Around midday, they watched the eastern slope dissolve — not fall, not slide, but vanish, swallowed by a blur that moved too fast to be fog. Not cloud. Not snow. Something between. A white so whole it cancelled shape. Then came the sound. A groan — not above, but below. Low and wide, like ice shifting deep beneath the roots. Old men called it ice-waking — when the land remembered the sea that shaped it. Not a storm. A reckoning. The wind struck a moment later, sideways and full of grit. Hoods yanked back. Torchheads flared out. Breath thickened in their chests. Every sound became snow. They pushed on, half-blind.

The slope that led to the longhouse came in and out of view. A shape, then a smear, then shape again. When they reached the yard, drifts had already formed around the storeshed, and the door creaked on its hinge. Snow drove sideways against the turf walls. The shutters groaned. Smoke reversed down the chimney and coiled through the rafters. The longhouse shivered like a hull in rough water.

Then the door slammed shut. The wind was outside.

Boots were kicked off. Cloaks peeled back, heavy with rime. The air inside still held the sharpness of damp wood and men's breath, but it was warmer than the gale, and dark enough to soothe the eyes. The fire hissed where snow hit it. A few men slumped near the walls, catching their breath, steaming.

Kristján stood, half-turned to speak, then thought better of it.

After a moment, Skagi crossed to the rear wall, muttering something to himself. He reached Ketill's bed-space, crouched low to pull the spare blanket, and stopped.

The furs were undisturbed. No steam. No boots. No breath.

He looked up, pale. "He's gone."

A few heads turned. No one moved.

Kristján frowned. "When did anyone last see him?"

"By the shore," said Oddi, voice thin. "He was squatting near the fish racks before first meal. Talking. Not loud. Just... words to himself."

"To someone," muttered Tyrkir, not looking up.

Skagi stood fast. His voice cracked. "We let him wander. We left him while we went hunting."

Kristján opened his mouth, shut it again.

"We should have seen—"

"No one saw," Leif cut in. Not cold, but final.

Someone near the back said, "You won't find him now. Not in this."

Another voice, older, almost whispered: "He's mostly gone already, if not all the way."

Skagi's fists clenched at his sides. No one met his eyes.

"We go."

Leif hesitated. Then nodded once. "Not far. Take rope. Take a torch."

Eight stepped forward.

Leif. Vidarbjǫrn. Ranhildr. Skagi. Tyrkir. Finnvið. Haukr. Vali.

They dressed in silence—two layers of wool under fur, oilskin wraps for boots, mittens stiff with cold. Scarves iced before breath could melt them. The rope came last—knotted between them in lengths of three arm-spans. Each knot marked a body's reach. Three pulls meant turn back. One short tug meant halt. A full jerk was for blood. Skagi led, jaw set, hands bare for grip. He knew where to go: west slope, near the old trapline, where Ketill had been found last time.

They moved into the white.

It was no longer wind, but pressure. The kind that pushed breath down into the chest and stripped sound from the ears. Snow came not in flakes but in blasts—needling, side-blown, blind. Shapes loomed, then vanished. Trees and rocks lost name.

Still, they moved. A line of eight souls dragged by need and rope into a storm that did not care.

The storm claimed them one by one — not with pain, but with silence. First their names vanished in the wind. Then their voices.

Drifts reached the thigh, then the hip. The rope stayed taut between them, tugging, adjusting, like the feelers of blind insects in a tunnel. Skagi broke the path, bent low, teeth bared to keep the ice from sealing his mouth. Ice crusted at his eyelids. Snot froze in his moustache. Fingers numbed in seconds despite the wraps.

Vidarbjǫrn followed close behind, one hand on the rope, the other at his axe. Each breath scalded the lungs. Snow clung to his beard, his brows, the fur of his hood. The world had no edges.

They spread without meaning to. Three steps too wide and the shape next to you vanished. Finnvið called once — no one heard him. Tyrkir slipped, yanked hard on the rope, and for a moment the whole line halted. Vidarbjǫrn felt the pull a heartbeat later. He turned, but saw only pale. The storm flattened everything. No sky, no earth. Only the rope in his hand, and Skagi's shape ahead, hunched like an ox against the drift.

They moved again.

The wind screamed around them. Not whistled — screamed. And somewhere behind the noise, Vidarbjǫrn began to wonder if it wasn't calling names.

They crested something — not a ridge exactly, but a heave in the snowpack, hard beneath their feet like buried stone. Then the land dropped.

It wasn't a slope so much as a cleft — ice-slick and hollowed by wind. They slid more than stepped, boots vanishing into powder, rope drawing them down one after another until the storm dulled above.

Here, it was quieter. Not still, but muffled. The howl of the wind circled above the hollow like a beast sniffing its own snare. And at the centre—

Ketill.

He was kneeling—head bowed, arms slack, snow circling but never settling. His white hair clung to his skull like threads of ice.

Not collapsed. Not crawling. Kneeling.

His arms hung slack. His axe lay beside him, half-buried. The wind curled around his body like a hungry animal, tugging at the edges of his cloak. His limbs were stiff. His skin white as tallow.

Skagi stepped forward, then stopped.

Vidarbjǫrn did not speak. He watched the way the snow moved around Ketill—always circling, never settling. Like something was still listening for breath that was no longer there.

Then the eyes opened.

Not slow. Not dim. Wide and white. Not milky, not blind— just empty. Staring straight through them, as if he'd forgotten what eyes were for.

He moved.

The motion was wrong — too fast for old limbs, too exact for any man undone by cold. Not the stagger of a frozen elder, but the angled twitch of something that had never truly stopped moving. His fingers closed around the axe as if they'd been waiting for it. His head turned — not seeking, but fixing. Like he saw something the others couldn't, or nothing at all.

For a breath, no one moved.

Then Finnvið shouted it from farther up the line, voice half-lost in the wind: *"Draugr!"*

Skagi ignored him, surged forward.

"Ketill!" he shouted — voice cracking, snow clinging to his lashes like salt to frost. His cloak had come loose at the clasp and flared behind him. He looked too slight for the cold, too pale, too bright. A boy still. But shining.

No answer. The kneeling figure didn't flinch.

"It's Skagi. We've come to bring you in. Like before. D'you remember? It's too cold out here. You don't need the axe. You're not alone."

He kept speaking, but the storm stole most of the words. Only the urgency showed — hands raised, body angled not in threat but pleading.

Ketill did not speak. Did not lower the axe. Did not blink.

Then he rose.

Not in a rush, not with anger — but with purpose. One knee, then the other. The axe lifted in his hand, slow and sure. His shoulders hunched forward, not from age, but from some stored force pressing toward release.

Skagi took another step closer. Then another. He raised one hand.

"It's me," he said, louder now, trying to hold his voice steady. "We'll go home. There's warmth, fish — people waiting. You don't — "

Behind them, Finnvið shouted again. Not a name. Just: "Too late."

The storm above the hollow howled again. Not louder, but closer. Like it had been waiting.

Ketill lunged.

The axe came down — not wildly, but with terrible direction, the kind used to split firewood or skull. It would have struck Skagi clean through the collar if Vidarbjǫrn hadn't yanked him back by the rope.

Skagi stumbled, fell hard, breath knocked out in a cloud of steam. His eyes were wide, mouth working to form words that wouldn't come. Confused. Terrified.

Vidarbjǫrn stepped forward, snow ghosting off his shoulders. His stance widened. In one motion, he unhooked himself from the rope. Then he drew his axe.

Not Bitabrjótur. Dökk Tönn — the blade for spirits and rites.

Skagi scrambled to his knees. "No — don't! He's freezing — he doesn't see us!"

Vidarbjǫrn didn't answer.

Tyrkir shouted through the wind, "The boy might be right!"

"No," Finnvið called back, already backing up the slope. "That's not him anymore."

Ketill stepped forward again. Each movement was deliberate now. Not lurching. Chosen. The axe rose to his shoulder. His path was clear—and it led through them.

He struck.

Vidarbjǫrn met the blow edge to edge, Dökk Tönn catching the haft of Ketill's axe in a burst of splinters and snow. The force jarred through his arms—more than a man that age should carry. More than any frostbitten body should still hold.

Skagi stumbled forward—boy-shoulders braced, teeth bared, voice breaking through the gale. He stepped between them, hands raised. His fingers shook, but he did not draw.

Ketill turned fast—too fast—and lashed out with the back of the axe. It caught Skagi's shoulder—edge of the collar, just above the heart. Not deep. But the blood ran fast in the cold, bright against the snow. For a moment, he didn't cry out. Just staggered, eyes wide. Then the breath came sharp.

Vidarbjǫrn swore, shifted his stance. He couldn't protect the boy and fight.

Ranhildr moved first—no hesitation. She grabbed Skagi under the arm, hauled him back with a force that nearly tore his feet from under him. Her voice didn't break—but her breath caught when she saw the blood. "Out!" she shouted, but her hands didn't leave him.

Then it was only Vidarbjǫrn and Ketill.

They circled — if it could be called that, sinking in snow with every step. Dökk Tönn was heavy, but sure in his hands. Ketill did not tire. He advanced without sound, lips cracked but silent, eyes dead.

Vidarbjǫrn blocked high, then low. Caught a glancing cut along the thigh—sharp and cold and wrong. He nearly slipped. Righted himself. Brought Dökk Tönn around in a low, rising arc.

Steel struck bone.

Ketill shuddered—but did not fall.

Vidarbjǫrn stepped in close, shoved him back with a shoulder, then drove the blade down again, this time with both hands.

The sound was not like splitting wood. It was quieter. Wet. Final.

Ketill folded.

The wind did not stop.

Somewhere in the gale, a name-cut—half-formed, shouted or thought—was torn from Vidarbjǫrn's mouth and screamed away by the wind.

Blood streamed in dark ribbons, steaming where it touched the ice. Snow drank it first, then the ice beneath— swallowing it in silence, as if it had been waiting. The body did not stiffen.

They did not speak on the return.

The wind pressed them back the way they'd come, though no one could say how they knew it was the same path. The rope pulled taut. The snow closed behind their boots as if the trail had never been broken. By the time they reached the slope above the longhouse, only the light through the smokehole told them they were near.

Inside, they stripped in silence. Ranhildr dressed Skagi's wound without speaking. Hallbjǫrn passed her the cloth — didn't kneel, didn't speak, just pressed it into her hand and moved on. The blood had slowed, but the mark was clear — a line just above the bone. She touched it once before wrapping. Skagi didn't flinch. But he didn't meet her eyes either.

No one asked what had happened.

When the storm broke the next morning — clear light, sharp sky — they went again.

Back to the west slope. Past the trapline.

They searched the drift, the rise, the edge of the hill where the snow had fallen different.

But there was no cleft.

No hollow in the ice.

No blood. No axe. No body.

No tracks. No blood. No hollow. Just white — unbroken, if

the land had closed its eye again. As if it had never been opened. As if nothing had ever been there at all.

Kristján opened the ledger that morning and laid it flat by the coals. The ink had warmed. The page waited.

He held the stylus poised — then lowered it.

There was no line. No measure. No place to mark what broke the count.

He closed the book.

If something else had taken him — better no mark be left.

If the gods had, they left none.

CHAPTER 15: THE THAWING

1001 A.D. – GÓA

The season had not broken—but it had begun to lean.

From the low rise east of the sod-wall, where spruce bent under salt-wind and ash stained the snow in greying crusts, one could see the whole curve of the inlet: the single turf-roofed longhouse crouched near the waterline, with the storage shed slumped to its west, the lean-to dark beneath wind-cut stone, and the knarr resting half-upright on its cradle. The church stood farther off—just visible on the rise above the inlet mouth, where the grass thinned and the sky opened wide.

Only the cold moved—thin and knowing, drawn through door-gaps and bone alike. It pressed behind the knees and under the nails. It found what the fire missed: the old frost-cracks, the scabs pulled open, the joints that once bent smooth. It whispered behind the ear, a soundless thing, the echo of wind against itself. This was not the bite of fresh winter, quick and keen. This was the patience of a dying season—one that knew it had nothing left to prove.

Inside the longhouse the barley had failed. What grain remained was dust-laced and pale, clinging to hulls like mould to bone. Barrel-lids cracked when pried. The sacks had to be struck with axe-flats to loosen them, and those who worked the grindstone coughed blood into their sleeves. Seal fat, hoarded since Yuletide, turned grey and thick. Used for tallow-lamps and smear-salve both. When stirred, it smoked; when cold, it cracked. It had to be stirred with bone-sticks to soften—when it congealed, it formed a skin the colour of bruised snow.

At last, the tide shifted and the cold began to withdraw.

This should have been the time to speak—when the land might still be softened by voice and vow, when the names of sea and soil could be called to witness spring. That had been the old way. But no name was spoken. Not for the gods. Not for the land. Christianity did not name such things, and Father Arnlaugr's presence hung over the longhouse like seal-wax pressed to parchment. The words stayed in the throat.

Rúni the Twice-Bitten had not returned. Ketill Flat-Nose had been taken by the ice and his body never found. They had searched the slope again when the weather cleared—no blood, no prints, no hollow in the snow. Only silence. No one spoke of what might rise if the land chose to give back what it never let go.

The ice did not shatter but it softened. First at the creek-bed edge, then beneath the inlet's black lip. A trickle between stones. A drip from the longhouse eaves. The snow thinned where ash had been buried. The thaw came not with grace, but with the slow reluctance of something old turning in its sleep.

The wind changed—from north to west. Birch buds split. Gulls wheeled overhead, silent first, then shrieking once. And the silence broke.

The men stepped lighter.

The frost let go of the basin rim where water once gathered.

Then the salt held. Just long enough. In the final gasps of

winter, the brine had betrayed them—thawed and re-frozen, it had soured what they thought preserved. Now, the barrels held fast. Meat stored without spoiling.

Kristján was the first to see it—the shift in tide, the thaw at the creek mouth, the black water rising without ice. He brought the bronze-bound ledger, the cracked cross, and a taper wrapped in lamb's wool. He stood at the hearth and waited. Only when the others had gone still did Arnlaugr rise.

Father Arnlaugr lit the taper from the hearth. He bowed his head—not deeply, just enough to remind the room that this was not his will, but God's. He said no words in council. No permission asked. He walked to the shore.

No one followed first. But when Kristján stepped after him, the others did too.

They gathered where a single stone had been raised in the tide-flats. Placed at mid-tide mark, where sea met salt-meadow. Heavy enough it took four to raise, set deep to keep it from frost-heave. No carving. No name. Just mass and memory. The surf breathed mist through its mouth.

Arnlaugr turned to them.

"You go down," he said, "in the name of the Son. And rise clean."

He lifted the cross. Spoke Latin. Named Christ. Marked the sea with ash from the taper.

No one spoke.

Skagi went first. He stripped to the waist—young shoulders

sharp, ribs lean as a bow stave. Pale skin scored only once at the collar, where the wound had long since sealed but not faded. His hands shook — not from cold, but from something older. He stepped into the tide. It caught him at the knees, the thighs, the ribs. He gasped. The mist swallowed the sound.

Then he ducked under. When he rose, steam curled from his shoulders.

Arnlaugr said the name aloud. "Skagi Arnkelsson." He made the sign.

But Skagi did not return to the others. He turned — slow, deliberate — and walked to the stone. Pressed his palm against it. Flat, firm. Just once. Then stepped back. Nothing said. Nothing explained.

Eysteinn went next. Then Sveigr. Not because it was asked. Not because it was their turn. But because death had passed too near them this season, and the water now seemed a place where something might be given back. The young men shouted half-laughs as they braced the cold, teeth clenched against the tide, half-proud, half-daring. One slipped and cursed, another bellowed like it was war. It wasn't mockery. It was relief — carried loud, raw, and shivering in the blood.

And when each rose — gasping, blinking salt from their eyes — they turned. As Skagi had. Not to the priest. To the stone. Not commanded. Not named. But necessary.

The stone took each touch in silence.

Father Arnlaugr did not stop them. But he did not look, either. His eyes stayed on the sea, where ash met foam. He held the taper aloft a moment too long, as if the mark might hold if he did not look away.

Tyrkir stood like driftwood, unmoving. He did not join them. He did not speak. He watched the sea as if he had seen such rites before — under other names, in other tongues — and each time, it had ended the same: with men colder than they expected, and something left behind in the salt. When Skagi touched the stone, Tyrkir's eyes closed — once, slow. Not in blessing. In recognition. The wind caught in his beard. As if the old names had risen, briefly, through a boy's hand.

Finnvið muttered to those around, sharp-nosed and half-grinning. "Holy water, brine, and no fish to show for it," he said under his breath, just loud enough for the younger men to hear. But his voice carried something else beneath the jest — something like hope, scraped thin and wry, but still there.

Vidarbjǫrn watched the water. Not the men. Not the priest. The way the tide moved. The way it took and gave. The way it did not pause. To him, it looked like the mouth of something older than Christ. Older than name.

The stone held the heat of each palm long after the men had turned away.

That evening, the warmth did not retreat. It clung to the doorposts and the rafters, worked into the seams of the longhouse like smoke that no longer sought escape.

Tyrkir made a feast — not by declaration, but by gesture. He soaked smoked trout in pine water until the skin broke with a crack like old fire, then mashed the flesh with spruce resin and salt-fat until it glistened. Seal blubber melted slow beside it, slick and briny, thickened with black weed dragged from the lowest tide. He crisped slivers of dried venison on a flat stone—meat curled dark at the corners, snapping between teeth with the sting of char and ash-salt.

He stirred cracked barley into marrow broth until it thickened, bittered with spruce ash. Turnips—stored deep in pit-earth—he mashed soft with dried angelica, sweet at first, then sharp. Spruce sap and honey followed, rolled between thumb and tongue, sharp first, then sugar-deep. Thin cakes of pine bark flour, bound with marrow, baked brief against stone—bitter, oiled, earthy. He laid out crowberries last—black-skinned, sour, the ghost of sun still clinging.

When all was done, he poured mead—thin and bright, warmth sharp as firewood turned liquid. Gave the first bowl to Ranhildr, the second to Kristján. No one waited for a blessing. But they sat close. Ate with both hands. Smacked lips. Licked grease from the rim of their bowls.

The snow had receded from the southern wall, and the thawed earth beneath showed its true colour—dark, wet, veined with root and charcoal, the ground where ash had been buried and not disturbed.

The doorway stood open. Not wide. Just enough to let the wind turn through without offence. The air it carried was sea-heavy, kelped and wet-edged. No one rose to bar it. Inside, the hearth held steady flame. Not strong, not large— but full, the coals rimmed in red, a low light that reached the bones without biting. The smoke lifted clean, curling through the opened vent without struggle, and no one cursed the wood. Someone had laid green alder to test it. It hissed, but did not fail.

Kristján brought the last barrel of mead. The stave bore old sail markings—reused from the coastal holdfast. The pitch-seal had to be reheated with coal before it poured. He did not speak over it. He simply rolled it in from the storage shed, scraped the frost from the lid with the back of his knife, and set it by the hearth as though it had always belonged there. The stave was split near the rim. The pitch-seal softened by age and ash from the last fire it had stood beside. The smell was sharp with ferment and smoke. But it poured clear. That was enough.

Ottar spoke first—nothing sacred, just a dry comment about fish returning to the traps.

Asleikr muttered about restacking the roof-beam come full thaw.

Hallbjǫrn only nodded. His face had colour again, and he no longer coughed into his sleeve. "About time the gods stopped wasting lungs," he muttered.

Eysteinn drank slow from a shared cup, his hand still raw from the sea's chill, wrapped now in fur and oilcloth. He winced when the warmth touched it, but he drank all the same.

At first they poured carefully—measured, deliberate, honouring the last of it. But once the rim turned warm and the staves no longer creaked in protest, the caution loosened. Cups passed from hand to hand. The rhythm broke. Someone spilled a ladle. Someone else refilled before it could be wiped. No one stopped them. The heat in the room rose—not sharply, not suddenly, but with a weight that settled into wool and sinew alike. The smoke stuck to cloaks and hair. The ash-smell softened to something older: hearth-warmth, horn-sweetness, the scent of wet bark and burned pine. Feet stretched toward the fire. Laughter came — not raucous, but real. Someone hummed an old tune and did not stop when the note faltered. Someone else clapped in time. It was not joy. Not yet. But it was the memory of it.

Leif drank the way a man drinks after weather has turned — carefully at first, then with the looseness of someone whose ribs no longer ache with every breath. His cloak was open. His braid had frayed at the edge. He drank as if each swallow might find something in him that had frozen over and melt it. When the barrel scraped low, he rose. Too fast. His boot slipped on the packed dirt, and he staggered once, then caught himself.

Across the hall, Ranhildr stood by the doorway — shoulders braced, braid damp, boots streaked in thaw-mud. Her silhouette cut clean against the grey outside. She was alone.

Leif stepped toward her — cloak open, braid loosened, boots soft on packed earth. Not swaying. Not squared. Just moving — like a man approaching coals left untended — still warm. Still dangerous. The warmth came sharp now: smoke-woven wool, salt still on his sleeves, the faint animal musk of shared breath in the longhouse air. He reached — not tenderly, not with claim, but with fingers rough from rope and thaw, open to whatever they found.

Her wrist was cool — bone close, pulse faint beneath winter-skin. She didn't pull.

He did not pull. He did not speak. But his eyes held hers, unmoving, steady as frost that does not melt, only waits.

The air between them held.

For a long moment, they stood — her framed by the open door where the wind crept in, him backlit by the hearth's low coals. Their breath hung between them, pale and mingled, rising and falling in the stillness like something tethered. Then he turned.

His boots scuffed grit into the floor-ruts as he crossed the hall, the turf sucking faintly at each step. He passed the place where her cloak still hung — wool gone stiff at the shoulders, the hem stitched with a scrap of sinew, looped in haste. He had done it that first night, after they pulled her from the ice, while she slept and her breath rasped in the dark.

She had never fixed it. Never removed it.

Later, someone called for Tyrkir to sing.

At first, he shook his head, muttering in his own tongue, eyes half-lidded behind the cup. But when Skagi clapped a rhythm and Kristján added a beat on the barrel-hoop, the old man relented. He did not sing a hymn. He did not chant a saga. He sang something older — sharper at the edge, vowels pulled long and wrong, a seafarer's tune shaped by bad winds and worse port. It traced a sailor's calendar: months marked not by moons, but by winds and wrecks. A rhythm born to bailing.

It caught.

The younger men picked it up in fragments, then full. Feet struck the floor. Palms hit benches. Someone tried to harmonize and failed. That, too, became part of the song. The roof-beams caught the echo and gave it back bent.

For a little while, the wind outside was forgotten.

Then Ranhildr drank. Not greedily. Not to forget. She drank like someone who knew the measure of her hunger—and took it. When the song dipped and the air swayed with it, she crossed to the barrel herself. The men stepped back—not in fear, but in deference, like trees parting for wind. No cup. Just both hands around the ladle—coarse grained, heat-darkened— dipped deep and lifted high. She drank from the vessel she made with her grip, water-bearer and oath-breaker both.

She crossed to where Leif sat by the fire-pit, his shoulders curled forward, head bowed, eyes half-lost in smoke and mead and something slower still.

She sank down beside him. Leaned close. Said something low—too soft for any ear but his.

He looked up.

She smirked—not wide, not for show— just a curl at the mouth's edge, sharp as a blade pressed flat. Her hand came up. She tugged loose a single braid behind his ear, slow and sure, like pulling thread from a seam she'd never agreed to wear. Then she rose. Turned. Walked back through the heat and the eyes and the noise, as if none of it belonged to her.

The barrel scraped hollow. The fire burned lower. The corners of the hall receded into shadow.

Finnvið moved to the centre of the floor.

His legs were crossed, his back arched like a stretching cat, one arm sweeping wide as if drawing the shape of his tale in the air. His voice carried—high, sharp-edged, slurred only slightly by drink— but clear enough to cut through mead-hum and crackling flame.

"There was a man once," Finnvið said, raising his cup high enough for the firelight to catch the rim, "who grew tired of rowing. Said it broke the back and stole the years. Said he'd trade anything—*anything*—to be free of the pull of water in his shoulders.

"So he found a woman on the shore. Not young, not old. Hair like eelweed, eyes like tide-rot. She said she'd give him an oar that rowed itself—but he'd have to pay with his shadow."

A few chuckles stirred. Someone muttered "always the shadow." Finnvið grinned.

"He agreed. Fool said he never needed shade, only shelter.

"And it worked. The oar dipped and rose, dipped and rose, smooth as breath, like it knew the way.

But it only pulled *against* the wind. Always.

"So wherever he set his eyes, the prow spun. He'd chase one coast, end up turned toward another.

"He saw his home once—just once—far off across the water. His brother's roof. The slope with the white stones. But the harder he reached, the more the oar bucked like a mule.

"And so he rowed in place for years. Years! Bones gone crooked. Skin turned salt-cracked and thin. No shadow to mark the days.

"And in the end," Finnvið paused, lowering his voice, "they

say he cursed every shoreline that drifted past. Said he'd been shown the whole world—but not one place that would let him land."

He drained his cup.

"Which is fair," he added, "since no one trusts a man without a shadow."

Laughter followed—real, from the gut. Haukr slapped his knee. Even Kristján laughed, half against his will. Someone muttered for quiet, but too late: the tale had teeth.

Vidarbjǫrn sat near one of the outer beams, his arms resting on his knee, watching the fire burn low.

The warmth didn't reach him, but he didn't move. He wasn't trying to get comfortable. He wasn't interested in joining the others. He sat apart on purpose—away from the noise, away from the heat. The cold didn't seem to bother him. Maybe he preferred it. Some men leaned toward fire. He leaned toward silence.

After a while, he looked up.

Ranhildr was gone.

Leif was gone too.

He remembered the way Leif had looked at her—open, hungry, certain—and how she had responded—not soft, but willing, like someone choosing danger with both eyes open.

He didn't know where they'd gone. But he knew what might follow. Their fire had never been quiet. It sparked in front of others—bright, reckless, seen. But this time it had slipped the circle.

The mead had gone to his hands. Leif stared at them now, loose on his knees, as if they belonged to someone else. Rime traced the edge of his boots from where he'd stepped outside to piss. When he'd returned, the warmth had not taken him back fully.

He looked up when he felt her near.

She eased herself down at his side, close enough that their sleeves brushed. Then leaned in, her shoulder pressing into his, the breath between them warming the space no fire reached. Her mouth near his ear, she said,

"You could've made me your wife. But you waited. You made camp, dug pits, raised walls—like that mattered more."

He looked up. He did not speak. He did not reach.

She let her mouth tilt—not a smirk, not quite—but something smaller, something almost tender beneath the blade. Her hand came up. She loosened a single braid behind his ear, slow and sure, like unpicking a knot she hadn't meant to tie. Then she rose. Turned. Walked back through the fire-warm air, her shoulders square, as if reclaiming her shape before the rest could see her softened.

He stood a moment later. Not in pursuit. Not in retreat. Just following the line she'd drawn.

The air cut sharp outside, but neither shivered. Their heat carried.

Near the knarr, where the ice had drawn back from the hull, they stopped. Wind stirred the pitch-ropes. Wood groaned, low and half-asleep.

Leif turned to her, sudden. Pressed her back against the slope of the cradle, fingers hard at her hips. The scent of earth rose — wet pitch, alder rot, salt. He kissed her without pause. Not rough. Just urgent. Like something that had waited too long.

She gripped his cloak and held him there a moment — tight, anchoring — then shoved him back.

"Not like this," she said. "Not here."

"I know," he said. But he stepped forward anyway.

"You haven't asked."

"Not yet."

"You should have asked."

"I will."

He kissed her again. Firmer. Her jaw stayed tight. Her breath caught — then steadied.

His hand found the back of her neck, where the braid met skin and the heat pulsed close. She didn't lean in. But she didn't pull away.

She didn't kiss him. She bit his lower lip, then let it go.

The moon hung wide above the inlet, bright and unclouded. The snow caught its edge but didn't hold it.

There were only two places with walls: the church, or the ship. He didn't ask. She didn't stop him.

The knarr smelled of ash and old fish, the pitch-sheen dulled with cold. When they ducked beneath the tarp-flap, she laughed once—dry and low, not for joy but from disbelief. Breath condensed fast beneath the tarp. Each exhale fogged the planks.

His cloak fell from his shoulders. Her fingers moved to the sinew tie at her waist.

"I'll curse you for this," she whispered.

"I'll deserve it."

Then silence. Only the creak of the hull, the shift of breath. A tangle of wool. The salt. The cold.

His hands found her hips. She let him. His mouth traced the salt at her throat. She arched, breath sharp, legs parting under his weight.

She bit his lip again—harder this time.

He grunted, pushed back, intent steady now, the mead hot in his blood.

Then—

A sound.

Just beyond the hull. A step, or something like it. Wood shifting on frost.

Ranhildr froze.

Leif did not. He pressed closer.

She pushed—flat-palmed to his chest. Harder this time.

"No," she hissed.

He stilled.

"Someone's close."

His breath caught.

Not far off, a step broke crusted snow. Or the wind caught the hull. It didn't matter. She heard it. It was enough.

She shoved him again—harder—twisting out from under, breath ragged, not from fear, but from hunger. Her braid had come loose across her collarbone. She shoved it back, tied the cloak at her throat with fingers still shaking.

The interruption had been enough. Enough for her to resist him. And herself.

She shoved the braid from her shoulder and tied the cloak fast. Her voice was level. "Ask it proper. Or not at all."

Then she was gone. Ducked out from beneath the tarp before he could speak. He lay where she'd left him, shoulders heaving, hands cold now where they had been warm. Outside, the wind moved west again. The ribs of the ship groaned. And the cold returned—not cruel, not kind. Just waiting.

CHAPTER 16: THE GROUND THAT ACCEPTS

1001 A.D. – SUMARMÁL

The thaw came not as warmth, but as relent. The snow rotted from beneath, softening first where boots had trampled it thin — around the latrine trench, near the meat-pit, by the knarr's cradle where moss pushed up in green fistfuls. Crust turned to slush. Earth showed in patches: black, wet, stubborn.

The sea broke open days before the lake. Ice heaved once, then cracked into slabs that drifted out past the inlet mouth, dragging debris and old blood-smear with them. Gulls returned first, screaming and wheeling. Then geese, in ranks that bent the sky. On the fourth morning, it was Skagi who found the print — long, heavy, fresh in the melt near the stream-path. He did not call out. Just knelt beside it, one hand hovering, not touching. Others came when he didn't rise.

Men moved with more purpose now, if not more ease. The wind still cut sideways, but the worst of winter had passed. No deaths. No vanishings. Only silence, and the weight of work.

Asleikr Thorgilsson spent his days beneath the knarr, hammering at the warped crossbeams with a rawhide mallet, calling for Sveigr to bring pitch or brace. He'd driven fresh alder stakes along the shoreline and soaked new planking in the meltwater trench. The keel might hold, he said. If not, he'd shape a smaller hull before midsummer. "But it won't carry all of you," he warned.

Stígandr Hroaldsson had fired the smithy two days before. Thin smoke rose from the lean-to now in sharp ribbons, carrying the scent of scorched bone and oil. Haukr moved steadily at his side, bellows strapped across his chest, face grey with soot. One of Ottar's fish-hooks had snapped in the cold—Stígandr made three more before sundown, muttering over the iron like it had betrayed him.

Kristján kept the new tally by the doorframe. Oddi stood beside him, charcoal-stained and silent. The list grew: repaired traps, usable grain, recovered tools, new growth spotted. All with dates, weights, and runes to mark condition. There were lines scratched out, too—men who would not return to claim their share.

By the forge, Vidarbjǫrn re-set the boundary stone. Not for any reason he could name—only that it had tilted, and needed to be upright again. He drove it deeper into the thawed earth with the butt of his axe, then stepped back, eyeing its lean.

Farther off, near the bluff, Arnlaugr stood alone at the church's edge. He had dug a trench around its foundation and lined it with small stones. The altar had been re-wrapped in linen, and the cracked gospel pressed flat beneath two pine boards. He did not speak of the coming wedding, nor of the gods that moved beyond his reach. But he did not leave the rise.

There was no council. No speeches. But the work had resumed.

And that meant the land had not yet claimed them.

They walked the stony strand below the bluff, just east of the church. Leif and his priest. The tide dragged out, slow and grinding. Ice cracked softly at the inlet's mouth. Gulls hunched on the rocks, still and watching.

"I've chosen my course," Leif said.

Arnlaugr kept his gaze forward. "Are we speaking of Ranhildr?"

Leif gave a nod. "I mean to take her as my wife."

The priest slowed his steps, hands folded in his sleeves. "This winter has not gone lightly between you. Nor for those caught near it."

"You speak true." Leif stooped, lifted a branch of driftwood, snapped it across his knee, and cast both pieces into the tide. "I came thinking I could leave the old ways behind. That I could think as I pleased, take what I pleased."

The wind turned then, coming down from the upland.

"But she will not yield."

Arnlaugr gave a narrow smile. "She may hold more wisdom than you reckon."

Leif gave a short breath of laughter. "Likely so."

The priest waited.

"She asked me to name her in the sight of God." Leif watched the mouth of the bay. "She will not give herself unless she is given honour. Then she will stand by me."

"Are you ready," Arnlaugr asked, "to bind yourself before God, and for the whole of your days, to this woman?"

"I am ready. I was not before. Now I am."

"And what of her? Will she submit to God's will?"

"She bears Christ's mark," Leif said. "And she asked me to wed her."

"She bears it, yes," said Arnlaugr. "But I think she bears it for your sake—for a hold upon you. Not for His."

Leif did not turn. "Can it not serve both?"

Arnlaugr was silent a while.

"Marriage is not flesh alone," he said at last. "It is a covenant. A yoke. Sworn aloud, with witnesses. Sworn before God. You must name her, and she must answer. There will be holy word. There will be vow. And there must be no falsehood."

Leif nodded. "You will stand before the cross?"

"We will."

Then Arnlaugr smiled—though the doubt had not left his eyes.

Leif found Vidarbjǫrn crouched by the meat trench, shoulders set, arms bare to the cold. The snow had hardened to a pale crust around him, but he didn't seem to feel it. A line of spruce boughs marked the edge of the buried pit. One corner had begun to sink.

He stood a moment in silence before speaking.

"I've just come from Arnlaugr."

Vidarbjǫrn did not look up. He shifted his weight, reached beneath the crust with a bone hook, and tested the buried lashings. "And?"

"I've told him I mean to take her as my wife."

A pause. The wind passed softly through the storage timbers.

"I've set it right," Leif said. "As it ought to be. No shadow-play. No claim without vow."

Vidarbjǫrn rose slowly. He brushed ice from his sleeve with the back of his wrist. His face was closed.

"I came before," Leif said. "But not in truth. I thought I could take what I pleased — as though the land, the people, even she, owed me for the blood I carry. But I see more clearly now. I see her."

Vidarbjǫrn crossed his arms. "And now you come seeking my word."

"I do."

They stood facing one another. No raised voices. No echo. Only the dry rattle of spruce and the slow drip of thaw from the eaves.

"She's your blood," Leif said. "And more than that — she

hears you. She won't heed Arnlaugr alone. If this is to be done rightly, it must carry your word."

A long silence followed.

Then: "What vow would you give?"

Leif's voice lowered. "To keep her. Not to break her. Not to make her mine by force or right. But to walk beside her — before men, before God, and before whatever else keeps watch in this land. If she'll have me, I'll hold fast."

Vidarbjǫrn didn't answer at once. He looked toward the longhouse.

Ranhildr stood in the turf-wall shadow, bone needle lifted, thread caught in her teeth. Her braid was loose, half-swept by the wind, but she didn't fix it. She had frozen mid-threading — still now, and watchful.

He stepped forward.

"I've known you since we were boys," he said. "We crossed to Norway together. I've not seen you fall as you've fallen for her."

He set a hand on Leif's shoulder — brief, firm. "I have worry in me. The two of you strike sparks. But if your word is clean, and this truly what you want — then I will not bar the way."

He gave a single nod, then turned toward the lean-to.

Leif did not move.

Across the yard, Ranhildr had shifted. Her gaze held first to her brother, then to Leif. A breath left her, small and visible in the cold.

He had asked. Her brother had not refused.

She did not smile. But she lowered the bone needle and thread to her side. Then she tucked it away.

Above the clearing, gulls wheeled once, then vanished inland.

Leif crossed the yard toward her.

Vidarbjǫrn stood by the lean-to, turned halfway, watching.

Ranhildr did not move. Her hands hung loose now. Her breath clouded the air, rising slow from parted lips.

One step, then another—he came to stand before her, the turf wall at her back, the storehouse behind him.

She had seen the touch. The nod. And the silence that held after.

He reached toward her, slow, as though she might vanish if he moved too fast. His hand found hers—raw-knuckled, half-curled, scarred from winter work. She didn't pull back. He looked at her. Not hungry, not proud—just open.

Her fingers tightened once, then stayed. She met his gaze without flinching. Her mouth pressed shut, but there was no hardness in it now. The wind caught a lock of her hair and pushed it across her cheek. She didn't reach for it. She let it stay.

Behind them, Vidarbjǫrn did not speak. But he watched—

one arm braced on the beam, his posture still.

No words passed between them. They had been spoken elsewhere — before the priest, before her brother. Now there was only this: her hand in his, and her breath, steady.

That night, she sat beside him — *not* apart, *not* in the space where unmarried women kept to themselves, but at his side, as a wife might. No words were spoken about it. No need.

Leif sat cross-legged by the hearth, shoulders loose now, firelight glinting off his copper-streaked beard. One hand rested on his knee, the other tracing the haft of his axe.

Ranhildr took her place to his left — between him and the hall wall, shoulder not quite touching his, but close enough that the shared heat passed between them. A scrap of linen lay in her lap, half-mended — likely his. But the thread remained idle. Her gaze followed the fire, then him. Once, she reached to touch the collar of his tunic — fixing nothing. Just resting her hand there, briefly. Her fingers curled the cloth between two knuckles, then released it. Leif turned slightly toward her, and that was all. They did not speak. But they breathed together.

The warmth had begun to spread before the sun was gone.

Kristján was the first to pass near them. He knelt at the hearth to shift the logs, but glanced up as he did. When he saw her at Leif's side, his jaw eased. He set the new wood in carefully, not with the usual brisk command. Sparks curled upward. He straightened with a grunt, dusted ash from his hands, and said — not to them, but to the fire —

"That's more like it."

Then he moved on, shoulders no longer braced as if waiting for fracture.

Skagi entered not long after, thumping the snow off his boots. His cheeks were ruddy from cold, the scar at his collarbone pale beneath the edge of his tunic. His eyes swept the benches and stopped. He blinked, grinned, and let out a breath he hadn't known he was holding.

"Looks like the roof's safe again." His voice was light, but it landed deep. He plopped down across from them with a length of dried fish, knocking his knee against the table leg like a boy settling in after a storm. The fire cracked, and someone laughed. Just once. But it stayed.

Finnvið had been working a strip of antler at the back of the hall. He didn't come forward—but he turned his head, blade paused in his hand. He saw them. Saw how they sat. He smirked.

"Gods. Took you long enough." Then, softer—almost to himself: "If I'd known silence was all it took, I'd've gagged the both of you a month ago." He went back to scraping, but there was no bite in it. Only approval, tucked beneath the mockery.

Tyrkir came in last, brushing sleet from his hood, cheeks red from wind. He stopped just inside the door, blinking at the scene before him.

"Ah," he said, smiling. "The land knows its own." He moved forward, slow and easy, eyes on Ranhildr first, then Leif. "It always goes better when two roots grow toward the same sun." He patted Leif's shoulder, once. "Now. Let the house breathe."

And it did.

Laughter stirred—not loud, but clean. The fire burned steady. No bracing, no strain. Even the dogs lay still.

For the first time, the longhouse held peace. Not emptiness. Not caution. But peace—with weight, with centre.

At its heart: her hand on his, his shoulders at rest.

Together.

They rose before first light, without signal.

The coals in the hearth still glowed beneath the ash when Ranhildr bent to stir them. She moved quietly—no hurry, but with purpose. She wore her hunting tunic, stitched in dark wool, the sleeves close to the arm, hem split for movement. Her belt carried only a skinning blade and a pouch of dried birch scrap for tinder. She laced her boots tight, wound a strip of hide around her calves, and pulled a fur cloak over her shoulders, not fastening it.

Leif met her at the threshold. He was already dressed— tunic and trousers plain, patched at the thigh, his spear strapped across his back with the point wrapped in cloth. A small axe hung at his side, haft worn smooth. He did not smile, but there was light in his eyes.

They stepped out into the dark together.

The frost had settled heavy overnight. Every branch hung

white with hoar. The sky above them was slate blue, the stars dulling at the edges. Overhead, ravens moved between trees — quiet, restless.

One passed directly above, circling twice. Its call cracked the morning stillness. A warning. But neither of them looked up.

They passed beyond the longhouse and headed for the treeline without waking the others.

The forest received them like a mouth. Cold and still. Their boots made no sound on the crusted snow.

Ranhildr moved ahead, bow in hand, her braid tucked beneath her hood. Her stride was long, sure, and lean with tension — like a wolf pacing its claim. The curve of her cheek was hard in profile, but her mouth was full, her eyes dark and clear under the fur rim. Her jaw was set, not tight, but held. The scar near her wrist caught a glint of morning light. Leif watched the way her shoulders shifted as she scanned the ground — deliberate, alert, entirely in command. She crouched to read a trail — fresh, perhaps a doe with yearlings still clinging late to the herd. She pointed, but did not speak.

He nodded, and they moved.

Their movements were trained, disciplined. But they were not clean.

He watched her too long when he should have watched the trail. She turned once to glance at him, and her lip twitched in the faintest curve — barely there, gone as quick as breath.

They flushed a pair of hares and missed both. Not because they weren't quick — but because they weren't paying attention.

Leif cursed under his breath. Ranhildr crouched, pressed two fingers to the snow, then looked up at him with a shrug. The hunt was failing.

Still, they went deeper.

The sun broke low over the eastern ridge by midmorning, casting long blue shadows through the spruce. Ice crackled in the upper branches. Once, she stepped through a patch of thin crust and her foot sank to the knee. He reached for her arm—not urgently, but with care—and steadied her. His grip was firm, fingers calloused and sure. She saw him fully then: the line of his jaw rough with frost-dark stubble, the cut of his brow shadowed by the hood, his neck thick where the tunic pressed. His presence was all weight and steadiness, the kind that held storms back by standing still. There was strength in him, yes, but also a kind of restraint that made it more dangerous. A man shaped to lead, not just by right—but by force of being.

She didn't pull away.

Near midday, they came upon the buck.

It stood broadside beneath a stand of birch, pale trunks leaning slightly where wind had pressed them all winter. Antlers hung with the tatters of shed velvet, dark and curling like old cloth. Steam rose in curls from its hide, thick where its breath met the cold air.

The ground beneath it was uneven—moss and hummock, with snow sunk in pockets and patches of thawed earth showing the red-brown of last autumn's leaf fall.

It turned its head slowly, not yet alarmed. Flanks shifted. One hoof pawed lightly at the softening crust.

Ranhildr raised her bow first. Her footing adjusted automatically to a patch of frozen duff. Leif shifted his grip on the spear, palm down the shaft, stance braced on a rise of root underfoot.

The moment held—silent, cold, still. Only the birches stirred, their upper limbs clicking softly against each other.

They loosed at the same time. The first arrow struck high in the shoulder; the shaft quivered, embedded to the fletching. The second—a spear with a fire-hardened tip—caught lower, just behind the ribs. The buck reared, hind legs kicking, then staggered and crashed into the underbrush.

They ran forward, breath tearing from their chests. Snow churned under their boots, spattering their leggings with slush and old leaf mold.

When they reached the body, it was still twitching. Its legs beat the air once, then stilled. Blood pooled quickly beneath the flank, dark against the pale melt crust.

Leif drew his knife and knelt. Ranhildr placed her hand at the base of the antler, grounding the head.

He opened the throat with one clean motion. The blood steamed into the snow.

They knelt there together, hands red, breath misting, eyes wide. Their chests rose and fell in rhythm. The scent of iron and moss filled the clearing.

Then came the silence. Not between them—around them.

The forest hushed. Even the birds held back.

Ranhildr looked at him. Her brow was still, eyes narrowed—not in challenge, but in focus. Wind lifted a strand of hair across her cheek. Her skin was pale from the cold, but flushed at the neck, where the wool of her tunic left a faint red line.

Leif reached for her. His hand came forward, palm up, unhurried. His eyes did not leave hers—gray, steady, rimmed with red from wind and long wakefulness.

The snow thinned under spruce canopy, rotted to a soft crust where the sun reached down. The light was low, amber through branches, showing the fine damp of melt along the moss.

She turned to face him, shoulders square. Her bow lay nearby, its string loose, forgotten.

He leaned close. He smelled of woodsmoke and pine pitch, with a faint trace of sweat under wool. His hand touched the edge of her cloak—coarse wool, woven thick, wet at the hem where it had dragged through snow. He didn't lift it.

She reached up and turned the brooch at her shoulder. Bronze, scratched and dulled, its pin stiff from cold. The cloak sagged and fell to her elbows. Then she reached for the clasp at his collar. A toggle of antler, worn smooth, bound through a loop of leather. Her knuckles brushed his throat—rough, warm, scarred.

No words passed between them. Her fingers moved with precision, practiced in winter. His breath caught. His lips parted.

Her fingertips lingered on his chest, where hair lay flattened under linen. His ribs moved beneath her hand, shallow and slow.

Between them, warmth gathered—body heat held in wool and skin, rising faintly with the mist of their breath.

She unhooked the clasp. The collar sagged open. Her hand slid upward—across linen, over his collarbone, to the side of his neck where his pulse beat hard.

Leif's hand came to her waist. Not firm, not tentative. He found the belt and followed it around with his thumb, feeling the seam of the fabric, the shift of muscle underneath.

She moved closer. Their foreheads nearly touched. Her breath stirred the hair at his temple. She smelled of wool, skin, salt, and the faint iron tang of the hunt.

His hand moved up her back, along her spine, to the base of her neck. He felt the bones there, sharp beneath linen, the heat rising from her skin.

Her hand flattened over his ribs. He was leaner than she had guessed. She felt the breath moving through his whole frame.

Their hands wandered now—sleeves, seams, shoulders, elbows, hips. They did not undress. They learned. When he pressed his palm flat to her belly, through tunic and shift, her breath caught—not from cold, but from nearness.

She leaned back slowly until her shoulders touched the tree. The bark was rough through the wool. Her eyes stayed on his—steady, waiting.

That was enough.

Leif stepped in. Their bodies met, thigh to thigh. He pushed the cloak from her arms—heavy, damp. It fell without resistance.

His hands went to her belt. Leather, looped and knotted, stiff from cold. He worked the knot loose roughly. It snapped. The belt slipped.

He did not wait. He bunched her tunic from the hem, pulling wool and linen up with both hands until his fingers reached bare skin—cool, then warm.

She arched slightly as the fabric rose. He pulled it over her head in one motion. The shift clung to her arms with sweat and heat. He pulled it down. Her breasts flushed from the cold, her skin mottled where the air touched it. He warmed each place his hands found.

He touched her throat, ribs, the inside of her arm. His mouth found her shoulder. She did not pull away.

Their breath grew ragged. Neither spoke.

She watched him. Her arms hung loose at her sides. She did not flinch.

Leif stepped back half a pace. He unfastened the brooch at his shoulder. His cloak fell with a dull thump. He stripped off his tunic, then his belt, then the sweat-stuck undertunic. Gooseflesh rose across his skin.

She saw his scars—small, old, smooth.

He untied the drawstring of his trousers. They slipped,

caught at the knees, then fell. He stepped free. Bare.

Her eyes held his. No sound between them but breath.

He stepped forward.

She reached back and dragged his cloak beneath them. The wool hissed over the moss.

Then she laid herself down, settling into it. The moss gave beneath her. It smelled of needles, loam, thawed earth. The forest was silent. No birds. No wind. Only the creak of bark. She bent one knee. Her hand guided him—sure, not gentle.

The cloak shifted beneath them. His weight pressed her into the moss.

She closed her eyes. The cold was gone. Only his heat, the press of wool, the ground giving way beneath.

They sank into the hollow where the moss lay thick and undisturbed.

When they came together, it was not quick, and not delicate. He held himself above her, one hand pulling her neck to his lips, as he moved inside her. She tasted of earth, sweat, desire.

Her hands reached for him. Her nails bit into his skin as she pulled him down.

The force of his need overwhelmed him. At first, he moved slowly. Then faster. Faster. Like a stag crashing through underbrush, wild to reach her.

She gasped—not from pain, not from shame, but from the

certainty: this was real. This was hers.

The moss shifted under them. The wool bunched. The soil was wet beneath. His hips drove low, hard, unrelenting. Her legs wrapped around him.

Their breath filled the space. His cheek scraped hers. Her mouth found his ear. His hand dug into moss, fingers full of earth. They moved without rhythm now — only drive, only heat. The world fell away.

Then he buried himself fully and stilled.

The wind shifted. A twig snapped upslope. A fox barked once and fled.

The moss held them. Above, the trees swayed, slow and tall. Far off, hunters called, their voices distant, softened.

He moved again — slow, certain. As though the act itself carried vow.

She pulled him down fully, arms tight around him, cheek to his temple. Their breath rose like offering smoke.

For a while they stayed joined. No hurry. No fear. Then he lay beside her. She turned to him and rested he head on his chest. One hand at his thigh. His fingers combed through her hair.

She looked up through the branches. The trees above her were older than names — crooked, tall, and watching. One creaked — a low, distant groan.

A smear of blood marked his knuckle — bark, or thorn, or her.

She touched it. Said nothing.

When they rose, she fastened his cloak first, then her own. He watched, silent.

They stepped back into the clearing where the buck lay cooling. Leif crouched and took hold of the antlers. The carcass was heavy, but he lifted it to his shoulders without a sound. Blood had dried along the flank; the body swung limp with weight and truth.

Ranhildr checked the bindings at its legs, then steadied the burden as he adjusted the sling of its weight.

As they climbed back to the trail, mist curled from the ground. A raven passed above, silent.

The woods had taken them. The kill was theirs. And the ground no longer held them as strangers.

As they walked back to the settlement together, the hollow stayed quiet. The moss still held the imprint of their bodies.

CHAPTER 17: WHAT WATCHES, WAITS

1001 A.D. – HARPA

They dug where the frost had loosened. It was Harpa still—though late, close to the edge of summer. The ground no longer cracked, only gave.

The old meat pit stank—salt-packs ruptured, sinew curling loose, the bone of some half-cured deer split and yellowing. Tyrkir had cursed low. His beard was still wet from the cellar's chill, his breath hanging in the air as he leaned over the mess. He pointed with two fingers, muttered something sharp in Saxon—frustrated, not panicked—and then turned toward Kristján, flicking a hand toward the treeline. It was direction, not dismissal. A better site lay beyond the rot. Kristján stepped forward, nodded once, and pointed out the rise near the alder line. Drier ground. Easier to seal.

Kristján had been about to assign the digging to Thorleifr and Hrólfr—strong backs, used to hard work. But Vidarbjǫrn had stepped forward.

"I'll take Skagi," he said. Not loud, but final.

Kristján paused, read something in his face, and nodded.

At the treeline, Vidarbjǫrn paused. Pressed the spade into the earth—not testing it, just leaning, like the weight might tell him something. Then moved again.

Skagi didn't speak. He carried the iron spade and a coil of rope.

No longer a green beardless boy, Skagi had come through the worst of the winter — frost-hunger, fireless nights, the weight of proving himself. But worst of all had been the loss of Ketill. The old man had been a solid foundation, rough but steady. And then gone.

Vidarbjǫrn had watched him drift since — listless, slower to speak, colder with the others. Not brooding. Just quiet, as if something inside had gone still. Vidarbjǫrn knew that look. It belonged to men already halfway toward the edge.

He was the one who struck Ketill down. Not the draugr. Not the sickness.

Skagi needed to speak the words. And work might help loosen his tongue.

The soil broke easier here. Sod split with clean sound. Underneath: dark, wet, rich with melt. They worked a while without words.

Then Skagi said, "He taught me to dig shallow at first. Let the roots show. Then go deep."

Vidarbjǫrn nodded once. Didn't look up.

Another spadeful. Another breath.

"He said the ground tells you things. If it resists too easy, you're in a flood bed. If it clings, it'll keep the cold longer. If it sags — " Skagi stopped. "He knew things."

"Aye."

Skagi brushed ash from his palm. "You didn't have to do it like that. Not in front of us."

Vidarbjǫrn paused. Straightened.

The wind had shifted. Alder clicked behind them.

Skagi's eyes didn't flinch. "He was sick." The word cracked. "He was lost. You could've bound him."

"He wasn't Ketill."

"You don't know that."

Silence. Then: "I do."

Skagi's hands curled on the spade shaft. The ground between them looked black.

"He held my shoulder that morning," Skagi said. "Told me I was growing into the kind of man he'd follow — mumbling a little, maybe called me by the wrong name. He was confused sometimes. But he was smiling all the same. I know he meant it."

Vidarbjǫrn didn't interrupt. Just stood, jaw tight.

"Then that night, you cut him like he was nothing."

"No," Vidarbjǫrn said, voice low. "I cut him because he mattered. If I'd waited, there'd have been nothing left to save. It already had hold of him. I killed what was trying to wear him — to keep his name clean. That wasn't Ketill anymore, not all the way. And I wasn't about to let the rest of him be dragged out screaming."

The silence after that held.

Then Skagi turned and drove the spade down hard. Broke a

layer of stone. It rang again. Skagi cursed and bent, fingers scraping at the edge. Not stone. Blackened firestone — stone hardened and darkened from many fires, used to ring a hearth or mark a site. Char-streaked, ash-caked, packed in a circle. This was where they had sat. Where Ketill had laughed. The winter snow had drifted deep, then melted, folding the ash under a season's weight.

It was not the land hiding him. It was the land remembering.

He sat back on his heels. Breathing harder now.

"This was his ring," he said. "The one we lit. The night before the storm."

Vidarbjǫrn didn't answer.

"I remember the way he laughed," Skagi said, brushing soot from his palm. "Said it would be his last drink before summer. I didn't think he meant it."

His voice caught — fond, but distant. The laugh he remembered hadn't been sharp or full. It had been cracked, half-toothless, broken by coughing. Ketill had been half-lost even then, forgetting names, muttering to himself, eyes sometimes tracking ghosts. But he'd raised the cup. He'd looked at Skagi like he meant it. And that was the part Skagi kept.

A gust took the edge of his cloak. He didn't pull it in.

Vidarbjǫrn knelt, slow. Ran his hand through the disturbed ash. Some still dry. Some wet. The bone of an old fishhook, half-buried. A cracked shell.

"He knew, then," he said.

Skagi looked over. "Did you?"

"No." He paused. "But I watched him unravel all winter. His eyes stopped settling. He talked to things that weren't there. The day before the storm, he stood at the edge of the knarr cradle for hours, just watching the ice. No one saw him go that night. But I think he'd already left."

The wind moved behind them again—not strong, but insistent. Alder shivered, and somewhere a gull cried once, then stopped.

Vidarbjǫrn knelt, slow. Ran his hand through the disturbed ash like he was reading something not written. Then pressed his thumb against the hook. Blood welled, small but sharp. He turned it once, then set it point-first into the ash ring. His other hand pressed flat to the soil. Not in prayer—just to feel if it still held memory.

"This is what was owed," he said. Not loud. Not soft. Just meant. "One life, given clean. Not stolen. Not twisted. Given." His gaze stayed on the alder. "We do not bind the dead. We do not raise them. We bury them whole, and speak their name without shame."

The wind stirred. The ash curled faintly around the hook.

Skagi shifted. Not in speech, but in stance. He reached into the ash, took one of the smaller firestones, and placed it back at the circle's edge—not perfectly, not where it had been, but with care. He pressed it into the thawed earth. Then he stood.

Vidarbjǫrn watched, but did not speak. The act said enough.

They said nothing more. Just dug. Slow. Deep. Until the fire-ring disappeared again.

The knarr lay half-shadowed beneath a lean sky, her rib-lines softened by moss and time. Asleikr stood beside her keel-cradle, thumb pressed to the grain of her hull. "Time," he said. "She needs her spine."

They brought the timber down at first light. Sveigr and Skagi led the pull, the birch beam lashed with seal-hide and dragging a wake through dew-dark grass. Grani and Hallgeirr hauled the tail. It had seasoned true: bark long peeled, ends tar-capped, the grain tight as woven gut.

Asleikr met them at the slope. He ran one hand down the heart-line, nodded once, and reached for his axe. "Split her."

Víg-Bjǫrn and Hrafn drove the wedges. One at each end, clean and steady. Haukr kept the tools sharp, a pail of water and grindstone at his side. The birch cracked like bone under pressure, then gave with a groan. Asleikr crouched to inspect the split. "No twist. Good."

They laid the halves side by side. Asleikr traced the scarf-line with a red chalk knot, marking the angle. "This joins here. Not again wrong."

Eindriði and Haraldr set the rollers while Hallgeirr and Skagi pried the hull from its cradle. The moss wrap peeled back in damp shreds. The winter patch came last — Víg-Bjǫrn scoring it loose with a chisel while Kristján made a mark on his tally-board.

The belly of the knarr exposed, Asleikr and Sveigr fit the new keel to the old join. The scarf held snug. Víg-Bjǫrn drilled through the join, then hammered in treenails soaked in pitch. The heads were pegged flat with bone mallets.

Pitch simmered over Tyrkir's fire. Hallbjǫrn stirred the moss, checking texture by pinch. Skagi drove the soaked mass into the seams, careful not to overswell.

Kristján watched with arms crossed. "That line splits, you die halfway to Helluland."

Oddi stood nearby, charcoal pressed tight to the tally board. His marks were steady—neater than Kristján's had been, once.
Kristján didn't correct him. Just nodded, almost to himself.

"Mark it. Spine's set."

Asleikr didn't look up. "Then it won't."

By dusk, the new keel was set. The hull stood level on fresh-packed rollers. The join ran true. The bone pegs held. Above, gulls circled but did not land. Asleikr stood back, arms streaked with pitch, his breath a slow fog.

"She's got her spine."

Kristján made a mark on the tally-board.

"Next comes skin."

They would not sail tomorrow. Nor next week. But the first answer had come. The hull no longer sagged. The first claim had been made.

Tyrkir did not work on the knarr.

While the others hauled timber and stirred pitch, he was behind the longhouse—on his knees, hands sunk in black soil.

He had cleared the plot weeks before: a wind-sheltered patch above the stream cut, where alder grew low and the frost came late. Each day he walked it, barefoot, marking where the sun rose warmest and where moss ran thickest. He turned the ground with a broken haft, scattered shell for drainage, and lined the rows with spruce tips to hold the wet. His thumb split at the cuticle from cold. The blood smeared the shaft, then dried. He didn't wipe it.

From a wax-sealed pouch he drew the seeds—caraway, angelica, bitter-leaf, and barley—brought from Greenland wrapped in wool. They smelled faintly of salt and old sweat. He pressed each into the earth with a thumb-callused finger, murmuring low in Saxland tongue.

Hallbjǫrn the Herbalist passed once and said nothing. But he watched. When he returned an hour later, he handed over two sprigs of crowberry, root-bound in clay. "They live through frost," he said.

Tyrkir nodded once, but did not rise.

Later, when Ranhildr came with a strip of dried seal and asked, "You're not sailing?" he only looked up and said, "Ships carry the bold," he said. "But the land needs someone slower."

She didn't argue.

By dusk, he had marked the row-ends with alder slats, each

cut with a rune—simple lines, not for warding but for memory. He laid his knife beside them and pressed his palms to the soil. It was cold still, but not dead.

Behind him, the longhouse stood. The beams were weathered, the turf dipped, the walls smoke-darkened—but it held. A hearth in the earth, and now a garden above it.

The land had resisted. But the rows held.

Now it would feed.

The wolf came at dusk.

Not slinking or howling—just there, still as stone atop a slight rise where the peatline broke into open gravel. The sun hung low over the waters of the strait, lighting the seagrass in brass-gold streaks. Salt wind pressed the moss flat. Gull cries came thin from the far shoals.

It stood alone. Young, but not lean like a pup—long in the leg, shoulders narrow, coat bristled from winter and shedding in uneven clumps. Its fur was a mottled grey-brown, dark along the back and light at the muzzle, ribs showing faint beneath the bulk. One ear notched near the tip. Its eyes were pale gold, almost green in the low light. Not soft. Not wild either. It watched like a thing learning.

It didn't flinch at the hammer strikes from the knarr's cradle. Didn't lower its head when Kristján shouted orders to the caulking crew. Just sat, still, the stiff grass around its haunches moving in the wind while it stayed planted— front paws even, tail tucked along one side.

Finnvið spotted it first while hauling a coil of gut-rope near the midden trench. He paused, fishbone in hand, then flicked it lazily across the peat toward the ridge.

The wolf didn't lunge. Just rose slow, walked in a circle, and took the offering from the grass with a small lift of its head. It chewed with care. Then it sat again.

The next night it came closer — edging along the seep where the peat-bog ran shallow, stopping by the old whale-rib marker near the piss trench. A place of habit and waste. It knew what scraps meant. And it was patient.

It sat tall, watching Finnið.

Skagi was the first to speak.

"That beast's watching you," he muttered, nodding toward the ridge where the wolf now stood half-shadowed.

Finnvið grinned, slow and crooked. "Someone ought to. Might be the only creature here who sees straight."

"You feeding it?"

Finnvið shrugged. "I've tossed bones."

Grani passed with a log across his shoulders and barked, "Name it and it'll follow forever."

Finnvið's grin widened. "Maybe I'll call him Fenrir."

That stopped movement. Even the gulls fell quiet.

Hrafn froze mid-stroke. Hallgeirr muttered something low in his throat. Ranhildr turned from the fire-line, eyes sharp.

"Your foolishness walks a dangerous line," she said.

"Why not? It watches. It waits. It knows us better than the priests do."

Hallbjǫrn didn't look up. "Speak that name, and something old listens," he said flatly. "Doors don't shut easy, once opened."

But Father Arnlaugr stood near the smoke-rack, arms folded into his sleeves. "A name is weight," he said. "But only to those who still bend their knees to it. Let him name the wolf. Fenrir's just a story. And this is our ground now."

Ranhildr turned away without another word.

Skagi shook his head. "Myths don't fade here," he said quietly. "They soak in."

That night, the midden was scattered—rinds, bones, the fatty core of a seal jaw cracked and licked clean. No one heard it come, but in the morning the prints were there: broad, soft-padded tracks sunk into the peat just beyond the piss trench, the shape of hunger with a mind behind it.

Kristján found the mess first and kicked Haukr awake. "Clean it," he said. "Before the flies nest."

By dusk the midden was reset, the trench raked, the scraps buried deep. But the next morning it was dug and scattered again.

Bones. Kelp. Even the sealed pot of boiled fat had been gnawed at the rim. Haukr came in red-faced, cursing. "It was back. Took the whole jaw this time. Dug out the bones like a man."

That's when the talk began.

"We need to end this," Grani said, hurling a split rib into the firepit. "Before it ends us."

"You going to track her through bog and rock at night?" Finnvið asked, arms crossed.

"If I have to."

"He's feeding off scraps, not hunting."

"For now," Hallgeirr muttered.

Ranhildr spoke then, quiet but clear. "You spill blood without need, you mark this ground with it. The old tales don't ask — they answer."

Skagi turned to her, eyes wide. "You think it's an omen?"

"I think it's watching. Waiting. And so are we."

Hallbjǫrn scraped a bowl clean with his thumb and said, "Wolves come for meat. Spirits come for names. You feed one, you get both." Then he went back to eating.

"Enough," Kristján said. "If it comes too close, we kill it. Not before."

Finnvið said nothing. But that night, he fetched a new strip of fish scrap and laid it by the edge of the trench. He stood a long while, glancing toward the ridge — but the wolf didn't come. Not that night. Something in him twitched like a misfired nerve.

The next dusk, the wolf returned. Again it sat upright,

watching Finnvið with almost human intelligence.

With a mischievous grin, Finnvið moved toward it, meat in hand. But as he closed, it moved off. He made kissing noises and waved the meat, but the beast wasn't enticed.

Several of the men laughed, but Finnvið only hammed it up — no apology.

When he finally gave up, tossed the meat, and stepped back, the wolf moved close, took the gift, and walked behind the peat bank. Still quiet. Still without fear.

Ranhildr didn't take her hand from her belt-knife. But she didn't draw.

"He's young," she muttered. "But not dumb. He won't strike unless he's starved."

"If he comes again," Finnvið said, "I'll toss him the head. Let him know we don't waste what we kill."

The wolf sat up again and looked at him — not long, but enough. Then it turned, tail low, and vanished between the saltgrass and rock flats, where the land ran wet before the sea-line.

Finnvið didn't move until the wind shifted. Then he turned back to the rope coils and said, just above the wind, "Let's see if he earns the name."

The next morning, near the alder rise where the ash-ring had been reburied, the earth was scuffed. A patch of soot exposed. One firestone turned. No prints. No sound. But something had come. Not digging. Just watching.

Skagi stood over the marks a long time, then turned and walked away.

The longhouse held warmth, but not comfort. Smoke hung low under the rafters, thick as wool. Thaw ran down the planks in slow weeping lines. Bowls passed hand to hand — boiled grain, seal fat, hard bread softened in broth. Knees touched. Shoulders hunched.

Leif sat near the fire-pit, Ranhildr at his side. Her hand rested lightly on his, but her gaze was elsewhere. She hadn't spoken since the meat was served.

Across the room, Finnvið raised a rib. "To the wolf," he called, "who eats better than Haukr."

Laughter stirred. Haukr growled, "If I ate like that, I'd blow out both ends."

"You already do," Finnvið shot back.

Grani thumped the bench. "A match of brains between beast and Haukr. My coin's on the beast."

Even Leif smiled.

Rúnar shifted. "Three weeks of clear sky," he said. "That won't hold. Wind's turning. If we don't leave by midsummer, we ride storm-wrath all the way to Helluland."

The air turned stiller than before.

Leif wiped his hand on his cloak and looked to Asleikr.

"How long to ready the knarr?"

Asleikr ran a thumb along the edge of his bowl. "If pitch holds and rain stays off—three weeks. Four, if we need to reseal."

"She'll carry thirty-three?"

"Not safely. Not with stores and timber."

A silence opened.

Hrafn set his bowl aside. "I'm not going."

Leif looked up.

"This land's got roots now," Hrafn said. "Hard ones. Deep."

Hallgeirr nodded. "I'll not risk another sea-crossing for a hall with no roof and hunger at the door."

Ranhildr's eyes shifted to Father Arnlaugr, who stood near the back wall, silent until now.

"There are souls buried here," he said. "That means soil to guard."

Leif blinked once. His spine didn't move, but his shoulders stiffened—as if a blow had landed lower than expected. His eyes found Arnlaugr's across the firelight, searching for some jest, some second phrase that didn't come. Then he nodded. Once. Slow. Measured. A movement that held in it the weight of more than agreement—acceptance, maybe. Or something like loss.

Víg-Bjǫrn stirred the dregs in his bowl. His voice was low

but certain. "You'll be sung for this, Leif. They'll carve your name above Erik's."

The others looked up. Not mocking. Not surprised. Just ready for it to be said.

Even Finnvið, who mocked everything, only gave a short nod. "Iceland was a feat. Greenland was a reach. But this?" He jerked his chin toward the low roof and the dark land beyond it. "This is legend."

"You'll outlive him in song," Skagi said. "And not because you're still breathing."

Leif didn't speak at first. He looked into the fire like a man checking his own shadow. The heat lit the line of his jaw, and for a moment he looked older — less son of Erik, more man made separate.

"I thought I'd never match him," he said finally. "When I left Brattahlíð, I told Vidarbjǫrn. That I'd always fall short." He turned then, not to Ranhildr, but to Vidarbjǫrn at the far side of the fire. "But here we are."

For a moment, Vidarbjǫrn didn't answer. Then, after a breath, he said, "You've found something. No one will argue that. But I still don't know if this land is gift or trap."

"You've seen what it asks," Ranhildr said quietly. Her voice didn't rise, but it cut clear. "It doesn't bless — it tests. It yields only to those who stay, who fight, who name it with weight and hold their claim."

Leif turned to her then — but the warmth was gone from his eyes. He was already holding the vision. Already shaping the tale that would return across the sea with him.

"You'll have your garden," he said. "Your rites, your ring of stone. But I'll have ships."

The silence after was longer than it should've been.

Leif sat straighter. "When I return," he said, "I'll bring more settlers. We'll lay beams. Raise stone. This land will answer our names."

He turned to Ranhildr. "You'll see it."

She stood without word. Walked past the hearth and out into the dark.

Vidarbjǫrn didn't follow. Nor did Leif.

He only looked after her a moment. Then down at his hands—still stained with pitch from the knarr.

CHAPTER 18: THE HULL BREATHES

1001 A.D. – SKERPLA

The sun struck sharp through broken cloud, carving light along the marshland's thawing edges. No frost lingered past dawn now. The alder had bloomed with midges, a slow cloud of wings rising where the earth wept underfoot. Spring's edge had softened the ground. Every step was a wager: rock to hold, or suckhole to swallow

The knarr stood firm on her rollers above the tide line, stern lifted slightly, bowline straight. For weeks she'd listed in the wind, her seams dry and tight as split bark. But now her timbers drank the air. She had begun to swell.

It was time.

They began at the seams.

Tyrkir boiled pitch down in two squat iron pots, built into an earth trench near the shoreline. He stirred slow with a pine bough, fat folded in from the winter slaughter—seal first, then bear grease to stretch it. The steam came thick, metallic-sweet. Midges drifted through it, landed, died.

Hallbjǫrn pinched the first batch between two fingers, then pressed it to his wrist like a healer with wound salve. He sniffed. "Still too thin." He jerked his chin at Tyrkir to stir again.

The others worked while the pitch thickened.

Skagi and Sveigr took the caulking: moss soaked from the

alder beds, beaten loose of insects, and softened over steam. They packed it seam by seam with bone wedges, hammering slow but firm. Each impact thudded—joint to joint, like bone meeting bone.. The ship groaned—responded.

The pitch hissed against wet seams. Its smell clung—sweet, tar-sharp, in the back of the throat. Asleikr followed behind them, thumb pressed hard into each bond, checking the seal by feel alone. He said nothing when it held. Only grunted when it didn't.

Near the beam-rig, Vigbjǫrn had stripped out two warped strakes—wood swollen uneven in the freeze-thaw. He knelt with his shoulder pressed to the hull, holding one replacement flush. Haukr crouched beside the forge, passing up the nails: soft-forged iron, their heads dipped in seawater and brushed with ash before being driven. Stígandr watched the hammer-falls. Not the hands. The angle of strike.

The hammer paused only once.

"You see that?" he said.

Vigbjǫrn leaned back. A splinter, hairline, had opened along the grain.

"I'll shave it." Haukr stepped forward with a drawknife, already in hand. No protest. No nod. The rhythm resumed.

Farther back on the ridge, where the wind was stronger and the smell of the shore gave way to woodrot, Hallgeirr unrolled the sail from its winter lashings. It spilled like muscle, taut and dark, patched with hide at the corner seams. With Ottar and Eirik, he bent the canvas to the yard, rethreading each rope through hemp loops and bark-twisted stays. His fingers moved stiffly — two had healed crooked from a frostbite break last year.

"No fray," he muttered, not to the men. "No gift to the wind."

They tested the knots, then tested again.

Lief came up the deck last, barefoot. The timbers were warm — alive under him. He walked the full length twice, arms loose, his weight shifting from heel to ball. Then he stopped near the tiller and stood silent.

"She lists even," he said. His voice was dry. "But she's thirsty."

Asleikr heard him. He didn't lift his head. "Then feed her."

They launched her on the evening tide.

The rollers were greased with seal-fat, the bow braced with alder trunks stripped of bark. Moss was packed tight at the stern to keep her upright as she slid.

Kristján read the timing by the shadow falling off the wooden cross they'd hammered into the bluff. "Now," he called.

Thirty hands heaved. Some grunted. Most didn't. The knarr shuddered once — then moved. Wet ground squelched beneath the rollers. The timbers creaked and pitched forward.

Then she slid.

The tide met her with a hiss. She rocked once, heavy, then righted. Ranhildr stepped forward, one hand on the rail, eyes narrow. No bubbles broke from her seams. The pitch held.

Asleikr waded thigh-deep, hand on the hull. "She floats."

Kristján scratched the tally board.

"Three days to load," he said. "Five to seal. Ten to settle the weather. We sail before the solstice."

No one answered. But they looked to the sky.

The cloudline was heavier now. Not yet a storm. But soon.

By the forge-lean-to, the wind had died just enough for the smoke to rise clean. The coalbed hadn't gone cold since early thaw. It wasn't hot enough for iron, but warm enough to draw hands near.

Stígandr knelt at the hearth, turning a bent rivet with his tongs. He rasped it smooth, slow and even — coaxing not metal, but rhythm. Not shaping. Tuning.

Haukr sat nearby, legs crossed, scraping pitch from the edge of a rewrapped caulking knife. His sleeves were soot-streaked to the elbows. One thumbnail had split at the quick. He rubbed it against the knife's spine without wincing.

The midden steamed behind them, low hill of rotted marrow and alder fluff.

Finnvið crouched upslope, half-shielded in the brush, one strip of dried seal meat in his outstretched hand. He didn't speak. Barely breathed.

A dozen paces off, shadowed beneath alder branches, the wolf stood still.

It didn't move. Didn't blink.

Just watched.

"Come on, Fenrir," Finnvið muttered, almost too quiet to carry. "You took the deer leg last week. Don't play the shy prince now."

The wolf yawned. Not quick—slow and vast, its back teeth flashed like wet stone. Then it turned its head slightly. Not away. Not toward.

A shift. Just enough to break the gaze.

Finnvið stood with a sigh. "Too smart for me," he said, louder now, brushing his tunic. "Too proud to admit it. Just like you, Stígandr."

Stígandr didn't turn.

"I don't yawn when threatened," he said.

"No," Finnvið agreed. "You just weigh the air down."

Haukr smirked. Didn't look up.

Finnvið leaned against the woodpile. It was damp where the moss had grown between the splits. He didn't care.

"So. You're staying?"

Stígandr didn't answer right away. He turned the rasp once more across the rivet, then held it up to the light, examining the edge. The rasp caught a flicker of sun and threw it sideways across the smoke.

"Seems so," he said.

"Thought you hated it here."

"I do."

"Then?"

Stígandr shrugged — one shoulder, barely a motion. "The forge draws. Wood's good. The land's stubborn. Suits me."

Finnvið clicked his tongue and turned to Haukr. "You always get the worst of it. First into the midden trench, last out. Don't you dream of a cleaner fate?"

Haukr straightened, brushing grit from his palms. "If he stays, I stay."

Finnvið rolled his eyes. "You could do less of it in Greenland."

Stígandr turned just enough to see Haukr full-on. "It's not like that," he said.

Haukr didn't flinch.

"You've got useful hands now," Stígandr went on. "Marketable. Could find a berth back home. But you won't."

Finnvið grinned. "Right. Expert midden-cleaner with marketable skills. I hear the kings of Norway are desperate for someone who can patch a piss-hole with flair."

Haukr wiped his hands on his tunic and stood. "I've seen home," he said flatly. "It's mostly rock and piss-wind. Greenland's colder and more crowded. Here, the forge is mine half the day."

A silence held there. Just long enough.

Then footsteps behind.

Ranhildr crossed behind them with a coil of sinew looped in one hand. Her other hand was red with old blood and fresh sap. She moved like she hadn't noticed the three men, or like they weren't worth stopping for. Her braid swung heavy behind her shoulder, wrapped tight in a strip of greased wool.

Haukr looked up.

Just for a moment.

His gaze caught the line of her throat, the hollow just above her collarbone. Something in him tightened—like breath taken too fast—and flushed. He scrubbed the back of his neck with his wrist. His hand came away smudged with pitch.

Stígandr looked too. Not openly. But he saw.

Then back to his rivet.

Even Finnvið, for all his noise, watched her go.

Then, smirking, "Gods save us. One woman walks by and every man in reach forgets his spine."

Haukr flushed deeper.

Stígandr rasped metal with a little too much pressure. The tool slipped. He regripped.

"We'll need women if it's to be a village," Finnvið said, more evenly.

Haukr glanced at him. "Leif says he'll bring three ships next time. With women. Maybe before winter."

Finnvið barked a laugh. "Three ships of brides and believers. And still no one to clean the forge trench."

He let that settle. Then added, glancing back toward where Ranhildr had vanished between turf walls:

"But not like that one."

His voice wasn't quiet. Just low. Not for secrecy. For irony.

"That one—any man she chooses, she leaves burning behind her. Just ask Leif. If he's still smouldering."

Stígandr didn't speak. Just set the rivet aside and picked up another.

Haukr went back to scraping the knife. The edge was dull. He worked it like a man who didn't want to hear anything else.

Finnvið pushed off from the pile and stretched, spine popping.

"Anyway. Fenrir's waiting."

He walked off—not fast, not straight. Like something not welcome, but not yet chased.

The wolf hadn't left.

It stood still beneath the alder fringe. Watching.

The air had shifted by dusk.

Smoke moved sideways again. The sky above the longhouse turned silver-blue, then bruised where the light bled west. Ground stayed soft underfoot—half-thawed muskeg, reeds at the ankles, gnats clinging to sweat.

Near the turf walls, Vigbjǫrn and Eindriði were hammering the last of the upright beams into place. The timber creaked against earth. The pegs held. The roof still leaked, but less.

Inside, Oddi scratched names into the tally ledger. No voice raised. Just stylus against vellum, sharp and final. Each name shut a door. Each line laid like stone on a burial path.

Outside the doorway, Leif stood with his arms folded and his face turned to the wind. He didn't read the sky. Just faced it—like a man waiting for the wind to choose for him.

Ranhildr passed by him with her bow slung across her back, hands red from sinew and binding grease. Her hair was tied back with a strip from her old hunting cloak—sweat-darkened near the scalp.

She didn't stop. Didn't look.

He didn't stop her.

Kristján stepped out next, the tally-board in one hand, charcoal mark still fresh.

He stopped near Leif. Nodded, respectful but dry.

"Four more declared today."

"Names?"

"Staying: Tyrkir. Vali. Stígandr. Ranhildr."

At that, Leif's jaw tensed.

Kristján waited. No protest. No request. Just wind and silence.

Near the fire-pit, Skagi crouched where Orm was skinning the last spring hares. The boy's hands were clean. He hadn't helped. But his eyes weren't on the meat. He was watching Ranhildr.

When she passed into shadow, Skagi stood. Didn't move. Just stood.

From the longhouse, Vidarbjǫrn stepped. The scent of pine smoke and old rot clung to his cloak. He didn't come fast, didn't come close — only far enough to stand, felt more than seen, between the dark and the dusk.

Leif spoke low. "She hasn't told me her mind."

Vidarbjǫrn's answer was slower. "You haven't asked."

Leif's throat moved, but no sound came. Then: "I thought

she might wait. To see."

"She has," said Vidarbjǫrn. Then, after a beat: "She's seen."

A cry broke the stillness—Finnvið and Grani at the racks, shouting something half-jest, half-wrestle. But even the laughter bent oddly tonight. Everything echoed too far. Too clearly.

Ranhildr came back across the compound, arms full of cut reed. Her boots were damp. Her stride didn't slow when she saw Leif. She dropped the bundle down beside the turf wall and straightened.

"You spoke of returning," she said. Her voice was steady. Even.

"I did."

"You haven't spoken to me."

"I thought—" Leif hesitated. "You wore the cross."

"I did," she said. "But I never named Vinland a wound."

Behind her, Skagi didn't move. Just watched her, like a child trying to see which way the fire leans.

Leif looked at her, properly. He had not until now.

"Would you stay without me?" he asked.

She didn't blink.

"Would you ask me to follow?"

His hand moved — toward hers. But it stopped at his belt. Not weakness. Not yet strength. Just unfinished.

"I would ask," he said, finally. "But not here. Not now."

She nodded. But her jaw set. Hard.

"I'll give you my answer," she said. "Soon. But not in your time."

Kristján, behind them, scratched another line into the ledger.

The dusk thickened. No stars yet. But the ground underfoot had stilled.

The air, though, carried the weight of futures being named — and of those who hadn't yet dared to ask.

Every seventh day, they climbed to the turf-roofed church on the bluff. It stood squat against the wind, its pine beams seasoned grey, its iron bell hung crooked but whole. The bluff itself was bare — no trees, only lichen-scabbed stone and grass that grew low and stubborn. From its edge, the sea could be seen in three directions. So could the sky. Up there, there was nothing to soften you — no trees, no shadow, no lie.

The bell rang once — sharp and flat as hammered iron. It echoed across the slope, over the timber walls and open hearths below. The men came as they would. About half.

Always Kristján. Always Oddi. Always Leif.

Kristján stood tall, hands folded. Beside him, Oddi mouthed the Latin—not fluent, but sure. They bowed together at the reading. Mouthed Amen in the final breath. No candles today—the wind curled through the narrow door too often. Smoke alone marked the altar.

When it ended, most left quick. Some with bowed heads. Some already talking trade, trench depth, or beam weight. Kristján stayed long enough to cross himself again. Then he too stepped out into the wind.

Leif remained.

Father Arnlaugr had begun folding the altar cloth—wool plain, red-dyed with ochre cross stitched centre. He moved with care, corners precise. When Leif did not move or speak, Arnlaugr looked up.

"Something weighs you."

Leif didn't answer.

There as no confessional. Father Arnlaugr merely gestured for Leif to kneel before the altar. "Come. Speak it plainly."

Leif hesitated. Then knelt before him and before God.

Arnlaugr murmured the invocation in low Latin, voice half-swallowed in the chill. He made the sign of the cross. Leif's hands stayed at his knees.

The priest waited.

"It's Ranhildr," Leif said.

A pause.

"You fear she'll stay," Arnlaugr replied.

Leif nodded.

"I must go back to Greenland. I have kin there. Duties. And…" He stopped.

The priest said nothing.

"She won't say it outright," Leif went on. "But I know. She looks at the woods like they're family. Like the land speaks to her."

Father Arnlaugr's jaw tightened slightly. Not frown. Pressure.

"You've not married her."

Leif's silence answered.

"Then it may be for the best," the priest said. "She is unruly. Pagan. Willful. You feel passion, yes. But that is not the same as faith. A Christian man must cleave to a Christian wife. One who fears God, not the wind."

Leif's gaze dropped.

"I know," he said.

Arnlaugr studied him. Then: "You've lain with her."

It was not a question.

Leif's mouth opened. Closed.

"Yes."

The wind pressed through the wall. The flame bent flat, then rose again.

Arnlaugr inhaled through his nose. "Then you are already bound in sin. Fornication poisons both bodies. Without sacrament, it condemns you both."

Leif nodded slowly. But there was no confession in it. Only confirmation.

The priest's voice did not soften. But it slowed.

"If you have taken her to your bed, you must take her to the altar. There is no halfway. You understand this."

Leif worked his jaw. He shifted, spine stiff from kneeling. His fingers tightened over his knees. The gesture was small. But he did not release it.

"I want to marry her," he said. "But —"

"But she does not obey," Arnlaugr finished.

Leif didn't correct him.

"She does not answer to you. She wears the cross, but not for God. She hunts, walks without guard, speaks when men do. That is not what the Lord intends."

Leif lifted his eyes. Just briefly. "She's strong."

"She is disordered," Arnlaugr snapped. "Strength without order is defiance. And defiance leads to damnation."

He stood, suddenly taller than the space could hold.

"Marriage purifies. It commands. And it protects. Once she is your wife, she is under your rule. That is the law — by man and by God."

Leif didn't move. His hand went to the small of his back, rubbed a place where old hurt still lingered. His mouth twitched. Not quite doubt. Not quite resolve.

Arnlaugr stepped closer. The taper's flame lit the bottom of his chin now, not his brow. "If she clings to the old ways, she will go to Hell. If you permit it, you walk beside her. And your children — should they come — will be born unclean."

That last word landed heavier than the others.

Leif looked up. "Will you marry us?"

Arnlaugr didn't hesitate. "Immediately."

Leif stood, slow. His joints cracked. The wind outside had shifted. He could hear it pushing around the turf walls.

"Name the day," Arnlaugr said. "And ensure she says yes. That is all the law requires. Her soul is the greater matter."

Leif nodded once.

But he did not leave right away.

He stood still as if waiting — for weather, or a voice, or some change in the earth underfoot. None came.

Outside, the sky had cleared. The light was bright, but not warm. A dry wind blew straight in from the sea, lifting sand from the bluff and sending it skittering along the path home.

CHAPTER 19: WHAT VOWS COULD NOT HOLD

1001 A.D. — HEYANNIR

Finnvið saw her by the ash-ring just after dusk, when the wind died and the air settled heavy with insects. Down in the hollow, where the ridges dipped and the ground held damp, the fog pressed low—thick and reeking of rot. The stone stood there, high grass grown up around its base, moss clinging dark to the cracks. Ferns crowded close on every side. The earth beneath looked bruised, wet with the day's heat, the soil open and breathing. Small gnats swarmed where water pooled shallow.

She knelt with no cloak.

Her hair had come loose—just enough to show it had been tied. Her shift stuck to her back and thighs, soaked through with sweat and damp from the ground. Barefoot, barehanded—her toes dug into the moss. Her hands were bare and bitten red from nettles or fly-strikes. Her belt was drawn tight, and the hem of her shift clung black with wet.

Finnvið stood behind a leaning pine, where the bark peeled in strips and sap hung thick as honey. He had come to check the fish-lines set past the marsh edge, but the path had drawn him here instead. The alder trail curved strangely this far in; the trees grew close, and their trunks leaned like watchers.

He meant to keep walking.

But then she knelt.

She wasn't alone, not truly. A rite makes witness, even without eyes. The air held still around her. No birds, no frogs. Just the throb of flies and the stink of heat-fat water. She bent forward and set something down—small, pale— into the hollow beside the stone. Birch bark, peeled and smoothed, marked with cuts he couldn't read from where he stood. It curled slightly in the humidity.

She smoothed it flat with her palm. Then she reached for a bone blade tucked into her belt. She pricked her palm— quick, clean—and let the blood fall into the hollow, where it met rainwater and mosquito spawn. The water took the red without resistance. A few drops spattered on the bark.

She placed her left hand to her belly.

Then she leaned forward and touched her brow to the stone. The breath she released was long. Her shoulders didn't shake. Her fingers did not tremble. It was not fear. Not shame.

It was offering.

A hot wind stirred the trees then, carrying the stench of standing water and cedar oil. The bark twitched in the pool. Her breath rose into the stillness, almost invisible in the dusk. A gnat landed on her temple. She didn't move.

She stayed kneeling long. Then stood.

She walked the long way back—along the edge of the marsh trail, where the cedar roots lifted and the boardwalk logs had been swallowed by green. Her footfalls were slow. The way she moved—upright, even, silent—marked no grief, no guilt.

It marked vow.

He waited until the insects bit. Then longer.

Only when the sweat ran down his ribs and pooled under his belt did he step back from the tree. His hands were shaking. He wasn't sure why. He checked the lines — two perch, one bloated and half-stripped. He cleaned it quick and headed back.

He didn't speak that night.

Not at first. Not while the sun still held behind the trees or while the longhouse still steamed from men's sweat and cookfire smoke. He waited until the pot was down to grease and no one had story left in them. Then he said it.

"She went to the ash-ring," he said. "No cloak. Just after dusk."

A few men shifted. One leaned forward. No one laughed.

"She cut her hand. Let it bleed into the stone hollow. Birch bark marked with runes. I think she spoke."

He didn't say to whom.

Didn't need to.

No one asked what the bark said. Or how close he'd stood. One of the younger boys, pale with scars across his neck, said: "Did she cry?"

"No," Finnvið answered. "She didn't."

The second telling came not long after. They were cutting

hide strips near the firepit, greasing them for boot-thongs, and the men were quiet. So Finnvið told it again. This time, she pressed her forehead to the stone long enough to leave skin behind.

The third time, someone said: "She called a name."

Another added, "Her eyes went white."

By the time the fog rolled in that night, she had bled deep into the stone hollow, laid runes to Freyja, and offered her vow to the land itself. Someone claimed she knelt bare-kneed, even on the grit. Someone else claimed a snake coiled near the base of the stone and didn't strike.

No one asked how Finnvið saw so much.

No one asked why he hadn't spoken sooner.

They took what they wanted, made the rest. Stories do that.

By morning, the story walked without owner. It passed between mouths like a half-remembered prayer. The older men scoffed, but none crossed the ash-ring after. The young ones carried it in posture—eyes sharpened, voices quieter.

But they looked.

And when Ranhildr passed, some pressed their knuckles tight into their own palms, as if to hold something still beneath the ribs.

It was no longer a tale.

It had become shape—carried in spine and breath.

By mid-afternoon, that shape reached Leif.

He was seated by the outer firepit, oiling his bowstring with seal-fat, the light low, the wind turned inland. His braid was undone from the salt air — dark rope against the collar of his tunic, still damp.

The younger men sat close, not speaking, but not leaving either. They passed knives between them for sharpening, watched the fat catch the firelight in his palms. They said nothing, but their stillness had shape.

The gossip came not as challenge. Not as insult.

Skagi brought it forward with the back of his voice — crooked and idle, as if he meant nothing by it.

"They're saying she called down Freyja."

He didn't answer.

Didn't lift his eyes.

But the cord stilled in his grip.

In the longhouse, Leif had moved his bedding beside hers, and she had not pushed him away. But there was no true privacy — just shadows and silence. Thirty-one men slept beside them, and Ranhildr would not take him there. Not with eyes and ears so near. Not with breath rising all around. He had tried. She had refused.

So the land became their refuge — every thawed hollow, every alder-shadowed rise. They came here to touch, to breathe each other without silence thick around them.

Now their bodies pressed close, skin steaming in the cold air. He lay behind her, his hand rested at the soft curve of her belly, his eyes running over her—the freckled slope of her shoulder, the red-copper tangle at her nape, the faint bruises his grip had left on her hips. Her breath was steady, chest rising slow. In that hush, she seemed carved from thaw itself—bare, rooted, claimed.

"We leave tomorrow," he said. Not urgent. Just spoken.

She didn't turn, just looked at the alder canopy above—fully leaved now, thick and green, the summer sun threading through in slow, shifting gold. But it wasn't just trees she saw. She saw a hush of branch and breeze, the hush of moss that held heat and memory. She saw the bond—rooted in her blood, answering her breath. The ground named her. The sky bore witness.

"You're on the ledger to stay," he continued.

She nodded.

He shifted his weight. The moss beneath them was damp. Moisture lingered from last night's rain, pooling in the dips where alder roots coiled. "You could come with me. Back to Greenland."

She turned to him then. Slowly. Her hair hung loose, fingers still marked with bark and damp soil, her body bare and unhurried in the golden hush. One knee bent, shoulder lifted slightly in the turn—freckled, streaked with leaf-dust. Her hair lay over the earth, catching glints of sun like copper wire woven loose.

"And if you stayed?"

He opened his mouth—but the words wouldn't come.

What he saw, when he looked at her, was not only her. He saw the land behind her. The sea behind that.

"I've already gone farther than Erik," he said quietly. "He gave Greenland. I've brought them farther."

She blinked. Not slow. Not soft.

"Your father's shadow does not fall here," she said, not unkind. "I stopped chasing. This place holds."

He faltered.

"I spoke to Father Arnlaugr," he said.

She frowned. "Why?"

"I want to marry you."

She blinked once. A slow, unreadable drag of the eye.

"We already are," she said. "You asked my brother. That was the vow. You laid beside me under oath and sky. I wore your mark on my chest. You think that wasn't a wedding?"

"No," he said. "Not before God. Not yet."

Her mouth opened slightly. Then closed. Her body stilled. Only her fingers moved, working against her palm like she was trying to feel something that had gone.

Still lying behind her, his chest to her back, he pressed his forehead briefly between her shoulder blades. Then he shifted, propping himself on one elbow.

"What we've done — it isn't clean. Not in God's eyes. But it can be made right."

She tilted her head. The gesture was birdlike, wary.

"I don't feel unclean," she said.

He pressed on. "If we stand before the altar — after your baptism — it will be done right. Blessed. Recognized. No one will question it. Not the men. Not the priest. Not Christ."

She pulled away from him — sharp, sudden, breath catching. Her bare shoulder slipped from his chest. The warmth between them broke.

She sat up fast and stepped clear. The damp moss gave underfoot, tearing softly as her heel sank in.

She stood bare. Her skin caught the light in streaks and shadows — breasts bare, thighs smeared with soil and bark, hip marked faintly where his hand had gripped. There was blood on the inside of one knee — thin, half-dried. Her hair, loosed from its tie, hung tangled and firelit down her back. She did not cover herself. Anger moved through her like heat through iron. Not shame — never shame. Just a clarity that burned.

"You think I need a priest to name what we already are?" Her voice was low. "You think I didn't mean it? That it was a game to me?"

"No," he said quickly. "I don't think that. But it isn't enough — not without God's blessing. Not for a Christian man."

Her jaw worked. Her shoulders rose—not defensively, but with something building beneath.

"I gave you my body," she said. "My blood. I named the god of my kin. I gave my vow to the land, and to you."

"I know," he said. "And I honour it. But—"

"No. You don't." Her voice was rising now. "If you did, you wouldn't ask me to kneel and wash it clean like a mistake."

He reached for her wrist. She pulled away fast.

She just stood over him—bare, backlit, burning. Her feet planted, her breath shallow, her mouth a tight line drawn hard. He rose to his knees now, looking up at her with the weight of her rage and the last light gilding the welt of her collarbone.

He reached—hesitant, open-palmed.

She struck him.

Not to startle. To hurt.

She struck him—flat and full. The sound cracked, clean and final. His head snapped sideways. He didn't rise.

"I spoke Freyja's name into the thaw," she said. "I bled. I gave what was mine. And you… you would call it sin?"

He reached toward her again. Not to touch—just to hold the moment steady, to keep her from vanishing entirely. But she stepped back, bare and seething, and her gaze cut through him—not with fear, but with the horror of someone seeing a beloved thing break. Not a man. A ruin.

"Ranhildr, I don't want to shame you. I want to make it right. In both worlds."

"No." She was shaking now—not from cold, but from heat beneath the skin. "You want it *clean*. You never saw what we already were. You never meant to marry me—not truly. Not in your heart. I gave you everything, and still, it's Erik you follow. It's Christ you answer. Not me."

She still wore it. The **wood-and-bone cross**, dulled by sweat and salt, lay against her bare chest—cool now in the air, smeared faintly from where it had pressed between them. The iron loop at its top was threaded by a leather cord, frayed at the edge. She had never removed it. Not in the longhouse. Not in sleep. Not even now.

He stood. Approached her slowly.

"We are bound. In flesh. In vow. I count it true," he said—sharper now, his voice tightening, not pleading but braced.

He reached for her. His fingers, colder now, brushed her neck—not asking, but claiming steadiness. His hand found the chain and lifted the cross off her body. It hung between them like a verdict.

"I would not ask you to change lightly. But the love between us must be made clean—not only in flesh, but in spirit. In the old way, we are bound. I do not deny it. But before God, we are not yet joined. Not until the Christian rite is spoken. That's the way it has to be."

Leif's jaw had gone hard. His hands curled once, then stilled at his sides. The muscle at his temple ticked. There was heat behind his eyes now—not grief, not doubt. A rising pressure that wanted to burn through reason. He was not used to being told he had failed. Not by her. Not here.

She stared at him. Just for a breath. Her chest rose and fell— fast now, but quiet. In the hush, a fly landed on her shoulder and she didn't flinch.

Then—

She wrenched the cross loose. The cord snapped with a brittle crack. She flung it hard. Not at him—through him. It hit, vanished in the muck. Her breath was ragged now, her throat tight.

"You witnessed the fullness of my offering—my blood, my body, my rite—and yet you let it pass without recognition or vow. As nothing."

"I was trying to bind both truths," he snapped. "What you gave—and what God commands. But you won't hear it. You'd see the world burn before yielding your pride."

"No," she said. "You were trying to bind your name—to your priest, to your god, to the story you think will be told after you're gone."

She crouched. Dug the cross from the muck with her fingers. Held it like a wound. Her breath stuttered—but her eyes stayed fixed. She gripped it between her palms. Turned it once. Then again. The leather pulled, warped. The bone creaked faintly—soft at first, then sudden, a dry crack as the tension gave way.

The wood split at the centre. Not loud—but final. White at

the break.

He didn't speak. His nostrils flared. His fists clenched again, harder this time, knuckles white. When he looked at her, it was through the narrowed eyes of a man who had offered what he thought was grace and been told it was dust. His breath came sharper now, chest rising with the effort not to shout.

She drew in one long breath. Her eyes pierced him. All the softness was leeched away, and ice filled her blood.

One breath to steady herself. Then: "Go back with your priest. Sail east when the knarr launches. Do not speak my name again. Do not set foot here if the land ever calls you back. I will not be waiting."

She turned. Walked fast, bare, her footing slipping once — but she didn't fall. At the edge of the alder rise, she stooped — still furious, still burning — and gathered her tunic and cloak. The cloth clung with sweat and earth. She wrapped them to her chest but did not dress. Not yet. Not for him. Her shoulders stayed squared as she disappeared into the trees.

"Ranhildr!" he barked, the name sharp with fury and disbelief. Not plea — command. As if saying it loud enough might bring her back, might undo the crack she'd split through his world.

The alder groaned — deep, wet wood shifting under thaw. As if something had been disturbed beneath. A single gnat dropped from the air, dead. The fog at the hollow's edge grew thicker. Something under the moss pulsed once, then stilled.

He crouched, groped through the moss. Found the broken cross.

He sat back on his heels—rough, not reverent. His breath came fast. The muscle in his cheek still twitched where she'd struck him. His hands, stained with moss and blood and bark, trembled with the effort not to throw the pieces after her, to shout into the trees, to demand the world reshape itself around his grief and fury. But the world held still.

The fragments rested in his hand a moment—bone pale, wood dark at the split. One edge was sharp enough to cut.

Then they slipped from his fingers.

The melt swallowed the pieces—slow, steady, like a thing that knew what didn't belong. The water took the cross as it had taken her blood—without resistance. But not without pardon.

He did not look up.

CHAPTER 20: THE TAKING SHORE

1001 A.D. — HEYANNIR

They gathered in the hollow by the waterline, where the tide pooled dark around weed-slick rocks and the knarr floated just off its cradle — patched, tar-streaked, and hungry for motion. The air held a late-summer thickness, wet with alder-sap and the brine stink of peeled kelp. Insects swarmed the shallows. Even the gulls were quiet.

Twenty-nine men stood in the cove, boots sank in damp gravel, the sound of low surf washing back and forth over unfinished farewells.

Leif stood nearest the keel — bare-headed, cloak loose at the throat. His hair was salt-stiff at the ends, gold caught with red, wind-drawn against his neck. One hand rested on the hull's beam, not steadying it — but steadying himself. Behind him, the last bundles had been stowed — cut spruce, alder, and pine, stripped and lashed for the crossing. Sap still wept from the grain. Enough for beams, for roofs, for coin. Wood the size of which Greenland hadn't seen in years.

It would make him wealthy. And the men aboard, too — each owed a share, if the sea held. The voyage would name them not just brave, but proven.

Those left behind would gain no such claim. No timber. No gold. Only land. Soil to guard. Roofs to mend. And names no skald would sing.

Kristján stood with his ledger. His boy beside him — Oddi,

precise even now—called names from the list. Those bound for Greenland stepped forward when called. Fifteen in all. They had left Brattahlíð with thirty-five. Four had died. One had vanished into the woods and not returned. Fifteen now left, and fifteen stayed. A clean severance.

But for the ship—fifteen was half a crew. No slack. No spare hands. Each man would bear double strain. Fewer for sail, for oar, for bail and repair. The sea would not pity them.

Each name met only boots shifting, sea-rope creaking, and gulls turning overhead.

Asleikr had loaded the last tool-chests himself. His tunic was pitch-stained, eyes rimmed red from smoke.

Stígandr stood beside him with arms crossed, one brow lifted, as if daring the keel-setter to thank him out loud.

Haukr hung back—half behind a frame post—but when Asleikr clapped his shoulder, he didn't pull away.

Hallbjǫrn and Tyrkir watched from the rise. Hallbjǫrn had dried willow bark and oxalis in hand; Tyrkir held a wrapped bundle of sea-rations and a skin of spruce syrup. Neither spoke.

When Leif passed them, he paused. "The herbs held," he said. "Because you took hold of the land—and didn't let go." He looked between them. "Keep it that way."

Hallbjǫrn shifted the bark in his hand. "What's left won't hold through spring rot," he muttered.

Tyrkir just patted his shoulder. The gesture said enough.

Messages were provided for delivery to Greenland. Ottar passed a roll of sealskin to Haraldr—marked in ochre, tied with net-line. "To my sister. Say Hafgrímr died clean." His voice caught only once. Orm handed nothing. Just gripped Asleikr's wrist and said, "Tell Dagrun the meat keeps. If she still wants the boy, send him." Then he stepped back without waiting for reply. Stígandr gave nothing, only stood with arms folded. But Haukr had tucked a carved fishbone token into Asleikr's pack—silent, shy, unspoken. Vali carried a carved stave all morning—runed on one side, sealed in spruce pitch. At the last moment, he fed it to the hearth.

When all was ready, Kristján stepped to Leif, a wax-sealed pouch in hand. For a moment, he did not offer it—just turned it in his fingers, the wax dull under sun.

"To Brattahlíð," he said. "For Herdis."

The name sat heavy in the air. Leif paused. It was the first time he'd heard it spoken in a year.

"You still claim her?" he asked.

Kristján's jaw worked once before he answered. "She keeps my house. She's owed my truth."

Leif took the pouch. The wax bore no mark—just a blade's flat press. Inside: birch bark, scraped and creased. Gut-bound. Measured.

"I'll give it to her," Leif said.

"See that you do." Kristján's voice stayed even. "And tell her the law holds. Even here."

He held Leif's gaze a breath longer, then turned. The pouch was gone from his hand, but the weight remained. He cleared his throat once. "The seal stores are tallied. Roof pitch will last till frost. If no rot sets in, there's margin for spring."

Leif nodded, but did not meet his eye. "And the law?" he asked, lower now.

The wind tugged at the loose vellum before Kristján closed it—one hand firm on the cover, as if sealing more than numbers. "What you set down, I'll keep. But what comes next—they'll need voice, not rule."

Leif looked at him fully then. "It's yours. The hall, the lines, the weight."

"I know," Kristján said.

They clasped arms, firm. Kristján stepped back. Oddi did not.

Leif looked down. "You're not coming?"

Oddi blinked. "I belong to the tally. My father says… the books won't sail themselves."

A smile nearly cracked Leif's mouth, but he only nodded. "Hold the weight true, then. For both of us."

Finnvið came next, bow slung, smirk already loaded. "You're leaving me with a priest, a ghost-biter, and thirteen axe-happy men. You sure this isn't cowardice?"

Leif exhaled. "I'm sure you'll talk them all to death before the winter turns."

"A fair plan." Finnvið leaned close, voice lower. "You should've asked her sooner. Before the land answered first."

Leif's jaw flexed. "You've never been quiet a day in your life."

Finnið grinned. "I'm quiet when I'm right."

Then Skagi—awkward, tall, too earnest. His pack was not on his back. His eyes kept drifting to the woods beyond camp.

"She's not coming," Leif said gently.

Skagi's brow furrowed. "But—she said—after the thaw—"

Leif shook his head. "The land answered her."

"I thought—" He stopped. The wind caught his hair and tossed it into his eyes. From behind, Grani muttered something and Finnið snorted.

"Don't listen to them," Leif said. "You've got good in you. Watch the ridge. Watch her."

Skagi didn't answer, but he nodded, slow. He wiped at his face, not quite hiding it, and walked back uphill.

The last man standing before Leif was Vidarbjǫrn.

Sixteen winters they had stood beside one another. Axe to axe. Storm to storm.

"You built this with me," Leif said. "Every stone. Every cut line."

"I didn't build it for you to leave."

Silence stretched. Wind tugged at their cloaks.

Vidarbjǫrn's voice was flat. "You go to be your father's son. Give them my name, when you reach the fjord."

Leif looked down. "I go to bring more."

"And claim? You mean to plant your father's flag, not just your foot?"

Leif's answer came quiet. "I'll send ships. And names. And claim."

Vidarbjǫrn nodded once, but the nod did not reach his chest. His gaze flicked toward the tree line.

"She didn't come."

Leif's voice dropped. "I know."

The two clasped arms, and this time neither spoke.

When the last name was called, Father Arnlaugr came to him—robe belted, eyes clear. He placed a hand on Leif's shoulder.

"You carry the Word. That's enough."

Leif's voice was tight. "Not without your strength."

"My strength is in staying. Yours is in going."

Their clasp was different. Not blood. But covenant.

Leif stepped toward the knarr. The tide had risen just enough to lift her.

The crew reached down—Hallgeirr with the rope, Haraldr at the plank. Eirik stood watch.

Leif turned once more toward shore. The wind had stilled.

Ranhildr was not there.

He touched the hilt of his knife, as he had the day they named the stream. Then he boarded without another word.

Ranhildr moved alone through the woods, bow in hand.

The air held the sour tang of crushed alder and wet lichen. Flies spun in the stillness. Above her, the canopy hung thick with late birch and black spruce, their needles whispering as the wind shifted seaward. Alder leaves—serrated and black at the edges from rot—shivered like teeth in the breathless light.

The sun stood high, but the light came slanting and slow, caught in the mist that hung low over the rootbeds and the midges that thickened where the moss held water. Her feet made no sound. The moss drank it all.

She didn't hunt for meat.

There was no pack on her back, only a quiver and a bow too tightly strung. Last week's blood still stained the fletching. She moved for no beast. She moved for breath. For what still burned behind her teeth. Rage cooled, not gone.

A hare broke from the rootline. Ash-grey, thin-flanked, too lean for winter meat.

She loosed without pause.

The arrow struck behind the shoulder. The hare twitched once, legs flailing, then dropped. Steam curled faintly from its belly. She stepped over the lichen and bent to it. Its fur was still warm, breath shallow at the spine. One eye dulled. The shot had been clean.

She should've ended it clean.

Instead, the knife flashed too fast. Her grip slipped. Bone cracked under the edge. She snarled low—not loud, but guttural, a sound from the chest. Her shoulders locked. She hacked at the belly, hands shaking. Guts spilled wet and hot, the reek sharp as bile. The moss darkened, steaming in the still air. Blood soaked the soft bed beneath.

The carcass was ruined.

She dropped it. Her breath dragged rough through her nose. A single tear burned down her cheek. She let it fall. Didn't wipe it.

The knife stayed in her grip.

She rose. Moved.

The light had begun to tilt west, and with it came the stench of low water and crushed fern. Horseflies thickened in the hollow. The sweat along her spine cooled without comfort. Her steps struck harder now. Each footfall met resistance — roots, stones, rot. Behind her, silence didn't mean peace. It meant aftermath.

She found height—an outcrop rimmed in crowberry and twisted pine, the stone slick with saltwind and lichen. Below, the inland channel spread wide and blue-grey, rimmed with spruce-shadow and low cloud.

And then—

A flash of red.

Canvas. A knarr's sail, pulled taut with wind, gliding north across the reach. Not fast. Not small.

Unmistakable.

She gripped the pine beside her. Bark peeled beneath her fingers. Her breath came in sharp, slow drag—pulled deep, until her ribs ached. Her jaw clenched. She watched until the sail vanished behind a headland of granite and fir.

Then she turned.

No cry. No word. Just the set of her shoulders, stiff. She drew the arrow from the ruined hare, snapped the shaft in half, and let the pieces fall. Then her feet found the slope down.

They watched from the rise above the strait, next to the church, where the wind ran cold despite the sun. The knarr had caught the tide clean—her patched red sail drawn full, ribs groaning as she cut forward into the blue-grey swell. Spray broke from her flanks—seal-greased wood meeting blue-grey swell. Her oarlocks were drawn tight, her stern braced low. She had weight—but she moved like she remembered the sea.

Leif stood near the tiller, back straight. One hand on the beam, the other on his belt. He did not look back.

Father Arnlaugr stood with the wind tugging at his sleeves, his hands hidden in the long fall of his robe. Kristján beside him, arms crossed, ledger closed beneath one elbow. Skagi crouched on a flat rock near the edge, eyes tracking every pitch of the hull. Vidarbjǫrn stood apart, axe on his back, jaw clenched so tight his neck corded.

No one spoke while the sail was still close.

When it crested the midpoint of the reach—when the red blurred in the sun haze—Kristján said, low: "He said he'd return. With settlers. With claim."

"He always says," Vidarbjørn muttered. "And he always means it."

"But?" Father Arnlaugr asked, not turning.

"But meaning isn't the same as staying."

The gulls wheeled wide over the bluff, but none cried. The wind dragged long across the stones, lifting dust from the cracks in the turf.

Skagi shifted, still crouched. "He brought us farther than anyone before. Farther than Erik. Maybe farther than any man will again."

"Aye," Kristján said. "He made all this."

"And left it," Vidarbjørn said.

Father Arnlaugr's gaze stayed on the line of water. "He

believes in legacy. In names carved after death."

"And do you?" Vidarbjǫrn asked.

"No," the priest said. "I believe in souls. And in what is kept whole."

"He won't stay whole," Kristján said. "Not out there. Not with half a crew and no wind past dusk."

"He doesn't need wind," Vidarbjǫrn said, bitter as salt. "Just a story."

Skagi's voice broke in: "He means to bring more. Means to build a new land."

No one answered. Below them, the knarr crested another swell, dipped behind the headland, and vanished.

Gone.

Not wrecked. Not blessed.

Just gone.

The bluff quieted.

Then Vidarbjǫrn spoke again, voice hard but not cruel. "He'll be sung. They'll speak of Leif Erikson who crossed the sea, who found Vinland, who bore the Word, who turned from it. They'll call him great."

"He is great," Skagi said.

"Yes," Vidarbjǫrn said. "And yet."

Kristján exhaled. "A man who builds and doesn't stay."

"He cut the path," Arnlaugr murmured. "But cannot walk it."

Skagi looked back once more—no sail now. Only water and the echo of red against memory. His hand curled around the edge of the stone, knuckles white.

"He said he'd come back."

Vidarbjǫrn turned from the sea. "Then let him find us here. Standing."

The four of them turned together—slow, shoulders squared, boots sinking into sun-warmed moss. Behind them, the settlement smoked: fifteen men, a warped-roofed hall, seal hides drying in the wind. No ship left to flee. Only soil, and blood, and the long pull of seasons.

The wind turned. Trees groaned—deep and slow. The air carried no omen—just sweat and ash, spruce-sap and salt. A world unfinished. Still watching.

They walked back to the settlement without another word.

The land said nothing. But it did not resist.

Somewhere beyond the ash-ring, a low shape moved through alder and pine. Not hunting. Not chased. Not claimed. It paused at the stream's edge, nose to water, then turned back toward the ridge.

The wind shifted. It did not howl.

Behind them, the hammer rang—once.

Not loud. Not a song.

Just the shape of staying: iron on wood, a dull note buried in moss and smoke.

Appendixes

Leif's 1000 Voyage – Crew Manifest

(34 Men & 1 Woman)

Name	Know n As	B or n	Role	Physiognomy
Leif Erikson		97 0	Captain	5'9", 190 lbs. Sun-browned skin. Bronze hair, clipped short at the sides, longer at crown. Full blond beard, kept trimmed. Grey-blue eyes. Scar under the chin from a snapped helm-strap. Hands callused from both rudder and blade. Wears a bronze cloak-clasp, gifted and claimed.
Vidarbjǫrn Ketilsson		97 0	Mystic/Figh ter axes	5'10", 200 lbs. Tanned skin. Dark eyes. Black hair (thick, tied). Full beard. Scar on right shoulder. Towering frame.
Kristján Eldgrimsso n		96 7	Quartermast er / Ledger-Keeper	5'7", 180 lbs. Fair skin. Grey eyes. Reddish-blond hair (tied neatly). Trim beard. Ink-stained hands. Neat posture.
Arnlaugr Asmundars on	Father Arnlau gr	96 5	Priest	5'7", 150 lbs. Sallow skin. Blue eyes. Blond hair (thinning). No beard. Gaunt frame. Long, bony fingers.
Ranhildr Ketilsdóttir		97 4	Hunter: bow and spear	5'5", 140 lbs. Fair, wind-rough skin. Green eyes. Red hair (long, braided). No facial hair. Pregnant. Scar on left knuckle.
Rúni Sveinsson	Twice-Bitten	96 9	Fighter/Sco ut: dual axes	5'5", 160 lbs. Pale skin. Blue eyes. Blond hair (unbound, shoulder-length). No beard. Scars at throat and collarbone. Moves barefoot even in frost. Narrow-hipped, light-footed, long-limbed. Back marked by scratches—some healed, some new.
Skagi	of the Far-	98	Fighter/Sco ut: bow and	5'7", 160 lbs. Fair skin, freckled. Blue-grey eyes. Flax-blond hair

Arnkelsson	Eyes	2	sword scout	(loose to collarbone). No facial hair. Long limbs, fine hands.
Ketill Hávarðsson	Flat-Nose	95 0	Fighter sword and shield veteran	5'6", 180 lbs. Broad shoulders. Coarse grey-streaked beard. Salt-crusted boots. Thick wrists. Weathered skin. Eyes grey, steady until they were not. Hands nicked from old blade-work.
Stígandr Hroaldsson		96 3	Smith	5'6", 170 lbs. Freckled skin. Brown eyes. Bald. Full beard. Slag scars on arms. Slight limp.
Finnvið Eilifsson	Snake-Tongue	97 1	Scout/Trader/Linguist	5'7", 150 lbs. Pale skin. Pale grey eyes. Ash-blond hair (tangled). Sparse beard. Scar over right brow. Smells of pitch.
Asleikr Thorgilsson	the Keel-Setter	96 0	Shipwright	5'8", 160 lbs. Weather-tanned skin. Grey eyes. Iron-grey hair (shaved sides, tied topknot). Broken nose, thick forearms.
Haukr Asleiksson	Half-Built	97 7	Apprentice to Stígandr (Smith)	5'4", 140 lbs. Fair skin. Brown eyes. Brown hair (tied back). Patchy beard. Broad chest, blunt fingers.
Oddi Kristjánsson	Ledger-Whelp	98 5	Apprentice to Kristján (Ledger-Keeper)	5'2", 120 lbs. Pale skin. Brown eyes. Brown hair (cropped short). No facial hair. Ink-stained fingers.
Eindriði Kolsson		96 0	Stone-placer / ditch-cutter	5'6", 165 lbs. Broad-shouldered, compact frame. Grey eyes. Dark brown hair (cropped close). No beard. Hands thick and square, scarred across the knuckles. Walks with slight weight to one leg — steady, not slow. Tunic always dirt-streaked from ditchwork and stone-setting.
Eirik Hrolfsson		97 9	Hunter: Spear	5'7", 155 lbs. Ruddy skin. Brown hair (shaggy). Hazel eyes. Clean-shaven. Spear-callused palms.
Eysteinn Kolbeinsson		98 0	Fisherman	5'5", 145 lbs. Pale skin. Sandy-blond hair (thin, damp-worn). Brown eyes. No beard. Hands raw from sea-chill, often wrapped in fur or oilcloth. Cloak always salt-darkened. Narrow across the shoulders, but

				wiry.
Geirr Thorgrimsson	of Hvalsey	94 8	Bowyer / Fletcher	5'9", 170 lbs. Weather-dark skin. Black hair (shoulder-length, tied back). Green eyes. Deep lines around mouth and brow. Broad hands with thick joints. Speckled forearms from old fletching cuts. Stooped posture in cold.
Grani Bjornsson		96 8	Fighter: axe and shield	5'7", 170 lbs. Ruddy skin. Chestnut hair (mid-length, loose). Blue eyes. Full beard. Broad-chested, thick neck, axe-callused palms. Scar on left hand from old edge-grind. Moves with compact force.
Hafgrímr Eldrsson		98 6	Water-bearer / Bandage boy	5'0", 100 lbs. Pale skin. Blond hair (uneven, wind-snarled). Blue eyes. No facial hair. Thin wrists. Cloak too big for his frame. Hands callused but still soft at the joints.
Hallbjǫrn Grimsson	Herbalist	96 1	Herbalist	5'6", 155 lbs. Pale, weathered skin. Grey eyes. Ash-brown hair (cropped). Thin beard. Long fingers, resin-stained.
Hallgeirr Herjólfrsson		96 9	Sailmaster	5'6", 160 lbs. Tanned skin. Dark blond hair (salt-bleached, rope-burned hands). Crooked fingers from rigging.
Hallkell Bjarnsson	Red	96 5	Fighter spear	5'7", 180 lbs. Tanned skin. Rust-blond hair (short, coarse). Hazel eyes — too bright. Sparse beard. Broad shoulders, rope-callused hands. Always forward in stance.
Haraldr Bjarnsson		96 0	Fighter: spear and shield	5'8"", 180 lbs. Tanned skin. Dark auburn beard (thick, short). Broken nose. Broad back, slow gait. Shoulders rolled slightly forward. Scar along the left temple. Gaze direct, flat.
Hrafn Sigurdsson		96 4	Log-wall & frame builder	5'6", 170 lbs. Medium-toned skin. Dark brown eyes. Black hair (coarse, mid-length). Stubbled jaw. Crooked right thumb.
Hrólfr Steinsson		96 2	Fighter: sword and	5'8", 180 lbs. Fair skin. Straw-brown hair (close-cropped). Green eyes.

Name				
			shield	Crooked front tooth. Heavy brow. Broad through the chest, with thick forearms from blade work. Scar at collarbone, left side.
Ketilbjǫrn Hallkelsson		972	Thatcher or turf-layer	5'6", 170 lbs. Wind-reddened skin. Straw-coloured hair (short, thick). Grey eyes. Full beard. Broad hands, cracked from turf and cold. Forearms speckled with old pitch-scars. Walks with a slight tilt from old back strain.
Orm Hallfredsson		968	Animal Tender / Butcher	5'6", 180 lbs. Ruddy skin. Hazel eyes. Brown hair (short, coarse). Stubble beard. Thick wrists.
Ottar Sigmundsson	Fish-Lord	975	Fisherman (lead)	5'5", 190 lbs. Tanned skin. Grey eyes. Dark brown hair (thinning). Coarse beard. Rope-scarred forearms.
Rúnar Thorsteinsson	Wind-Ruler	960	Navigator / Weather-Reader	5'8"", 165 lbs. Pale skin. Storm-grey eyes. Black-streaked hair (loose). Bearded. Sea-scar under jaw.
Sveigr Sorkvirsson		981	Apprentice to Asleikr (Shipwright)	5'7", 165 lbs. Fair skin. Blond hair (short, often sweat-clumped). Grey-blue eyes. No beard. Shoulders broad, wrists scarred from adze work. Right thumb nail split from pitch-burn. Walks with a slight forward lean, from hauling timber too young.
Sveinn Brandsson		981	Fisherman	5'7", 155 lbs. Fair skin. Blond hair (ragged-cut). Pale grey eyes. No beard. Narrow shoulders, long limbs. Belt often double-knotted to hold a tunic too wide. Right arm amputated at mid-bicep; stump bound in birch pitch and ash-moss. Skin faintly sea-salted even far from shore.
Thorleifr Audunsson		973	Fighter: spear and shield	5'8", 175 lbs. Tanned skin. Dark brown hair (cropped). Brown eyes. Scar across left eyebrow. Strong-legged, with spear-callused hands. Long chin. Crooked fingers from an old shield-break. Wears a fur-lined mantle patched at the hem.

Tyrkir Thjodolfsson	Saxlander	955	Cook / Provisions	6'2", 280 lbs. Olive skin. Brown eyes. Black hair (greying, shoulder-length). Full beard. Fingers stained with malt and herb oils.
Vali Skeggjasson		970	Hunter: archer	6'0", 180 lbs. Pale skin. Hazel eyes. Black hair (tied back). Clean-shaven. Tattooed right forearm (runes).
Víg-Bjǫrn Arnesson	the Joiner	974	Carpenter (fine work)	5'4", 155 lbs. Stocky frame. Weather-dark skin. Balding crown. Grey-flecked beard. Squat posture, fingers broad and flattened from decades of carpentry. Right hand bears deep chisel-scars along the knuckles. Often seen with a drawknife tucked in his belt and a wooden wedge behind one ear

Old Norse Calendar

As used in Iceland and Greenland around the 10th–11th centuries. It is a **lunisolar calendar** *with a clear division into* **two halves: summer and winter**, *each with six months. The year begins around mid-April with* **Sumarmál**, *the start of summer.*

🜚 SUMMER HALF (Six Months)

Month/Marker	Modern Equivalent	Notes
Sumarmál	Mid-April	First day of summer. Marked by gatherings and omens.
Harpa	Mid-April – mid-May	Start of summer. Possibly named after a forgotten goddess. Time of thaw and planting.
Vármót (poetic)	Early May (within Harpa)	Spring assembly. Optional or regional. May appear in saga or poetic usage.
Skerpla	Mid-May – mid-June	Early growth, hunting, gathering. Often vague in source; transitional.
Sólmánuðr	Mid-June – mid-July	"Sun Month." High summer. Hay growth begins.
Miðsumar (ritual)	Around June 21 (not a full month)	Midsummer solstice. Often used for rites or omens, not a named month.
Heyannir	Mid-July – mid-August	"Haymaking Month." Peak labour and harvest.
Tvímánuðr	Mid-August – mid-September	"Second Month." Transitional. Hay storage, travel ends, signs of decline.
Haustmánuðr	Mid-September – mid-October	"Autumn Month." Final harvest. Slaughter season begins.

❄ *WINTER HALF (Six Months)*

Month/Marker	***Modern Equivalent***	***Notes***
Vetrnætr	*Mid-October*	*"Winter Nights." First day of winter. Often marked by sacrifice (blót).*
Gormánuðr	*Mid-October – mid-November*	*"Slaughter Month." Animals killed for winter stores.*
Frostmánuðr (regional/poetic)	*Late October – early November*	*Used in Icelandic and Greenlandic texts to mark onset of freeze.*
Ýlir	*Mid-November – mid-December*	*Named for Yule. Deepening cold. Prepares for darkest days.*
Mörsugr	*Mid-Dec – mid-Jan*	*"Fat Sucking Month." Food stores thin. Feast or famine.*
Jól (festival)	*Late December (Solstice)*	*Yule. Twelve-night midwinter celebration.*
Þorri	*Mid-Jan – mid-Feb*	*Harshest winter. Male rites (Þorrablót). Ice-thick months.*
Góa	*Mid-Feb – mid-March*	*Named for a feminine figure. Hope, light returns.*
Einmánuðr	*Mid-Mar – mid-April*	*"One Month." Last of winter. Ice softens, lambing begins.*

🛠 Key Notes:

- Frostmánuðr and Torfmánuðr are not core calendar months, but poetic/regional terms for late autumn or early winter (mainly in Iceland/Greenland).
- Miðsumar, Vármót, and Jól are ritual or calendrical points, not official month names.
- Calendar uses half-month shifts (starting mid-April), not Gregorian month boundaries.

The Saga of the Greenlanders

Excerpts from: Flateyarbók, Arthur Middleton Reeves, Finding of Wineland the Good

"The Saga of the Greenlanders" was recorded in Iceland towards the end of the 14th century by an anonymous scribe. It tells of the accidental discovery of hitherto unknown lands south and west of Greenland. The discovery was made in 985 or 986, the same year that Greenland was settled, by a crew on an Icelandic merchant ship en route from Iceland to Greenland. The ship was owned by an Icelander, Bjarni Herjólfrsson. Returning to his home in Iceland from a trading voyage to Norway, he found that his father had emigrated to Greenland with Erik the Red. Undaunted, he set out for Greenland, despite lacking familiarity with the route and the fact that it was late in the season. Rounding the southern tip of Greenland, now called Cape Farewell, they were hit by a storm and tossed unmercifully on the sea for some time. When the weather cleared, they sighted land. Realizing that he was too far south for this land to be Greenland and that the landmarks did not correspond to what he had heard of Greenland, Bjarni set course first northward, then east, and eventually made his way to his father's place in Greenland in time to spend the winter there.

Word of Bjarni's discovery spread fast. People were interested in finding out more about this new land, but it was not until fifteen years later that anyone did anything about it. The first to launch an expedition was Leif, son of the paramount chief of Greenland, Erik (Eirik) the Red. Retracing Bjarni's route in the opposite direction, Leif created the names *Helluland, Markland, and Vinland* for three regions with distinct characteristics first observed by Bjarni. They established a base in Vinland and called it *Leifsbúðir*, Leif's Camp. From there they explored in several directions and discovered wild grapes for which Leif named the area.

Bjarni's Voyage in "The Saga of the Greenlanders"

Chapter 1

- 636-637 -

[...]

Bjarni steered his ship into Eyrar in the summer of the year that his father had sailed from Iceland. Bjarni was greatly moved by the news and would not have his cargo unloaded. His crew then asked what he was waiting for, and he answered that he intended to follow his custom of spending the winter with his father — 'and I want to set sail for Greenland, if you will join me'.

All of them said they would follow his counsel.

Bjarni then spoke: 'Our journey will be thought an ill-considered one, since none of us has sailed the Greenland Sea.'

Despite this they set sail once they had made ready and sailed for three days, until the land had disappeared below the horizon. Then the wind dropped and they were beset by winds from the north and fog; for many days they did not know where they were sailing.

After that they saw the sun and could take their bearings. Hoisting the sail, they sailed for the rest of the day before sighting land. They speculated among themselves as to what land this would be, for Bjarni said he suspected this was not Greenland.

They asked whether he wished to sail up close into the shore of this country or not. 'My advice is that we sail in close to the land.'

They did so, and soon saw that the land was not mountainous but did have small hills, and was covered with forests. Keeping it on their port side, they turned their sail-end landwards and angled away from the shore.

They sailed for another two days before sighting land once again.

They asked Bjarni whether he now thought this to be Greenland.

He said he thought this no more likely to be Greenland than the previous land — 'since there are said to be very large glaciers in Greenland'.

They soon approached the land and saw that it was flat and wooded. The wind died and the crew members said they thought it advisable to put ashore, but Bjarni was against it. They claimed they needed both timber and water.

'You've no shortage of those provisions,' Bjarni said, but he was criticized somewhat by his crew for this.

He told them to hoist the sail and they did so, turning the stern towards shore and sailing seawards. For three days they sailed with the wind from the south-west until they saw a third land. This land had high mountains, capped by a glacier.

They asked whether Bjarni wished to make land here, but he said he did not wish to do so — 'as this land seems to me to offer nothing of use'.

This time they did not lower the sail, but followed the shoreline until they saw that the land was an island. Once more they turned their stern landwards and sailed out to sea with the same breeze. But the wind soon grew and Bjarni told them to lower the sail and not to proceed faster than both their ship and rigging could safely withstand. They sailed for four days.

- 638 -

Upon seeing a fourth land they asked Bjarni whether he thought this was Greenland or not.

Bjarni answered, 'This land is most like what I have been told of Greenland, and we'll head for shore here.'

This they did and made land along a headland in the evening of the day, finding a boat there. On this point Herjolf, Bjarni's father, lived, and it was named for him and has since been called Herjolfsnes (Herjolf's point). Bjarni now joined his father and ceased his merchant voyages. He remained on his father's farm as long as Herjolf lived and took over the farm after his death.

Chapter 2

Following this, Bjarni Herjólfrsson sailed from Greenland to Earl Eirik, who received him well. Bjarni told of his voyage, during which he had sighted various lands, and many people thought him short on curiosity, since he had nothing to tell of these lands, and he was criticized somewhat for this.

Chapter 2

- 638 -

[...]

Leif, the son of Eirik the Red of Brattahlíð, sought out Bjarni and purchased his ship. He hired himself a crew numbering thirty-five men altogether. Leif asked his father Eirik to head the expedition.

Eirik was reluctant to agree, saying he was getting on in years and not as good at bearing the cold and wet as before. Leif said he still commanded the greatest good fortune of all his kinsmen. Eirik gave in to Leif's urgings and, when they were almost ready, set out from his farm on horseback. When he had but a short distance left to the ship, the horse he was riding stumbled and threw Eirik, injuring his foot. Eirik then spoke: 'I am not intended to find any other land than this one where we now live. This will be the end of our travelling together.'

Eirik returned home to Brattahlíð, and Leif boarded his ship, along with his companions, thirty-five men altogether. One of the crew was a man named Tyrkir, from a more southerly country.

The Saga of Erik the Red

Excerpts from: 1880 translation into English by J. Sephton from the original Icelandic 'Eiríks saga rauða'.

Chapter 5

Eirik had a wife who was named Thjodhild, and two sons; the one was named Thorstein, and the other Leif. These sons of Eirik were both promising men. Thorstein was then at home with his father; and there was at that time no man in Greenland who was thought so highly of as he. Leif had sailed to Norway, and was there with King Olaf Tryggvason.

Now, when Leif sailed from Greenland during the summer, he and his men were driven out of their course to the Sudreyjar. They were slow in getting a favourable wind from this place, and they stayed there a long time during the summer ... reaching Norway about harvest-tide.

He joined the body-guard of King Olaf Tryggvason, and the king formed an excellent opinion of him, and it appeared to him that Leif was a well-bred man. Once upon a time the king entered into conversation with Leif, and asked him, "Dost thou purpose sailing to Greenland in summer?"

Leif answered, "I should wish so to do, if it is your will." The king replied, "I think it may well be so; thou shalt go my errand, and preach Christianity in Greenland."

Leif said that he was willing to undertake it, but that, for himself, he considered that message a difficult one to proclaim in Greenland. But the king said that he knew no man who was better fitted for the work than he. "And thou shalt carry," said he, "good luck with thee in it." "That can only be," said Leif, "if I carry yours with me."

Leif set sail as soon as he was ready. He was tossed about a long time out at sea, and lighted upon lands of which before he had no expectation. There were fields of wild wheat, and the vine-tree in full growth. There were also the trees which were called maples; and they gathered of all this certain tokens; some trunks so large that they were used in house-building. Leif came upon men who had been shipwrecked, and took them home with him, and gave them sustenance during the winter. Thus did he show his great munificence and his graciousness when he brought Christianity to the land, and saved the shipwrecked crew. He was called Leif the Lucky.

Leif reached land in Eiriksfjordr, and proceeded home to Brattahlíð. The people received him gladly. He soon after preached Christianity and catholic truth throughout the land, making known to the people the message of King Olaf Tryggvason; and declaring how many renowned deeds and what great glory accompanied this faith. Eirik took coldly to the proposal to forsake his religion, but his wife, Thjodhild, promptly yielded, and caused a church to be built not very near the houses. The building was called Thjodhild's Church; in that spot she offered her prayers, and so did those men who received Christ, and they were many. After she accepted the faith, Thjodhild would have no intercourse with Eirik, and this was a great trial to his temper.

Chapter 8

…

Now, before this, when Leif was with King Olaf Tryggvason, and the king had requested him to preach Christianity in Greenland, he gave him two Scotch people, the man called Haki, and the woman called Hækja. The king requested Leif to have recourse to these people if ever he should want fleetness, because they were swifter than wild beasts. Eirik and Leif had got these people to go with Karlsefni. Now, when they had sailed by Furdustrandir, they put the Scotch people on land, and requested them to run into the southern regions, seek for choice land, and come back after three half-days were passed. They were dressed in such wise that they had on the garment which they called biafal. It was made with a hood at the top, open at the sides, without sleeves, and was fastened between the legs. A button and a loop held it together there; and elsewhere they were without clothing. Then did they cast anchors from the ships, and lay there to wait for them. And when three days were expired the Scotch people leapt down from the land, and one of them had in his hand a bunch of grapes, and the other an ear of wild wheat.

950 A.D.	Birth of Erik the Red
	Born in Rogaland or Jæren, Norway. Son of Thorvaldr Ásvaldsson.
960s A.D.	Exile of Thorvaldr Ásvaldsson
	Thorvaldr is outlawed for manslaughter. The family migrates to northwest Iceland.
970–980 A.D.	Erik Settles in Iceland
	Marries Thjóðhildr and settles at Eiríksstaðir in Haukadalr.
	Children: Leif, Thorvald, Thorstein, Freydís.
970 A.D.	Birth of Leif Erikson
	Born in Eiríksstaðir, son of Erik the Red and Thjóðhildr.
970 A.D.	Birth of Vidarbjǫrn Ketilsson
	Born in Greenland (or possibly late Icelandic period), not kin to Erik the Red. Family background: Kuerlander stock; raised in hardship on the outer coast. Becomes boyhood companion to Leif Erikson—a loyal and quiet counterpoint to Leif's charisma.
971 A.D.	Birth of Thorvald Erikson
	Born in Eiríksstaðir, son of Erik the Red and Thjóðhildr.
972 A.D.	Birth of Thorstein Erikson
	Born in Eiríksstaðir, son of Erik the Red and Thjóðhildr.
974 A.D.	Birth of Freydís
	Born in Eiríksstaðir, son of Erik the Red and Thjóðhildr.
	Birth of Ránhildr
	Vidarbjǫrn's younger sister, born in Greenland.

	Ambitious, sharp-minded, with early leanings toward sea rites.
981–984 A.D.	Erik's Exile from Iceland Erik is outlawed and explores Greenland. Names it to attract settlers.
985–986 A.D.	Colonization of Greenland Erik leads 25 ships west; 14 arrive. Settlements: Eastern and Western.
986 A.D.	Bjarni Herjólfsson Sights Mainland North America Sees unknown lands west of Greenland; does not land.
999 A.D.	Leif Erikson Acquires Bjarni's Ship Leif sets sail west Vidarbjǫrn joins the voyage as trusted shipmate. Ránhildr joins as well. Lands at: Helluland (likely Baffin Island), Markland (likely Labrador), Vínland (likely Newfoundland)
1000 A.D.	Founding of Leifsbuðir in Vínland Settlement established at what is today L'Anse aux Meadows. Vidarbjǫrn helps build shelters, scout terrain, and manage supplies. Leif winters there; abundant wild resources reported.

Lief's Journey 1000 A.D.

Christianity and the Old Faith in the Northern World, 1000 A.D.

The religious confluence reflected in the Vidarbjǫrn Saga

Vidarbjǫrn Saga is set during one of the most pivotal centuries in the history of the Norse world: the era of Christianization. By the year 1000 A.D., the older polytheistic faith of the Norse — a religion of many gods, oaths, and ritual offerings — was coming under pressure from the expanding power of Christian Europe. This conflict of faiths was not merely theological. It reshaped law, kingship, daily life, and the very language of loyalty and identity.

The saga's characters — Leif, Father Arnlaugr, Ranhildr, Vidarbjǫrn — live at the sharp edge of this transition. Their choices, their oaths, their names, and their struggles reflect the deep tensions between two worldviews that were not easily reconciled. This appendix offers readers a concise study of that religious conflict, to illuminate the context that shapes the narrative.

The Norse Faith: Gods of Oath, Sea, and Kin

The pre-Christian Norse religion was polytheistic, with gods who were not distant creators but immediate powers in the world. Odin, Thor, Freyr, and others governed aspects of life and nature: wisdom, storm, harvest, war, and fate.

Faith was not a matter of doctrine or abstract belief, but of practice:

- **Sacrifice and Offering:** Worship took the form of gifts — blood sacrifices of animals, offerings of treasure, ale, or labour. These bought the favour of gods, secured luck in battle, harvest, or voyage, and maintained balance between men and the divine.

- **Oaths and Rites:** The sacred bond in Norse culture was the oath — sworn before gods, stones, or the sea. Oaths bound men to their kin, their lord, and their gods. To break an oath was to invite ruin upon oneself and one's house.

- **Burial and the Dead:** The dead were honoured through ship-burials, mounds, or cairns, sent on their way with goods for the journey to halls beyond. The rites ensured peace for the dead and protection for the living from wandering spirits.

- Names held profound significance in this belief system:

- Ships, swords, and sons were named with care, as names were thought to bind the named to their destiny.

- Renaming was seen as inviting misfortune, for it disrupted the fate woven at the naming.

- Names could also be protective, invoking the strength of ancestors or gods.

Christianity: The Expanding Faith

Christianity arrived in the Norse world not only through missionaries, but through kings and the politics of power. From the late 10th century, rulers like Olaf Tryggvason of Norway and later Olaf Haraldsson (St. Olaf) enforced Christian conversion, seeing in it a means to unify their realms and align with Christian Europe.

Key features of Christianity in this context:

- **Monotheism:** Christianity's single, almighty God stood in contrast to the Norse pantheon.

- **New Moral Law:** Christianity forbade blood sacrifice, temple rites, and vengeance-killings. It introduced concepts of sin, penance, and salvation through Christ's sacrifice.

- **Burial and Worship:** The dead were interred in consecrated ground, facing east, awaiting the resurrection. Sacred groves and stone circles were replaced by churches and chapels.

- **Hierarchical Structure:** Christianity introduced a clerical order — priests, bishops, popes — which replaced the more diffuse spiritual authority of chieftains and godi (pagan priests).

- The spread of Christianity was uneven:

- **Iceland:** In 1000 A.D., the Althing (national assembly) officially adopted Christianity, but with the compromise that private pagan worship could continue to avoid civil strife.

- **Greenland:** Leif Erikson, after converting in Norway, brought Christianity to Greenland. His mother, Thjodhild, established the first church, while his father Erik the Red remained attached to the old faith.

- **Syncretism:** In practice, many Norse combined Christian and pagan practices: making the sign of the cross at sea while offering coins to wave-spirits; marrying in Christian rites while invoking runes for protection.

Points of Friction Between the Faiths

The two religions differed not just in belief, but in their vision of law, loyalty, and the structure of the world.

Norse Faith	Christianity
Polytheistic: many gods with specialized domains	Monotheistic: one God, omnipotent
Oaths sworn before natural powers: sea, stone, gods	Oaths sworn before God, cross, relics
Blood offerings and feasts to honour gods	Sacrifice replaced by prayer, penance, charity
Ship-burial, pyre, or mound for the dead	Burial in churchyard, facing east
Kin-loyalty paramount, vengeance honourable	Universal brotherhood, forgiveness enjoined
Sacred sites: groves, stones, springs	Sacred sites: churches, altars, relics

The arrival of Christianity threatened not just personal faith, but the social order. Old rites were forbidden; temples were destroyed or converted; legal systems shifted to reflect Christian moral codes.

The Power of Names

In Norse culture, names were believed to hold inherent power — binding identity to fate.

- **Personal Names:** Often invoked ancestors, gods, or qualities (e.g., Thorstein, "Thor's stone").
- **Ship and Sword Names:** Ships were named as one might name a child: to bind them to luck, to honour, to protection. A sword's name reflected its deeds and its master's standing.

- **True Names:** The idea of a hidden or true name — which could grant power over the named — echoes through Norse myth and saga.

Christianity did not share this mystical view of naming. Names marked identity and baptismal belonging but were not thought to bind or shape fate in the same magical sense.

The Expansion of Christianity in *Vidarbjǫrn Saga*

The saga reflects these historical realities:

- Leif bears the weight of conversion as duty and burden, reflecting the historical Leif Erikson's mission to Christianize Greenland.
- Father Arnlaugr embodies the harsh, uncompromising edge of conversion — a man who believes the soul's salvation may demand blood in this world.
- Ranhildr stands for the old ways, unbowed by king or priest, representing those who clung to the gods of their ancestors.

The saga does not present the religious conflict as simple victory or loss. Christianity does not so much conquer as entangle with the old faith, leaving a world divided in loyalty and practice.

The Christianization of the Norse world was not a clean or swift conversion, but a centuries-long negotiation of faith, law, and identity. Names, oaths, and rites were not literary colour, but the language by which men and women bound themselves to the powers they believed shaped their lives.

The saga's world is one where the old gods fade, but do not yet fall; where the Cross rises, but does not yet rule uncontested; and where every name and oath carries the weight of a people caught between two destinies.

Glossary of Terms

A

Alder (wood, ribs, trail) – *A flexible, clean-burning wood used in fire-starting, ship repair, and building. Alder groves often mark spiritually charged terrain. "The alder trail curved strangely this far in".*

Alder ash – *Used to preserve fabric; when mixed with seal grease, makes cloaks water-resistant.*

Angelica – *Native herb with culinary and medicinal uses; valued for both sharpness and sweetness. Used in fumigation and boundary rites.*

Antler tine – *Sharpened point of antler used as a tool in Norse daily life.*

Ash rod – *Flexible, salt-tolerant wood used in fish-stringing, spear hafts, and tool handles.*

Ash staining snow – *A practical act of fire waste disposal; common near hearth sites.*

Ashes kept in pouch – *Used for protective or warning marks; part of Norse magical and funerary rites.*

Ash-ring – *A natural or carved circle of ash trees or stumps used as a sacred space for offering or witnessing. Not metaphor, but sacred ground in Norse tradition.*

B

Barley and sea-biscuits – *Standard provisions on Norse voyages.*

Bear grease / seal *fat – Rendered fat used to stretch pitch or grease runners, ropes, and weapons. Central to ship maintenance and winter survival.*

Berserker (óðr) – *A warrior in a state of divine madness, linked to Odin.*

Birchbark with runes – *Used for votive or magical inscriptions in seiðr rituals.*

Bitabrjǫturr *("Bite-Breaker") – Vidarbjǫrn's work axe. A named tool, not ceremonial but ritually respected.*

Blood-offering / blood rite – *Sacrificial blood, usually pricked from the palm, offered in a stone hollow or onto earth or bark. Associated with vow-making, spirit invocation, and fertility.*

Bone tools – *Needles, pegs, charms, blades—tools and spiritual items fashioned from animal bone.*

Boundary stone – *Often treated as sacral; resetting one carried spiritual implication.*

Bronze brooch / antler clasp – *Common Norse fasteners, often inherited or ritually charged.*

C

Capelin – *A small, oily fish vital to North Atlantic Norse diets.*

Caulking – *Ship-sealing method using moss, bone wedges, and stretched pitch. Vital to survival in northern crossings.*

Charcoal and driftwood ash — *Fuel sources; ash reused in medicine and dye.*

Charcoal trench – *Long pit fire used to heat pitch or forge tools. Fed with seal grease or resinous wood.*

Christian rite (*marriage / baptism*) – *Defined by public vow before God, altar, and priest. Contrasts sharply with Norse vows sworn under sky, in blood or breath.*

Clinker-built — *Overlapping-plank ship design used in Norse knarrs.*

Crossbeam — *Structural ship rib; symbolically tied to Leif's relationship to his ship.*

Crowberry and twisted pine — *Real Newfoundland flora, marking altitude or sacred ground.*

D

Dökk Tönn ("Dark Tooth") — *Vidarbjørn's long axe. A heavier, more reserved blade, associated with combat or judgment.*

Draugr — *Norse undead; dangerous revenants bound to land, oaths, or unrest.*

Dream-fungus — *Requires guidance from a seiðr-woman; tied to spiritual boundary crossing.*

F

Feather choice — *Carried symbolic weight; osprey implies swiftness, seen in Vali's ritual gesture.*

festarmál — *A public, legally binding betrothal. Without it, a woman remains unclaimed.*

Fire-ring — *Hearth-marking of stones; the social and spiritual centre of any Norse dwelling.*

Fishbone charm / token – *Carved bone figure or amulet used for protection, memory, or silent farewell.*

Fish-glue / gutline — *Repair and storage materials; glue made from boiled fish, cordage from intestines.*

Fog omen – *Heavy mist over moss or water often signifies spirit presence or spiritual "watching." A motif of unsettled judgment.*

Freyja – *Norse goddess of fertility, love, war, and magic. Invoked by Ranhildr in rites of bodily vow and territorial claim.*

Fylgjur — *Animal-formed spirit-followers in Norse cosmology, tied to fate or kin.*

G

Ghost pipe (Monotropa uniflora) — *A folklore-rich plant, used in death rites.*

Ghost-biter – *A local nickname for a man associated with spirit-facing work or second-sight. Used derisively or fearfully.*

Grain rationing – Barley was precious and used sparingly in broth or bread.

Gull-silence – An atmospheric omen. Absence of birdcall where noise should exist suggests spiritual presence or tension.

H

Hammer-song – The sound of iron-on-wood or iron-on-iron.

I

Ice-heave / frost-crack – Natural forces that warp structures or soil; spiritually interpreted in Norse culture.

K

Keel – The ship's backbone. Splitting or repairing it carries structural and spiritual weight. Keel-setting is both practical and sacred, often done by named builders.

Knarr – A Norse merchant ship designed for long sea voyages. Central to both trade and colonization.

L

Land claim stake – Placed by settlers to legally and spiritually claim territory.

Leifsbúðir – "Leif's Huts." The saga name for his settlement at L'Anse aux Meadows.

Longhouse construction – Sod-roofed, trench-set, ribbed with local wood. Insulating and communal.

M

Moss-bed – Used for sleeping, burial, and sealing offerings. Holds moisture, scent, and blood. "The moss drank it all."

Moss-caulked hull – A hull sealed with moss and pitch – flexible and sacred to Norse shipwright tradition.

N

Naming the wolf (Fenrir) – Not just symbolic; it's an act of spiritual defiance or invitation.

O

Oarlocks drawn tight – A readiness gesture; the ship prepared for hardship.

Offal offering – Ritual use of viscera; raw for seers, burned for gods.

Offering (blood / bark / breath) – A personal rite involving bloodletting, birch bark, and posture. Seen as a vow and invocation of land, gods, or both.

P

Pine pitch — *Sealing agent for wood, containers, and wounds. Handled hot, dangerous work.*

Pitch boiling — *Toxic, smelly, but essential — symbolizes necessary discomfort for survival.*

Pitch-work - *Hot pine or spruce resin blended with fat or grease to seal ship seams or rooflines. It stains hands and skin; symbolic of survival and labor.*

R

Red thread — *Used in warding, ritual binding, or protection charms.*

Rime / hoar frost — *Early winter signals; shape the settlers' rhythm and perception of time.*

Rite of blood and breath - *A private Norse rite to vow self, body, and land. Ranhildr performs it alone, and it is later misinterpreted by men into myth.*

Rope-and-fire rituals — *Used for rescue in blizzards or for symbolic passage rites.*

Runes on bark / driftwood — *Practical communication and spiritual protection.*

S

Seal oil / seal-hide — *Key materials for lamps, salves, mittens, and preserved foods.*

Seal-ration / seal pouch - *Preserved meat in fat or skin pouch, used in winter or voyages. A mark of shared survival.*

Seax — *A common Norse blade, used daily.*

Seiðr — *Norse spiritual practice, primarily feminine; includes divination, trance, and ritual.*

Shipstone - *A stone marked by blood, bark, or bone, used to name a site, bless a vessel, or vow an oath.*

Smokehole / hearth — *Central to longhouse life; poorly drawn smoke signals spiritual or material failure.*

Spruce syrup - *Used for nourishment and preservation. A concentrated sap, rich in sugar and resin. Served in leave-taking.*

Sword-vow / axe-oath - *A binding statement spoken under sky, witnessed by steel and silence. Often replaces formal marriage.*

T

Tally share - *A legal entitlement to profit or claim. One's "name on the ledger" indicates belonging, status, or inheritance.*

Tally-board — *Kristján's ledger, marked with ink or notches; reflects Norse-Christian bureaucracy.*

Tar-sealing / sod roof – *Proper sealing prevents winter draft and collapse.*

Thaw rites - *Spring rituals to open hunting, break ground, or mark changes in vow or loyalty.*

Thing – *Norse council assembly; legal and ritual authority.*

Threshold rituals – *Doors mark liminal space; crossings matter spiritually.*

Turf layering – *Root-side down turf, laid like shingles, insulates and drains.*

V

Vættir – *Land spirits. Disrupting stones or cutting green wood without offering invites danger.*

Vatnslaugr – *A Norse toponym ("water hollow"); blends naming, mythology, and terrain.*

Vow beneath sky - *A Norse marriage custom: no priest, just sky, silence, and bodily presence. Valid by kin witness and oath. Rejected by Christian law.*

W

Whale bone / piss trench / midden – *Authentic camp structures. Each had spiritual and functional purpose.*

Wolf's-head – *Legal term for outlaw; such a man may be killed without retribution.*

AUTHOR'S NOTE

Most of the time, I write fantasy—worlds of my own making. But one day I started reading the Viking sagas, and I couldn't put them down. They're short, sharp, and packed with little fragments of lives: voyages, quarrels, triumphs, deaths. They're not full novels, but they feel like doorways, and once I stepped through, I couldn't stop imagining.

Erik the Red had four children, each with their own story. Of course, Leif is the most famous. But I wanted someone who could stand with them all, a voice to carry their weight. That's how Vidarbjorn was born. Then Ranhildr arrived—strong, fierce, entirely herself. And from there I found myself with thirty-five souls crammed into a sixty-foot knarr, one sail above them, bound for a land no Norseman had ever seen. To picture them crossing the Atlantic that way still amazes me.

I wrote this book for my wife, who loves historical fiction. It's also my first attempt at a romance. (Although some have said it doesn't qualify, since there's no "happily ever after." My answer: it's a Viking saga—shouldn't everyone die in the end?)

Thank you for picking up *The Taking Shore*. If you're curious about what comes next—the rest of Erik's children, or even a prequel about Leif's charge to bring Christianity to Greenland and beyond—you can find me at www.harwoodjones.com. I'd love to hear from you.

—Troy

www.ingramcontent.com/pod-product-compliance
Lightning Source LLC
Chambersburg PA
CBHW070737120726

47910CB00001B/127